ALL *the* FLOWERS *in* PARIS

Center Point
Large Print

Also by Sarah Jio and available from Center Point Large Print:

Goodnight June
The Look of Love
Always

This Large Print Book carries the Seal of Approval of N.A.V.H.

ALL *the* FLOWERS *in* PARIS

A NOVEL

SARAH JIO

CENTER POINT LARGE PRINT
THORNDIKE, MAINE

This Center Point Large Print edition
is published in the year 2019 by arrangement with
Ballantine Books, an imprint of Random House,
a division of Penguin Random House LLC.

All the Flowers in Paris is a work of fiction. Names,
characters, places, and incidents are the products of
the author's imagination or are used fictitiously. Any
resemblance to actual events, locales, or persons,
living or dead, is entirely coincidental.

The text of this Large Print edition is unabridged.
In other aspects, this book may vary
from the original edition.
Printed in the United States of America
on permanent paper.
Set in 16-point Times New Roman type.

ISBN: 978-1-64358-347-1

The Library of Congress has cataloged this record
under Library of Congress Control Number: 2019944751

For Evangeline and Petra

AUTHOR'S NOTE

Dear Reader,

This is my ninth novel to be published in the United States, and my tenth in the world. In all of my years of writing and traveling, I have always been drawn to Paris. And while life circumstances have never allowed me to move there (a dream since college), I have always known that I would one day write a story set in Paris. While bits and pieces of my past novels have taken place in the City of Light, I've never fully planted my characters there in the way I have in this book, which, for me, was exhilarating in its own right.

While tending to my three young boys in Seattle in my daily life, I tagged along with my characters to the most charming cafés, beautiful balconies, and beloved sights of Paris. The journey was a memorable one: climbing the steps of Montmartre, admiring the colorful produce on the rue Cler, sipping espresso in secret cafés on little side streets.

But this story delves far deeper than chocolate croissants and the Eiffel Tower on a spring day. It tackles heartbreak and trauma head-on, both in war-torn 1940s Paris and in the present day, with

7

characters who have the ability—or inability—to resist, forgive, and love.

This book is my love letter to Paris, and maybe someday there will be another. For now, I hope you enjoy the little story I have dreamed up, its characters, and all of Paris, down to the very last petal.

xo, Sarah

ALL *the* FLOWERS *in* PARIS

CHAPTER 1

CAROLINE

SEPTEMBER 4, 2009
Paris, France

How could he? My cheeks burn as I climb onto my bike, pedaling fast down the rue Cler, past the street vendors with their tables lined with shiny purple eggplants and bunches of flowers, pink peonies and golden sunflowers standing at attention in tidy buckets, past Café du Monde, where I sometimes get a coffee when I'm too tired to walk to Bistro Jeanty, past an old woman walking her tiny white poodle. Despite the bright sun overhead, she pessimistically clutches a sheathed umbrella, as if at any moment the skies might open and unleash their fury.

Fury is the emotion I feel. *Furious,* rather. *He* was the last person on earth I expected or wanted to see this morning. After everything that's happened, does he not have the decency to respect my wishes? I told him I didn't want to see him, now or . . . ever. And yet, here he materializes, at Café du Monde of all places, smiling at me as if nothing has happened, as if . . .

I blink back tears, careful to regain my

composure, the way I didn't last night, when I threw down my napkin, shouted at him, and stormed off. A Parisian woman, in contrast, would never lose her cool like that.

While I have a lot to work on in that department, on any given day I might pass for French, at least from a distance. I look the part, more or less. Scarf tied loosely around my neck. On a bike in a dress. Blond hair swept up in a high bun. No helmet—*obviously*. It has taken three years to semi-master the language (emphasis on the "semi"), but it would easily take a lifetime to become adequately versed in French style.

But what does any of it matter now? Over time, Paris has become my hiding place, my cocoon, my escape from the pain of the past. I blink back tears. And now? Does he really think he can just waltz in and expect me to behave as if nothing happened? That everything should just magically go back to the way it was?

I shudder, glancing over my shoulder to make sure he isn't following me. As far as I can tell, he's not, and I pedal faster around the next corner, where a man in a leather jacket catches my eye and smiles as though we've met before. We haven't. Saying that Frenchmen are notoriously forward is an understatement. The truth is, they believe the world, and every woman in it, should be so lucky to be graced by their special good looks, charm, and intelligence.

I've barely dipped my toe into the pool of French dating, and the experience hasn't been great. There was dinner with the hairstylist, who couldn't stop checking himself out in the mirror behind me; lunch with the artist, who suggested we go back to his apartment and discuss his latest painting, which, by chance, hung over his *bed;* and then the professor who asked me out last week . . . and yet I couldn't bring myself to return his calls.

I sigh and pedal on. I am neither American nor Parisian. In fact, these days, I don't feel as if I'm anything. I belong to no country or person. Unattached, I am merely a ghost, floating through life.

I wend past the rue de Seine, zigzagging down a lamppost-lined hill, the grandeur of the city at my back, my pale-blue sundress fluttering in the breeze as more tears well up in my eyes, fogging my view of the narrow street below. I blink hard, wiping away a tear, and the expanse of cobblestones comes into focus again. My eyes fix on an elderly couple walking on the sidewalk ahead. They are like any older French couple, I suppose, characteristically adorable in a way that they will never know. He in a sport coat (despite the humid eighty-five-degree day), and she in a gingham dress, perhaps in her closet since the afternoon she saw it in the window of a sensible boutique along the Champs-Élysées in 1953. She carries a basket filled with farmers'-market finds

13

(I notice the zucchini). He carries a baguette, and nothing else, like a World War II–era rifle held against his shoulder, dutifully, but also with a barely detectable and oddly charming tinge of annoyance.

My mind returns to the exchange at the café, and I am once again furious. I hear his voice in my head, soft, sweet, pleading. *Was I too hard on him?* No. No. Maybe? No! In another life, we might have spent this evening nestled in a corner table at some café, drinking good Bordeaux, listening to Chet Baker, discussing hypothetical trips to the Greek islands or the construction of a backyard greenhouse where we would consider the merits of growing a lemon (or avocado?) tree in a pot and sit under a bougainvillea vine like the one my mom planted the year I turned eleven, before my dad left. Jazz. Santorini. Lemon trees. Beautiful, loving details, none of which matter anymore. Not in this life, anyhow. That chapter has ended. No, the book has.

How could I forgive him? How could I ever forgive him . . .

"Forgiveness is a gift," a therapist I saw for a few sessions had said, "both to the receiver and to yourself. But no one can give a gift when she's not ready to."

I close my eyes for a moment, then open them, resolute. I am not ready now, and I doubt that I will ever be. I pedal on, faster, determined.

The pain of the past suddenly comes into sharp and bitter focus. It stings, like a slice of lemon pressed to a wound.

I wipe away another tear as a truck barrels toward me out of nowhere. Adrenaline surges in the way it does when you're zoning out while driving and then narrowly miss swerving into an oncoming car, or a light post, or a man walking his dog. I veer my bicycle to the right, careful to avoid a mother and her young daughter walking toward me on my left. The little girl looks no older than two. My heart swells. The sun is bright, blindingly so, and it filters through her sandy blond hair.

I squint, attempting to navigate the narrow road ahead, my heart beating faster by the second. The driver of the truck doesn't seem to see me. "Stop!" I cry. "*Arrêtez!*"

I clench the handlebars, engaging the brakes, but somehow they give out. The street is steep and narrow, too narrow, and I am now barreling down a hillside with increasing speed. The driver of the truck is fiddling with a cigarette, turning it this way and that, simultaneously swerving the truck across the cobblestone streets. I scream again, but he doesn't seem to hear. Panic washes over me, thick and overpowering. I have two choices: turn left and crash my bike straight into the mother and her little girl, or turn right and collide directly into the truck.

I turn right.

CHAPTER 2

CÉLINE

SEPTEMBER 4, 1943
Paris, France

A utumn's coming," Papa says, casting his gaze out the window of our little flower shop on the rue Cler. Despite the blue sky overhead, there are storm clouds in his eyes.

"Oh, Papa," I say through the open door, straightening my apron before sweeping a few stray rose petals off the cobblestones in front of the shop. I always feel bad for fallen petals, as silly as that sounds. They're like little lost ducklings separated from their mama. "It's only the beginning of September, my oh-so-very-pessimistic papa." I smile facetiously. "It's been the most beautiful summer; can't we just enjoy it while it lasts?"

"Beautiful?" Papa throws his arms in the air in the dramatic fashion that all Frenchmen over the age of sixty do so well. I've often thought that there's probably an old French law stating that if you're an older male, you have the irrevocable right to be grumpy, cantankerous, and otherwise disagreeable at the time and place of your choosing. Papa certainly exercises this right, and yet I love him all the more for it. Grumpy or not, he still has the biggest heart of any Frenchman I've ever known. "Our city is occupied by Nazi soldiers and you call this summer . . . *beautiful?*" He shakes his head, returning to an elaborate arrangement he's been fussing over all day for Madame Jeanty, one of our more exacting clients. A local tastemaker, and owner of one of the most fashionable restaurants in town, Bistro Jeanty, she funnels many clients to us, namely, new admissions into the high-society circle who want their dining room tables to look as grand as hers. As such, Papa and I know we can't risk losing her business, and her demands must always be heeded, no matter how ridiculous, or how late (or early) the hour. Never too much greenery, but then never too little, either. Only roses that have been snipped that morning. Never peonies, only ranunculus. And for the love of all that is holy, no ferns. Not even a hint of them. I made that mistake in an arrangement three years ago, and let's just say it will *never happen again.*

It's funny how different a child can be from a parent. Her son, Luc, for instance, is nothing like her. We've known each other since secondary school, and I've always thought the world of him. We have dinner together each week at Bistro Jeanty, and I've valued our friendship, especially during this godforsaken occupation. Luc and

I might have been sweethearts under different circumstances. If the world weren't at war, if our lives had taken different paths. I've thought about it many times, of course, and I know he has too. The Book of Us remains a complicated story, and neither of us, it seems, knows the ending.

I sigh. Who has time to think of such things now, when so much is at stake? Some of our friends have lost their businesses, others have been roughed up on street corners. And yet, so far, our little family has managed to avoid any significant personal or financial harm, and I'm grateful for that every day. I like to believe (pretend?) that we are immune to it, that this war could come and go and we'd continue being our little family of three: Papa, me, and my little girl, Cosi. As the storm rages, we'll manage to stay in its peaceful eye.

I'm no fool, however. There's cause to be concerned, all kinds of it. But caution is a very different thing than paranoia, and I refuse to be ruled by fear. After all, we are French citizens, with the papers to prove it. Even though Papa's mother was half-Jewish, she's long since passed away in a small village outside of Normandy, miles from here. Though unashamed of his ancestry, he has never been defined by it. His father was Catholic, and his mother converted. As far as I know, no one is aware of Papa's ancestry or could trace his bloodline. Besides, the

Germans love our shop, stopping in for special bouquets for their wives or mistresses, or any pretty French girl they hope to woo. We will be fine. All three of us.

The bells on the door jingle as Luc appears. He kisses my cheek, then shakes Papa's hand.

"What are you doing here?" I ask with a smile.

He produces a perfect pink grapefruit from his coat pocket. "Look what I found at the market."

My eyes light up. "Luc, really?"

He nods. "I thought you'd be pleased."

"I haven't had a grapefruit since—"

The doorbells jingle again, this time ushering in Madame Bernard, who walks up to the counter in a huff. "I need four dozen tiger lilies," she says to Papa, out of breath. "We're entertaining some of Paris's most important people tomorrow tonight."

Papa furrows his brow. He knows as well as I do that tiger lilies are hard, if not impossible, to come by.

"Madame Bernard," he says, clearing his throat. "Lilies are a rarity these days. May I suggest roses, carnations, even—"

"I said lilies," she barks, holding her hand out as if to halt any further discussion on the matter.

"Madame Bernard," Luc says suddenly. "How nice to see you."

"Why, Luc!" she exclaims. "I didn't see you there."

19

He smiles. "How is your husband? I'm told he was ill recently."

"Well, thank you. He made a fine recovery."

"Good," he says.

Madame Bernard looks at me, then Luc, and then back at Papa again. "Roses will be fine. I don't mean to make a fuss." She glances back at me, then Luc. "Especially in these times. Three dozen roses. Various shades of pink will do."

Luc blows me an air kiss, then heads out the door. Papa transcribes the order into his notebook as he always does. "And shall we bring them by at three? Four?"

"Noon," she says. "Last time your delivery boy was late. Make sure he isn't again."

"Of course, madame," Papa says.

"And the flowers were a bit wilted." She shakes her head. "If you're not careful, you'll lose your best customers, including myself."

"With respect, madame," I interject. "We don't sell wilted flowers. Perhaps your memory is what has wilted."

"My memory?" she huffs, turning to Papa. "It's a shame you didn't manage to teach your daughter any manners. On second thought, cancel that order."

After she's gone, I fall into the chair behind the counter with a sigh. But it's apparent Papa doesn't find any of this funny.

"Céline, you can't let your temper get the better of you like that."

"And let people like Madame Bernard boss us around?" I shrug. "We have plenty of customers, Papa. We don't need her."

He sighs. "And what if she tells her friends and they all stop ordering?"

"They won't," I say. "Our customers are loyal. Madame Bernard, on the other hand, is a known Nazi sympathizer."

Papa looks tired and unconvinced. "All the more reason we should keep her happy."

Just then, Cosi barrels into the shop, my little eight-year-old, with the spirit of a lion and the heart of an angel, and just like that, Madame Bernard's nonsense evaporates into thin air. "Mama," she says, throwing her arms around me. "Look what I made in school!"

She produces a piece of paper from her satchel, a watercolor painting of a beach scene. "Do you recognize it?" she asks, wide-eyed and expectant. "It's Normandy!" she blurts out with gusto, too excited to wait for my reply. "Where you were born, Mama!" Beaming with pride, she points to the rocks she's painted along the beach and the tide pool to the right, just as I'd described to her on so many nights before she drifted off to sleep. My childhood home, Normandy remains deeply embedded in my heart. We lived there in a little cottage by the sea before my mother passed away, the year I turned twelve. After that, Papa moved us to Paris. It's been so long, but if I close my eyes and let my mind travel back, I can still smell the sea air, the blossoms on Mama's lemon trees on our back patio. It's as if I never left. I suppose part of me never did.

"Do you miss it?" my daughter asks, studying my face.

My eyes are misty, so I turn away and pretend to busy myself with a bucket of greenery that will end up in one of Papa's arrangements, for one fancy party or another.

I collect myself, then turn to Cosi, nodding. "Yes, love," I say with a smile. As much as my heart aches for Normandy, it aches for Mama more. As magical as our little seaside life was, we could have lived anywhere, in the desert or the darkest forest—as long as my mother was there, we'd have been happy.

As such, nothing was the same after her death. Much of the joy had been snuffed out of our lives, like the flame of a candle, especially for Papa. Our sweet life in Normandy made way for a busy life in Paris, where people moved faster and smiled less. Papa opened the flower shop and we forged a new existence without Mama.

A stoic man, Papa has cried only once, as far as I've seen: on Christmas morning, the year I turned thirteen. Just after breakfast, I had given him a photograph I'd found of Mama in a box buried deep in the attic. She couldn't have been older than eighteen, so beautiful, with her wavy dark hair, just like Cosi's, falling over her shoulders. I found the perfect frame for it at a secondhand store and wrapped it for Papa. To this day, I'm not sure if he'd ever seen the photograph before, but when he set his eyes on it, he wept.

Yet, despite Papa's efforts to keep his sadness at bay all these years, it's still there. He wears it like a scarf, permanently tied around his neck. The truth is, as big as Papa's heart is, Mama took half of it when she passed. When you lose a love as deep as they had, can the void ever be filled?

"Mama?" Cosi asks, jarring me from my memories.

"It's beautiful," I proclaim, turning my eyes back to her little watercolor masterpiece before planting a kiss on her cool, rosy cheek. "You've captured it like a true artist. It's just as I remember."

She tucks a lock of her dark hair behind her ear and looks up at me with a confident smile. "Will you take me there someday?"

"I promise," I tell her.

"And can we get a *tarte normande*, the kind you used to love as a little girl?"

The mere mention has my mouth watering and my heart aching. I can almost taste the tarts my mother used to make, with apples from the trees in our garden, loads of freshly grated cinnamon, and a dollop of whipped cream on top.

"And can we look for treasure on the beach?"

"Yes, sweet child."

"And can we throw rocks in the water and look for starfish in the tide pools?"

I nod, fighting back tears. She's as much like her father as she is like me. An optimist through and through who sees the good in all people, with a fierce, determined spirit. Pierre would be so proud. I clutch the gold necklace he gave me on our wedding day, with the tiny diamond pendant reminding me of the life we once had together.

His death was sudden, just as Mama's was, but unlike her, he wasn't struck by illness. Six months after our wedding, just after I'd discovered I was pregnant with Cosi, I awoke to the sound of him opening the closet door, then the rustle of fabric as he pulled on his trousers. The clink of a belt buckle, feet slipping into shoes. I opened my eyes with a yawn. "I'm sorry, darling," he said. "I didn't mean to wake you."

"Come back to bed," I said groggily. That evening, I'd planned on telling him the news of the baby I carried. First, I'd stop by the butcher and select a special steak to accompany his favorite dish, *gratin dauphinois*, a simple yet inexplicably divine mixture of thinly sliced and layered potatoes, garlic, Gruyère cheese, and cream. I'd watched my mother make it a hundred times, but it would be my first attempt in my own kitchen.

I remember the look on his face that morning. I always will. So handsome, his eyes filled with passion, just as much for me as for life in general. Pierre had such dreams, and a plan for all of them. When his business picked up, a little wine shop in Montmartre, he planned to open a second, and then a third, with the ultimate goal of becoming the most successful wine merchant in Paris. After that, he said, we'd buy a country house in Provence and spend our summers lounging beside a mineral-rich pool, breathing in lavender-scented air. Papa would come, too, of course. Pierre's success would allow my father to finally retire and rest his weary, arthritic hands. A beautiful life and future to look forward to, and it was ours, all ours.

That morning, full of all those big dreams and love, he'd walked back to bed, lowered his majestic body, and pressed his lips against mine, sending a rush of energy through me like only the very best espresso can. No man had ever had that effect on me, and sometimes I wondered if it could really be possible to love someone so much that you might burst.

"Don't leave," I said.

"I won't be gone long," he replied with a wink.

"But it's so early," I muttered from that foggy place between sleep and waking, glancing at the clock. Half past six. "Where could you possibly need to be at this hour?"

"It's a surprise," he said. "Go back to sleep, my love. When you open your eyes, I'll be back, and you'll see."

Just as he instructed, I closed my eyes and my exhausted, newly pregnant body drifted back to sleep in moments. But when I awoke an hour later, Pierre hadn't returned. The morning hours dragged on, and by afternoon, he still hadn't come home. I busied myself preparing dinner, pulling off the *gratin dauphinois* without a hitch, thankfully. I poured the wine. I set the table. And by a quarter past six, the apartment smelled heavenly. But Pierre still hadn't come home.

Panicked, I inquired at nearby cafés, the barber on the corner, and with Madame Benoît, who was just closing up her bakery. I still remember the bit of flour on her cheek. "Sorry, Céline," she'd replied with a shrug.

No one had seen Pierre.

Then the call came. The ring of the telephone had never sounded so loud or frightening. I ran to it, not a second to waste. It would be Pierre. He'd let me know that he'd taken a detour to check on the shop, just as a new shipment of Bordeaux had come in. His assistant, Louis, young and inexperienced, was not capable of categorizing the bottles and stocking them on the right shelves, so he had to do the job himself. The life of a business owner, of course. I knew it well. I would be mildly annoyed, but understanding. I'd encourage him to bicycle home as quickly as possible. *"Dinner is getting cold! I've made your favorite dish!"* He would calmly say, *"Sorry to keep you waiting, my love. I'll be home in a flash."* And there he'd be, fifteen minutes later, standing in the doorway, with that handsome, expectant smile. He'd beg my forgiveness and he'd have it, in an instant.

The voice on the phone was not Pierre's but a police officer's, calling from the sixteenth arrondissement. "I'm sorry to inform you, madame, that your husband . . ."

I don't remember what he said next, not exactly. The officer's words felt like bullets, but at one one-hundredth of the normal speed—so slow, I felt each one hit my body and tear through my heart.

Pierre's body had been found wedged between a delivery truck and a brand-new gray Renault. When the truck hit him, he'd been thrown from his bicycle and pinned against the other oncoming vehicle. The medics said he died instantly. He hadn't suffered.

That night, I jumped on my bicycle and pedaled to the street where he took his last breath. I fell to my knees when I saw the most heartbreaking scene of my life: a badly mangled bicycle left lying on its side, and pink peony petals scattered on the cobblestone street like fresh snow, the remnants of what could only have been an enormous bouquet.

My surprise.

Losing Mama, and then Pierre, was like getting hit by lightning twice. After that night, there were dark moments when I felt I couldn't go on. I looked over the edge of my balcony more than a dozen times wishing for a quick exit to end the pain, but the little life inside me kept me hanging on. Papa helped, too, as best as he could. He spoon-fed me broth when I was too nauseated, or distraught, to eat, and held me when I cried so hard I soaked the collar of his shirt.

But, Cosi, my sweet Cosi, was ultimately the bandage my heart so badly needed. With her, I could go on, and I have. She is the reason I wake up in the morning and say my prayers at night. She's also the reason I can see the beauty in every day, even this one.

"*Bon après-midi*," our delivery boy, Nic, says, appearing in the doorway. He's about twelve and very tall for his age. A sweet, hardworking boy, he holds down several jobs, including helping at Jeanty and a nearby bakery to ensure that his family makes ends meet.

Cosi blushes. I know she has a crush on him, but I dare not say anything to embarrass her. "Anything for me to take out this afternoon, monsieur?" he asks.

Papa nods and hands him an arrangement that's ready for delivery. "Sure thing," he says, smiling at Cosi before patting her on the head as he rushes out the door.

Cosi beams as she watches him leave, then turns to me, tugging at my apron. I look down at my little girl. "Can I go play in the park with Alina?" she asks.

Papa casts a concerned look my way. "A child of eight should not be playing in the park in these times. She should—"

"It's fine, Papa," I interrupt him before he can say anything further that might frighten her. Of course, I share his concern for her safety in our war-occupied city, but I am also keenly aware of Cosi's need to be a *child,* to live openly and as carefree as possible even if the world around us seems to be falling down before our very eyes. Despite Papa's concerns, I've tried my best to shield her from fear. Her life saved my own and gave my world new meaning. In return, I color hers in shades of joy and happiness. Where there is darkness, I cast light. Where there is worry, I provide relief.

She'll be fine at the park. It's just around the bend from the shop. And as cruel as the SS soldiers are, we have yet to hear a single story of a German officer harming a French child. There is still dignity in the world, and as long as there is, I intend to cling to it.

"Yes, honey," I say, ignoring Papa. "But be back by six for dinner."

She kisses me and dashes out of the shop and across the street. I watch her skip along as she disappears around the corner.

Papa mutters something under his breath.

"What?" I ask, folding my arms across my chest. "You disagree with the way I'm raising her. Just say it."

He's quiet for a long moment. When his gaze meets mine, I can see that his eyes are misty, his expression tender, not cantankerous. "It's only because I love her, and you, so much. I couldn't"—he pauses to compose himself—"I couldn't . . . live with myself if anything ever happened to either of you."

I walk closer to him and place my hands on his shoulders, kissing both his cheeks. "Oh, Papa, I know you worry," I say. "But nothing will happen to us. We are fine. We always will be."

He smiles. "You're just like her."

I know he means Mama, and it's the best compliment he can pay me.

"You see the way she did. Always through rose-colored glasses."

I grin. "It's more fun that way."

We both turn around when we hear the jingle of bells on the door, alerting us to a customer. This one I don't recognize. A German officer, clearly, and high ranking, as evidenced by his decorated shirt pocket. He's taller than the others who have come in, at least six feet four, with exceptionally broad shoulders. He has dark hair and a square jaw. His eyes are cold, steely, and his figure casts an intimidating shadow on the shop floor. I greet him with a cheerful *bon après-midi*, in the same manner that I greet all of our customers. It's my one rebellion, showing no special treatment for the Germans and often regarding them with indifference.

He grunts something at me, and I wait a long beat to respond. "May I help you?" I finally say.

He ignores me as he paces slowly around the shop, inspecting every corner suspiciously, as if the very flowers and their petals might be spies. I watch as he pulls a red rose from a vase, raises it to his nose, then tosses it on the ground. Papa and I exchange a worried glance.

"What has happened to roses?" the man asks. His French is good, even if tinged with a heavy German accent. The question appears to be as much to himself as to us. Neither Papa nor I venture a response. "In the Fatherland, a rose smells like a . . . rose. These French roses smell like shit. French shit."

I open my mouth to speak, but the officer does first. "And these?" he asks, pointing to a bucket of hydrangeas, variegated, purple and pink. They're very hard to find this time of the year unless you have connections with the best gardeners in the south. "What the hell are these?"

"Hydrangeas," I say. "May I interest you in an arrangement, for a special someone? They'd look lovely with a sprig of—"

"No," he grunts, turning his gaze to Papa. He walks closer to the counter, where Papa stands. With each of his slow, heavy steps, I feel my temperature rise a degree. "What is your name, sir?"

"Claude Moreau," Papa replies. If he's worried, he shows no sign of it. Just the same, my heart pounds wildly in my chest.

"Moreau," the officer says. "A proper French name."

Papa remains quiet, his face emotionless.

The officer laughs to himself. "The führer himself loves the French, so much so that we spared Paris. He'll be living here before long, you know, setting up residence just up the way. The French are, you might say . . . special." He turns to me and smiles. "And, I might add, very attractive."

I shiver as Papa clears his throat. "Monsieur, if we may help you with an order, please let us know your requirements so we may begin assembling it for you." It's an offer of service as much as a man-to-man warning. While it's true that we've always remained somewhat guarded when a member of the German Army enters the shop, this is the first time I feel any real sense of fear.

"Oh yes," he says, glancing at Papa, then turning his gaze back to me. He seems amused by something neither Papa nor I understand. "You may help me." He walks toward me, stopping at an uncomfortably close distance. He reaches his large hand to my collarbone and, with his index finger, traces the outline of the gold necklace from Pierre, then smiles at Papa. "I'll take two dozen of those shit roses." He laughs. "French girls like anything."

I nod. My hands tremble as I select the roses from the bucket beside me and carry them to the counter for Papa to arrange.

"What's your name?" the officer asks me.

I look at Papa, then back at him. I know I have no choice but to answer his question. "Céline," I finally say.

"Céline," he says, as if both perplexed and amused. "Such a forgettable name for such a very *memorable* girl." He pauses to think, then nods to himself. "You look more like a Helga to me, a fitting name for a very beautiful *Fräulein.*"

Papa's hands work at lightning pace, and in a moment's time, he extends the bouquet to the officer. "Will that be all?" Papa asks, his tone firm—I worry, too firm.

"Yes, sir," he says, reaching into his pocket, then tossing a wad of cash on the countertop.

"Goodbye . . . Helga," he says with a laugh, tipping his hat to me. He walks to the door, turning to us once more. "Like I said, your daughter is a beautiful woman." He shakes his head. "A shame, sir, that you have such a prominent Jewish nose."

The door closes with a slam, and after a long pause, I run to Papa and throw my arms around him. "Do you think he—"

"Don't worry about him," he says. "He's just trying to scare us. That's what they do. They prey on people's fears so they can control them." He pulls me to his chest. "Don't you worry, my Céline. He has no power over us." And with that, he turns back to the cash register and deposits the money in the till. We both notice the officer has underpaid us by many reichsmarks, but we don't discuss it.

I reach for my jacket as a shiver runs down my body. "I'm going to go get Cosi for dinner a little early," I say, heading to the door.

"Good idea," Papa says. "And, Céline?"

I turn around to face him before exiting the shop.

"Be careful."

Looking over my shoulder two or three times, I walk with a brisk stride to the park to find my daughter. It feels colder than usual, and I pull the collar of my jacket up a bit higher.

Somehow summer seems like a distant memory. Papa is right; autumn is coming, whether we like it or not.

CHAPTER 3

CAROLINE

FIVE DAYS LATER

I open my eyes and blink away the most terrible dream. There were sirens and lights. There was blood. A child. I sit up in bed and gasp for air. Everything aches.

Where am I?

The white walls and fluorescent lights are harsh, and I squint to make out my surroundings: industrial tile on the floor, drab, sun-faded curtains shrouding a window looking out to a strange city. I notice a familiar monument out the window. The Arc . . . de Triomphe? And then it hits me.

Paris. Good Lord, why am I in Paris? But the more pressing question is . . . *Who am . . . I?*

I glance down at my arms, pale, a little freckled, foreign looking. My hands are thin, and my nails are painted pale pink. The polish on the right thumb is chipped. There's dirt under the nail. I will my right hand to touch my left, like a stranger—the skin feels foreign—then sit up, heart racing. I'm in a hospital bed.

"Hello?" I call out, both to anyone who can

hear me and, I suppose, to myself. I am deeply and sorely lost. I am a strange soul trapped in an even stranger body. The only thing I know is that I am alive, and that I am in, well, Paris.

A thin, middle-aged woman dressed in white bursts through the door. "You're . . . awake," she says, dabbing a napkin to her face and swallowing the remnants of something. Apparently I've just interrupted her lunch break. I don't have the discernment to tell if she's annoyed or not. But, to be frank, I don't have the discernment to tell if I'm, well, alive or not. I close my eyes tightly, and I am at once in some other place, some other level of consciousness, where trade winds blow through palm trees, making that unmistakable sound that only rustling palm fronds can. Wind blowing through evergreens is an entirely different thing—more of a low howl, a dull but reverent power, pushing through a wooded forest, haunting and enigmatic. But this? This sound is electric. It reverberates in my ears. It is the sound of something on the cusp. It is the sound of my past, and it's the sound of something about to *happen.*

Wind chimes clang as a little girl cries. I open my eyes, heart beating fast.

"Madame," the woman in white says, hovering over me. "Madame, you are *awake?*"

I blink hard. "What happened?" I mutter. "Why am I here?"

"You were in an accident." I notice her high cheekbones, overplucked eyebrows, and freckles on the bridge of her nose. She has a thick accent, and I strain to understand each of her words. "It was a bad accident."

I was in a *bad accident?*

Another woman enters the room, this one somewhat regal looking with dark hair pulled back, not a strand askew. "Hello," she says, also in a thick accent, taking a seat in the chair beside my bed. "We're so happy to see you awake and conscious."

I reach for her hand, clutching it with a firm grip. "Please, tell me who I am. Tell me what happened to me. How did I get here?"

She nods. "I'm a doctor," she says. "You are in the Pitié-Salpêtrière Hospital, in Paris. You were in a bike accident; well, you were on a bike when a truck hit you. You endured a serious injury—how serious, we don't know yet." She places her hand on my arm and smiles for the first time, and the reflection from the window makes her white teeth glisten. "But it's a good sign that you are awake. A very good sign."

"Injury?" I ask, sitting up. I don't know if it's winter or summer. Monday or Friday. If I am a good person or a bad one. I know nothing. Absolutely nothing.

The doctor nods. "You have been unconscious for five days."

I move my arms and legs. "I'm not paralyzed."

"No," she says, leaning into me. "But you did have a great deal of swelling on the brain, which appears, from the scans, to be improving. Tell me, what do you remember?"

I take a deep breath, trying to distinguish reality from dream. "I . . ." I stammer. "I'm not sure." My head pounds. My mouth is dry.

"It's okay," the doctor says. "Memory is a funny thing. It can return in bits and pieces, or in one huge wave, or . . ." She pauses and looks out the window.

"Or what?"

She swallows hard. "Or never at all."

"Oh," I say, eying the thin gold ring on the middle finger of my left hand. *Who am I?*

"We will help you," the doctor continues, "to get settled, regain your life."

My life. *What* life?

"The paramedics retrieved your purse at the scene of the accident," she says. "We made some phone calls but haven't come up with anything concrete other than the fact that you have an apartment on the rue Cler. Once you're stable, we'll have a hospital staff member take you there."

I nod solemnly, blinking back a tear. "Do I have a . . . family?"

The doctor shakes her head. "Not any relations in Paris who we can find. You appear to live alone." She stands up. "I know it's hard," she adds. "You must be feeling so scared. But you must try to be happy that you survived. So many people don't. You've been given a gift."

The nurse hands me a glass of water and a pill. I swallow it and then close my eyes as they both leave the room.

I do not feel as if I've been given a gift. I feel as if I've just stepped into a nightmare.

THREE DAYS LATER

"You've been cleared for discharge," the nurse—Aimée—says. I've come to enjoy her company since I've awakened from this strange abyss. Each night, I am tormented by nightmares of a bike accident that supposedly wiped the hard drive in my brain. The repetitive dream has me winding down a narrow street, a truck barreling toward me and a mother with her young daughter walking ahead. Dr. Leroy has said each day that she is hopeful my memory will improve, but for now, this is all I recall. And while I can tell you the colors of the rainbow or the days of the week or the sixteenth president of the United States, I can remember nothing of my life.

The mother and her daughter survived, I was so happy to hear. They'd left flowers for me at the hospital while I was sleeping yesterday afternoon. Yellow roses. Claudine and Jeanette are their names. Two-year-old Jeanette drew me a picture, and for reasons I cannot explain, it made me weep, so hard, in fact, that Aimée gave me a Valium.

"You must have been quite a fancy lady," Aimée says, smiling as she hands me a black leather purse.

"Fancy lady?"

"Yes," she says, pointing to the emblem on the side of the handbag. *My* handbag. "Chanel."

"Oh," I say, running my hand along the quilted diamond pattern and eying the gold clasp at the center. "So apparently I'm a . . . snob?"

"No, no," Aimée says, laughing a little. "Just good taste."

And a posh address, apparently. My credit card, the hospital staff informed me, was traced to a three-bedroom apartment overlooking the Eiffel Tower on the coveted rue Cler, which, apparently, I have rented for the last three years. Police went to the apartment to notify any potential family members, but found none. Further interviews with neighbors in the building rounded out my résumé: I live alone and rarely go out. In fact, no one seems to know me at all.

"I don't understand," I say to Aimée. "I'm an American in Paris. I live in a fancy apartment with a fancy handbag. And I have no family, no friends?"

"I'm sure you have family . . . somewhere,"

she says. "And, well, no friends in the building, anyway. But those buildings are often filled with old people who care for nothing else but their miniature poodles, and their taxidermy." I imagine mounted antlers as she continues on. "A friend of mine has a grandmother who lives near you. I visited her for lunch last April. She said my hair displeased her." She pauses to smooth an unruly curl. "Maybe you didn't want to be friends with those type of people anyway?"

"Maybe," I say. My eyes widen. "Aimée, what if *I'm* one of those people?"

"No, no," she says, reassuringly.

"Tell me the truth," I say, locking my eyes to hers. "Do I seem like the cantankerous type?"

"No," she insists. "People who are cantankerous don't ask if they're cantankerous."

I force a smile. "I guess you have a point."

"Here." She hands me a shopping bag. "Your clothes were ruined in the accident, so I brought these from home. You're about my size. I thought you could find something that would work." She smiles. "I mean, they're nothing fancy, but we couldn't send you home in a hospital gown."

"Wow," I say. "Thank you."

I select a gray sweater and a pair of black leggings and tan, nondescript cotton panties, then Aimée hands me a white sports bra. "Hope this one fits all right," she says before turning her back to give me some privacy. "You've got a bit, well, more up there than I do."

I grin, letting my gown fall to the floor, exposing the naked body I'd only seen parts of in the bathroom since I've been conscious. Lean, strong legs (Dr. Leroy commented that I must be a runner), a firm belly with a faded scar above my bikini line, full breasts with nipples the size of quarters, and strong, slim arms. This is me.

I run my hand through my medium-length blond hair, then hold on to the side of the bed, threading my legs through the panties, then the leggings. I squeeze into the bra and pull the sweater over my head.

"Thank you," I say, staring down at my outfit as Aimée turns around. "This was . . . incredibly kind."

I open the Chanel bag and sort through its contents. I see a tube of red lipstick, a little cash, a receipt of some sort, a phone number scrawled on the back of a napkin, and a pack of gum.

"Ready?" she says, looking at me while reaching for the door handle.

I shake my head. "Aimée," I say, "what's my name?"

She smiles. "I've been waiting for you to ask," she says. "Caroline. Your name is Caroline Williams."

I swallow hard and follow her out the door and down the hallway, to a life I know nothing of. My heart pounds in my chest.

I am Caroline Williams.

"Here we are," Clément, the man from the hospital, says, pointing to a stately building outside the car. "Your home."

"Really?" I ask in disbelief, touching the window glass, then looking up at the centuries-old gray stone building with elaborate moldings, window dormers, and little balconies trimmed in intricate wrought iron. Quintessential Paris. Could this really be my *home?*

"Yes, mademoiselle," he says, stepping out of the car, with a sack in hand, and helping me with my door.

"But it's so . . ."

"Chic?" he says with a smile.

I nod.

"Yes, it is. One of Paris's most admired addresses."

I shake my head and exhale deeply. "How did I end up *here?*" I say under my breath.

Clément casts a worried glance my way. "Are you sure you're ready to"—he pauses to find the English word he's looking for—"assimilate?" I give him a blank stare as he adjusts the wire-rimmed glasses on his nose. "Dr. Leroy said you—"

"What did she say—" I begin, but stop when

I hear my tone: desperate, scared. "I'm sorry." I take a deep breath. "I'm just so . . ."

"Lost," he says, finishing my sentence. "I know. But you're home now. Let's get you settled."

I follow him into a foyer and together we enter a small elevator, which jerks upward after he presses the fourth-floor button.

"Here we are," he says, proceeding down the hallway. He inserts a key into the lock and nods as it releases. The hinge creaks as the door opens, beckoning me into a home that is foreign to me. My hospital companion flips on a light switch, illuminating our surroundings.

"Wow," I reply, running my hand along a modern blue velvet sofa—tufted, with brass legs. "It's . . . very nice."

Clément smiles. "I'll say."

The apartment is spacious but decorated minimally, which makes it look grander some-how, and also lonely. Three large windows in the living room lead out to a balcony, where I expect to find potted plants and a chair or two, but when I unlock the three separate latches and open the French doors to inspect the space, only a lone pigeon sits on the ledge, startling and flying away as I walk out.

"Funny," I say. "It's lovely out here. Why would I have kept it all locked up and sparse, as if I hated the idea of a balcony?"

Clément shrugs. "I don't know. But my wife

would die to have gardening space like this." He points to the corners of the balcony. "She'd fill every square inch with flowers."

Why didn't I?

I walk through the other areas of the apartment, which wraps around the right side of the building's top floor. There are three bedrooms. Two are empty; the third must be mine. I sit down on the queen-sized bed, blankets pulled tight and tucked so precisely around the edges that I worry about leaving a wrinkle when I stand again, as if the indentation I've just made might somehow disturb my former self.

"Looks like there's a bathroom down the hall, and the kitchen is just beyond," he says.

I turn back to face him, pulling my attention away from the dresser. *Why do I feel anxious about opening the drawers?* They're mine, or so I'm told. And yet, somehow, I don't feel ready, or right, about digging through the most private contents of *my* life. What sort of bras do I wear? Do I have a good sense of fashion? Are there letters or a secret photo of an old lover hidden inside a sock?

"I'll just leave this bag of groceries here," he says, clearing his throat. "One of the nurses went to the market earlier and picked up a few things for you as you get settled." I see a baguette poking out of the paper sack he sets down on the wood floor.

"Thank you," I say, feeling my heart pound inside my chest.

"If you need anything," he says, turning back once more, "just call the hospital and page Dr. Leroy."

I nod, swallowing hard.

"You're going to be just fine," he says with a smile that does little to reassure me.

A clock ticks somewhere in the distance. I sit down on the sofa, then stand again, walk around the living room examining a strange and yet eerily familiar painting on the wall, of a scene from a California backyard, perhaps: a pool edged with palm trees and a bowl of lemons on a wooden table. I touch the corner of the frame as if wishing it could speak. Had this painting been special to me?

I sigh. Everything evokes a feeling of déjà vu. The fruit on the counter. The clock ticking on the wall. The smell of the soap in the bathroom. I don't remember encountering any of it before, and yet I feel that I somehow have.

I scan the apartment once more. *Where do I begin?* It feels like moving, when the movers deposit the last box and leave you there alone with all your stuff. I am so paralyzed by the monumental task of unpacking my life that I have no idea where to start. The kitchen? The bedroom?

Inside all of the unseen boxes here are memories that need to be unpacked. I have so much to do, but I feel weary. I retreat to the couch, where I rest my head on a pillow. I let my heavy lids close. Tomorrow will be less hazy, I tell myself. I hope.

CHAPTER 4

CÉLINE

I stare at my reflection in the mirror above my dressing table, noticing a few new lines beneath my eyes. No longer fresh-faced and girlish, the way I was when I married Pierre; I'll be thirty-three before long. I sometimes wonder what he'd think of me now, almost a decade older. So much has changed since his passing, for good and for bad: the birth of a daughter he never knew, our city pinned down by the terror of occupation, and my heart's desire, though it be slow and cautious, to yield to love again.

Luc. I smile to myself. I've been harboring feelings for him for some time, feelings I pushed back for one reason or another (timing, Cosi, the war), but now I'm beginning to feel clarity—even more, a sense of urgency to tell him how I feel, before it's too late. Would he share my feelings or find them foolish?

I reach for a tube of lipstick and carefully apply a coat before giving myself a final look in the mirror, then fluffing the pillows on my bed.

The apartment we share with Papa, the same

one I've lived in since moving to Paris the year I turned twelve, isn't anything you might call grand, but it's larger than most, with two bedrooms and a sunny living room with windows facing out onto the rue Cler. Down the hallway is Papa's study and bedroom, and the one I share with Cosi, which overlooks the back-alley garden between buildings, where Cosi and I tend a little plot of land. The butter lettuce and carrots fared quite well this year, as did the broccoli (even if Cosi turned up her nose at it). The sweet peas were also so glorious this past spring that Papa even snipped a few for arrangements for extra-special clients. No matter the state of the world, or how dark the shadow that has fallen on our city, I find it curiously comforting to know that if you plant a seed and give it sunlight and water, it will grow.

All these years, the apartment has been our comfort, too. When Papa first laid eyes on it, pleasantly situated on the rue Cler, he knew it would be our home. His checklist was simple: sunny, clean, and with a balcony where he could have his coffee in the morning. We couldn't smell the sea or hear the seagulls squawking their morning hellos, and it would never be Normandy, but still, our modest perch over Paris was special in its own way.

Back then, the residence hadn't been a fancy address by any means. But in the almost twenty years we've called these walls home, the neighborhood has grown in popularity, which the Germans have quickly taken note of. Since the occupation, in fact, most high-ranking officers choose to live in nearby apartments. While, to date, no law-abiding French property owner has been displaced, many immigrant families have, most notably a few of our nearby Polish and Jewish neighbors.

In May, I watched in horror as a family of six across the square—with a little boy and three girls, one a primary school classmate of Cosi's—were forced from their apartment in a violent raid. I rushed Cosi to Papa's study and turned on the radio so she would be spared the scene of porcelain dishes, glassware, and family heirlooms shattering in splintered pieces onto the cobblestone streets below. My heart surged with every hysterical scream from the mother, who was losing everything she held dear, and then, something I will never be able to erase from my mind: a young German soldier, no more than nineteen, ripping a teddy bear from her little boy's grasp. In knickers and a tweed cap, he was a child I'd seen at the market with his mother occasionally. I always made a point of playing peekaboo with him, loving the way he would hide his little face behind his teddy bear, just like Cosi did at that age.

I heard from one of our customers who lives

on the top floor of that very building that the father was sent by train to a work camp far from here, the type described in the smuggled foreign newspapers circulated by the city's boldest members of the Resistance. The mother and children were believed to be taken to the Jewish ghetto across town, which we've all heard is teeming with filth and disease. She had kind eyes, the mother. My heart aches to think of her now. Will she see her husband again? Could I, or anyone else, have done something?

Evil has seeped into Paris like a cancer. And while there is strength in carrying on— sending your children to school in the morning, humming a tune on your bicycle, baking your bread, playing your piano, making your flower arrangements, being home by curfew—it also feels false when lives are being ripped apart right before our very eyes. Is it fair to carry on when others don't have that same right?

I don't have any answers, nor the means to make any real difference. That day in May, I'd suggested to Papa that we might try to shelter a family at risk. He'd dismissed my idea, but not for lack of compassion. "I won't risk your safety or Cosi's," he'd said. He was right, I suppose. And yet, my heart never stopped aching for that family across the square, and the thousands of others just like them.

"Luc will think you look beautiful tonight,"

Cosi says, peering in from the doorway. She has a big grin on her face, oblivious to the worries that play out like a dark novel in my mind. She leaps onto the bed, rumpling the velvet coverlet I'd smoothed just a moment ago. By the time I return home tonight, she'll be fast asleep in my bed, clutching her well-worn teddy bear, Monsieur Dubois (she gave the bear the distinguished name herself at the age of three), in a mangled torrent of sheets and covers. A wild sleeper like her father, my Cosi.

Cosi adores Luc, and Luc is crazy about her, too. I knew him long before Pierre, which is strange to think about. In fact, we were schoolchildren together. Kind and quiet, he wasn't like the other boys, who would chase and tease my girlfriends and me in the schoolyard, pulling our braids until we screamed. Luc was different. The winter I sprained my ankle, he offered to carry my book bag to and from school. I didn't accept, of course, knowing I'd be ridiculed by my best friend, Suzette, who was anti-boy at that moment, but I always wished I'd had the courage to accept his offer.

He'd been away from Paris for university and then worked in London before returning two years ago. He came to the flower shop with a pastry for Cosi and a dinner invitation for me. With his soft smile and gentle demeanor, he was still the same Luc of my childhood, but the years had molded him into a man who made my heart flutter.

So we had dinner that night, and the following week, and the one after that. We continue to see each other, and I love my weekly dates with Luc. The only son of Madame Jeanty, the owner of Bistro Jeanty, he avoided the family business and became a high-ranking member of the French police. I feel safe in his presence and enjoy our conversations about everything from childhood memories to the dismal state of France. Like me, Luc cares deeply about those suffering in our city, and we talk endlessly about ways we might make a difference. And while my feelings for him are real, and always have been, I sometimes don't know quite what to make of them. After all, where can this courtship possibly lead? I love my life with Cosi and Papa and have no interest in disrupting our home because I, selfishly, have fallen in love again. And Luc certainly wants to start a family of his own. Can I give him that? And even so, would it be fair to him when he might have a less complicated life with some other woman, a woman who could make him happier than I could?

I suppose that's why I've kept my feelings at bay for so long and steered our conversations away from matters of the heart. "Did you see that Madame Toulouse has painted her door green? The absurdity!"

Luc remains a mystery to me. He has more patience than the moon, and I feel that he cares about me deeply, even if he hasn't said it explicitly. Sometimes our eyes meet across the table, or on an evening walk, and I wonder if he's thinking what I am: that I could wander the streets of Paris, the world for that matter, for the rest of my life and never find a better home for my heart. If he feels the way I do, he doesn't say it. Perhaps we're each waiting for the other to pull back the curtains that shroud our hearts. In any case, each week I put on a pretty dress, a little red lipstick, and we have dinner.

I sigh, taking a final glance at myself in the mirror. I study my gaunt cheeks and these new fine lines around my eyes and wonder what Luc sees in me. I am thirty-two years old, not a young woman anymore. I will be forty in the blink of an eye. Surely, with his good looks and position in the community—not to mention his family name—he could be courting any woman he liked.

"Do you think Luc will bring me a chocolate?" Cosi asks expectantly.

The answer is always yes, and when the doorbell rings five minutes later, he arrives looking handsome and well groomed and, as usual, holding two squares of fine dark chocolate wrapped in gold foil. "One for you," he says to Cosi, on cue. "And one for Monsieur Dubois."

She hugs him, which is always followed by

my warning for her to brush her teeth and be in bed by half past seven. Papa nods at Luc from his chair by the fire, and then we leave and find our usual candlelit table waiting for us at Jeanty. While the world itself is drowning in uncertainty, I have come to find comfort in the certainty of *this*.

"Is that a new dress?" Luc asks as we sit down at the restaurant.

"No," I say, smiling. "I just haven't worn it in a while."

I notice his mother, Madame Jeanty, at a far table, entertaining some very fancy ladies in very fancy hats. If she sees me, she doesn't let on. It's no surprise that she doesn't approve of Luc's interest in me. I knew she'd long imagined her only son, heir to the family's substantial wealth, marrying a woman from a proper upper-class family rather than wasting his time with the widowed daughter of a simple florist, with an eight-year-old in tow.

An exceptional eight-year-old, I would argue. I hear Cosi's voice in my ear just then. "I'm almost nine!" She's been saying that since the week after her eighth birthday, of course. And indeed so. Born with an old soul in the very best way, my little girl is almost-nine going on twenty-three.

When I bring her to Bistro Jeanty on the first Sunday of every month, which is our tradition, she first locates Nic, our part-time delivery boy, who also helps in the kitchen and behind the bar at Jeanty. She'll wave at him shyly before walking over to the miniature compartment in the wall Luc told her about. Painted on its door is a French nursery rhyme and a whimsical little scene featuring animals and a hot-air balloon. As a boy, Luc had kept his most treasured toys inside its door. Upon discovering it, Cosi was instantly smitten. Knowing this fact, Luc, with the help of Nic, leaves little surprises for her—and, of course, Monsieur Dubois—to find: sometimes a spool of red satin ribbon for her doll's hair, other times a perfect orange from the market, or a peppermint stick. Whatever object he places inside, Cosi delights in it, even if Madame Jeanty does not.

Luc is a devoted son indeed, but one thing is certain: he has no interest in his mother's uppity aspirations, nor does he ever hide or apologize for his affection for Cosi and me.

"Céline?" he says when I don't respond. "Is everything all right?"

I look up and force a smile.

"You seem lost in thought tonight."

"I'm sorry," I say. "I suppose I'm just a bit tired. It's been a . . . busy week, that's all."

"Well, tired or not," he says, "you're a vision tonight."

"Thank you," I reply, shyly deflecting my gaze.

A waiter approaches, and he and Luc exchange

pleasantries before Luc examines the menu with great focus, the way he always does, then orders us the same bottle of Bordeaux, the finest on the menu.

"Very nice choice," the waiter says. He's new and apparently doesn't know that Luc is the son of Madame Jeanty. "And good timing, as that vintage won't be on the menu for much longer."

"Oh, is that so?" Luc asks.

"Indeed," the waiter replies. "I know for certain that there are no more than four cases left."

Luc's eyes flash. I recall him saying just a few weeks ago that his mother, a good friend of the winemaker's, had ordered enough of this particular wine we so enjoyed to last until at least Christmas, which was saying a lot for wartime.

Luc shakes his head. "Are you sure about that?"

The waiter nods, then leans in. "Madame Jeanty sold most of the lot to a German officer the other day," he says in a hushed voice. "Wine for his party."

Luc frowns, casting a glance at his mother's table as the waiter refills our water glasses. Luc has long worried about her associations with the Germans. At first he accepted it as business preservation, which was understandable to some degree. But he'd been disheartened to learn about regular customers being displaced from their tables to please groups of rowdy German soldiers, who were also given the best cuts of meat even when they frequently "forgot" to pay their bills. But now Luc's fears have heightened, especially since learning yesterday that his mother had attended a costume party alongside the city's highest-ranking members of the Third Reich.

"Thank you for bringing this to my attention," Luc says to the waiter. "I'll be sure to have a word with my mother about that. We can't give all of our finest wines to the Germans." He smiles. "What would we drink then?"

The waiter takes a step back and dabs his handkerchief to his forehead nervously. "Forgive me, monsieur," he says. "I . . . I had no idea you were Madame Jeanty's son."

"Please," Luc says graciously. "Think nothing of it. I'm glad you told me." He winks. "And I won't tell her it was you."

"Oh, thank you, monsieur," the man says. "Thank you ever so much. It's just that . . . my wife is expecting our third child, and I need this job."

"And you shall keep it," Luc says with a kind confidence that makes my heart stir. "Now, see if you can go find us that bottle of wine before it vanishes."

Madame Jeanty's table is too close to ours for us to risk discussing the matter further, so we do our best to settle back into our usual rhythm, but tonight feels different somehow. When I stare into Luc's eyes a bit longer than normal, he's nervous in a way he usually isn't. He drops his butter knife not once but twice and knocks a glass of water over with his left elbow.

"Céline," he finally says, "I . . . I need to talk to you about something very important."

I nod cautiously and take a long sip of my wine. In the dim light, I can't quite read his expression. Is he in trouble? Sick? In some kind of danger?

"Céline, I have to leave Paris soon, for training with . . . the police force, in the south. I'll be gone a month, maybe more."

"Oh, is that all?" I say, smiling. "You had me worried that it was something more . . . serious."

Luc doesn't share my sense of relief. His face is solemn, focused. "Paris is getting more dangerous by the day," he continues, his voice hushed. "Just last week, the captain of my department was ousted from his position. They took him away. His wife and children haven't heard from him since. Today, his replacement arrived, handpicked by the Germans."

"Wait," I say, fear creeping in, "that's not what's happening to you, is it? They're not taking you to—" "No, no," he says. "I mean, yes, traveling anywhere in the country right now comes with its own dangers, but that's not what I'm getting at. I'm not worried about me. I'm worried about you and Cosi here on your own."

"But I have Papa," I say cheerfully. "We'll be fine."

"Yes, but maybe not. What if something happens? What if they find out that—"

"Luc, you mustn't speak of that, here or anywhere," I say, my cheeks burning. Luc always said that in restaurants, the walls have ears. I've begun to wonder if they do. I look to the table to our right and gauge whether the couple beside us is eavesdropping; I'm relieved to see that they appear to be engaged in a heated argument.

"I'm sorry," he continues. "I can't help but worry about your safety. I want the best for you. I want . . ." He reaches his hand out to me, and I let him take it.

There are so many things I want to say, but in this moment, I can only utter his name. "Luc." Tears sting my eyes.

"Céline," he whispers, squeezing my hand tighter, just as a blast of cold air filters into the restaurant from the open doorway. I glance over my left shoulder and notice the group of German officers who have just arrived, a half dozen at least. Their dark gray overcoats make the restaurant seem that much darker.

Before I turn back to Luc, one of the officers, the largest in the group, catches my eye, and the hair on the back of my neck stands on end. *It's him—the man who came into the shop.*

Before I can explain to Luc, the officer approaches our table. Luc stands, the way French police officers do out of strained respect for the Germans. "Good evening, monsieur," he says. "I'm sorry, have we met?"

The officer smirks. "No, but I've met your lady here," he says, staring at me like a very fine steak that has just been wheeled before him on a dome-covered plate.

Luc glances at me, then back at the officer, confused.

"Oh yes, hello again," I say as calmly and politely as I can. "Luc, I waited on this gentleman at the shop the other day."

"You most certainly did," the officer says, grinning. He reaches for Luc's half-drunk wine on the table. "Mind if I have a taste?"

He takes Luc's silence as permission to take a sip.

"Very nice," he says, setting down the glass. "I picked up a truckload of this very vintage from your mother recently." He gazes around the bistro, with its trademark deep-red walls and polished brass trim. "She runs a fine establishment here. One of the best in Paris."

"She does," Luc says, his voice steady and without emotion.

"Well," the officer says, stepping back and switching expressions like only the very best actor can. Frightening one moment, he now seems somehow jovial. "I shall leave you to your charming dinner date." He looks at me for a long moment before turning back to Luc. "You are a very lucky man."

Luc nods, face solemn.

The officer extends his hand. "Kurt Reinhardt," he says.

"Luc Jeanty."

"Yes, I already knew that," the officer says in a way that sends a shiver through me.

We remain completely silent as the officer and his colleagues stop at Madame Jeanty's table. We can't make out their conversation, but her expression is as animated as it would be if Groucho Marx and a bevy of other Hollywood elite had come to dine.

When they leave a few minutes later, it's as if the entire restaurant, including the very walls, let out a collective sigh.

"That wasn't good," Luc says.

Although the encounter has left a bad taste in my mouth, I don't want Luc to worry any more than he already is.

"Let's try not to let it ruin our night," I say. "So what—an officer recognized me from the flower shop. They do all the time."

"No," Luc says. "That one is different."

"Sure," I continue. "His ego is as big as the Eiffel Tower, but—"

"No," he adds. "I saw him beating an elderly woman in the ninth arrondissement last week." He lowers his head.

I swallow hard. "Are you sure it was him?"

He nods. "I'm certain. After he took off, I drove the woman to the nearest clinic. Broken collarbone, likely. Bruised from head to toe."

I shake my head. "Why did he . . ."

"Brutalize her?" Luc sighs. "Because she looked at him the wrong way? Because the color of her dress didn't please him? I don't know. What I do know is these men believe everything and everyone is theirs for the taking." His eyes narrow as he looks deeply into mine. "Which is why I'm worried about you. And that German officer?" He shakes his head. "You do not want him paying you any sort of attention."

I nod. "What should I do?"

"You're going to have to keep a low profile, now more than ever," Luc continues. "Stay in as often as possible. Maybe have your father handle the flower shop for the next few months, or at the very least, never be there alone."

"But that's impossible," I say, shaking my head. "Papa can't manage on his own, with his arthritis and—"

"He can manage," Luc says.

I shiver, blinking back tears so no one detects the fear that grips me like a thorny vine.

Luc keeps his arm draped tightly around me on the walk home, frequently looking over his shoulder. Instead of saying good night outside, the way we always do, I invite him in, and he follows me up the stairs. Papa and Cosi have long since gone to bed. I hear the faint sound of snoring down the hall.

I sit on the couch and Luc nestles in beside me. Close, so close. I don't recall my legs ever touching his before, and for the first time in all the years I've known him, I want to be even closer. Like an avalanche brought on by spring, or this surge of love brought on by war, I feel as if the walls around my heart are beginning to come down. One crack, then three, then twenty, and all at once, the ice has melted and with it all of my fears, reservations, and insecurities. I move closer to Luc, first finding his hand, then his mouth.

We've kissed before—small pecks in greeting and farewell—but nothing like this. My heart races as he pulls me closer to him, his fingers caressing my hair, my face, my neck. I touch him, too, feeling the outline of his cheekbones, his strong jaw, the lines of his collarbone under his dress shirt after I undo the top buttons.

"I love you, Céline," he whispers to me. "I have always loved you."

"I love you, too," I say, the words slipping out of my mouth easily, like a reflex. *I love you, too.* It's a catharsis to release these words, long held in my heart, into the space between us, and Luc practically eats them up.

He pulls me closer, kissing me again with such

64

passion, I wish we could be anyplace other than here. I want all of him, and I know he wants all of me.

"I don't ever want us to part," I whisper, running my hand slowly down his torso.

"Me either," he says, pulling my hand to his lips and kissing each of my fingertips. "And that time will come soon, my love."

I nod, eyes fixed to his, hanging on his every word.

"When I return, we'll get married. I'll care for you and Cosi, your father too. I'll buy us a beautiful home. You'll have everything you wish for, and Cosi will too." He smiles and reaches for a peony stem in a vase on the coffee table. The work of Cosi, to be sure. She loves peonies. He hands me the flower, and I hold it to my nose with a smile. "My love," he continues, "I'll give you anything your heart desires. All the flowers in Paris, if you'd like them."

I grin, twirling the stem between my fingers. "All the flowers in Paris," I say, loving his sentiment.

He nods.

"But I only want . . . you," I whisper, blinking back tears.

"And you have me," he says, kissing my forehead. "You always have."

I smile. "Why me, when you could have any other woman?"

He shakes his head. "No other woman would do. It's you. It's always been you."

I wipe away a tear. "Thank you for waiting for me."

"I wouldn't have waited for anyone else," he says, standing. He kisses me once more before reaching for his overcoat and heading to the door.

Now I will be the one waiting, in a Paris so different from the one of our childhood. Luc will be out there, somewhere, and I'll be here, waking and sleeping; putting one foot in front of the other; keeping my head down until the joyful day he returns.

"I'll be home before you know it. Promise me you'll be safe."

He stands in the doorway, hair a little askew, a big smile plastered on his face, eyes beaming with love, so much love. If I owned a camera, I'd photograph this moment, just like this. Instead, I capture it with my mind.

"I promise," I say a beat later, memorizing the image of Luc and tucking it away in a safe place in my heart.

"I love you," he says. And then he is gone.

CHAPTER 5

CAROLINE

Light streams brightly through the living room windows as I open my eyes, gazing around the strange apartment that is apparently my home. The events of the last few days, and nothing else, hover like a fog stubbornly lingering on the horizon, blocking my view of the world around me.

I stand up and stretch, peeling off the jacket I fell asleep in, then tossing it on the back of the sofa. I find my way to the kitchen, where I rummage through the bag of groceries from the hospital. My stomach growls as I survey the contents: one baguette, a wedge of hard cheese, two peaches, a carton of cream, which I should have put in the refrigerator last night (oh well), a small bag of coffee beans, a hunk of salami, and a brown paper bag containing two chocolate croissants, one of which I reach for. My mouth waters as I sink my teeth into the flaky confection studded with chunks of dark chocolate. But as I swallow my second bite, I'm hit with a pang of doubt. Do I even eat sweets? I catch the reflection of my very thin figure in the kitchen window and envision the real me subsisting on carrot sticks and hummus. I consider setting the croissant down, but it tastes like heaven, so I finish it anyway.

I peer into my refrigerator, surveying its meager contents: a dozen eggs (expired), a shriveled apple, a moldy block of cheese, and a lonely jar of jam. In the back is a carton of milk and a box of what looks like old takeout, which I dare not touch.

There is no butter. No container of leftovers from a previous night's homemade dinner. No dessert left chilling before a dinner party. Clearly, I do not cook. And maybe I don't even *eat*.

I wipe a croissant crumb off my face and survey the rest of the kitchen. It's well appointed, with custom white cabinets fitted with brass knobs, black granite countertops, and an antique brass lantern hanging over the small island. Shiny copper All-Clad pots and pans, presumably never used, are stacked in the cabinets below. The pantry is bare, except for a box of oatmeal and an unopened bag of rice.

I scour the kitchen drawers for any clues to the life I once led but only find a stack of junk mail, some pens, a lone clothespin, and, curiously, at least two dozen unsharpened pencils in varying colors. I feel a sudden tinge of . . . a memory? But as quickly as it appears, it disappears again.

I sigh, defeated, then peruse the drawer beside the kitchen sink. Inside is a box of matches from a place called Bistro Jeanty and a phone number written on a scrap of paper, which I study for a long moment then tuck in my pocket along with the matches. Clues. They're all I have now, I guess.

I find my way to a tiny den beside the bedroom and notice a laptop, which I open and turn on. Of course, it's password protected. I make a mental note to take it to the Apple Store. Maybe if I explain my situation they can help me unlock it?

I smile to myself. It's funny that, even with such a massive lapse in my life memories, I can still think of things like the Apple Store or know what a fork is or that a bed is for sleeping, or how to hard-boil an egg.

"This is called passive knowledge," Dr. Leroy has explained. "Knowledge that is embedded in you, but not personal *to* you."

Whatever this meant, or means, for now, I am currently a person without a story. But I feel more like a person without a soul.

I walk out to the balcony facing the street and shiver as the cool morning breeze touches my skin. The sun shone so bright during these past days, one could almost forget that it is actually autumn. I watch as a single tawny-colored leaf falls from a maple tree on the street below, sailing in the breeze until it lands on a cobblestone in front of a café with a green awning.

I take a deep breath and walk to my bedroom,

where I bypass the stiff-looking black dresses in the closet and rummage through the dresser until I find a pair of jeans and a light blue T-shirt. I slip them on, then take in my reflection in the bathroom mirror. My eyes are blue, and my nose turns up a little at the tip. Do I look like my mother? My father? Are they still living?

I wash my face, then brush my hair and pull it up in a bun, then find a canvas bag and collect my laptop before sliding my feet into a pair of sandals by the door. It feels silly to be surprised that they fit, but then again, everything feels surprising.

"Hello there," I say to a portly concierge when the elevator deposits me in the building's foyer.

He sniffs and turns to the door, busying himself with his pen and notebook.

"I'm sorry," I say, my voice a bit louder. "I just wanted to say . . . hello."

"Hello," the man says quickly, as if my very presence is causing him a sharp pain.

"I'm Caroline," I say, extending my hand.

He looks at me as if I am certifiably crazy.

I smile, tucking my hand back in my pocket when he doesn't take it. "You'll have to forgive me. I was in an accident, and my memory's a bit unsteady."

He sighs dismissively. "I heard."

"So we're acquainted, then?"

"Mademoiselle," he says, without a shred of

emotion. "I've been taking care of this building for thirty-five years. You've lived here for the last three. Yes, we are acquainted."

"Well, good then," I continue. "Will you remind me of your name?"

He gives me a long stare. "Monsieur de Goff."

"Is that what I should call you? Or do you go by—"

"You may call me Monsieur de Goff."

"Of course," I say as he opens the door for me. "Well, I'll just be going now."

"Good day," he says, though he might as well have said "Good riddance."

I shake off the grouchy doorman as I head out to the street. I have bigger things to worry about. But first . . . coffee. I don't even know if I drink it, but it sounds like heaven right now, so I look around for a café. I remember the book of matches I'd found in my kitchen and tucked in my pocket. Bistro Jeanty. I eye the address and walk ahead, rounding one block, then two, until I see its sign in the distance.

I place my hand on the door, cautiously, then walk in. At once, it feels familiar and foreign, with its little wooden tables and walls painted a deep crimson. Customers form a line at the counter, where a number of swift-moving waiters buzz to and from a shiny chrome espresso machine. Steam wafts in the air, along with the smell of freshly ground coffee. A woman in a navy suit jacket orders a double espresso and a pastry from the case. A couple walks in hand in hand behind me, requesting a table by the window. The place has a hum to it, a pulse, and for some reason, I feel a part of it.

The hostess regards me cautiously. She's pretty, about my age, but her eyes look very tired, as if she hasn't gotten a good night's sleep in far too long. She whispers something to another employee, who looks up at me, then hurries through the double doors leading to the kitchen. "Good morning, madame," she finally says, her words stiff. "Your usual table?"

My usual table? I suppose I must have come here often . . . before the accident. I look around hoping that some person, some table or light fixture, might jog my memory, but like everything else, it's all a blur. "Uh, yes," I finally say, and she leads me to a table tucked away in a dark corner in the back.

"May I please order an espresso?"

Her eyes widen. "You never have coffee."

"Oh," I say, smiling. "I guess I just feel like it today."

"Very well," she says, looking at me strangely.

"Wait," I say. "What's your name?"

She studies me quizzically. "Margot."

"I know we may have met before, but . . . I had an accident, and my memory is . . . well, it's gone."

She nods at me as if I've just told her that I have a pet unicorn, then returns with a coffee, but no menu. Before I have a moment to inquire, a timid-looking man in his twenties deposits a plate before me. "*Bon appétit*," he says, scurrying back to the kitchen.

I look down at what is, presumably, my usual breakfast order: one poached egg, with nothing more than a dusting of black pepper, over a bed of wilted spinach. I notice the couple at a nearby table enjoying a quiche that looks freshly pulled from the oven. At another table, a man reads the newspaper between bites of a mouthwatering plate of eggs Benedict. I survey my breakfast with disappointment, then take a sip of coffee, just as a man wearing a white apron approaches. He's distinguished-looking, with handsome, chiseled features and wavy dark hair, speckled with a little gray at the temples.

"I trust we haven't made any mistakes today," he says with a cautious smile. His eyes are kind, if not familiar.

"Mistakes?" I search his brown eyes. "Oh, no, no," I say a moment later, glancing at my untouched breakfast and then back at him. "No, it's . . . perfect. I'm just . . ." I sigh, gesturing toward the chair across from mine. "Do you have a minute to . . . sit down?"

He seems surprised, even a little confused, but nods and slips into the chair at my table.

I lean in and lower my voice. "The thing is," I say, "I assume you know me, and that I'm a regular customer here. But I don't remember you. I don't remember anything. I had an accident and in the process, well, I lost my memory. I'm trying to piece together my life."

"Oh," the man says. "I'm very sorry about your accident, and of course, I am at your service."

I extend my hand to him. "I suppose I should start with an introduction." I feel the hostess's eyes burning a hole through my right side. "I'm Caroline."

He takes my hand, equal parts amused and guarded. "I'm Victor. I own the place—at least, as of recently. Big shoes to fill, but I'm up for the job. I do most of the cooking, too, though I have a few excellent sous-chefs, which means I never have to chop onions, which I hate."

I smile, then point toward the hostess. "And Margot? Am I reading into things, or does she want to throw a menu at me right now?"

Victor grins.

"So that proves it. I'm a jerk."

He laughs. "No, no, you're not a jerk."

"Then what am I?"

He looks at me curiously. "I don't know you well enough to say."

I sit back in my chair. "Fair enough. But if I owe anyone an apology, I hope someone would tell me."

"I'm sure there are no apologies necessary," Victor says with a smile. "And don't worry about Margot. She's a single mother and commutes from the farthest part of the city. She has a lot on her plate."

I suspect there is something more he isn't saying, but I don't press him. I glance at my plate and frown. "If my breakfast order is any judge of my personality," I say sarcastically, "I must be *loads* of fun."

Victor laughs. "Maybe you are."

I sigh, looking around the restaurant. "So you recently bought this place?"

Victor clears his throat. "Yes, it's a Paris landmark, you might say, owned by the same family for nearly one hundred years." He pauses. "Stop me if I'm being redundant, or if you . . . remember something I've already told you."

"Do you know how badly I wish you were being redundant right now?"

"Okay," he says, grinning. "Anyway, I was shocked to see it come on the market and snatched it up as quickly as I could. I updated the menu a bit, but other than that, I didn't make any big changes."

"Nor should you," I say, looking around. "It seems . . . perfect."

"And loaded with history, too," he continues. "Gertrude Stein, Hemingway, the Fitzgeralds— they all dined here. And when the Nazis pillaged

Paris, these walls stood strong. The menu's changed with the times, but we've always served a mean steak, a memorable breakfast, and a perfect martini."

"What more can you ask for?" I say with a smile.

He nods. "I used to come here as a boy—every Sunday, with my mother. I looked forward to it all week, because it meant I could have crème brûlée for dessert and stay up past my bedtime."

"And did you always dream of buying it?"

He shakes his head, turning his gaze to a spot on the wall behind me, or rather, a place in his memory, far, far away. "No, not really. I never thought it would be a possibility. Besides, life took me in a different direction." He pauses for a long moment. "But, yes, when the opportunity presented itself, it seemed like the right thing to do. Now, enough about me. It's you we need to talk about."

I nod, taking a long sip of my espresso. "It seems so strange to ask someone I don't know to tell me about myself. I wish you could fill in more details."

"Details, I'm not so sure. But I can give you a sketch."

"Please," I say.

He nods. "I know that you come in each morning at precisely seven-thirty A.M., not a minute before, or a minute after. You order the same thing." He points to my plate. "A poached egg over a bed of spinach. You talk to no one."

I grin. "Clearly, a party animal."

He pauses for a long moment, looking at me as if I've just said the most peculiar thing.

"What is it?"

He shakes his head. "It's just that . . . you're smiling."

"And that's strange . . . because?"

He searches my eyes. "You never smile."

I rub the spot on my head that had been hit hardest in the accident. It's still a little tender, but not painful the way it had been in the hospital. "Gosh," I say. "I sound miserable."

He forces a smile. "I wouldn't say miserable."

I grimace. "I sound pretty miserable."

"No, no, please, that isn't the case," he says reassuringly.

"Then what? I'm just a recluse?"

"No, Caroline, if you want my humble opinion . . ."

"I do, please. Anything you can tell me."

He nods. "I think you're just very . . . sad."

"Why?" I ask, leaning in closer to him as if this stranger somehow holds the key to unlock my memories—but, alas, he doesn't.

"Sorry," he says with a shrug. "I wish I could be more helpful." He stands up when he hears his name called from the kitchen.

"Wait," I say. "Is there anything else, at all, that

you can tell me? How could it be that I'm such a sad, miserable, grouchy person?" I glance at Margot again and shake my head regretfully. "I must have snapped at her at some point."

He tightens his apron. "When working in restaurants, you learn a lot about humanity. You see it all, from the beautiful to the ugly, and all the various shades in between. One thing I've come to learn over the years is that hurt people hurt people."

"Hurt people hurt people," I say, repeating his words. "Wow."

He nods. "You may not know why, Caroline, but you are hurting."

I expectantly hang on his every word, but he offers me no more. "I'm sorry. I have to get back to the kitchen. But I'll see you tomorrow for poached egg over spinach."

I may be a hurt person, but I decide that I won't be one who hurts others. Not anymore. And it's time I begin eating food that *tastes good*. "Thank you, but tomorrow, I think I'll have quiche instead."

"Excellent idea," he says with a smile.

The streets of Paris feel like a maze. I gaze up at the apartment buildings hovering over the narrow streets, balconies brimming with pink geraniums. Do I turn right, or left? It's hard to believe I have apparently succeeded in living

78

here for three years. I stop and ask an older woman for directions in French; my words sound sophisticated and savvy as they pass my lips. I wonder what other latent skills I possess. Perhaps I can do splits or recite the Pledge of Allegiance backward. The more I discover about myself, the more confused I feel.

I spot the Apple Store in the distance and find my way through its doors and to a female sales clerk with a nose ring and hair streaked with blue. I explain my problem, in English, as she looks at me skeptically. "You'll have to wipe it," she finally says in French.

I shake my head. "But you don't understand. I have amnesia. I had an accident, and I was in the hospital for a week." I hold up my laptop. "I need to access this computer."

She stares at me blankly, as if I have just walked in and told her that I am Steve Jobs's daughter, and I would like her to box up one of every device in the store and charge the company account, thank you very much.

"Please," I say.

She radios to someone on her headset, and a man in his fifties appears a minute later.

"I'm sorry," he says robotically. "I'm afraid we can't help you, as your device is password protected." He opens my laptop and points to the screen. "While you won't be able to access the password-protected area, you can log in as a guest user. In this way, at least the device will be functional."

"Thanks," I mutter dejectedly as I head to the door.

I walk for a long time, aimlessly, until the streets start to look familiar again. My inner compass must know how to get me home, and eventually I see Bistro Jeanty in the distance. It's almost seven o'clock, and my stomach is growling. I think of the owner, Victor, and how kind he'd been to me this morning. Would it be weird to go back for dinner?

I remember what he said about steak and set aside my hesitation. A different hostess greets me when I walk in the door, this one older and with dark hair. I can't tell if she knows me or not. "Just one?" she asks. I nod. The restaurant is busy, but I notice an open spot at the bar, and she leads me over to the counter, leaving me with a menu and a glass of water.

I pull my phone, freshly charged at the Apple Store, from my bag and am grateful it isn't password protected. I open my messages, but all of my texts appear to be deleted. My contacts don't provide much interest, either—only a list of names I don't recognize. There's no Facebook or Twitter app to comb through, so I open the photo folder, only to find two lone images: one of the backyard of a house, with palm trees and a pool. It reminds me of the painting on the wall in the apartment, the one with the bowl of lemons. The next photo is of two figures on a beach somewhere. A man and a little girl, holding hands, backs turned to the camera.

Strange. Why just these photos and no others?

"Excuse me," a man behind me says, tapping my shoulder. "Caroline?"

"Yes," I say, tucking my phone in my bag and turning around to face him. "I'm sorry, have we met?"

"It's me, Jean-Paul." He's tall and well dressed, good-looking, to be sure. "You may have had a few glasses of wine the other night, but surely you remember."

"Oh yes, of course," I say, playing along. I don't want to be rude.

"Is that seat taken?" he asks, pointing to the stool beside me.

"No, no," I say.

"Great," he says, smiling and taking the seat beside me. "It's good to see you again. Did you get my message?"

I study his face cautiously. Obviously, we are acquainted. But how? I scan the restaurant for Victor, hoping he might be able to connect the dots, but I don't see him. "Oh, no, I'm sorry," I say awkwardly, fumbling with my purse.

"I called you a few times."

"I've been . . . busy."

"That's okay," he continues, grinning. "Can I get you a drink?"

"Sure," I say, just as Victor walks out from the kitchen. His eyes meet mine immediately, but he doesn't approach. Instead, he hands something to the hostess, then slips back behind the double doors.

My companion motions for the bartender and orders us each a martini. The first sip hits me like a punch to the face, but it feels good. I take another sip, and then another, and in a few minutes, I'm warm all over, and a little numb.

"What did you say your name was again?" I ask.

"Jean-Paul," he says with a laugh. "You must have had more wine than I thought the other night." He orders us a second round of drinks and begins to tell me about the lecture he gave today at the university, where he is a professor of one subject or another. I half listen, but really, I'm watching the kitchen to see if Victor will appear through the double doors. By the time my third drink has arrived, so has my steak, and I devour each bite as Jean-Paul discusses the merits of existential thinking in the modern age, or something like that. After the first martini, I'd given up all hope of following his very big ideas. By half past nine, I feel lighter than a feather, and I hardly notice when his hand slips under the bar and touches my leg.

"This has been so fun," he says.

Has it? I wonder. I barely remember saying anything other than "oh," "yeah," "no," "that's great." Frankly, I barely remember anything he said. But there's music playing, and he's nice to look at, and who else do I have to sit beside me at a bar?

"May I walk you home?" he asks, leaning closer to me, just as Victor appears behind the bar.

"Well hello again," Victor says, refilling my water glass, then nodding at Jean-Paul. I can't tell if they know each other, but something about their exchange is . . . tense.

"We'll just settle up the bill now," Jean-Paul says.

"No dessert?" Victor asks.

"Not for us," he says.

"A shame." He looks at me. "Not even crème brûlée?"

"Yes, please," I say. "At least, for me."

Victor rattles off our order to the kitchen, and within moments, the most heavenly caramelized confection sits before me.

Jean-Paul dips his spoon in first, then sets it down. "A bit too sweet for my taste."

I try it next and close my eyes as the flavors swirl in my mouth. "It's perfect."

"How about another drink?" Jean-Paul suggests.

Before I can reply, Victor pipes in, looking right at me. "Don't you think you've had enough?"

His intention may be coming from the right place, but his tone reads as judgmental, and it rubs me the wrong way.

"You make a good point," Jean-Paul says, handing Victor his credit card. "Why have another drink here when we can go back to your apartment?"

I think I detect a fleck of regret or concern or . . . something . . . in Victor's eyes, but it's gone in a flash. Jean-Paul stands and heads to the door as I fumble for my bag. The martinis have kicked in, and I steady myself as I rise to my feet.

"Be careful," Victor whispers to me across the bar. "That one's a shark."

I let his words sink in, and yet I wonder: If Victor is genuinely concerned about me, why isn't he offering to walk me home himself? Besides, Jean-Paul seems nice enough, if a little self-absorbed.

"Good night," I say to Victor as Jean-Paul slips his arm around my waist.

"Here we are," I say when we arrive in front of my apartment. "Thank you for dinner. It was a fun night."

"What, you're not going to invite me to come up? You know I have a thing for the historical spaces on the rue Cler. You're torturing me."

For a brief moment, I consider shooing him away, but then I see a flash of movement to my right. Though it's hardly detectable in the dim street light, I think I see someone's shadow peering around the building ahead, but it quickly vanishes.

"Did you see that?" I ask Jean-Paul.

"What?"

"Well," I say, stumbling a little, "I've had way too much to drink."

"Then let me help you up," he says, reaching for my hand before tucking his arm firmly around my waist. Suddenly everything begins to spin. The lamppost above me strobes, and as Jean-Paul's face comes in and out of focus, my body goes limp.

I open my eyes and gasp, momentarily confused about my whereabouts, but then the scene comes into focus: I am on my living room couch, with a blanket draped over me. I sit up, clutching my head, and glance at the clock on the wall: 3:34 A.M. The previous evening's memories come screaming in. Jean-Paul. Martinis. Bistro Jeanty. Victor's disapproving gaze. I must have passed out. Did Jean-Paul carry me upstairs? I look down at myself, grateful to see that I am still fully clothed but also horrified that I risked my own safety. I vow never to drink martinis again and quench my parched throat with three glasses of water in the kitchen.

I let out a defeated sigh as I walk to my bedroom, where I take off my clothes, then select an oversized T-shirt from the top drawer, which smells like lavender, and . . . something I can't quite place. I pull it over my head, and before I shut the drawer, a fleck of green catches my eye. I reach to the back and pull out a carefully folded man's linen button-down shirt. It's short sleeved, with a faded palm print, like something a guy would wear on a tropical vacation, or in an ad for Tommy Bahama. *Whose is this, and why have I kept it in my drawer?*

A phone rings from what sounds like the kitchen—the landline I didn't know I had. I run down the hall as it continues to ring. It might as well be a fire alarm or air-raid siren, because the shrill sound sends shivers up my spine.

"Hello?" I say, heart racing as I wait for the caller to speak, but there is only faint breathing, and then a click.

I hang up the phone and stare at it for a long moment. Who would call at this hour? I decide to put it out of my mind and walk back down the hall, but before I turn to my bedroom, a flash of light catches my eye. The door to the third bedroom at the end of the hall is cracked open, and a spray of moonlight projects onto the floor, enticing me to peek my head in.

The hinges squeak as I open the door wider and walk inside. About half the size of the master bedroom, it contains just a double bed and one side table and a small desk by the window. Something about the space doesn't fit the rest of the house, but I can't quite pinpoint why. Perhaps it's the light fixture, which looks more dated than the modern selections in the rest of the apartment? I run my hand against the plaster wall, feeling the peeling paint and deep cracks beneath my fingertips, and then it hits me. While the entire apartment has been remodeled, this room remains veritably untouched. Why? I peer out the window, where the moon hangs low over the rue Cler, and for a moment, I could be anyone, at any time in the history of Paris. A little girl wishing on a star before school the next morning. An expectant mother humming a song on Christmas Eve. An old woman praying for safety during the Nazi occupation. Whoever had once lived here, in this very bedroom, somehow, I can feel her presence.

As the moon slips behind a cloud, I switch on the little lamp on the bedside table, which immediately casts a menacing shadow above the closet. I pull the two brass knobs, opening its doors and releasing a blast of stale air, which smells like an old attic layered in dust and forgotten memories. There are no clothes inside, just a few lone hangers and the remnants of floral wallpaper that has long since faded and peeled. I reach up to the top shelf, displacing an avalanche of dust, before kneeling down to have a look at a decorative wrought-iron grate in the wall, the remnants of an old heating system that has long since been updated. I press my hand against the grate, and when it pops back into the space behind the wall, I crouch in closer to retrieve it, extending my fingers into the dark crevice, where I detect an object of some sort. I extend my hand deeper, until I am able to grasp a small wooden box, which I set on the bed and examine in the light.

It appears to be an old cigar box. I blow a thick layer of dust off its surface and carefully release the delicate clasp. Inside is a tidy stack of yellowed envelopes tied with a strand of twine, which I pull loose. I examine the first envelope, which is addressed to a Mr. Luc Jeanty. The next one is, too, and the next. But there are no stamps or postmarks on the letters. In fact, they appear to have never even been sent. *Who left these here, and why?*

I slide my finger along the seam of the first envelope and pull out the two carefully folded pages inside, studying the beautiful handwriting as I move closer to the light. The words are in French; I read them easily.

My dearest Luc,
    While you're away, I have decided to

write you letters to pass the time. Time is all we have now, and I cling to it. Every second, minute, day until you are home, and we are reunited. And we will be, I know it. I feel it. If not on this earth, in heaven.

It's challenging to stay positive in these grim times, to hold firm to the idea that good will eventually overcome evil, that in the end, love will always overcome hate. But we must persevere. We must draw on the love we have for each other and let it be our strength.

I don't know where you are, but I pray you are safe. I pray for you every day, in the morning when I wake, and at night when I close my eyes. It gives me comfort to think of you praying for me, too. I know you must be.

I need your prayers now more than ever. I am in trouble and deeply afraid. I don't know if this letter will ever find its way to you, but I will continue to write to you just the same. I long for the day when this is all behind us, when we are together again.

I love you with every ounce of my being.

Yours forever,
Céline

Before I tuck the letter back into the envelope, I return to the first page to examine the date—October 18, 1943—and my eyes widen. That was wartime and, if I'm correct, the height of the occupation of Paris. I return to my bedroom and set the cigar box on my bedside table before crawling under the covers. I shiver as a draft of cool air hits my skin, and I pull the blanket around me tighter. I feel like a stranger in my bed, and also in the world. I'm too exhausted to think about my life, my problems. Instead, I think of Céline. Who was she, and how did her letters end up in my apartment?

My eyelids are heavy, and when I close them, I feel myself slipping into that space between sleep and waking. It's as if I'm standing at the center of a bridge that connects each side. In the distance, I hear the distinct sound of palm fronds in the breeze, and then the giggle of a little girl. "Look, Mama, look!" she says, jumping into a pool with a noisy splash. I feel the droplets of water hit my face. It's enough to make me open my eyes, to sit up in bed, but I don't. I want to stay here, just a little longer. My eyes flutter closed as a man appears in the distance. I can't see his face, but I know him. A wind chime hangs from the eaves of the house, jingling in the breeze.

The rustling of the palm trees fades away as quickly as it came, and when I open my eyes the next morning in my strange Paris apartment with secrets seemingly hiding in every corner, I blink back tears. I have no memory or understanding of the life I once led, but for the first time, I am acutely aware that I sorely and deeply long for it.

CHAPTER 6

CÉLINE

SEPTEMBER 30, 1943

Don't you love autumn, Mama?" Cosi asks, nestling her head into the crook of my arm.

"Yes, love," I say, smoothing her raven-colored hair. I don't tell her that this is the first autumn that I haven't loved—in fact, that I've even despised. Yes, there are pumpkins at the market and the trees are starting to turn glorious shades of crimson, yellow, and burnt orange, but the city is not ours anymore, and Luc is not in it.

I received a letter from him a week ago. It arrived last Tuesday, with no return address, and our postman, Gustave, handed it to me with a wink. "A special one for you today, Céline."

But as excited as I was to tear open the envelope, my heart sank when I read his words— cold, brief, and utterly foreign.

> Dear Céline,
> A beautiful day in the south of France.
> Nothing is like home, however.
> Give my best to Cosi, and your father.
> Every day, there are so many changes.

Remember that there is still so much
    beauty in the world.
*"La vie est un sommeil, l'amour en est
    le rêve."*
        Ich werde dich vermissen, always,
                                    Luc

I must have reread his letter fourteen times.
*Whatever in the world does he mean? And what
is this cryptic quote, "Life is a long sleep and
love is its dream"?* He obviously wrote it under
duress. I scour the letter again and again. *Luc!
What are you trying to tell me?*

I sigh, retreating to my bed, where I collapse in
a heap.

"What's wrong, Mama?" Cosi asks when she
gets home from school an hour later.

I rub my eyes and glance at the clock. "I must
have dozed off."

Her eyes are big and filled with concern.
"You're crying."

"No, honey," I say, collecting myself. "I'm
fine."

She finds Luc's letter on my dressing table, and
I immediately regret not tucking it away.

"I don't understand," she says, the letter in her
hands. "What does Luc mean?"

"It's nothing, dear," I say. "Nothing at all. A
joke. A silly joke."

My words don't faze her. Wiser than any child

I've ever known, Cosi turns back to the letter undeterred. She's quiet for a few moments, then turns to me with a satisfied nod. "It's a riddle," she finally says, smiling. "Luc is very smart. Mama, don't you see? He's left you a *secret code*."

"It's okay, love," I say, dismissing her sweet attempt to console me. "This is a grown-up matter that you don't need to worry about."

Her eyes widen, and I think of what a gift it is to be a child and to see the world through such a simple lens. I don't want Cosi to lose that gift because of this war, or because of me.

"No, Mama," she continues. "I *get it!* The little door at Bistro Jeanty! You know, the secret cabinet with the hot-air balloon and circus animals painted on it, where Luc always leaves a treat for me to find—one for me and one for Monsieur Dubois?"

I shake my head. "I don't understand."

"Mama," she says, pointing to Luc's letter again. "*La vie est un sommeil, l'amour en est le rêve.*" Her eyes flash. "These are the *same words* painted on the door."

I take the letter in my hands again, looking at it with a fresh perspective.

"Of course!" I say. "How could I have been so shortsighted? Luc is giving me a—"

"Secret message!" Cosi says, finishing my sentence. "And this," she continues, pointing to the first letter of each sentence. "It's an acrostic code."

"A what?"

She smiles. "Luc taught me," she says. "Only secret spies like us understand it, but, here, let me teach you, Mama." She plops onto the bed beside me and shows me how the first letter of each sentence spells out a word. "See," she finally says, her face suddenly ashen. "D-A-N-G-E-R."

I want to tell her that everything will be fine. That this is just a game, and that she should run along and play hopscotch in the street with one of her girlfriends while I quietly carry the burden of all of this and keep her little world just as she knows it—safe, beautiful, and joyful. And while I might have been able to pull off that perfect charade yesterday, and in all the days before, I know I cannot anymore. Evil has seeped into our world. I see it in Cosi's eyes as she leans in and wraps her small arm around my waist.

"Everything will be okay, Mama, no matter what," she whispers, "won't it?"

"Yes, sweet one," I say, fighting back tears.

We are in this together now.

I make crêpes for dinner, but Cosi hardly touches hers, as does Papa. The three of us sit by the fire after I finish the dishes. Even after the sun sets and darkness falls on the city, we don't bother turning on any lamps, settling instead for the warm glow of the fireplace. It feels safer that way, somehow, to be cocooned in the protective blanket of darkness.

Later, after Cosi and I are in bed, and she's fast asleep beside me, I lie awake for a long while thinking about Luc's letter. Had his training been a guise for something else? Something darker? And the riddle he'd left, hinting at danger and the little cabinet at Bistro Jeanty . . . Could he possibly have left something there for us? A message? Instructions? As soon as I can, I'll go and have a look.

I snuggle in beside Cosi. I'm too exhausted to get up to close the drapes in our bedroom; as a result, the moonlight pours in, casting its cool light on Cosi's cheek and the left ear of Monsieur Dubois. Somehow it feels good to remember that the moon, this very moon, has been around longer than Hitler and his army of terror. Over the course of history, it has seen as much evil as it has seen good. And it's the same moon that Luc might be looking up at this very moment, wherever he is. I cling to that thought and let it comfort me until I finally drift off to sleep.

"Shakshuka!" Papa says cheerfully the next morning at breakfast, setting a hot cast-iron skillet on a folded kitchen towel at the table. Cosi's legs dangle off her chair, and I smile to myself. As much as I want her to grow into the beautiful young woman she is meant to be, I know I'll always mourn the day that her feet finally touch the floor.

"Shakshuka?" Cosi studies the foreign meal.

I recognize it in an instant, of course. Eggs in a mildly spicy tomato sauce with a tiny dusting of parsley and Parmesan. I smile nostalgically at Papa, remembering the first time Mama made it for me.

"It was your grandmother's favorite dish," he says to Cosi.

"Really?" Cosi dips her fork in and takes a bite without any hesitation. "It's good," she says, smiling.

"Yes indeed," Papa says. "Careful, the skillet is very hot."

"Look at you." I smile at Papa. "What's gotten into you? You haven't cooked breakfast in . . . years." But then I remember. "It's Mama's birthday—of course!"

Cosi studies Papa's face. "Do you miss her the way Mama misses my father?"

"Every day," he says without faltering. "Every single day."

He walks to the radio on the side table in the living room and switches it on, turning the dial until he hears an orchestra: clarinet—Glenn Miller, of course—that jazzy blend of happy and sad. Mama loved music. She'd have danced with Papa right now, in her slippers, in the kitchen.

She gets up from the table and walks to Papa, peering into his eyes as if searching for something. "Are you sad?"

His smile acknowledges both his pain and her concern. Both tug at my heart, each emotion hitting me with equal force. "I suppose I always will be, sweet child." He pulls her small body toward his, placing his right hand on her waist, left hand on her shoulder. And they dance to Glenn Miller, in the middle of the living room with dishes from breakfast piled high in the sink, at the center of a war-torn city, and the very heart of a war-torn world.

There is no certainty for us, for anyone. None whatsoever. There is no assurance that our little family will be spared heartbreak or pain. And I have no sense of what today will bring, or tomorrow. But I do know that this sight, my papa dancing with my little girl on a Wednesday morning, is perhaps one of the most beautiful things I have ever seen.

And for now, that's enough.

I watch from the window the street below, sighing as Papa and Cosi set out on their way. He'll walk her to school, stand at the gate until she waves from her classroom window, then take his usual path to the shop, unlock the old door, and begin his work for the day. I wish I could join him. I miss being out in the world, feeling the fresh air on my cheeks, breathing in the scents of the city, taking in the cacophony of Paris—a barking dog, the scent of pastries baking, a school-boy humming a song on his bicycle, a couple quarreling on a third-floor balcony. I miss all of it, but especially the old rhythm of my life.

Luc has been gone for three weeks now, but it feels more like an eternity. After the final goodbye we shared, time feels slow and torturous. A fluttery feeling comes over me each time I think about our final night together, which is about nineteen times a day. I like to turn that moment over and over again in my mind. *When did I first see that spark in his eyes? At what moment did our lips first meet? Did he lean in first, or did I?* The steady, comfortable, fond friendship we'd had for years was infused with an electric energy I cannot explain. All I know is that I think of him morning and night—while I'm braiding Cosi's hair after breakfast, tying a pink ribbon around her locks, or while I'm wiping the last dish clean from dinner, the embers of Papa's fire sparking like the butterflies in my stomach when I recall the way Luc looked at me that night. *That night.*

And though only weeks have passed, it feels more like years. *Is he safe? Will he return soon or be forced to be gone longer?* I took his advice to heart and kept a low profile, staying home, save one morning when Papa was overwhelmed at the shop. And even then, I wore a cloak with a hood and managed to weave through side streets and alleyways so that when I made it to the shop, I did so almost invisibly.

Alone with my thoughts all day, I often wonder if any of it really matters. Perhaps I've been overly cautious. Perhaps Cosi was wrong and Luc's letter isn't a warning of any kind, but rather a rushed note from a busy officer with little time to write? To my disappointment, I haven't received any more correspondence from him, but if he had some important information to impart, surely Gustave would have delivered another envelope by now.

I hang my apron on the hook in the kitchen and watch a bird flying outside the window. It flaps its wings, then swoops down to an awning across the street before taking flight again, sailing off to its next destination. I want to be that bird. I want to be free.

So what if there's a German officer out there who fancies me? I'm not the first French woman to have a German suitor. It will blow over in time, just as soon as he finds someone prettier at some other café. And while I promised Luc I would make myself scarce, it doesn't mean forever. Everyone knows that German officers are as fickle as the weather on a spring day. For all I know, that man has completely forgotten about me.

The phone rings and I run to the living room, where it sits on the little marble-top side table by Papa's wingback chair.

"*Bonjour*," I say into the receiver, catching a glimpse of my pale face in the rectangular brass-framed mirror on the wall. Dark, hollow circles hover under my eyes.

"Céline, it's Suzette." Her voice is urgent, hurried.

Suzette and I have been friends since childhood. When I moved to Paris she was the only girl in my new school to venture a smile at me. "Two things you have to know about Paris life," she'd said that first day. "The girls are mean, so don't take it personally. And, when a boy shows interest in you, *always* pretend you don't care, even when you do." We've been friends ever since.

Suzette and I remained inseparable, scaling the steps of the hilly Montmartre neighborhood to and from school each day. With her good looks and striking auburn hair, she always had a line of boys vying for her attention. But it was her confident, irreverent nature that I most admired. Only Suzette could convince someone that it was a good idea to throw a pebble at the living room window of the school's headmistress, or stand in the rain outside the Ritz for a solid hour because she heard Cary Grant had checked in (he, in fact, had not), or sneak a spoiled egg into the desk of the meanest girl in school. While the majority of her antics were harmless enough, when they weren't, I was Suzette's much-needed voice of reason. At the age of sixteen, I talked her out of accepting a dinner invitation from a man at least her father's age (even if he was quite handsome). The following year, while employed to look after the children of a wealthy family for the weekend, she snuck out after dark to meet a boy at a nearby café, only to return to find herself locked out. After a frantic phone call to me, which, miraculously, did not wake Papa, I pedaled my bike for a mile and met her in front of the house, where she climbed on my shoulders and broke in through the second-floor window. I made her promise never to do anything like that again.

We survived each other's first crushes: hers, the very arrogant Jean-George, three years her senior, and mine, a quiet fellow named Jacques who moved to Provence with his family the year I turned sixteen. I wrote him two letters; both went unanswered. We shed countless tears over our respective unrequited loves, a fact that now gives us hours of comic relief.

"Can you believe I actually found him *attractive?*" Suzette said once over coffee.

"I know," I agreed. "That nose! And Jacques! What was I thinking?"

While one might say that our friendship revolves around the superficial—crushes, fashion, and the like—Suzette has been a constant in my life. Despite her shortcomings, her loyalty runs deep. She stood beside me when Cosi was born, holding my hand as I cried out in pain and reminding me that I wasn't alone.

Like me, Suzette had also been unlucky in love. Ever since a particularly devastating broken engagement (it turned out that her very handsome, and wealthy, fiancé from a fine family in Lyon preferred . . . men), she had found herself on the exhausting and seemingly never-ending search for her one true love, or at least someone who would do. The journey, sadly, had been a perilous one, with many unfortunate stops along the way—most recently, the country home of a married restaurateur whose wife happened to pop in with their daughter while Suzette and her lover sipped coffee in bed. Needless to say, things did not end well that afternoon.

"Please tell me you're free for lunch today," she says persistently.

"I'm sorry," I reply, twirling the cord of the phone between my fingers. "I just . . . can't today."

But Suzette isn't someone who takes no for an answer. "Come on, Céline, it's been too long. I haven't seen you in at least two months. You might have grown a beard or a third eye."

I laugh.

"I miss you," she continues. "We need a proper catch-up."

"I miss you, too," I say, "but it's just that I'm—"

"Let me guess. You're busy at the flower shop. I know, I know. Darling, I'm telling you, the flowers can wait. Please, sneak away for lunch. Your father will understand. Besides, I . . . need to talk to you about something important."

I recognize the worried tone in her voice. "Is everything okay?"

She sighs. "I'd rather talk in person."

I hope she hasn't gotten herself into a predicament. What she doesn't need is another angry wife in Paris who has it out for her. I fidget with the telephone cord and consider Suzette's proposal, thinking about how nice it would be to put on some lipstick, get out of the house, and order a Niçoise salad, even if it lacked *haricots verts* and tuna due to wartime rations. I was so weary of my own cooking, any restaurant meal would do. And I'd be careful getting there. I could take a less conspicuous route to the restaurant and keep my head down. What would be the harm in that?

"All right," I finally say.

Suzette squeals with delight. "Great. Café du Monde at noon. See you then."

I pull on my cloak, lifting the hood over my head, then lock up the apartment. It's only eleven, and I have plenty of time to run an errand

104

before meeting Suzette. I remember Luc's letter and decide to stop at Bistro Jeanty on the way. Madame Jeanty never comes in until at least five, and there will be a lull between breakfast and lunch service. Besides, all the waitstaff know me, so no one will question my presence. I'll order a coffee and distract the young woman at the counter while I peek inside Cosi's precious cabinet to see if there is anything to the riddle she claims to have pieced together from Luc's letter.

"*Bonjour*," my favorite waiter, Jon, says in greeting as I enter the restaurant. "We haven't seen you and Cosi in a while. We missed you last week."

"Yes," I say, "we've been . . . so busy."

"Ah, but of course," he says. "Shall I seat you by the window?" He scans the restaurant. "Your usual table is available."

I shake my head. "No, not today," I say. "I'd just like a cup of coffee at the counter if that's all right."

"For you, mademoiselle, anything is all right."

While he fiddles with the coffee maker, back turned to me, I inch closer to the little cabinet in the wall.

"You must miss your fellow," he says, talking to me as he works. "It's a mystery what he's doing out there. If I didn't know him better, I'd guess that he's in some sort of German training facility. Police officers are turning every day, of their own accord, you know. It's a shame."

"Luc would never . . ." I begin, standing up suddenly just as he turns around.

"Of course not."

It bothers me that Jon would speculate in such a way about Luc, whose character is unwavering. And yet these dark times have everyone looking over their shoulders.

He turns away, and I crouch again, opting not to press the matter further. I am within arm's reach of the cabinet door. "I have to say, as tough as Madame Jeanty is, she hasn't been the same since he's been gone."

The hinges creak as I pry the little door open. Inside is a thick envelope, tied with twine. I reach for it and tuck it into my purse, slipping back into my seat at the counter just as Jon presents my coffee. "*Voilà!*"

"Thank you," I say, smoothing my hair in the mirrored wall beside me. My heart races. *Did he see me tuck the envelope in my purse?* "What is this about Madame Jeanty?" I ask, deflecting attention away from myself.

Jon casts a cautious glance toward the kitchen and then back at me. "I know Madame Jeanty can be a tyrant at times, but I'm worried about her. She broke down in tears last night during dinner service."

"What was the matter?" I ask, taking a sip.

"I don't know," he says, "but it can't be good."

My eyes widen. "You don't think Luc is in trouble, do you?"

"I hope and pray it is not the case," he says. "But, mademoiselle, the truth is, these days we're *all* in trouble."

He's right, of course. We're all sailing in a ship that's taking on water. Life rafts are sparse.

I finish my coffee, then place a few coins on the counter before setting out again. *What has Luc left for us? What is happening?* I want to tear open the envelope immediately, but I know it would be unwise. I'll wait until I'm home, and safe.

I arrive at Café du Monde without incident, slipping into a table in a quiet corner, where I wait for Suzette (usually late) to arrive. True to form, she rushes in at a quarter past the hour begging my forgiveness. "I ran into that gossip Madame Simon on the way, and she would not let me out of her clutches!" She sinks into the chair across from me and sets her handbag on the table. "I'm so glad you could meet me!"

Suzette is as beautiful as ever, with her high cheekbones, big green eyes, and hair swept back in the way I could never manage to do mine, even with a thousand bobby pins.

She reaches across the table and squeezes my hand. "I've missed you so," she says. "Thank you for coming."

"The truth is," I say, "I've been a bit . . . cooped up at home lately. It's good to get out."

Suzette scrunches her nose as she reviews the menu. "Cooped up?"

"It's a long story," I say as the waiter approaches. After he records our order of two Niçoise salads and a carafe of Burgundy, Suzette leans in to continue our conversation.

"How's Cosi?" she asks, though I can tell her mind is elsewhere.

"She's great. You ought to come by and see her one evening. You know she adores you, especially when you do her hair. Lord knows her mother is challenged in that department."

Suzette nods, looking around the restaurant distractedly. "Right, yes, anytime."

"What is it?" I ask with the sixth sense that only a lifelong friendship can provide.

She ventures a smile. "So . . . I met someone."

"Oh?" I say playfully. "And is this someone, by chance, a man?"

She grins coyly. "Maybe."

"And are you going to give me the details?" I ask, smoothing my hair. I'd curled it for the first time in days (weeks?) and even put a little lipstick on. It felt good to be out in the world again, if only for a brief afternoon. For a moment we are not two women in an occupied city plagued with fear, but rather, two old friends having lunch in the city we love.

"I'll get to all that later," she says uncharacter-istically. It's unlike Suzette to not jump to the chase, but I don't press her. "You first. How's Luc?"

I fill her in on the developments of my relationship with Luc, most notably on how things had taken a serious, and beautiful, turn. Her eyes widen. "Finally," she says with a smile. "After all these years."

"Yes, apparently I'm a bit slow-moving when it comes to love."

"Well, if you didn't make up your mind by next year, I was going to swoop in and marry him myself," she says with a laugh, in the way only Suzette can be forgiven for.

"You two were," she adds, pausing to let out a wistful sigh, "written in the stars."

I smile. "Yes, I think so, too."

I recall Suzette's fairly recent debacle with the married restaurateur and wonder if she's recovered.

She reaches for a slice of bread and butters it. "Will you have children, the two of you?"

"I think Luc wants to," I say, smiling at the very thought of him. "We'll see."

"Well, if you do," she continues, "you'll have pretty babies, that's for sure."

The thought of our future, and the possibility of having a family together, warms me. Suzette is right. They *will* be beautiful, with Luc's brown eyes, my Norman cheekbones. If we have a little boy, I can imagine the plump curve of his face, his eyes big and curious. Joyful like Cosi, but also a bit of a rascal, in the very best way. I smile to myself.

"You will, too," I say, reassuringly.

"How can you be so sure?" she says with an air of defeat. "All the good ones have been taken. And the rest? They're off fighting this damn war, or . . . worse." She shakes her head. "I may never have a child if I don't . . ."

As her voice trails off, I pause to consider what comforting words I might offer my discouraged friend, but I have none. Instead, I reach across the table and squeeze her hand as four German officers enter the café. A hush falls over the room, and anxiety rises in my chest, at first a slow simmer, and soon a full-fledged boil. I tell myself I have nothing to worry about. I am a law-abiding French citizen having a normal lunch with an old friend. The Germans, they say, can smell fear. I refuse to give them a single whiff.

After refilling our wineglasses, the server places two salads before us. I eye the soft-boiled egg, but I am no longer hungry. Instead, I take a nervous sip of my wine as Suzette leans in closer to me, looking over my shoulder out at the tables behind us. "So the thing I wanted to tell you about is . . ." She pauses.

"The man you met."

"Well, yes," she says after a long moment. "But he's not the usual sort of man I date."

I smile. "As in not married, or otherwise a scoundrel."

She forces a smile. "That's not what I mean. This one is *different*."

"Different? How?"

She takes a deep breath, then closes her eyes tightly before opening them again. "His name is Franc," she continues. "He's . . ."

I shake my head in disbelief, piecing together the details before she has a chance to finish. "Suzette. What are you telling me, exactly?"

"I mean, if you asked me two years ago if I'd ever go out with a German officer, my answer would have been a flat no, but . . . I don't know, I met Franc, and . . . well, he's really great, different than you'd expect. We've gone on a few dates, and Céline, he's truly a gentleman. All this time, I thought they were a bunch of monsters, but the thing is . . . that's not true at all."

At first, I'm in too much shock to speak, but then I find my voice. "I understand that you have feelings for this man, and I understand that the Nazi uniform doesn't necessarily make someone a monster, but Suzette, do you understand the seriousness of what you're doing?" I lower my voice to a whisper. "Do you understand the risk?"

My friend furrows her brow as if my words have wounded her, deeply. She'd wanted me to encourage her, delight in her news, even, and here I am scolding her. "I should have expected that you couldn't be happy for me," she replies. "I mean, look at you, having the good fortune of having not one but two great loves in your life. Love has come so easily to you, you haven't any idea how hard it's been for me."

My eyes flash with pain. "That's not fair. How can you accuse me of not wanting happiness for you?"

"I'm sorry," Suzette says quietly. "That came out wrong." She sighs. "I only wish for the kind of love you have. You're lucky."

I nod, composing myself. "Of course you long for love," I say. "But at what cost?"

Suzette's eyes drift off.

"I'm scared, just like everybody else is," I continue. "I'm scared for Cosi. Scared for Papa. Scared for you."

"Yes, I know," she continues. "But Franc isn't scary. He's wonderful, really."

"Are you out of your mind?"

She seems impervious to my concern. "I saw Marguerite Leon at the market yesterday. You know, that half-witted girl from school with the horse-shaped face?"

I nod. But I don't care about Marguerite, her horse-shaped face, or anything else right now other than reasoning with Suzette.

"She's been going out with the most handsome

officer. He takes her to the theater and buys her practically anything she wants."

I shake my head, exasperated.

"You know those silk stockings they used to sell at La Boutique Rouge that everyone was clamoring for and now no one can get?" She doesn't wait for me to respond. "He bought her *three pairs.*"

Suzette has always fancied the finer things in life, but this? I sigh. "And that's what you want? To be *paid* for your . . . company?"

"Don't be such a prude, Céline. The facts are the facts. Paris isn't the same, and it may never be. You know as well as I do that there's a very good possibility of the Allies losing the war."

I shake my head. "That's not going to happen."

"But it might. And if it does, why wouldn't I want to be on the winning team?"

She continues to talk, but I struggle to listen. What's happened to my friend? On the exterior, she looks like any other prosperous woman of Paris, with her up-to-date wardrobe and perfectly coiffed hair, but I happen to know the truth. Her family is in financial crisis and has been for some time. The care and treatment for her older brother, Élian, who was born with severe medical problems and is confined to a wheelchair, has drained much of the family's meager discretionary funds. The family's future well-being and financial security rests on Suzette's ability to marry well, and I know she feels the pressure.

I reach my hand out to hers once again. "Oh, Suzette. These are such hard times, for all of us. There are things you can sacrifice, but your dignity is not one of them, nor is your heart. Cut it off with this man. You'll meet a good Frenchman before you know it. Just you wait and see."

Suzette doesn't look convinced. Instead, she sheepishly lifts the cuff of her burgundy velvet dress to reveal a diamond bracelet more beautiful than anything I've ever seen her wear.

"Where did you get *that?*"

"He gave it to me the other night when he came to the house to meet my parents, and Élian."

My eyes widen. "Wait, you let him meet *Élian?*"

"Yes."

"Suzette, haven't you heard the rumors of what they do to—"

"Cripples?" Suzette finishes my sentence. Her eyes flash. "Go ahead and say it."

"Suzette, you know I love Élian. How can you act as if I'm not on your side, as if I'm . . . against you?"

Something about her expression tells me that my words are useless. Her mind is made up.

"Do you think I'd actually go out with him if I was worried that any harm would come to Élian?" Suzette exclaims, the color rising in her cheeks.

"Franc is as gentle as a lamb, and besides, he told me all about Hitler's plans. Once the war is over, they will build quality homes for those like Élian, where they can live peaceful lives." She smiles to herself. "Contrary to what you may think, not everything about the Nazis is bad."

I can hardly stomach her words. Of course, we've all heard of French citizens turning, taken by the charm of friendships with German officers who promise them lavish rewards, high-ranking positions, and other special treatment once the war was over. Rumor has it that on any given night at the Ritz, fashion designer Coco Chanel even shares a bed with a blond officer half her age. But my lifelong friend? I cannot bear it.

"Stop this nonsense at once," I say, eyes fixed on hers. "I beg of you. Give him the bracelet back. Because if you keep it, you are his possession. Do you understand that? Tell him you're sorry, but your heart is elsewhere right now. Tell him your mother is sick. Tell him you have diphtheria. Tell him anything. Whatever you need to say, say it, and end it and get him out of your life, and Élian's. Please, Suzette. You are in danger, and you don't even know it."

She tucks her arm under the table as though retreating to the opposite side of an imaginary border.

"Even if this officer, Franc, is one of the good ones, if there is such a thing, what about the others he works with?" I press her. "When they find out about Élian . . ."

"You're being paranoid," she says, fingering the bracelet on her wrist.

"And you're being a fool!" I throw my arms in the air the way Papa might about something completely asinine, like the married men who come into the shop to buy flowers for their mistresses and wives at the same time and mix up the names on the cards and hardly care. "That bracelet," I continue, pointing to her wrist and looking closer at the diamonds, which are really quite large. "Have you considered where that even came from?"

"He bought it for me, obviously."

"We both know that didn't come from a jewelry shop."

"Stop, Céline," she says, as if she herself cannot bear the truth.

But I don't stop. "I'll tell you where it came from."

"I told you to stop," she says again, this time in a louder voice, drawing attention from the other tables. Tears fill her eyes.

I feel like crying, too, but I take a deep, steadying breath. I remember my promise to Luc. We mustn't cause a scene. "Please," I say. "Let's talk rationally."

But Suzette isn't listening. Instead, she bats her eyes and smiles at someone behind me. "Franc!"

116

she says, leaping to her feet as a handsome officer walks toward us with another man. She smiles coyly as Franc reaches for her waist, pulling her toward him in a nauseating embrace. A hush falls upon the café like a suffocating muzzle. Everyone, it seems, is watching us.

"Céline, this is Franc," Suzette says. "Franc, my old friend Céline."

Franc smiles. "A pleasure," he says before introducing his colleague, Ralph, to me. At best, I come off as cold, and very obviously uninterested.

"You two should join us at the theater tonight," Franc suggests. "We have tickets to the cabaret show at eight." Eight. In our occupied Paris, the theater, a dinner reservation, or any other event at eight is out of the question, as it collides with the citywide nine o'clock curfew, of course. A proper French meal takes at least two hours, preferably three, so at any given café or bistro, the last seating begins at seven these days. However, if you're in the company of a German officer, the world is your oyster. As such, most restaurants and high-profile entertainment establishments stay open to cater to the Germans in exchange for protection and special treatment.

"What do you say, Céline?" Suzette asks. I am heartbroken by the look in her eyes.

"I, I . . . I'm sorry," I say, taking a step back. "Thank you for the invitation, but I have a . . .

prior commitment tonight." I smile as politely as I can, reaching for my purse to pay for the meal, but Franc intervenes.

"Beautiful ladies should never pay," he says, holding out his hand, barring me from depositing my cash on the table. Suzette beams as he reaches into his pocket and pulls out several crisp bills, fanning them like a peacock's tail. It is more than enough to cover our salads and wine; he leaves an obviously generous tip for our server, which only seems to elevate Suzette's affection for him.

"You're too generous, Franc," she says with a moony expression that makes my stomach turn.

"I'm sorry," I say. "I've lost track of time. I must go."

"Well," Suzette says, pursing her lips. "It was . . . nice to see you." For a moment, I detect a flash of regret in her eyes, but another moment, it's gone.

I search her face unsuccessfully for any trace of my old friend, the one who didn't stand for injustice, who once confronted a gang of boys twice her size when they'd picked on her brother.

Papa always said that the Germans have a way of spreading their evil like a disease, and that some of us are more susceptible to it than others. I suppose I've never really believed that until now, when I see it happen with my very eyes.

Suzette has been infected.

CHAPTER 7

CAROLINE

In the morning, I lace up a pair of sneakers that look as if they've never been worn. While a run would be out of the question, a brisk walk might do me some good. Dr. Leroy said that exercise is one of the best things I can do for my brain, and she reiterated that on the phone earlier when she called to check in on me.

"I've been having these . . . flashbacks, I guess you could call them," I told her, describing the recent episodes I'd experienced. "But I can't really make much sense of them."

"That's normal," Dr. Leroy said, "though annoying, to be sure. Think of it this way. All those memories, all of your past, is there and intact in your brain. It hasn't gone anywhere, you just don't have access to it yet. As it downloads—or rather, as your brain's pathways repair themselves—it will seem strange at first."

Strange indeed. I select a pair of black athletic leggings and a gray T-shirt from the dresser, cinching the fabric into a little knot at the side, then pull my hair into a loose ponytail and head to the elevator.

Monsieur de Goff looks startled to see me when I arrive on the lobby level.

"Good morning," I say cheerfully between bites of a juicy apple I picked up at the market yesterday.

"Hello," he says, eying me cautiously as if I might detonate.

"Nice day," I say.

He nods.

"May I ask you a question?" He doesn't respond, so I launch right in. "My apartment, on the fourth floor, do you know anything about its past?"

He studies me for a long moment. "In all the years you've lived here, why do you suddenly ask now?"

I think of how many times I must have come in and out of Monsieur de Goff's foyer over the years, perhaps treating him with indifference, barely uttering a hello. No wonder he's suspicious of me.

"I know I must seem a little nuts," I say, "given my accident and memory loss. I'm trying to make sense of . . . everything, I guess. Like how I came to live here."

"I'm afraid I can't help you there."

I nod, considering whether I should tell him about the letters or not, and I decide against it—for now, at least. What if he demands I turn them over to him, or the landlord, before I have a chance to read them?

"The other night, I noticed that there's something different about the bedroom at the end of the hall. The apartment has been remodeled, but that bedroom is literally untouched. Anyway, I thought you might know why, or have some information about the history of the apartment."

"History?" he scoffs. "All of Paris is history."

"Of course," I say, turning to the door. "I'm sorry." If he knows anything of importance, he has little interest in sharing it with me. And, in his defense, why should he? I haven't earned his trust in these past years.

"Your apartment remained vacant after the war for years, even after I came to work here," he finally says. He looks out to the street for a long moment, perhaps deliberating about whether I deserve any further explanation. The wrinkles on his face are amplified by the morning light, and it occurs to me that he is quite advanced in age—at least seventy, perhaps even seventy-five.

"Nobody could ever understand why such a remarkable residence in one of the finest buildings in Paris would remain locked up and empty all those years," he continues, eying the lines of the ceiling with admiration. I can tell that his devotion to these walls runs deeper than a mere paycheck. "But I understood."

"Understood what?"

"Then, about fifteen years ago, the apartment came on the market. A nice young couple fell in love with it. I tried to warn them, but it was no use. After all, I'm just a doorman."

"Warn them of what?"

He continues on in his own way, revealing only what he chooses. "They were going to raise a family there. But . . ." He pauses and shakes his head. "That never happened. Partway through the remodel, they sold it to a rental agency."

"I don't understand. I thought you said they loved the apartment."

"It's hard to love a place where evil has lurked," he says, glancing up at the ceiling as if he can see straight into my apartment.

I shiver. "What do you mean by *evil?*"

"Like I said, I'm just a doorman. If the apartment suits you, that is good. But I'd never live there."

My eyes narrow. "Why?"

"With all due respect, mademoiselle," he says coldly, turning his attention to the mailroom door, "I don't have the time to indulge you any further."

"Yes," I say, taking a step back. "Yes of course."

Victor studies me quizzically as I walk into Bistro Jeanty forty-five minutes later. My cheeks flush when I remember leaving with Jean-Paul the night before. I'm a little out of breath from my brisk walk. When I notice how pretty one of the waitresses looks in her fitted black dress and carefully applied lipstick, I make a self-conscious, and futile, effort to improve my appearance by wiping the sweat from my brow and readjusting my ponytail.

"Have fun last night?" he asks with a coy smile.

"Sure," I say, avoiding his gaze. "He walked me home and that was that." I nod to myself, then rub my forehead. "My only real mistake was thinking that three martinis was a good idea."

Victor grins. "Four martinis."

I groan. "What was his name again?"

"Jean-Paul."

"Right. And he talked about himself incessantly."

Victor's smile disappears. "I want to apologize."

"For what?"

"For not walking you home myself."

My cheeks feel warm.

"I should have insisted. I shouldn't have let you leave, in your state, with, well, anyone."

"Well, nothing happened, and you don't need to—"

"Just the same, will you forgive me?"

I study his face carefully. "Why do you care? You don't even know me."

He stares at me for a long moment. "I care about all my customers." He pauses, then waves to a pretty woman in her late twenties who has just been seated at a nearby table.

I nod. "Of course."

Victor takes a deep breath, glancing toward the kitchen. "Will it be quiche today?"

"Yes, please," I say, turning to my usual table in the corner, then stopping suddenly. "You know, I was just thinking, maybe I could sit closer to the window? The sunlight feels so good."

"As you wish," Victor replies with a playful smile, setting a menu on a particularly sunny table by the window.

As I wait for breakfast, I quietly watch the hostess, Margot. She seems anxious, repeatedly glancing at her phone, then sighing.

"Excuse me," I say, approaching her cautiously. "I couldn't help but notice that you seem a little . . . worried. Are you okay?"

She squares her shoulders and straightens her posture, lifting her chin higher. "Everything is fine," she says in an icy voice. Her eyes are red. I can tell she's been crying, but it's obvious I'm the last person she'd dream of sharing her concerns with.

I nod, heading back to my table. When my breakfast arrives, I devour every bite, then order a second espresso. I wonder what the old me thought of this place. Did she take comfort in the hum of plates shuttling in and out of the kitchen, cutlery clinking, savory scents drifting in the air, friends greeting each other with double-cheek kisses? Or did she simply sit in her dark corner table, eat, and rush out? What was she hiding from? And why on earth was she so sad?

A fleck of color in the distance catches my eye, on the side wall leading to the kitchen. It looks like a painting, but when I notice a little brass knob, I see that it's some sort of cabinet built in the wall. I leave my coffee and walk over to have a look. As I crouch to pry the little door open, Victor rounds the corner from the kitchen.

"Shall I notify the police that we have a thief?"

"I'm sorry," I say. "I don't know what came over me. I just noticed this little compartment and I couldn't help but have a look inside."

"No harm," he says. "It's pretty special, isn't it?"

I nod, examining the words painted on the door: *La vie est un sommeil, l'amour en est le rêve.*

"Most people don't even notice it." He kneels down to point out the intricate detailing on the miniature door, with painted circus animals and a hot-air balloon.

"What is it?"

"One of the many mysteries of this place," he says. "It was here when I was a boy. Rumor has it that Monsieur Jeanty himself made it for his son, something fun for a child who spent his entire life in a restaurant, no doubt. Anyway, it always piqued my curiosity when I was young,

125

and one time when my mother wasn't looking, I snuck over and opened it. I thought I might find treasure inside."

"Did you?"

"Yes," he says, eyes sparkling. "I found a chocolate. After that, I kept looking, and each week, there would be another, and another."

"Who left them there?"

"Maybe one of the servers," he says with a shrug. "Maybe Monsieur Jeanty himself. I'll never know. But for a boy of nine, it was . . . magic."

I smile.

"You could ask Monsieur Ballard to tell you more. He used to work here as a boy, back when Madame Jeanty herself ran the place."

I recall Victor telling me about the history of the restaurant. After Madame Jeanty's death in the 1950s, her son took the reins until the mideighties, when he succumbed to cancer. A distant cousin picked things up from there, a time that Victor calls the restaurant's "dark age." Beloved menu items were changed or removed altogether, and while customers remained loyal, a part of the restaurant's soul had been deeply wounded.

Victor seems to have brought it back to life, however, to the delight of its long-standing customers, Monsieur Ballard included.

"His memory is fading a bit," Victor continues, pointing to the old man at a table by the window.

"That makes two of us," I say with a grin.

"Even so, he knows this place better than anyone. He comes in for breakfast every morning and every night for dinner. Breakfast varies, but dinner is always the same. A steak and salad and bottle of good Bordeaux. Here, let me introduce you."

I wish I could have gone home to shower and change before meeting the restaurant's oldest patron, but I follow Victor anyway, to a table where the elderly man sits with a newspaper and coffee. A well-worn cane is draped over the side of his left leg.

"Monsieur Ballard, there's someone I'd like you to meet."

He looks up at Victor, then at me. He's in his late seventies, perhaps even older. His eyes look as tired as they do wise, but I can also detect a spark of youth that never died out. At once, I imagine him as a rosy-cheeked boy of seven standing beside his mother at the restaurant, or a few years later, as a teenager, polishing glassware and shuttling hot plates out to customers, balancing a tray of wineglasses, and then as a young man, with the world at his feet.

I open my mouth to speak, but Monsieur Ballard does first. "I've seen you here for years," he says. "It's about time you said hello."

"I'm sorry I didn't—"

"Don't apologize," he interjects. "We all have our reasons."

I explain my accident and lost memories. "I don't really know much about myself right now." I smile. "But last night, I found a man's shirt folded up in the back of a drawer in my bedroom."

"Wait, what?" Victor interjects. "What sort of shirt?"

"It's terrible, actually, one of those loud tropical-print shirts you buy at tourist shops on vacation."

"That's funny," he says.

Monsieur Ballard clears his throat. "Your illness is as much a gift as it is a curse. There are parts of my life I'd rather forget."

My eyes meet Victor's, and recognizing the old man's discomfort, he steers the conversation in another direction. "I was just telling Caroline that you used to work here, as a boy in the nineteen forties."

Monsieur Ballard's eyes are clouded with memories, which he begins to share. "That's correct. I was just eleven when I came to work here. My parents needed the money, so I did odd jobs. Peeled potatoes after school. Washed dishes. Swept up at night. I had a lot of odd jobs like that during the occupation."

My eyes widen.

"I made deliveries for a nearby bakery, a local flower shop, too. But I loved being here the most, always have. There is no place like Jeanty."

I point across the room to where Victor and I were just standing. "That little cabinet over there, do you know how it . . . came to be?"

"I do," he says. "Do you know about yin and yang?"

"Yes, I mean, I guess I do."

"Opposite and yet compatible forces," he says. "You might say that the Jeantys, Monsieur and Madame, were like that. Monsieur Jeanty was all heart. He'd have given away free dinners all night were it not for his wife. Madame was just the opposite. All business, no play. Very strict. When her husband died, a lot of the whimsy died with him. But that cabinet . . . it remained. He made it for their son, Luc, who stored his wooden figurines inside."

"Luc," I say, remembering the letters I'd discovered last night addressed to someone of the same name. I want to ask him more about his wartime experiences, but he stands abruptly, setting his napkin on the table.

"Forgive me, but I must be going now," he says. "Good day to you both."

After he's gone, I tell Victor about the letters I'd found in the apartment and the conversation I'd had with the concierge, Monsieur de Goff. "What do you think?"

"I think he's just trying to scare you off," he says. "He's probably one of those old snobs who doesn't like Americans."

I nod. "But the letters I found. Why would they be in my apartment? I just feel like there has to be more to the story."

"Listen, you could find a story in every apartment in Paris if you wanted to," he says. "I hate to say it like this, but don't you already have enough on your plate trying to piece together the story of your own life?"

"True," I say. "But I have to admit, it's rather comforting to take my mind off my own problems."

"I see your point. Maybe it would be therapeutic to delve deeper, learn a bit more about this letter writer, or at least, whatever you can find."

I nod. "Thank you—for being a friend to me."

He smiles. "How about this: since you're sort of discovering Paris for the first time, why don't I show you around tomorrow? The kitchen will be well staffed, so I can break away. We could . . . walk around Montmartre, find a grassy spot somewhere and have a picnic. I'll be your own private guide." He grins expectantly.

I love the idea, but before I can respond, he interjects. "That was a stupid idea. I'm sorry, I—"

I reach out and touch his strong forearm. "No, it's not stupid at all. It's a wonderful idea. And I'd love nothing more than for you to show me around."

His face brightens. "Good. Let's meet here at noon and we can go from there."

He looks at me for a long moment, then shakes his head as if snapping out of a trance.

"What?" I ask.

"Nothing," he says with a smile.

I look at him quizzically.

"I'll . . . see you tomorrow."

"Yes, see you tomorrow."

I feel rather light and fluttery as I leave the restaurant and begin my walk home. Victor. I smile to myself, then immediately repress the thoughts that follow. This is silly. I am in no place to develop feelings for any man until I find out who I am. I sigh. What if I have a terrible past? What if I am a horrible, unlovable person? What if I'm . . . married? Yes, Victor would be my friend, and nothing more. Besides, he's much too handsome to ever be interested in me. I notice the way women look at him at the restaurant. Surely he could have his pick of Paris. And that's fine; we are merely embarking on a friendship.

I stop suddenly in front of a shop window not far from my apartment, where a painting of a palm tree hangs inside. It's an art studio of some sort; about a dozen people sit at easels. *Le Studio des Fleurs*, the sign above reads. THE STUDIO OF FLOWERS. I smile. And the text beneath: SPÉCIALISÉ EN ART-THÉRAPIE POUR LA GUÉRISON: specializing in art therapy for healing.

Art therapy? Healing? I venture inside as if pulled by a magnet.

"*Bonjour,*" I say to the dark-haired woman at the desk. She's a little older than I am, and very beautiful, with big blue eyes and pale-pink lips. "I'm sorry to interrupt, but I was just passing by and saw . . . well, I was just curious. What's art therapy?"

She extends her hand out to the small studio. Soft jazz music plays in the background. "*This* is art therapy."

"I guess I don't understand," I continue. "Aren't they just *painting?*"

"Yes, but they are painting their troubles away."

"Can you really . . . do that?"

She smiles. "Yes, and it really works. Maybe you'd like to try?"

I step back. "I don't know. I'm not really artistic."

"Everybody's artistic, in their own way," she says, walking over to an easel with a blank canvas, beside an empty stool. She gestures to me. "Here, why don't you try a free session?"

I take a seat, cautiously. I'm skeptical and regret poking my head in the door, but when she hands me a paintbrush, I feel a shift deep inside.

"There are no mistakes, and only two rules," she says. "You must tune everything else out and create from your heart."

I nod, dipping my brush in red acrylic, then white, before mixing the paints on the palette until they form a perfect pink.

I paint a peony, and then another. I somehow recall a garden, far away from here, where there were (are?) peonies. I remember the way the blossoms are so heavy that they flounce over, and I reach for another brush and dip it into green to get the stems just right.

I don't notice when the session has ended and the other students have gone. I don't notice my hunger pangs when lunchtime comes and goes or hear the church bells chiming. I am wholly consumed with this painting.

"How are things coming?" the dark-haired woman asks, placing her hand on my shoulder.

I gasp, as if being released from a trance or a session of hypnosis.

"This is really beautiful," she says, looking over my canvas. "In fact, it's extraordinary."

To my surprise, I agree. It's actually . . . good.

"Have you painted before?" she asks.

I shake my head. "Not that I recall."

"Well, then you must do more of it."

I smile.

"How do you feel?"

"Tired," I say.

"Like you've just run a marathon?"

"Or something like that." I reach for my bag.

"Good," she says. "That's how the healing

133

happens. I hope you'll come back again, at least to pick up your work once it's dry. You're welcome here anytime."

I nod, still stunned that something so beautiful could come out of me. "You must be the owner?"

She nods. "My family has had this building for as long as I can remember. I finally convinced my mother that I could put it to good use."

"Oh, is she an artist?"

"No," she says. "But she appreciates it. At least she used to, when she was in better health."

"I'm sorry."

She nods. "Life is full of challenges. We all have them. Art has helped me through my own deep valleys. That's exactly why I opened this studio." She smiles. "You'll get there."

"Thanks."

"I'm Inès."

"Caroline."

"It's so nice to meet you, Caroline."

I pass the market on the way home and stop to admire the late-fall hydrangeas brimming from buckets along the street, their edges tinged with purple.

"May I have six stems, please?" I ask the vendor, an older woman with dark-rimmed glasses, seated on a stool. She nods, and I watch as she expertly trims the stems, and a few leaves, then wraps the ensemble in crisp brown paper before tying it with twine.

I thank her and give her my card.

Home in my apartment, I find a vase under the kitchen sink and fill it with water, placing the flowers inside. They look stately in their spot on the dining room table, and I am struck with the sudden urge to . . . paint them, but with what? And then, like a flash of lightning, a memory surfaces. I run to my bedroom closet. I know what is tucked away in the far right corner: colored pencils and pastels beside a sketchbook. In my mind's eye, I see my old self. Sobbing, she shoves these art supplies high up on the shelf, banishing them from her presence, before falling to her knees and weeping.

Why? Why was I weeping?

I collect the pastels and sketchbook and study the flowers in the vase on my table. Hardly looking at the sketchbook, I let my hand take a path of its own on the page.

I close my eyes and hear wind rushing through palm trees again. And then laughter. The scene is foggy at first, and then it comes into sharp focus. I am standing in a kitchen. It's one of those big, well-appointed spaces you see in magazines, but this one is well loved, not just staged. A cake bakes in the oven. Carrot. There are matches and a box of birthday candles at the ready by the stove. Stan Getz's smoky-sweet saxophone filters from a speaker somewhere nearby. I'm stirring a pot of marinara sauce; a bit has splattered onto the marble countertop, but I don't care. I take a sip of wine and sway to the music. A little girl giggles on the sofa. I don't see her face, just her blond ponytail. And then, warm, strong arms around my waist as he presses his body against me. I breathe in the scent of rugged spice, fresh cotton, and love. I turn around to face him, but when I do . . . my eyes open.

I am at my dining room table in Paris, alone. The sun is setting, and I have sketched a vase of hydrangeas in intricate detail. I don't know much of anything right now, just that I so desperately want to go back to that kitchen. I so desperately want to go home.

CHAPTER 8

CÉLINE

As I leave the café, I try to put Suzette out of my mind, for now anyway. I've spoken my piece and that's all I can do. Besides, I have enough to worry about in my own life—namely, Cosi and Papa.

I pull my scarf higher around my neck. The wind is brisk, cruel even, with a bitterness that wasn't there last week, or even yesterday—the unrelenting kind that weasels its way between buttons and underclothes and seeps through woolen caps.

The first snow would be upon us soon, leaving Paris awash in white. I've always loved the city in winter, particularly the way the rooftops look as if they've been dusted with a heavy layer of confectioner's sugar, turning the formerly anemic balcony gardens of winter into scenes straight out of a fairy tale.

Luc will be home before long, I assure myself. We'll get married and sort everything out. The German officer who I feared would be a problem for me, and for all of us, hasn't returned. We'll carry on as we always have, Papa making his beautiful flower arrangements, boxing them up

137

for delivery by Nic; me tending to Cosi, helping at the shop when I can.

I cut through a side alley, bypassing the rue Saint-Placide, where so many Nazis loiter, then exiting for a brief moment on a quiet side street. Just six more blocks and I'd be home.

I glance at my watch: half past one. The gold antique timepiece belonged to my mother, and I've worn it since I found it in a jewelry box in Papa's shirt drawer when I was fourteen.

I look right, then left. I'm eager to make it home so I can open the envelope I found at Bistro Jeanty in a safe place, but I decide to make an unplanned detour to the flower shop to see Papa. There's plenty of time before Cosi's home from school, and Papa could use some cheering up. He's been so quiet lately, hardly saying a word at dinner. Last night, before I could even think about serving dessert, he turned in for the night. He works so hard. Too hard. Luc asked me to be careful, but at what expense? Papa's health? Our business?

Each morning, my father wakes before sunrise, and he comes home after dark, exhausted and with shadows under his eyes darker than the day before. I can't let him continue like this for much longer. Yes, I'll go see him at the shop, I decide. I'll bring him a pastry from the bakery around the corner, because he probably hasn't eaten anything since breakfast, which he barely touched anyway. I salvaged the eggs for reheating tomorrow.

"Good day, mademoiselle," a young man behind the counter says, his back turned to me. When he turns around, I see his flash of recognition.

"Nic! I didn't know you worked here, too. Between Jeanty and our deliveries, when do you rest?"

He smiles, deflecting my concern. "My family needs the extra income."

"Well," I say, "as long as you're not working yourself too hard." I order two *pains aux raisins* and a chocolate croissant for Cosi, and Nic packs them carefully into a bag, ignoring the coins I hand to him.

"It's on the house," he whispers.

"Are you sure?"

He nods, shooing me away with a wink as another customer walks in. "Please tell Mademoiselle Cosi I said hello."

"I will," I say with a smile and set out along the street that leads to our shop, expertly avoiding wedging my heels into the cobblestones as only lifelong Parisian women can do. ("Step on the balls of your feet," Suzette's mother, Madame Claudine de Bont, had said when teaching us how to navigate a city in delicate shoes, "like a low tiptoe.") I admired her in so many ways—for her effortless beauty, her spirit, and the fact that she took me under her wing and taught me the things my mother would have,

139

had she survived. Claudine could have married any man she wanted. She could have been a countess, an heiress, a first lady. She could be clad in Chanel, right now, at the finest hotel, entertaining dignitaries and the like. But none of that mattered, not to her at least. She fell in love with Suzette's father, Bertrand, the son of a farmer, and that was that.

Even at the age of thirteen, I could see the love in her eyes. Claudine chose a life of financial instability to be with a man she loved so fiercely. But she hasn't been rewarded for choosing the path of love, by any means. Her eldest, Élian, was born with severe medical challenges. And while Bertrand loved his wife deeply, he was frequently out of work and struggled to provide for the family.

I think of my recent encounter with Suzette and let out a defeated sigh. I shiver when I recall the way the German officer had looked at her, with lust in his eyes. *How could she not see it? How could she not see the danger lurking?*

The shop is just a few paces away, and I'm warmed by the familiar sight of our sign hanging from the awning. I remember when Papa hand-painted it, on the balcony of our apartment, when I was twelve. He'd asked for my input on the business name, ultimately settling on my suggestion: BELLA FLEUR. And so it was, Bella Fleur, painted in curly pink lettering on a forest-green background. I thought it was perfect then; I still do now.

"Papa," I say, walking into the shop, holding up the bag of pastries. "Surprise!"

But he's not behind the counter, where he usually is. I proceed to the back room, where I expect to find him trimming the thorns and leaves off a new delivery of roses, or sweeping up stems from yesterday's orders. But he's not there, either. In fact, the shop seems entirely empty, and also . . . askew. A bucket of greenery has been knocked over and water pools on the floor. Shards of porcelain, remnants of one of our finer vases, lie in a defeated pile nearby.

"Papa?" I cry, this time louder. I tell myself not to panic. With Nic working at the bakery today, Papa is maybe out on an important delivery, perhaps to Madame Lumière's apartment, where she is, no doubt, having one of her fancy dinner parties. She is notorious for phoning in impossible last-minute orders that Papa never says no to.

Yes, he'll be back soon, I assure myself. But then I hear a faint groan coming from somewhere near.

"Papa!" I see him now, lying on the ground, beside the front window. I must have walked right past him when I came in. I run to him and fall to my knees. "You're hurt." I rip a strip of fabric from the hem of my dress and gently dab

141

the blood from his brow, then carefully tie the strip around his forehead, securing it tight enough to control the bleeding.

"Can you move?" I ask, placing a gentle hand on his leg.

He bends his legs, then his arms. "Yes, I'm just fine, dear. No broken bones." With my help, he sits up. "I must have lost my balance and passed out for a spell."

"Who did this to you?"

"It doesn't matter," Papa mutters.

"It *does* matter," I say, wiping away a tear.

"When they . . ." He attempts to stand, then winces in pain.

"Where does it hurt?"

"I'm afraid it's my back," he says. I place my hands under his arms as he carefully rises to a stand. "Nothing that a little ice can't fix."

"Papa, what happened?"

"I just got a little roughed up," he says.

"Who did this?"

"Nobody," he says, brushing off the incident.

"Papa, what sort of nobody?"

He looks off into the distance.

"Was it a German?"

He remains quiet.

"Papa, please. Talk to me." I look into his tired, sad eyes. The laceration on his eyebrow oozes blood through my makeshift bandage. It will surely require stitches. I make a mental note to call Dr. Bennion, who has been our family physician for years. "Tell me so I can protect you. Tell me, so we can be *safe.*"

Papa remains quiet.

"Was it the officer who came into the shop, the tall one who—"

"Céline," he says, "I told you not to worry. It's only a scratch—"

"But I do worry," I say. "And I have to know. Was it *him?*"

He lowers his head and nods.

The phone rings and Papa moves quickly to answer it, but I stop him. "No. Let it go. You are in no condition to continue for the day. I'm taking you home. You need a doctor."

Except for the day Pierre died, Papa hasn't closed the shop early in all the years since its opening. I can read his mind: staying is not safe, at least, not this afternoon, but closing the shop early feels like a defeat.

As he deliberates, I reach for the broom leaning against the side wall and begin cleaning up. I kneel down and pick up the shattered remains of the vase that was once my favorite. I let out a sigh as I toss it in the wastebasket then walk to the alley to dispose of the mess, looking over my shoulder three times.

Back inside, I glance at my watch, and when I do, my heart seizes. "Cosi! I was supposed to meet her at the apartment fifteen minutes ago!"

By now she must be wondering where I am. *What if she wandered off? What if she . . .*

Just then, the door jingles and I nearly collapse with relief when Cosi runs in. "Mama! There you are! I went home like you said, but you weren't there so I came here." She searches my face. "Are you cross with me?"

"No, no, honey," I say, kneeling down to hug her. I squeeze her harder than usual. "I'm so sorry I wasn't home, love. I hope you weren't worried. I lost track of time."

"It's all right, Mama," she says quickly. "I wasn't worried. I . . ." She pauses when she sees Papa's face, and runs to him. "What happened?"

He forces a smile. "My dear child, it seems I need to get a better pair of glasses. Somehow this silly grandfather of yours managed to walk straight into a wall today."

Cosi's worried expression melts into a smile. "Silly, silly Papa! You ought to be more careful!"

"Yes, I ought to," he says.

She smiles, then walks to the front window, slowly studying something that's caught her eye. "That's strange," she says, pointing ahead. "Mama, what's that on the window?"

"What, honey?"

Cosi stares ahead. "The yellow star."

I look up, and the hair on the back of my neck stands on end. For a moment, I don't believe my eyes. This is not real life but a terrible nightmare. And yet, my eyes aren't lying. The paint is still wet. I hadn't noticed the crude-looking and hastily painted star when I arrived, and by the look on Papa's face, he hadn't noticed it, either.

"Mama?" Cosi asks again. "Why did they do that?"

She knows what the yellow star means. Every man, woman, and child knows. I want so desperately to tell her that, just like Papa's "silly" accident, this is also a silly mistake, one she needn't worry herself over. We'll scrub it off with a little soap and water, and *voilà*, good as new.

But I don't say anything. I have no words. Instead, I take her hand in mine, and Papa and I exchange glances. "I'll just get the keys and lock up," he says.

Papa finds his coat and satchel, and for the second time in the history of his business on the rue Cler, he turns the sign to CLOSED and locks the door before six o'clock.

I've seen Papa cry two times in my life. This is the third.

Papa needs a doctor, but we can't risk taking him out in the light of day, so we decide to wait until after dark, when most officers are too distracted with their personal dinner plans to notice an old man with facial injuries. After I've made a quick meal for Papa and Cosi, I reach for the address book beside the phone and dial Dr. Bennion's number. He's made house calls here before and has always been kind to us. His mother was also from Normandy, and he's enjoyed sharing stories with Papa of boyhood summers by the sea. Surely he'll help us now.

"Dr. Bennion, it's Céline Durand," I say in a hushed voice, so as not to startle Cosi.

"Yes, hello, Céline," he replies.

"I'm sorry to bother you after hours, but my father's been hurt and needs attention."

"Oh, I'm very sorry to hear that," he says, his voice strangely void of any warmth.

"He was beaten, quite badly. He needs stitches. Could you possibly pay us a visit, or, if that's an inconvenience, may we come over?"

"Céline," he says, after a long silence that makes my heart sink. "I'm very sorry, but it's so late, and, you see, my . . . schedule is dreadfully full. And . . ."

"And what?" I say, tears stinging my eyes. Dr. Bennion walks along the rue Cler each day, from his apartment to his clinic. "You saw the star, didn't you?"

"I don't know what you're talking about," he says.

"Of course you do," I say. "Everyone does."

"Céline."

"Don't pretend that I don't understand, Dr. Bennion. It's just that . . . I thought that you, of

146

all people, would see through what's happening. But I guess I am mistaken."

Papa looks anxious. He motions for me to hang up the phone.

"Goodbye, Dr. Bennion." I set the receiver down with a thud, then walk to the sofa and collapse beside Papa.

"My girl," Papa says, shaking his head. "I know you're upset, but you can't talk like that, not to Dr. Bennion, not to anyone, do you understand?" He lowers his voice to a hush. "We have to be careful—now more than ever."

Our Jewish heritage has always been a concern, but only a whisper in the back of my mind. Papa's father was French, after all, and so are we. "We're French citizens," I say to Papa. "They have no right to—"

"We *are* French citizens," he says. "But that doesn't matter now. Obviously they know the truth about my grandmother. Someone must have reported us."

There's no use trying to figure out who. Papa's wound is still bleeding. "We have to get you help," I say. "There has to be someone who can stitch you up." My eyes widen. "Wait, I have an idea. Do you remember that woman who lives in the apartment downstairs? Esther. She's a nurse. Let's go see if she can help."

Papa looks unsure. "Can she be trusted?"

"Yes," I say, recalling the time she knocked

on our door last year to present a bundle of mail, containing several checks, that had been misdelivered to her address. She'd met Cosi that day and seemed nice enough. "We have to get that wound closed up," I continue, taking his hand. "It needs to be cleaned properly and stitched, or you'll risk infection. Esther will help us.

"Cosi," I continue. She looks up from the breakfast table, where she's busy writing in her journal. It's filled with the accounts of her days, little poems and sayings she finds amusing— curated by Cosi, and Cosi alone. "I'm just running downstairs with Papa to . . . drop something off for one of the neighbors." I hate to leave her, but I also can't bear to have her see Papa in pain, nor do I want her to hear us speak to Esther. She'll be safe at home. "We'll be back in fifteen minutes."

She nods, and Papa and I walk to the door.

"Mama?"

I turn around again. "I'm not scared," she says with a smile that brings tears to my eyes. "You know why?"

"Why, love?" I ask, trying to keep my voice from cracking.

"Because I have Monsieur Dubois!" She squeezes her beloved bear, heavily matted and showing more signs of age than ever. I must remember to sew his left ear in place—again.

"Yes, dear one. You are never alone." I blow her a kiss.

"Say it," she says.

I smile, knowing immediately what she wants to hear, the very same words my mother would say to me when we parted. She'd look at me with her big, loving eyes and say, *"Ne pas s'envoler, mon petit oiseau."* Don't fly away, my little birdie.

"Ne pas s'envoler, mon petit oiseau," she repeats to me.

I blow her a kiss and close the door behind me. Esther's apartment is on the ground floor; I hold Papa's elbow as we slowly make our way down the stairs to her door, where I knock two times. A moment later, I hear footsteps, then an extended silence before the door creaks open, letting out a slow sliver of light, which pierces the dim hallway. A pair of brown eyes peers out at us.

"Céline?" Esther says, opening the door a bit wider.

"Yes," I say, "I'm here with my father, Claude. I know it's late, and I hate to disturb you, but . . . we need your help."

"Of course," she says, without a moment's pause, opening the door wider and cautiously eying the staircase behind us. "Come in right away," she says, whisking us over the threshold then, closing the door and securing the latch.

Her apartment is much smaller than ours, but charming in its own way. Perched toward the back of the building, it abuts the garden where Cosi and I tend to our little plot of land.

"Please, sit down," Esther says warmly, pointing to a sofa. The apartment is much more stylish than I imagined, with its walls painted a pleasing shade of burgundy and an assortment of unique furnishings, including a vase of peacock feathers, which I am certain Cosi would love.

Esther isn't what you'd call a fashionable person, or high society in any way, with her cropped haircut and muslin dresses, and yet there is something quite smart about her, odd as she is. She's my age, or maybe a few years younger, but in the ten years since she's lived below us, I've never once seen her in the company of a man. Sad, some might think. But Esther has always seemed effortlessly content working her shift at the hospital each day, then coming home to her cat, Gigi.

I notice a little writing desk by the window, with a typewriter and a rather thick stack of typewritten pages bound with two rubber bands. Esther sees me looking at her desk and nods. "I'm writing a book," she says with a confident smile.

"A book?"

"Yes," she says. "Well, a collection of stories. I've heard so many things from my patients over the years. I needed a place to put them all." She smiles. "So I decided to write them."

I grin at Papa, trying to lighten the mood. "Look, we might end up in a book!"

"Indeed so," Esther says before Papa can muster a half-hearted smile. "Look for a mention in chapter nineteen." She frowns as I recount Papa's injuries while she examines his wounds. "We'll get you fixed up as good as new. But before I get started, may I make you a cup of tea?"

"No," I say. "We wouldn't want to trouble you."

"It's no trouble," she says. "I think I'd like one myself."

I've been so consumed with worry over Papa that I hadn't noticed that she's in her nightdress and robe. We have woken her, or at the very least caught her just as she was retiring for the night. And yet she is not the least bit inconvenienced. In a few moments she returns, carrying a hot teapot in one hand and three stacked teacups in the other.

"You're too kind," I say to Esther. "We are very grateful for your help. I called Dr. Bennion earlier and . . ."

Esther quietly shakes her head as she pours the tea. "Say no more," she says, handing Papa a cup, then me. "I'm glad you came to me. Dr. Bennion is not a trustworthy man."

I think of all the times he treated Papa, Cosi, and me. He'd been friendly then, hadn't he? Did I have him pegged all wrong?

151

"Sadly, this war has brought out the worst in some," she says. "And that Dr. Bennion is one of them." She shakes her head. "No medical provider should turn away a person for any reason, especially because of their race."

I assume she's talking about Papa, but then she continues. "Last week, a child of only three came in with a deep chest cough. The poor dear could hardly breathe. She needed oxygen immediately. She was Jewish; I noticed the star on her mother's coat. Dr. Bennion turned her away. He said his schedule was booked." She shakes her head gravely. "It wasn't. I was the charge nurse on duty that day and I saw the clipboard."

"I don't understand," I say with a sigh.

She nods. "Some things are impossible to understand. Like evil."

"But Dr. Bennion isn't . . . evil," I say.

"He may not be," Esther replies, "but he's succumbed to it nevertheless. And who knows why? Because he wants to protect himself, or his wealth and position? Because he's scared? I don't know." She looks off into the distance, where her cat is purring on the little dining room table.

As hard as all of this is to stomach, how can I fault Dr. Bennion? Isn't every one of us trying to hide from the Nazis, keep our heads down, avoid confrontation of any kind—all so we may protect what is dearest to us? I'd been doing that very

152

thing by heeding Luc's advice and staying away from the shop for a time.

And then there are people, like Esther, who say to themselves, "I *don't* want to end up arrested by an SS officer, but I *do* want to help this person in need—this person whose association with me could cause me much personal trouble."

She reaches for her medical bag and switches on the lamp beside Papa. "Now, let's have a look," she says, peeling back the bandage I wrapped around his forehead earlier today.

Tears sting my eyes as I lean toward Esther and whisper in her ear (on Papa's right side, where his hearing is diminished): "They put the star on our shop window today."

"I know," she says without emotion. "I saw it."

I wipe away a tear. Of course she did. Esther and everyone else in our neighborhood. Word has surely gotten out now, far and wide. I begin to think of all of our wealthy patrons, French citizens who have managed to keep their lives functioning as if Paris were not under siege, as if, despite the impending threat of world takeover, the lavish life continued—the dinner parties and luncheons with elaborate floral arrangements. Yes, for some time we have been able to weave in and out, undetected, but only because we cloaked ourselves with a fictitious sense of security. But now the cloak is off, and we have been branded, and for that, others will disassociate.

"We'll be out of business before Christmas," I whisper.

"No," Esther says. "You won't be. You have plenty of good and noble French clients who respect your father and will stand by you."

"Like Dr. Bennion?" I say, shaking my head.

She takes a deep breath. "The good ones will stand tall," she says, fixing her eyes on mine. "Don't you forget that. Don't let all this evil make you forget that there is still so much good." She smiles. "There are still more flowers than there are weeds."

She hands me a handkerchief and I take it. It's been embroidered with the initials LRJ, and I wonder if it once belonged to someone she loved. "Thank you," I say, dabbing my eyes.

Here's a woman who works at a war-embattled hospital day after day, caring for French and Germans alike, and yet she seems to have no fear. I decide that I want to live the way Esther does, fearless and heart-forward. Can I?

I explain the assault Papa sustained, and Esther frowns as she pulls a box of gauze from her medical bag. "Now," she says to Papa, steadying his chin with her hand. "This may hurt a little."

Esther cleans his wound, then begins stitching his skin back together in the same way I did needlepoint as a girl. Papa only winces once.

"There," she finally says, stepping back and examining her work. "As good as new."

154

"You are very kind," I say as Papa and I stand and walk to the door. "Thank you ever so much."

"You come to me whenever. Whatever I can do, I will." I am overwhelmed by her kindness. She looks at Papa for a long moment, then at me. "We're all in this together, you know?"

"Yes, indeed we are," Papa says. His voice sounds so tired.

I reach for Esther's hand and squeeze it. "Please, let us make you dinner one night."

"I would love nothing more," she replies with a smile.

Papa and I turn to the stairs to walk back to our apartment but stop suddenly when we hear voices on the floor above.

"You know they shut their flower shop down," a woman says.

"It's about time," another replies. "I just hope they get them out of our building. The last thing we need is another Jewish family causing trouble."

Papa and I exchange glances as the two women continue to talk before disappearing into a door on the second floor. We both know which one: the home of Francine and Maxwell Toulouse. Their daughter, Alina, attends school with Cosi and has been over to our home many times. She has always been kind, unlike her parents, who have never seemed to warm to us. I figured it was because my dresses weren't fashionable enough, or something silly like that, given Francine's elaborate wardrobe. Maxwell is the only son of one of France's most successful railroad entrepreneurs. But his rumored laziness did not please his father. And so, he was given just enough money each month to live comfortably, and no more. The rest would come upon his father's death. And by the sound of Francine's frequent complaints about the apartment building, it is obvious to anyone who knows the couple that they can't wait for that day.

"Don't worry about them," Papa whispers to me as we continue up the stairs. "Just harmless gossips."

"But what if they—"

"Shhh. It will all be fine."

I glance at my watch; more than a half hour has passed, and I immediately regret leaving Cosi home alone. I could have brought her with us, but . . . I didn't want to frighten her. And yet, we've been gone longer than I had hoped. I walk a little faster up the last flight of stairs, rounding the corner toward the hallway that leads to our door, which is . . . gaping open.

"Cosi?" I cry, racing into our apartment. I hadn't left the door open, and Cosi knows better than to leave.

"Cosi!"

"Cosi!" Papa chimes in.

Her coat, her shoes. They're all there. I run to

156

look in her bedroom, and mine. Empty. I scour the living room and find Monsieur Dubois lying on the floor. I pick him up and pull him to my chest and burst into tears.

"Papa, they took her," I sob. "They took Cosi!"

He reaches for his coat on the hook by the door. "I'll go out and ask if anyone has seen her. Maybe she—"

"No," I say, frantically. I want to find my baby girl more than anything in the world, but if Papa goes out after curfew, especially after today . . . I can't bear to think of what might happen. "Not after curfew. They'll . . . arrest you. Let me go instead. I'm a woman. I'll draw less suspicion."

"I won't have it," he says in protest. "I won't let my only daughter—"

"Oh, there you are," Cosi says, appearing in the doorway holding the little blue ball she brought home from school yesterday.

I run to her and fall to my knees. "Cosi! Cosi! Darling, we were so worried! Where did you go? What happened?" I search her face. "Are you hurt?"

"No, Mama." She tosses her ball in the air, catching it with both hands. "I know you might be upset with me, but I opened the door just a smidge, because"—she pauses to collect her bear from the floor—"naughty Monsieur Dubois dared me to do it." She giggles. "We were playing a game. But then my ball fell down the stairs, so I ran to go get it. When I saw you and Papa walking up the stairs, I was worried you'd be cross with me, so I waited and tried to sneak in behind you."

"We were so worried," I say, squeezing her tightly.

"Sorry, Mama," she says. "I didn't mean to frighten you."

My heart still pounds wildly in my chest as I hold her close to me. That night, after Papa is settled in bed, and I tuck Cosi in beside me, listening to the way her breath changes as she drifts into a deep sleep, I think about all the things I've lain awake wishing for before slipping into slumber, when the mind wanders and the heart yearns. A handsome husband with a kind smile who calls me "dear" and begs me to make cassoulet because he insists my recipe is even better than his grandmother's. A house by the sea in Normandy with linen drapes that catch the breeze when the windows are open. A scarf like the ones I saw in the fashion magazines at the salon. A new set of fluffy pillows with silk cases.

But when I think of these things now, they mean nothing. There is only one wish that matters at this moment, the most important one of all: safety. For Cosi, Papa, Luc, and myself. Tomorrow we will wake up, and we will make breakfast like we always do, and we will carry on, with the hope that we can wake and make breakfast the next day, and the next, and the next, until there's finally an end to this madness.

That is my one wish.

CHAPTER 9

CAROLINE

The autumn sun shines through my bedroom window as I sit up in bed and yawn. Today I'll meet Victor at Jeanty for a walk and a picnic. I peruse my closet for something to wear, settling on a white off-the-shoulder linen sundress and sandals. Thanks to the unseasonably warm temperatures, I won't need to bother with a sweater, but I toss a blue pashmina in my bag just in case the wind picks up later.

I take a quick glance at my reflection in the bathroom mirror, then walk closer, daring to lean in and inspect my face on a micro level. I have good-enough cheekbones, not razor-sharp like so many women in Paris (every other one you pass could be a professional model); my eyebrows have a nice arch; a few wrinkles on my forehead, oh well; dry skin; and lines around my jaw—whether they're from frowning or smiling, I may never know. My lips look pale, so I open the drawer to my left and fumble around until I find a tube of lipstick. It still feels strange rummaging through my drawers and shelves. It's all my stuff, of course, and yet I feel like a party guest who peeks into a medicine cabinet that is not hers, or a little girl sneaking into her mom's makeup bag to steal a swipe of lipstick.

The lipstick I swipe is red, *bright* red. At first, I consider wiping it off, but I purse my lips in the mirror, then smile. Why not?

I think of the letters I'd found in the cigar box and wonder if the woman, Céline, had ever applied lipstick in this very bathroom. I decide to open another letter and read it before I start my day.

Dear Luc,

How I wish I could write to you with good news, but I'm afraid our situation here has worsened. Papa was badly beaten today, by the Germans. He'll recover, though our business, I fear, will not. We've been branded with the yellow star. Everything I'd prayed wouldn't happen is happening now. It's like we've been pulled into the storm, and the winds are too powerful to withstand much longer.

I desperately wish that you'd come home. I'm so scared.

Yours,
Céline

Heart reeling, I read the letter once more, then tuck it back into its envelope. Never mind my own problems; I only wish I could transport myself to 1943 and help this poor woman. *Whatever became of her?*

My curiosity is intense as I tuck the letter back in the cigar box. I'm about to pull another out when my cellphone rings. It's Victor.

"Hi," I say, smiling.

"Hi. Are we still on for today?"

"Yes." I glance at the clock. "Sorry, I guess I'm running a little late. I'll be there in a few minutes. Is that okay?"

"Yes, great."

I tuck the cigar box back in the drawer of my bedside table, then grab my bag and head to the elevator.

In the lobby, Monsieur de Goff is on the phone, and I'm a bit relieved, given his dismissive tone with me yesterday. Perhaps Victor is right about his prejudice against Americans and, apparently, my apartment.

I head out to the street and don't give the matter a second thought.

"Hi," Victor says to me when I arrive at Jeanty. "You look . . . beautiful."

I feel my cheeks flush a little. "Oh, thanks."

"I'm just about ready," he says, reaching for a basket. Inside are a few paper to-go boxes, a baguette, a small blanket rolled into a perfect cylinder. He runs to the kitchen and returns with another small box, a bottle of wine, and two small glasses, which he tucks inside. "There," he says, holding the door open for me. "Shall we?"

I pretend not to notice the hostess and bartender smiling at us. Why would they be? This is not a date, after all.

"So, I was thinking I'd take you up to the Montmartre neighborhood. It's a bit of a walk, so I wanted to check first to see how you're healing."

"No more aches and pains," I say. "And my doctor called to say that I'm cleared for exercise, so let's do this."

"Good," he says. "I promise, you won't be disappointed."

I smile.

Victor wears a pair of jeans and Converse and a tailored linen shirt the color of the summer sky. He looks different in street clothes, in a good way. He's trimmed his beard, and all that remains is a soft shadow of stubble around the edge of his strong jaw.

"I—" We both speak at once, then stop and laugh. For some reason, I feel a little nervous, and he seems to be too.

"You go first," he says.

I smile. "I was just going to say that I'm happy to be spending this day with you."

"Me too," he says, smiling. As we round the next corner, he begins to tell me about his life growing up in Paris. He points out the park where he took his first steps, the apartment where his parents brought him home from the hospital after his birth, the bench where he had his first kiss (her name was Adèle, and she had braces), his favorite bar, and the best bakery, where we stop and order two *pains aux raisins.* I listen and laugh and take it all in. Victor's Paris is colorful and vibrant. Every corner has a story. Every café a memory.

"You love this city so much," I say as we make our way down an alley so narrow that a passing car nearly scratches its side mirror against the stone building. "So what made you want to leave and spend time in the United States?"

"Well," he says, "that's a bit of a long story."

"I'd love to hear it."

He nods. "First it was for education. I wanted to go to culinary school, but I wasn't interested in any of the stuffy classical French schools here. I was fascinated by the cuisine coming out of Northern California, specifically Napa and Sonoma. Fresh ingredients with such style and personality. Wine food." He laughs. "At least that's what I call it. I wanted to cook like that. So I went and studied there for four years, then worked off and on in kitchens in California, New York, before coming back here again around the time my mom got sick."

"Oh, I'm so sorry."

He nods. "Breast cancer. But she recovered."

I place my hand on my heart.

"After that, I did a lot of soul-searching. And I ended up back in California."

"What brought you back this time?"

"A special lady," he says. There's a glimmer in his eye that tells me he was once bewitched by her, and perhaps still is.

"How did you meet?" For some reason, I want to know everything about the person who captured Victor's heart.

"By chance, really," he says, staring out at the street ahead dreamily. "She was on a summer trip with a few of her girlfriends, just after graduating from college. She walked right up to me and asked for directions, in Montmartre, actually." He smiles. "And just like that, I was . . ." He pauses for a moment. "What is that American saying? Oh yeah, I was putty in her hands."

I smile. "So the two of you were together for a long time?"

"Years, yes," he says, his face awash with memories. "I've never met anyone like her. She could light up a room just by stepping foot in it. And her laugh," he pauses and laughs, "it was magic."

I hate that I feel a pang of jealousy. I imagine that Victor's long-lost love must be tall and beautiful, with thick dark hair and a functioning memory. She's probably wearing a chic outfit and doing something very important right now, like editing a magazine in New York City or completing her neurosurgery residency.

"What happened then?"

His face changes suddenly. "Life happened, I guess you could say."

"Surely if you loved her that much, you could have worked out your . . . differences?"

He shakes his head. "No, not with her. Sadly, some things cannot be fixed." He clears his throat. "Anyway, sorry to go on about that. Besides, here we are." He points to a rather steep staircase and bows with a cheeky smile. "At the top of the hill, my lady, I give you . . . Montmartre."

I grin, adjusting my bag on my shoulder. "Race you to the top?" I smile and take off ahead of him.

"Hey!" he says, chasing after me. "Unfair advantage!"

I forge ahead, laughing. I'm entirely out of breath when I reach the top, with Victor just behind me.

"Hey, I had to carry the basket," he says, grinning and equally out of breath. He sets it at his feet, then places his hands on my shoulders, turning me around to face the expanse of city below.

"Have you ever seen anything more beautiful?"

I shake my head.

"I've traveled the world, and this . . . this is the pinnacle. And it's home." He reaches for the basket again. "Come on, I know a great place for us to throw a blanket down and eat."

We walk through what feels like a small village punctuated with shops, cafés, art galleries, then a bit farther. Victor points to an iron gate. "Right through here," he says, unhooking the latch.

"What is this?" I ask. It doesn't look like a park. Maybe someone's residence?

"You'll see," he says, motioning me through the gate.

We dip beneath an underpruned flowering vine that threatens to overthrow the very trellis that has given it life. A crimson flower tickles my cheek as I duck under it.

The scene just ahead is like something out of a fairy tale, or at least a fairy tale I'd like to read: at our feet a patch of wooly thyme, so soft it looks like a green pillow, and all around, roses, hydrangeas, alliums as large as dinner plates— flowers everywhere. But the view of Paris from this magical little perch is what really takes my breath away.

"Wow," I say, stunned.

"Isn't it something?" Victor says, setting the blanket on the bed of thyme and sitting down. He tucks his knees to his chest as I sit down beside him.

"Yes. How did you find it?"

"It's a long story." He winks at me. "But let's just say I don't share it with many people."

I smile. "Well then, I'll take that as a compliment."

He opens the wine, Burgundy, pours us each a glass, then lays out a selection of cheeses and meats, pickled vegetables, an orzo salad with Greek olives and cherry tomatoes. It all looks divine.

We drink and eat as the early autumn sun makes its journey across Paris. Between bites, I tell Victor about the art class I stumbled into. I reach for my bag and produce my sketchbook, showing him my drawing of the hydrangea.

"That's . . . really good," he exclaims. "It almost looks professional. Hey, maybe we've solved the mystery of your identity. Maybe you're a famous artist."

I shake my head. "I highly doubt that."

"Well, even if not," he says, pointing to the open page, "it's still a clue."

"I guess," I say with a sigh. "I mean, I've been trying to make sense of who I am, but is it weird to admit that I'm a little scared to find the answers?"

"Not at all," he says. "What you're going through is monumental. Anyone would be feeling apprehensive."

I nod. "I know there are so many things I could be doing to get to the bottom of my identity. I could go to the embassy. I could do a background check, then fly to my hometown and interview every resident until I learn who I am. But to be completely honest, Victor, I don't want to."

"Tell me why?"

I feel my eyes getting misty. "Being in the dark about my life is weird and scary and kind of lonely. But what if the alternative is . . . worse?"

Victor refills my wineglass.

"What if my memory comes back and I hate my life, or worse, hate myself? From all I can tell, I was miserable before. I don't want to be that woman."

Victor places a finger to my lips and shakes his head. "Then don't. Be you. You don't ever have to go back."

I look out at the horizon, thinking about the words he just uttered.

"You know what I believe?" he says, turning to me. "That no matter what we try to make of our lives, much of it isn't under our control. Yes, we can study and work hard and be good friends, lovers, citizens, parents. But what happens will happen. There's a lot of freedom in believing that all of it is already written in the stars."

"That's . . . beautiful," I say.

He nods, leaning closer to me. "Like this afternoon, this moment. We were meant to have it. The stars already knew it would happen."

"There's definitely something freeing about that," I say.

"It's true," he continues, reaching for my hand

and examining my fingers carefully, as if meeting them for the first time. After a moment, he raises my hand to his lips and kisses the top of it, which sends an electric sensation up my arm and through my entire body. "Maybe your accident wasn't such a tragedy after all," he continues, turning his eyes to me. "Maybe it was a *gift*."

I nestle closer to him. As the late-afternoon sun casts shadows across Paris, somehow that's all the assurance I need.

It's too late to walk back; it will be dark soon, so we take a cab to my apartment. I consider inviting him in, but decide against it. This has already been a perfect day.

"I had a lot of fun today," he says.

"Me too. Thank you."

I wave as the cab drives off, then turn to the entrance to my apartment building. Monsieur de Goff doesn't look up from his post as I head to the elevator, and I tell myself not to let his grumpiness ruin a beautiful day.

"Wait," he says before the doors close. I hold my hand out to keep them open. "Someone came to see you today."

"Oh? Who?"

"A man."

"Did you get his name?"

"No, he wouldn't leave any information."

I shrug as he hands me a small stack of mail,

then head upstairs. Inside my apartment, the air is stuffy and warm, so I open the balcony doors and let some fresh air in before sorting through mail, mostly bills, but a hand-addressed envelope catches my eye. I open it immediately.

Dear Ms. Williams,

I'm sorry to reach out once again, as I know you told me no already, but given the importance of my project, I wanted to try once again to see if you might, please, allow me to have a moment of your time. Even just 15 minutes.

With my greatest gratitude for your
consideration,
Estelle Olivier

I scan the contact information below her name. A phone number, and an email address indicating she is a student at Sorbonne University. What did she want, and why had I apparently turned her away?

I notice the blinking light on my phone and press a button to play a voicemail from Dr. Leroy, who wants me to come in for a follow-up visit. I decide to call back the college student instead.

"Hi, this is Caroline Williams. I received your letter and I thought I would—"

"Yes, Madame Williams!" she practically

squeals. "I'm so very glad to hear from you." She sounds young.

"How can I help you?"

She clears her throat. "I'm studying journalism, with an emphasis on history. For my final project before graduation, I'm working on a piece about 1940s Paris during the occupation of France. I'm interested in sharing stories from that time that have never been told, and I've settled on one in particular."

"I'm sorry," I say. "Why is it that you need *my* help?"

"I'm interested in some of the older residences on the rue Cler, particularly yours, and I'm hoping you wouldn't mind if I stopped by to have a look and take a few photos for my project. I promise not to consume too much of your time."

"Of course," I say. "How about . . . this evening? Seven o'clock?"

"Yes, thank you!"

"Perfect."

I reach for my sketchbook and colored pencils, then head to the balcony, where I begin sketching the view of the rue Cler below. People bustling across the cobblestone streets. Bicycles weaving this way and that. Colorful produce laid out seductively on tables, enticing passersby. Old stone buildings standing guard.

In a moment, there it is again, the sound of wind chimes and palm trees in the breeze, just as before. This time, I am on a beach. I hear the waves crashing on the shore before I can see them, and when I do, I watch as they hit the sand, exploding into a million bubbles before retreating. Mesmerized, I walk closer to the water's edge, plunging my bare feet into the sea as a wave pummels my ankles and splashes my legs. I laugh to myself as another wave comes, this one completely soaking my dress.

"Mommy, come on!" A little girl's voice calls out behind me.

I turn around and see a small figure in the distance. The blond ponytail. A pink and white polka-dot bathing suit. Little tanned legs. She's running hand in hand with a man, the same one who wrapped his arms around me in the kitchen.

"Come chase us, Mommy!" she calls to me. "Daddy says you can't beat us."

Their backs are turned; I can't make out their faces. "Run, Alma, run!" the man says, his voice muffled by the crashing waves.

Alma. Her name is Alma.

I know them, these two ghosts running on the beach ahead, and yet I . . . don't. Regardless, the pull to be near them is magnetic. "I'm coming!" I cry, running from the next wave, plunging my feet into the sand, one after the other, forging my way down the beach toward them. But the faster I run, the farther away they seem. Tears sting my eyes. "Wait, I'm coming!"

My eyes shoot open involuntarily, ripping the scene from my view. There is no beach. No waves. No sand. Just Paris.

"I'm coming, Alma," I mutter. "I'm coming."

I am emotionally exhausted when the doorbell rings later that evening, and I regret agreeing to meet the Sorbonne student, but it would be rude to cancel now.

I do my best to smooth my messy hair as I walk to the door. A young woman stands in the hallway outside. She's tall and pretty, with short brown hair that's cut to a blunt bob. "You must be Madame Williams," she says, extending her hand. "I'm Estelle. It's so nice to finally meet you."

"Please, come in."

"Wow," she says, placing her hand over her mouth. "It's just as I imagined one of these old apartments would look. So . . . grand."

I watch as she strolls slowly around the room, marveling at everything from the ceiling to the floorboards.

"Would you like to sit down?"

"Thank you," she says. "I don't want to take up too much of your time, but, Madame Williams, can I just say what a special opportunity it is to be here."

I nod, a little confused. "Call me Caroline."

She nods.

"Tell me about your project."

"Well," she continues, producing an old book from her satchel and handing it to me. "I found this in the university's archives. It's a notebook kept by a French nurse who worked with the Resistance during the occupation of Paris. She lived nearby, and she writes about an apartment in this building."

My eyes widen. "*My* apartment?"

"Well, maybe. I'm still piecing it all together, but from what I can tell, a high-ranking German officer lived in the building. He was a terrible man, linked to all sorts of despicable crimes against humanity." She opens the notebook. "As you can see, the pages are badly damaged and faded. I'm working with a graduate student in the science department to see if I can make out the text under a special ultraviolet light. I'm not sure if it'll work or not, but it's worth a try. As it is, I can only make out a few words. And a name." She points to a badly water-stained page. "Céline."

"Wait," I say, my eyes wide. "*Céline?*"

"I know it may sound crazy," Estelle says, "but I don't think I'll be able to rest until I know what Esther was trying to say. I have to know what happened."

I glance down the hallway toward my bedroom. "Wait a second," I say. "I have something you might be interested in seeing." A moment later, I return with the cigar box.

"What's that?"

I open the box. "Letters from Céline, to the man she loved."

Estelle gasps. "Where did you find these?"

A chill erupts on the back of my neck and travels downward, sending a trail of goosebumps along my arms. "In the closet of the guest bedroom. It was wedged behind the wall. I have no idea why they were left here, or by whom. I've read several. They're heartbreaking. I'd planned to go through them all, but I've been so consumed with my own life that, well, here." I pull out the stack of letters and hand them to her. "Why don't you take them and see if they might help you with your project."

"Wow," she says. "This is . . . truly remarkable."

I smile. It feels good to help solve a mystery, even if it isn't my own.

"I know it might seem futile," she says, closing the box and tucking it into her bag, "to find the truth about this one story after so many years have passed, and also when so many other stories have gone untold. Céline is just one among thousands, but for some reason, I feel drawn to her." She sighs. "My roommate, Liesel, doesn't understand my fascination with occupied Paris. 'There'll never be another Hitler again,' she said, 'so what's the point?' But I don't see it that way."

"That may be true," I reply, "but even if we think that something like that could never happen again, we don't know it. Besides, I'm with you. I think there's value in learning from the past."

"Thank you," she says, standing. "I'll leave you now. As curious as I am about having a look in that guest bedroom you mentioned, it's getting late and I should go. Besides, I'd like to do a bit more research first. Do you mind if we meet again?"

"Of course not," I say.

"Thank you."

As the door clicks closed, I can't shake the thought of Céline. In this strange twist of fate, my life is inextricably entwined with this woman from another era whose past is as murky as my own.

CHAPTER 10

CÉLINE

The telephone calls begin, initially at a slow trickle, and then like a faucet turned on full speed. First, Madame Laurent. "I'm so sorry to bother you at your home, but your shop seems to be closed and, well, I will need to cancel my order for Saturday night. Nothing personal, you know. It's just a very important dinner, and I've placed my order elsewhere."

"Of course, madame," Papa says, without the slightest hint of disappointment. "We understand completely."

And then Madame Clément, who, five years ago, sent us business from more than fifteen people in her circle of wealthy friends: "Dear me, I regret to say that I have decided that I no longer need flowers for Sunday brunch."

"Yes, Madame Clément," says Papa, setting the phone down in its cradle with a defeated click.

And then Madame Fontaine, who has always been so kind to us, bringing Cosi a gift on her birthday every year: "Seeing that it's wartime, I've decided that it isn't right for me to be spending money on flowers when I could be giving more to those in need. Surely you understand."

"Yes, Madame Fontaine," Papa says.

Recognizing Papa's despair, I handle the phone calls after that. At least a dozen more.

"Yes, madame."

"Of course, madame."

"If you should reconsider, we will be here."

"Indeed, madame."

"We understand, yes."

Our customers are leaving us in a mass exodus, but can we even blame them? Associating with Jews is risky, everyone knows that. And yet, *we* are the Jews. The very Jews they turned to for the most beautiful arrangements for the most important moments of their lives: weddings, luncheons, christenings, births of babies, deaths of loved ones, engagements. If they trusted us then, why don't they trust us now? We haven't changed, but Paris has. And now our business is finished.

Papa has some savings—not much, but enough to get us by for a few months until I can find work. Perhaps Nic could help me find work at the bakery. How hard would it be to serve pastries or wait tables, maybe even at . . . Bistro Jeanty! Madame Jeanty may not love me, but for Luc's sake, she'll surely allow me to wait tables until Luc returns.

Papa stands, his face awash in pride. "I won't be put out of business like this."

"We can't keep our doors open without customers."

"They're just rattled right now," he says. "They'll come back."

I shake my head. "We can't count on that. You know as well as I what our expenses are. Without orders, we'll be throwing money down the drain, money we need to . . . survive."

Papa stares off into the corner of the living room. His eyes are determined, distant. I imagine he's thinking of life in Normandy, before Hitler, before Mama's death. I think of those times, too, and I wish I could relive them. But we are living now, and we must carry on. Papa knows that, and I can tell that he is embroiled in a battle with his pride.

I remember the envelope from Luc and run to my bedroom to retrieve it from my bag. I can't believe I've forgotten about it, but I've been overwhelmed by Papa's injuries and the incident at the shop.

"Wait, Papa," I say, holding up the envelope tied with twine. "Luc left this for us."

He shakes his head, confused.

"In the little compartment at Bistro Jeanty." He doesn't understand. "Never mind how. Just look." I pull off the twine and tear the seal open. Inside is a thick stack of German marks, which I fan and count quickly. "There's at least five hundred here, maybe more. And look." I pause to produce some papers that have been folded into a tight square. "Oh, Papa, it's paperwork. Official paperwork. Our names have been changed, yours, mine, and Cosi's. Look, different surnames. We are now the Le Blanc family. Papa, do you know what this means?"

He stares ahead, frozen, as if all this information is too much for him to process.

"Papa, it means we can get out of here! It means we can find a train to the south, maybe cross the border there into Switzerland, or better yet, book passage to America."

"America? Switzerland?" He shakes his head. "I will never leave my home."

Cosi skips down the hallway clutching Monsieur Dubois. "Are we going to America? Really? I heard it's nice there."

I smile at my beautiful daughter. "We'll talk about it later, my little birdie. Now run along and go finish that puzzle you started this morning while Papa and I talk."

"Okay, Mama," she says with a smile, turning to look over her shoulder once more before running down the hallway. "I hope we move to California. They have palm trees there."

I nod playfully. "They do, love."

"Papa, you must listen," I say, sitting beside him on the sofa. "We can't stay here. People like . . . us are being arrested at every turn. Men are disappearing. Women and children are being . . ." It's all too awful to say. "Luc is trying to protect us. We must make a plan."

Papa's eyes meet mine. "I know, my dear. I know. And you are a fighter, just like your mother. It's just that . . ." He pauses, and closes his tired eyes for a moment. "I don't know if I have much more fight in me."

Papa will turn seventy next month, and he looks older now than ever before.

I fall to my knees beside him. "Then let me fight for you," I say. "For all three of us."

"I can't ask that of you, Céline." He pats my hand. "You go, with Cosi. Luc will find you."

"I don't understand, Papa. What are you saying?"

He takes a deep breath. "I'm staying. I'm not leaving my home."

I know in this moment that there is no amount of convincing or pleading that will change his mind.

"I'm not leaving you."

"You must," he says. "Take your papers and do as Luc has advised."

I shake my head. "No. I won't abandon you like this. I could never do that." I nod, resolutely. "It's decided then. We'll stay here. We have the money from Luc to keep us going, and I'll find work. In fact, I'm going to go see about that today."

I rest my head on Papa's shoulder, glancing out the window beside us. "Look," I say. "It's snowing."

"Early for the year," Papa says. His smile

warms me. "Almost makes the city feel . . ." His voice trails off.

"The way it used to feel?" I offer, finishing his sentence.

He nods, and I squeeze his hand.

Tomorrow the city will be dusted in powdered sugar, and Cosi will squeal with delight, and I will rejoice that we have survived another day.

I kiss Papa good night, then nestle in beside Cosi, who is fast asleep, before turning to my bedside table and reaching for a pen and paper. By moonlight, I compose a letter to Luc. I don't know where he is, or if he'll ever read my words, but it gives me great comfort to write to him.

I tuck the letter in an envelope and set it beside the others I've written. When we're reunited, I'll give them all to him, an account of our days apart, and a reminder of the beauty of reunification.

CHAPTER 11

CAROLINE

The accident has left me with the strangest dreams. Although it's fair to say that maybe I've always been this way; I'm just not sure. I do know that each night, my mind is filled with the most elaborate plot twists, and when my eyes open in the morning, I am hard-pressed to make sense of any of it.

I think of Céline again. She'd made an appearance in my dream, or my imagination's creation of her has, anyway. She stood on the balcony on a cold night, wrapped in a shawl, the stoic full moon perched over Paris, illuminating her sad face. I recall the last of her letters that I'd read before turning the bundle over to Estelle, and I can almost hear Céline's voice.

Dear Luc,

Thank you for the provisions to get us out of the city. I know we must go, and soon. Each day that passes is a gift when people like us are being rounded up day and night. I want to go so badly, but Papa refuses. He will not leave his home, and I just can't bear to abandon him. Oh, Luc, I wish you were here to advise what to do. I'm so very, very lost. Your love sustains me, though. I feel it all the time. I feel it now.

I miss you terribly.

Yours,
Céline

Did they ever reunite? Had fate been kind to them? I sigh, reluctantly pulling myself out of bed and my head out of the past. It's time I face matters of the present.

I dress quickly and head out the door to the elevator. In the lobby, Monsieur de Goff is engaged in a conversation with another tenant in the building, a woman in her sixties with short gray hair and a friendly smile. When our eyes meet, he looks away, then continues exchanging pleasantries with the woman—American, judging by her accent—before she walks out the door behind me.

"Excuse me," she says. I turn around to find her smiling at me curiously. "I'm new here, and I don't think we've met." She smiles. "I'm Anna."

I extend my hand. "Caroline."

"Is it just me," she continues, "or does our concierge disapprove of Americans?"

I grin. "I'm glad to know I'm not the only one he despises."

"Well," she says, adjusting the Hermès scarf

around her neck, "perhaps we're being too critical of him." She leans in closer to me. "The other day, I met a couple on the second floor who told me he's had a rather harrowing life."

"Oh?"

"I guess he lived right here as a child, on the rue Cler." She points across the square. "I didn't get the whole story, but I'm told that he was just a boy of four or five when the Germans rounded up his family and took everything." She sighs. "I'll never be able to understand that kind of evil."

"I had no idea. . . ."

She nods. "Maybe we should forgive him the next time he snaps at us."

"Yes."

My heart is heavy as I walk to Jeanty. To think that all around me—the letters in my apartment, Monsieur de Goff—are remnants of such an ugly time in history. It makes my amnesia pale in comparison. In fact, for those who suffered trauma, as Monsieur de Goff reportedly has, amnesia could even be a gift.

"Hi," I say to Victor. My cheeks warm when I remember the way he kissed my hand yesterday.

He smiles. "Hi, you."

"I have an art class at ten, so I don't have a lot of time, but I wanted to come in to say hi." Inès called last night and encouraged me to attend; I'd cautiously agreed.

"An art class? That's wonderful!"

We slip into a booth on the left side of the restaurant, and Victor motions to a waiter to take my order. "Just espresso today," I say. Victor orders one, too.

"How are you feeling?" he asks.

"Okay, I guess."

He analyzes my face like a treasure map. "Any new—"

"Memories?" I shake my head. "Well, just more visions, or flashbacks, or whatever they are that I've been having."

He listens expectantly.

"I'm in California, or somewhere warm and coastal like that. There's a little girl. Her name is . . . Alma." Saying the name aloud feels equal parts refreshing and painful, like an acupuncture needle twisting in the skin.

Victor stares at me for a long moment. "Wow," he says. "I . . . don't know what to say."

I look into his eyes. "What if I—"

"Alma," he says. "That's a really cool name." He scratches his head. "I may be mistaken, but I think there's a hotel in Mexico—yes, Tulum, actually—called the Alma Inn or something like that. I ended up there years ago during that travel period of my life I told you about. Have you ever been to Tulum?"

I shake my head. "No—at least not that I can remember."

"Listen," he continues, his face tender. "These visions you're having . . . try not to let them get to you too much. Didn't the doctor say something about your memory repairing in fits and starts? Some of these episodes might be memories, but what if others are merely your mind's creations, or even scenes from movies?"

"I guess you could be right," I say, nodding. "But something about it all feels . . . so real."

"Yes, perhaps," he says. "But you know what's *really* real?"

I search his brown eyes, grateful for his friendship, his kindness.

"This," he says. "Right here, right now. We can spend our lives chasing the past, turning our regrets over and over again, replaying painful memories, wishing we had done this or that differently, wondering why someone failed us, or why we failed them and whether we might have prevented it somehow." He shakes his head. "I used to live in the past. Not anymore. I live for today. And that's my wish for you, too, Caroline."

I blink back tears.

"Promise me that you'll at least try?"

"Yes," I say, forcing a smile. "I will. But . . . just one question."

"Okay."

"Do you think she would have been amazing?" I ask, my voice cracking. "If I had a daughter?"

Victor turns back to the kitchen, and I worry

that I'm taking up too much of his time, or being too needy.

"I'm sorry," I say, standing up, then taking a long sip of the espresso I've neglected. "I should go. The class starts soon, anyway."

"There's no question," Victor says, turning to me again.

"No question of what?"

"No question that any child of yours would be a phenomenal human being."

"Thanks," I say with a smile.

"Now go paint a masterpiece."

"Wait," I say, turning back from the door. "It's probably nothing, but when I got home yesterday Monsieur de Goff, my building's concierge, said a man had stopped by asking for me. As far as I know, I don't have any male friends."

"Did he leave his name?"

I shake my head. "What if it's Mr. Tropical Shirt?"

Victor smiles, but I can tell he's more troubled than amused.

"It's probably nothing of concern, but it did leave me curious, especially since . . . I don't think I told you. . . . That night that professor walked me home, I had this weird feeling that someone was following me."

"That settles it, then," Victor says. "I'm coming over tonight to make sure the boogeyman doesn't get you."

I smile. "I'd like that."

"How about seven?"

"Perfect."

I turn to the door, but then remember the little nosegay of freesia and stock I'd bought this morning on my walk. I'd been unable to resist the flowers' beautiful scent, even if they'd be long wilted before I made it home later in the day. I reach into my bag and hand it to Margot. She looks wearier than ever. "Just a little something to brighten your day," I say with a smile.

Stunned, she holds the little bunch of blossoms to her nose. She opens her mouth to speak, but nothing comes out.

"See you tomorrow," I say, reaching for the door handle.

"Thank you," Margot says, her voice cracking a little.

"This is quite lovely," Inès says, peering over my shoulder as I put the finishing touches on the painting I'd begun earlier this morning. "Promise me you'll consider being a part of our art show next month."

"I don't know," I say, setting my brush down.

"All you need are three or four pieces, and at this rate, you'll have plenty of time." She smiles at me. "Besides, I think it would be a good goal for you."

"Maybe," I say with a cautious smile, washing

my palette and brushes. I thank Inès, then head to the corner market and pick up a baguette, a few wedges of cheese, and a bottle of wine for Victor's visit this evening.

As I head for home, the wind picks up, ushering in an army of dark clouds. I feel a raindrop on my cheek, prompting me to quicken my pace. After a long streak of sun, Parisians, me included, are allergic to clouds. Shopkeepers peer out of store windows, gazing up at the sky with concern. Passersby zip up their coats and cinch their scarfs.

I cross the street to my apartment, but turn sharply to my right when I sense someone close behind me. Of course, no one's there but a baguette-carrying older gentleman turning to round the next corner. I tell myself to stop being paranoid, and yet I can't help but pick up my pace to a light jog until my apartment building is in sight. In the lobby, I set my bags down, winded. I'm grateful to see Monsieur de Goff standing at his post.

"I'm sorry," I say, catching my breath. "I . . . got spooked."

For the first time, I think I detect concern on his face.

"It was nothing, of course." I turn to the elevator.

"Mademoiselle," he says, prompting me to turn around. "The man who came to see you yesterday returned again today. Just like before, he didn't leave his name."

I shiver.

He reaches in his pocket and pulls out a scrap of paper, then hands it to me.

"What's this?"

"The name and phone number of the couple who remodeled your apartment. You seemed curious, so I . . . Anyway, in case you wanted to contact them."

"Thank you. So much." I am touched by the gesture. "Monsieur de Goff, I just want to say that I'm sorry if I have ever been unkind or—"

"We all have our reasons," he says.

I nod, turning to the elevator.

"Mademoiselle," he says again. "Do be careful."

"Yes," I say, forcing a smile.

I tell myself not to worry as the elevator jolts upward. I look over my shoulder as I unlock the door to my apartment. *Everything is going to be fine.* Just the same, once I'm inside, my hands move quickly to secure the deadbolt.

CHAPTER 12

CÉLINE

"I'll only be gone an hour at the most," I say to Papa the next morning as I button my coat. The snow is falling heavily, and by the looks of the heavy clouds above, there doesn't appear to be an end in sight.

"I'm not sure you should go out in this weather," Papa says.

"Well, we won't have anything to eat for supper if I don't, and besides, if this weather continues, the market will close. I'll be quick. Don't you worry about me."

"Take side streets," he says, finally relenting and kissing my cheek.

I nod. "Tell Cosi I'll be back in a snap."

Outside, Paris is awash in white. I breathe in the crisp, cold air and pull my hood over my head. My boots crunch through the fresh powder with each step, reminding me of the days I was a schoolgirl, walking home with Suzette, with Luc a short distance behind. Luc. How I wish he were here now.

Normally bustling at this time of the day, the market is quiet. Besides me, a lone elderly man hovers over a barrel of pockmarked potatoes, inspecting one after the next, ultimately setting all back. A mother picks through a table of onions, most of them bruised and visibly rotten, before giving up and turning to the carrots. Her young son kicks the snow beneath his feet, and I smile at him. He reminds me of the little boy I used to play peekaboo with at the market. The little Jewish boy whose home has been taken and family dispersed, his teddy bear left in the street. I sigh, selecting a few decent zucchinis. I'm grateful to see that there are eggs and milk available, which I grab, along with some salad greens and cherry tomatoes for Papa. This will certainly be the last of them for the season now that we've had the first snow. Basil, yes. A block of cheese. A squash, which I'll roast for Cosi. I pay Monsieur Duval, whose hands are red and chapped from the cold, then purchase two baguettes at the nearby bakery, along with three pastries for breakfast.

I sling my bag over my shoulder and continue on to Bistro Jeanty to speak to Luc's mother about the possibility of waiting tables to supplement our income. I haven't told Papa, of course. I don't want to worry him. He'll argue that Madame Jeanty will do us no favors, but I think he's wrong. Despite her feelings about me, she loves her son, just as I do. I will appeal to her as a mother and as a woman. The position will be temporary, of course. Luc will be home soon, France will be liberated, and this will all be a distant memory.

My mind turns to Suzette and her German officer. She called me in tears yesterday, but Cosi was sitting beside me in the kitchen, and I didn't want to frighten her. When I phoned her back an hour later, there was no answer.

I hope her tears are merely the result of a silly lovers' quarrel and nothing more serious. I pray that I am wrong about Suzette's beau, and that, as she explained, he's one of the "good ones."

I'm pleased to see the lights of Bistro Jeanty in the distance. Under the awning, I pull my hood down, dust the snow off my shoulders, and smooth my hair before stepping inside. A blast of warm air hits my face as I inspect my reflection in the mirrored wall. I need to look my best when I speak to Luc's mother, who is always meticulously groomed, even in a snowstorm.

The restaurant is empty, aside from a busboy polishing a rack of glasses at the bar. I don't recognize him, but then again, why would I? Madame Jeanty burns through help faster than Cosi does a chocolate bar.

I nod at the boy and walk to the rear of the restaurant. I can hear Madame Jeanty's voice in the kitchen, and I'm happy to catch her here. While she typically doesn't arrive until the dinner service begins, I know from Luc that she comes in early once a week for the wine delivery. I decide to wait just outside the double doors until she emerges. I'll then give her a double kiss and tell her she looks lovely in whatever new dress she has on. We'll talk about our hopes for Luc's return, make some small talk, then I'll explain that the flower business has been difficult in wartime. I won't tell her why, exactly, though I'm sure she already knows. Madame Jeanty knows everything. But that doesn't matter. I am Luc's sweetheart. She won't turn me away. I'll ask if she can carve out a position for me to wait tables, or even help at the hostess station. The Germans who come in won't bother me, because they respect Madame Jeanty. It will be safe.

I pause my stream of thoughts when I hear a male voice in the kitchen. I detect the thick German accent immediately, followed by laughter from Madame Jeanty. While I've seen her engaged in friendly conversation with plenty of soldiers, I've never known her to welcome them into the restaurant's most intimate spaces. *Who is she speaking to?* I inch closer to make out the conversation as best I can.

"I don't know what dreadful things my son is tied up in down there, but can you get him home, once and for all, like you promised?"

"Soon, soon."

"But it's already been longer than you said."

"You wanted him out of the city long enough for us to take care of things with the girl."

"Yes," Madame Jeanty says, "but I didn't realize it would take this long. I want my son home."

"I assure you, we are working on it. We'll need to pay a visit to the home, arrest the father. We'll send him to a work camp with the next roundup."

"When will that be?"

"A few days at most."

"Good," Madame Jeanty says. "And the little girl?"

I gasp.

"Up to you," the man says.

"Luc shouldn't have to care for another man's child. He deserves his own. If she stays, he'll try to take her in. I can't have that."

"Understood."

"I could never understand what he saw in her," Luc's mother continues. "It would be one thing if she was beautiful, but she's really rather plain. And there's something distinctly Jewish about her face. Luc deserves so much better. He doesn't see it now, but he will, in time."

"Come here and let me have my way with you," the man says.

"Oh, Gerhard, you're a scoundrel. Not in the kitchen!"

"Why not? We've never tried that before," he says.

197

Suddenly, there's silence, then giggling, followed by a pot or pan hitting the tile floor with a jarring thud. I race to the door, running out to the snowy street without stopping to button my coat.

I run home as quickly as I can, passing all the places I might have stopped in happier times: Madame Caron's boutique, the cake shop Cosi loves, Luc's favorite patisserie, which is where I hear a man shouting and see a woman stumbling out to the street and falling into the snow as if she's been pushed. The door slams shut behind her.

I run ahead and kneel beside her, brushing the snow from her face and neck. "Are you all right?" I ask, as she turns to look at me. I recognize her instantly. Suzette.

"Céline!" she exclaims, rising to her feet.

"What are you doing here?"

"It's Mother's birthday and I wanted to get her a cake. But"—she pauses and gestures toward the bakery—"I guess our family isn't welcome here."

"Why on earth . . ."

I notice that her lip is trembling. "He said he doesn't serve families with . . . cripples." She shakes her head. "I don't understand. We used to take Élian here often, and it was never a problem." She brushes the snow off of her coat. "What's wrong with the world?"

"I'm sorry," I say, tucking my arm in hers. "I've missed you."

"Me too."

"Shall we walk together?"

She nods as we set out on the snowy streets. For a moment we could be the two schoolgirls we once were, talking about hair ribbons and giggling about boys. But the world has changed, and so have we.

"I'm scared," Suzette whispers.

"I am, too," I say.

"What will become of us, Céline? What will become of Paris?"

I don't ask her about her beau, or inquire about her brother, or tell her anything of my own problems. Instead, my mind turns to a woman named Antoinette, the wife of a jeweler who kept a shop on the rue Cler, where my late husband had purchased my necklace. I ran into her at the market earlier and learned that the business was recently shuttered and looted by the Nazis. Our conversation was brief but meaningful, and I share Antoinette's story with Suzette. Raised in orphanages, her parents died when she was a child. Her life was altogether miserable until the summer she turned eighteen and met Mendel, the son of a jeweler. For Antoinette, marrying into a big, loving Jewish family was a dream come true until the Nazis arrived in Paris. The day they arrested her husband, his brothers, and his father, they raided the jewelry store and sent the entire family to a work camp. Even his mother, and his sister with her newborn baby.

Suzette holds her hand to her heart. "I can't even imagine."

I nod, explaining the way Antoinette had pulled back the sleeve of her dress to reveal a scabbed-over wound, a crude star of David, on the lower part of her right forearm, carved into her flesh, just like the one hastily painted on our shop window.

I recall the way she'd closed her eyes tightly, telling me how much she'd wished they would have just taken her too. "My punishment," she had said, "was far worse. Being separated from the family I love is like being orphaned all over again."

Suzette shakes her head.

"I told her not to lose hope, that she would see her beloved Mendel again, in this life or the next."

I stop and lock eyes with Suzette as we round the next corner. "And that rings true for both of us, Suzette. You know why Antoinette will persevere, just as you and I will?"

"Why?" she asks, searching my eyes.

"Because she's a lotus, and so are we."

"A lotus?"

I smile to myself, recalling the story Papa told me as a girl. "The flower. Have you seen one?"

She shakes her head again.

"They're gorgeous," I say. "But my point isn't about their beauty. Lotus flowers lead harrowing journeys. Their seeds sprout in murky swamp water, thick with dirt and debris and snarls of roots. For a lotus to bloom, she must forge her way through this terrible darkness, avoid being eaten by fish and insects, and keep pressing onward, innately knowing, or at least hoping, that there is sunlight somewhere above the water's surface, if she can only summon the strength to get there. And when she does, she emerges unscathed by her journey and blooms triumphantly." I place both of my hands on her shoulders. "Suzette, *you* are a lotus."

She forces a smile.

"You may be deep in the murky water right now. But you will bloom."

"I wish I had the confidence that you do. The truth is, Céline, I'm scared. All the time."

"We all are, dear friend," I whisper.

My apartment building is just ahead, and at the next block we say our goodbyes. I turn right, she turns left, each of us on our own journey, but with the same goal: to emerge through the murky waters and bloom in the sunlight.

With the remaining potatoes, I make a simple soup for dinner and carefully ladle it into the blue-and-white china soup bowls that my mother used to love so, then call Cosi and Papa to the table. There are no leeks, nor crème fraîche, but it's a fine meal just the same.

"How was your day?" I ask Cosi.

So far, Papa and I have decided to let her continue at school, despite our family's troubles and fears. Cosi's school is just across the square, and she knows to avoid stopping along the way or drawing attention to herself in any way. Besides, she loves school, and it would break her heart to leave her friends.

Normally cheerful, Cosi stares silently into her soup bowl.

"Is something wrong, love?"

She nods, looking up at me a moment later, tears in her eyes. "Alina says she can't be my friend anymore."

"Oh, honey," I say, reaching for her hand, thinking of our neighbors on the second floor.

"Because of the yellow star," she continues, tucking her knees to her chest. "I hate the yellow star."

Papa and I exchange worried looks.

"I hate it, too, my sweet girl," I say, trying to console her.

Her eyes search mine for answers, or at least some semblance of hope that everything is going to be okay. "Mama," she begins again, tearfully, "what if no one wants to be my friend? Then what?"

I sit up straighter in my chair. "Then they are silly little girls, and you're better off without them. Besides, you have me, Papa, and Monsieur Dubois. We will always be your friends."

She nods, cracks a tiny smile, and returns her attention to her soup bowl. A few minutes later, I excuse her to the living room, where she tucks herself under a blanket with her book.

"How did your outing go?" Papa whispers.

"I'm afraid I don't have good news to share."

Papa's eyes widen as I recount the scene at Jeanty. I know he's as discouraged as I am. Each day brings more bad news. Each hour, a greater sense of fear. I stiffen every time I hear footsteps in the hall, or the creak of the staircase outside our door. Are they coming for us?

We need to make an escape plan, and soon. But at the mere mention, Papa sighs and retreats to the sofa, as if the best defense mechanism is to pretend that everything will be all right. He sits beside Cosi: two silhouettes in the dim light beside the crackling fire. If only I could freeze this moment forever.

By the time I'm done tidying up the kitchen and preparing for tomorrow's breakfast, Papa and Cosi have both dozed off on the sofa, he with his reading glasses half on his face and an open book in his lap, she with her beloved journal, which has fallen from her grasp onto the floor. I smile at the sight and tap Papa on the shoulder. He sits up, disoriented, sets his reading glasses on the table. "Good night," he whispers, heading to his bedroom as I lift Cosi into my arms and carry her to bed, tucking Monsieur Dubois against her chest. She pulls the bear to her face and rolls over in peaceful slumber.

As I tidy the living room, the phone rings. *Strange,* I think. *Who'd be calling at this hour?* I'm quick to answer so as not to let it wake my sleeping family.

"Céline?" It's Suzette, and I can tell she's been crying.

"Suzette? Are you okay?"

"No," she says. "Céline, you were right, about everything." Her voice is beyond frantic, it's hysterical. "Franc betrayed me. Céline, he *betrayed* me." She sobs so hard, I can barely make out her words. "When I came home tonight . . ." She is hysterical. "They . . . Élian. Céline, Élian!"

"Wait," I say. "Slow down. What happened?" My heart beats faster.

"They took him away," she cries. "They came to the apartment. Céline, they *arrested* him."

My legs feel weak and I collapse into a chair at the table. I don't know what to say. I can only weep. He'd been born with a compromised body, but no one had a bigger or more perfect heart. I can picture his face now, smiling up at me from his chair, trying to say my name, which always came out sounding like "Shell-ene." Their mother, Claudine, loves him with such intensity. I shudder to think of how she is coping in this moment. And now he's gone, and Suzette is the reason. There is nothing left to say, so we sit at our respective kitchen tables in Paris, and we cry, and we cry.

CHAPTER 13

✣

CAROLINE

Before Victor arrives, I try on three different dresses, then settle on jeans and a white blouse that drapes off the shoulders a bit. I nervously set out the cheese, bread, and wine, hoping he'll be pleased with my selection.

"Nice place," he says, looking around.

I smile. "I have no idea why I would have chosen something so large. Seems a little silly."

"Silly, or awesome," Victor says. "Check out the detailing in the ceiling." He marvels at the intricate woodworking above. "I've seen plenty of fancy Parisian apartments in my life, but this is . . . in a class of its own. And with real estate so tight and competitive, you must have been very lucky to sign the lease."

"I suppose so," I say, nervously tucking my hands in the pockets of my jeans. "Monsieur de Goff, the concierge, acts like it's cursed or something." I relay what I've learned, and Victor shrugs.

"Who knows," he says. "Maybe he's just trying to spook you so you'll leave and he can rent it himself."

I shake my head. "I highly doubt that. I don't think he wants anything to do with this apartment. Anyway, would you like a glass of wine? I picked it up at the market today. Apologies if it's a terrible choice. I admit, I know next to nothing about wine."

He eyes the bottle. "Wow, a 2005 Château Margaux? I'd say that you've made a very fine selection, Ms. I Don't Know Anything About Wine."

My cheeks flush. "Well, I did ask the wine merchant to steer me in the right direction."

"May I?" he asks, reaching for the corkscrew.

I nod, watching as his strong hands expertly uncork the bottle.

"Do you have a decanter, by chance?"

"Oh," I say. "I . . . really don't know."

"Shall we go have a look in the kitchen?"

"Sure." I lead him down the hall, past the dining room.

"Look at this kitchen!" he says, stunned. "We could move the whole restaurant here."

I smile. "Feel free to pillage my cabinets. I have no idea what's in there."

He pokes around in the pantry first. "I take it you don't do much cooking."

I shake my head. "I guess not."

He grins. "Well, then, stick with me, kid." He checks some of the upper cabinets next, then crouches to open a drawer beneath the island, pulling out a cylindrical glass vase of sorts with a narrow opening. "*Voilà!*"

"So I don't have a proper set of water glasses, but I have a wine decanter," I say, shaking my head.

"A woman with her priorities right," Victor teases.

Back in the living room, he pours the wine into the decanter. A half hour later, we decide we can't wait any longer, and he reaches for the glasses, which I've set out earlier, pouring us each some to try.

"It's . . . marvelous," he says after taking a first sip.

"Yes," I agree, having another.

"Wine tastes better in France," he says.

"Oh, does it?" I ask playfully.

"I know you probably think I'm being a snob, but trust me. I've worked all over the United States, a little in Canada, too, when I was getting my training, and there's no way around it. Wine just tastes better in France."

I give him a cheeky smile. "So you're telling me this same bottle, opened in, say, Los Angeles, wouldn't taste the same?"

"Yep," he says, swirling the wine in his glass.

We laugh about this, and many other things, and by the time the bottle is empty, I'm feeling lighter and less inhibited.

Victor sets his glass down on the coffee table.

The city lights sparkle outside the windows. "I imagine it must be pretty crazy to be locked out of your memories."

"It is."

"What's the weirdest thing you've learned about yourself since the hospital?"

"The weirdest thing?" I stop to think. "Oh, I don't know. You mean, aside from the fact that I apparently was practically a recluse?"

He laughs.

"Well, I have this birthmark," I say, pointing to my lower back, "that looks sort of like a heart."

"You're saying you have a heart on your ass."

I laugh harder. "No. Well, yes, I guess I do." I shake my head. "All these strange discoveries. At least I'm not a hoarder!"

He laughs. "There must be something else."

"Well, I already told you about that man's shirt in my bedroom drawer," I say. "Want to see it?"

He nods, and I lead him to my bedroom and open the top drawer, reaching all the way to the back. "Here it is in all its glory." I pull it out and hand it to him. "What's your take?"

He grins. "Two thoughts. You once had a man in your life with very bad taste. And I think you might still care for him."

I raise an eyebrow. "I'm not so sure about that."

Victor takes the shirt in his hands and

thoughtfully inspects the buttons, the pocket. "I bet you loved him," he finally says. "And that you miss him, whoever he is."

Then who *is* he? *Where* is he? I pause for a moment to consider that I might have been married, or might still be.

He cracks a smile. "But aren't you relieved that your true love has such an impeccable sense of fashion?"

I laugh.

"I mean, I'm thinking to myself, How can I convince Caroline to cut her losses and give this fine specimen of clothing to me?"

"All right Giorgio Armani," I say, grinning as I snatch the shirt from him, folding it quickly, then tucking it back in the drawer.

"Look at the view from your bedroom," he says, marveling at the way the moon shines down on the rooftops all around.

"It's pretty great, isn't it?" I climb onto the bed and set my head on the pillow. "If you lie right here, you can see the moon."

He nestles in beside me. "Wow, look at that." We hardly know each other, of course, but being in his presence feels natural somehow, easy. He may only be a sketch for now—in black and white, and only foreground, no background—but somehow I can already envision the painting to come, and I rather like it.

"That garden in Montmartre," I say suddenly.

"Did you take *her* there, the girlfriend you spoke of?"

He's quiet for a long moment. "Yes," he finally says.

"You loved her very much."

"Yes."

"Do you still?"

"Now, now," he says, turning over on his side and propping himself up on an elbow. "Where is this all coming from?" He grins. "Am I not allowed to have had any semblance of a life before you?"

Before me . . . I like that he considers me a landmark in his life.

I smile. "Sorry," I say. "I'm just . . . trying to know you better, I guess."

"It was a very long time ago," he says.

"Was she anything like me?"

He swallows hard. "Yes in some ways, no in others." I feel his hand searching for mine, and when our fingers meet, a rush of energy courses through my body. "All you need to know is that nothing makes me happier than being here with you now." When our eyes meet, he leans over and moves closer to me, kissing me softly. It feels so natural, so good. I breathe in the scent of his skin as his lips move down my neck. I don't want him to stop, but something inside me says we should, even if I can't quite put my finger on why.

"I'm sorry," I say, pulling back. "I don't know if I'm quite . . . ready."

His eyes are tender. "Don't be sorry. Please." He kisses my forehead and leans back against the pillow beside me. "This," he says, reaching for my hand, "is enough."

I smile.

"Here, come closer. Let me hold you."

I lay my head on his chest, listening to the sound of his heart beating.

"A friend of mine has a home in the south," he says. "He's never there. I was thinking, well, maybe we could . . . spend a weekend there sometime."

"Really?"

"His family owns the place. It's a gorgeous old stone house that's been completely redone. Big airy spaces. Lavender and rosemary growing like weeds. A pool. They hardly ever use it. We could go next weekend, even, if . . . you're up for it."

"That sounds amazing," I say. "And I'd love to."

I close my eyes as he pulls me closer to him. For a moment, everything feels all right. Better than all right.

CHAPTER 14

CÉLINE

The next morning, I set the table for breakfast. Coffee for Papa and me, milk for Cosi. Pastries for us all. The sun glistens on the fresh snow outside. Cosi is eager to bundle up, put on her mittens, and make snow angels with her friends. I haven't yet told her that I've decided to forbid her from leaving. I had hoped it wouldn't come to this, but I fear that even school is too dangerous now. She'll stomp her feet and cry. She'll hate me for the morning, or maybe even the whole day, and I'll hate myself for it. But I can never let her leave the apartment. Not now. Not anymore. I swallow hard, thinking of Élian again. I decide not to mention it to Papa. No point in him worrying about something he can't do anything about.

I gulp down my first cup of coffee and pour a second. I didn't sleep at all last night. And how could I? The conversation I'd overheard at Bistro Jeanty had pulled the rug out from under me and changed everything, squelched what little hope I'd clung to. There isn't much time left; two days at most. We need to leave, all of us, before it's too late.

I decide to wait until after breakfast to discuss this with Papa. Surely when he hears what I have to tell him he'll realize that staying in Paris is not only foolish but possibly a death warrant. He'll listen then.

Yes, today will be about mobilizing, forming a plan. Tomorrow we will leave.

I clear the breakfast dishes, and Cosi tells me she is going out to play in the snow before school. I tell her no, and that she must also stay home from school, and as if on cue she stomps her feet, runs to her room, and weeps.

"I hate you!" she screams.

I hate the world we live in, and how it's affecting my sweet child.

"I feel awful for her," I say to Papa as she slams the bedroom door. "I wish there were another way."

He nods.

"Listen to me, please," I say, reaching for his hand and beckoning him to look in my eyes. "We have to get out of here. It's not safe for us, and you know it, Papa. There's an afternoon train that departs for the south. With any luck, we can be having dinner tomorrow night at a little café far from here, under the protection of our new names. We'll stay away until the war ends, or cross the border into Switzerland."

Papa just stares ahead.

"Please," I cry, wiping a tear from my cheek.

214

"You go, dear," he finally says, patting my hand the way he might have done when I was Cosi's age and had just recited some silly idea about wanting to move to the moon and set up a candy shop. "Dear child, this is my home. I will not leave."

My heart feels as if it is being pulled in two directions and might sever. How can I choose between Papa and Cosi? Could I even make such an impossible decision?

Before we can continue our conversation, Cosi runs into the room and leaps into my lap. "I'm sorry that I said I hate you, Mama," she says, nestling her head into the crook of my neck. "I really don't hate you. I'm just . . . sad."

"You are forgiven," I say, "my naughty little birdie."

"You're only trying to make sure I'm safe," she continues. "I know that. It's just that"—she turns to look at me, her big green eyes sparkling—"I love snow *so* much!"

I smile, her enthusiasm as contagious as influenza. "I do too, love."

She bounces her bear on her lap playfully, then freezes in a moment of terror. "Mama! Mama!" she cries.

"What is it, honey?"

"Oh no, oh no, oh no!"

"What in the world is going on? Tell me."

She leaps to her feet. "It's a terrible thing, just

terrible." She points to Monsieur Dubois. "His necklace. It's gone!"

I'm immediately relieved. In my mind, Cosi's burst of anxiety could have been much more serious: a child of German sympathizers who had threatened her at school, a rock thrown at our window, or something much more concerning.

But I know how special the bear's necklace is to her. A locket, engraved with the letter "C," which matches the one she's worn around her neck every day for the last three years. Papa gave her the set for her fifth birthday. A necklace for her, and one for Monsieur Dubois. I don't think I'd ever seen her so happy.

"We'll find it," I say. "It's sure to be hiding somewhere."

"No," she says, shaking her head gravely. "I know where I left it."

"Where?"

"The flower shop," she says. "I took it off when you and Papa were talking. I was going to put a sunflower seed in it. Monsieur Dubois loves sunflower seeds. But then you said we had to go." Her eyes are frantic. "I set it on the counter when I leaned down to tie my shoe, and, oh, Mama, I left it there!" She wipes a tear from her eye. "Do you think . . . someone might have stolen it?"

"Certainly not, love," I say. "The shop is all locked up."

"But what if someone breaks a window?"

I don't tell her that the last thing someone would want to steal would be a little girl's necklace for her bear, nor do I tell her that this is the last thing I can deal with in this moment when there are a million other much more important things to attend to in the name of our safety. And yet here is my little girl, who only has one worry in the world. And it's a worry I can alleviate.

"All right," I say after a long pause. "I'll go get it for you."

Her face beams with gratitude as she throws her arms around my neck. "You're the best mama in the entire world!"

Papa flashes me a look of concern, which I dismiss. I can read his mind, of course: he doesn't want me to leave. I wouldn't want him to, either, but I can be there and back in under fifteen minutes with Cosi's precious bear's necklace, and it will make her heart happy. I reach for my coat.

The sun is warm, and it's beginning to melt the remnants of yesterday's snow, but many icy patches remain, and I'm careful not to slip on the cobblestone streets as I make my way to the shop.

I see it just ahead. The little green sign sways in the morning breeze, and I feel a pang in my heart. Our shop has been more than just a business; it has also been a family member of sorts. I've

217

found beauty and comfort within its walls, and purpose. So has Papa. I study the crude yellow star on the window, painted with hatred, and I shudder at the sight. Since we left, someone has thrown a rock at the right front window, leaving a dozen cracks in the glass that look like a jagged spiderweb.

I push the old brass key into the lock and step inside, breathing in the familiar scent of flowers, sprigs of baby's breath, brown paper and twine, and Papa's aftershave. I hope I'll never forget what this smells like. Home.

Papa would be horrified to know that the white roses have turned brown, and the stock has all but dried up from lack of water. Instinctively, I walk to the sink, ready to jump into action and breathe life into our little storefront, but I stop myself. There isn't time for anything more than what I came for: Cosi's necklace, which I'm relieved to find on the counter, just as she described. I tuck it into the pocket of my coat, which is when I notice . . . someone standing in the doorway.

It's *him*. Reinhardt. I could never forget his name, or his face. "Well, hello again," he says.

My heart beats wildly in my chest as he walks toward me.

"Céline, isn't it?"

I open my mouth to speak, but nothing comes out.

"Yes that's right, Céline." He smiles. "You know, I haven't been able to get you out of my mind since we met." As he paces closer to me, I inch away, until my back hits the counter.

He looks at his watch. "Closed for business, I see?" He gives me a reprieve from his gaze and walks to a vase of carnations, stopping to hold the flowers to his nose, before setting it down again. "Fortunately for you," he continues, turning back to me again, "I am a generous man, and I've come to help you." He walks closer. "You see, I need a new housemaid, someone to tidy my apartment, keep things looking smart. It's been hard to find the right . . . woman." He is so close to me now I can smell his rancid breath. "I live at eighteen rue Cler. You'll start tomorrow at eight A.M. sharp." He begins walking to the door, then turns around a final time. "And Céline," he says, studying my face. I clutch Cosi's necklace tightly. "It would be such a shame, particularly for your father, if you disappointed me." He tips his hat to me. "Good day."

When I reach our apartment building, I am out of breath. I slipped on the ice, and now my knee throbs under my dress. I didn't stop to see how bad it was but feel blood trickling down my leg to my ankle.

I startle when I feel a hand touch my shoulder from behind.

"I'm sorry," Esther says, her face tinged with concern. "I didn't mean to frighten you."

"Sorry," I say, exhaling deeply when I see her face.

"Everything all right?"

I could tell her about my encounter just now, or what I've overheard at Bistro Jeanty, or my fears for Cosi and Papa. I could tell her of the hundreds of worries that plague me. But why? She has her own. Everyone does. I won't burden her with mine.

"As well as can be," I say, forcing the corners of my mouth to turn upward.

"And your father? I trust his wound is healing nicely?"

I nod. "Yes, thank you again."

"Good," she says. "Send him to me in about ten days and I'll take out the stitches."

"I will," I say, waving goodbye as I climb the stairs to the third floor, my knee aching with each step.

That night, after Cosi is asleep, Papa and I sit up by the fire. I tell him about what happened in the shop, and he buries his head in his hands.

"I won't let you go to him," he says.

"And the alternative?" I say. "I don't want to begin to imagine what might happen if I don't." I take a deep breath. "Listen, it might not be as bad as we think. If he's happy with my work, it will buy us more time."

"No, Céline," Papa says. "I will not send you to a monster." He nods. "We'll leave at dawn, catch the early train to the south. We'll be gone before he even knows it."

I blink back tears. "I love you so much."

"I love you, too, my precious daughter."

"I know you don't want to leave home," I say.

"No," he corrects me. "I've been conflicted about that for some time, and then I realized. A home is a refuge from the world, a place of safety. We don't have that anymore here." He clasps his hands together. "So, we'll find a new one."

"Yes," I say, my voice cracking. "Yes we will."

I wake Cosi at half past five. She yawns and rolls over. "Honey," I whisper, "I need you to get up."

"Why, Mama?" she asks. "It's still dark out."

"We're going on an adventure, love," I say. "On a train."

Her eyes shoot open. "Really?"

"Yes," I say, helping her out of her nightgown and into the dress and cardigan sweater I'd laid out for her the night before.

"Are we going to California?"

"Maybe," I say with a grin. "You'll just have to wait and see."

I tuck the letters I've been writing to Luc in the inside pocket of my coat, along with some paper and envelopes.

"What about breakfast?" Cosi asks.

"We'll eat on the train."

She scratches her head. "Shouldn't we pack a suitcase?"

"Don't you worry, love," I say. "Papa and I have everything figured out." I don't tell her that a suitcase would draw attention, and that we'll have to purchase the things we need later.

"All I need is Monsieur Dubois, anyway," she says cheerfully, giving her bear a squeeze. "And my journal." She tucks her precious book into the pocket of her coat. I'm pleased to see that it fits.

Papa surveys the apartment a final time. For all we know, it might be the last time any of us lays eyes on these walls. He stops at the bookshelf and picks up the framed photo of Mama. "Do you have room in your purse for this?"

"Yes," I say, pulling the photograph from its frame.

"We aren't ever coming back here, are we, Mama?" Cosi asks with wisdom far greater than her eight years.

I kneel down beside her. "Maybe someday," I say. "A long time from now."

She nods and turns to the door. "I'm ready now."

"Can I have a back ride?" Cosi asks Papa on the street below. We have about an hour until the train leaves, plenty of time to purchase our tickets, two coffees, and a snack for Cosi at the station, and yet I'm anxious and want to get there as soon as possible.

"No, Cosi," I say. "That will slow us down, and besides, you know Papa's back has been bothering him. Your legs are strong. You can walk."

Papa hears none of it, however. He crouches, and Cosi climbs onto him, giggling happily.

"All right you two," I say. "Let's go."

I don't remember Paris ever being so quiet. It's as if the entire city is asleep save us. We walk ahead, beginning the fifteen-minute journey to the train station, but before we can round the first corner, the beam of a flashlight and a loud, startling whistle stop us in our tracks. Just ahead, a group of German soldiers approaches. There are six or seven of them, and when I see that one is Reinhardt, my heart sinks.

"Well, well," he says, walking toward us with four other men. "Going on a little *outing,* are we?"

Papa opens his mouth to speak, but Reinhardt silences him. "Save your breath, old man. You'll need it where you're going."

"Please," I say, attempting to buy us some time. Even a few seconds. "We are just out for a morning walk."

He holds out his hand to catch the falling snow. "In this weather?" He turns to one of his counterparts. "A perfect day for a family walk, wouldn't you say?" The men laugh. "When I told you to arrive at my apartment at eight A.M. today, it was a test," he continues. "And you failed."

"But it's not even six yet," I say, glancing at Cosi, who clings to Papa tightly. "I was going to come. I . . . I still am."

Whatever I say makes no difference. We are mice, and these are great big cats before us. With guns.

"Céline," Reinhardt continues, "I warned you how much I hate to be disappointed." He looks at Cosi.

"Please," I beg, falling to my knees. The right one is still sore from yesterday, and it smarts when it hits the cobblestones.

Reinhardt smiles. "I like it when you beg." He touches the nape of my neck where my necklace from Pierre drapes over my collarbone, then rips off the gold chain as Cosi lets out a scream of terror. I look up at her, my eyes welling with tears. "I don't like clutter on collarbones." He grabs my arm and jerks me to a stand. As he does, my purse falls to the street and the photo of Mama spills out. Reinhardt turns to the men beside him and nods. "Take them."

He smiles. "Wondering how I caught you? Well, it was thanks to my sharp instincts, of course, but I wouldn't have intercepted you at precisely the right moment without help from Monsieur Toulouse."

My cheeks burn. The neighbors on the second floor have turned us in.

"A little tip," he continues. "When planning your escape in an old, drafty apartment building such as yours, be sure to avoid divulging your plan beside the radiator vent." He laughs. "Sound carries. People might hear you."

Papa quickly thrusts Cosi down from his shoulders and into his arms, slinging her over his shoulder, and turning down the street. I watch Monsieur Dubois flap against Papa's back as his tired legs work as hard as they can to carry them out of danger. It's a futile attempt, but I love Papa all the more for it.

"Papa!" I cry.

Cosi screams for me. "Mama! No, Mama. No!"

I fight against Reinhardt's grasp in vain, twisting this way and that, screaming Cosi's name over and over again.

Right before the men reach Papa, his legs give way. He breaks Cosi's fall, and a moment later, I watch her jump to her feet and dart to the left, clutching her bear. She gets four paces away before one of the soldiers captures her. Her little legs kick wildly. Two others lift Papa to his feet, just as a truck arrives. I sob, falling to my knees again as the men push Papa and Cosi inside.

I watch in horror as the truck drives off into the early-morning light, taking away both halves of my heart.

CHAPTER 15

CAROLINE

The next weekend, Victor and I stop at the restaurant briefly before heading to the train station. Just like a new mother fretting over an impending separation from her baby, he is nervous about leaving the restaurant, I can tell, even if it will be in capable hands. His kitchen staff, headed up by the very talented Julien, will take care of the back end; Raoul, the bartender, along with Margot, will handle the front of the house, although, when I see her this morning, she looks worse than ever. I can detect a faint bruise around her left eye, which she's obviously tried, unsuccessfully, to cover up with makeup.

When Victor heads to the kitchen to talk to Julien, I stay and check on Margot.

"Please," I say softly. Her eyes are red, misty. "Do you need help? What can I do for you?"

She turns away, attempting to hide her tears, then faces me, collecting herself. "He's a good man, he really is," she says, smoothing her dress. "But when he drinks . . ." She shakes her head, looking away again. "I only worry about my little boy."

I reach for her hand.

"Do you have somewhere safe you can go?"

She doesn't reply, so I reach into my bag and pull out the keys to my apartment. "Why don't you stay with me until you get back on your feet? I have the extra space, and my apartment is very close to the restaurant. It would take some strain off you, at least for a little while." I hand her my keychain.

She examines it, then hands it back. "I wouldn't think of troubling you like that."

"Where is your son right now?"

"With my boyfriend's sister. She runs a day care center outside the city. She watches my son while I work. I thought about staying there, but he would find me for sure."

"That settles it then," I say. "You'll stay with me. It's no trouble whatsoever." I smile. "Besides, the apartment is much too large for just one single lady." I hand the keychain back to her. "I could use the company." I squeeze her hand. "What is your son's name?"

"Élian," she says.

I smile. "You and Élian will be my guests. Eighteen rue Cler. The concierge is Monsieur de Goff. He's a little prickly around the edges, but I'm certain there's a teddy bear under all those thorns. Tell him I sent you."

Victor loads my bag onto the train, along with his duffel, tucking them both in a luggage-holding area before we find our seats.

227

"It'll be nice to get away for a while," he says. "It's been nonstop since I took over the restaurant." He reaches for my hand. "I think you're really going to love the south. It's so peaceful."

"I can't wait," I say, taking the seat beside him.

"When I was growing up, my family and I took the train down every few months to visit my grandmother in Lyon."

"Tell me about them, your family."

He nods. "My mom's name is Babette. She grew up with wealth and never quite got over it when her father lost most of his money in a bad investment when she was sixteen. They had to move out of their posh apartment to a much less prestigious address. You would assume, given the trauma of losing her nearly endless monthly allowance from Daddy, that she'd have sought out a wealthy man to marry, but instead she chose my father, Charles. He's a college professor. For every one hundred words my mother speaks, he speaks three."

I grin.

"She's flighty, he's grounded. She stays up late into the night, he's up at five A.M. You'd think that after all these years they'd have ended up divorced, but you know what? I think they're actually perfect for each other."

I smile. "Ah, I love that."

I look out the window wistfully, wishing I

could make my mind release the memories it stubbornly keeps of my own family, wherever they might be.

Victor's eyes meet mine. "Oh, I almost forgot to tell you about Hugo."

"Hugo?"

"My crazy brother. He's four years younger than me, devilishly handsome, and a favorite among the ladies."

I laugh.

"Last I heard from him, he was in Portugal, on the yacht of some heiress."

"Did Babette ask to join them?"

He grins. "Very good," he says. "You catch on quick."

"I'd love to meet them all," I say, then suddenly wish I hadn't let the words slip out. My cheeks feel hot. How completely ridiculous to talk about meeting his family when we've only gone on a handful of dates, if you could even call them that. "I mean . . . someday, if they ever come to the . . . restaurant or anything." I want to crawl into a hole and stay there for a thousand years.

"You'd love them all," he says, seemingly unfazed as he gazes out the window. "Look," he continues, pointing. "A castle."

I see it in the distance. A castle indeed, but very run-down. The entire left wall has collapsed, and its perimeter is encircled in weeds and tall grass. A few broken-down cars are scattered nearby.

"It's so funny that people can actually own and *live* in those old buildings," I say, marveling.

"Yeah," he says. "They're everywhere in these parts. Look, there's another."

I see it ahead. A bit better kept than the last, but still very modest, with a rusty aluminum swing set and plastic slide to its right.

"My cousins and I would play this little game we made up called Castles and Sheep."

I laugh. "Castles and Sheep?"

"The thing is so ingenious, I really should have branded it," he says, smiling. "I know you're dying to know how to play it, so fear not, I'll tell you." He looks out the window. "As you've probably noticed, even as we've just begun our journey, this great country of mine has a lot of castles, and a lot of sheep."

I smile at the hilarity of this but play along, pointing out the window to my first sheep. "There, at three o'clock!"

"Good," Victor continues. "Now, sheep get you two points, and castles five. Inevitably, it's neck and neck, the castles and the sheep. Whoever has the most points after the train ride wins. No cheating."

"Castle!" I point out as we pass an old stone home with a spire.

"Sheep!" Victor counters with an animal on the left side of the train.

Fifteen minutes later, and after a lot of

laughing, we've lost count and give up, opting instead to head to the dining car to purchase a bottle of wine and some snacks, which we bring back to our seats.

Victor uncorks the wine and pours us each a glass. I take a sip, then turn to him. "What if my memory comes back, and it . . . changes everything?"

He looks at me with tender eyes, waiting for me to continue.

"It's just that . . ." I pause to look out the window again, then back at him. "I like this. I like my life, just the way it is right now. Does that make any sense at all?"

He nods, giving me the space to go on.

"I'm getting used to the unknown." I swallow hard and reach for his hand. "I'm getting used to *this*. I don't want anything to change."

He looks at me like he doesn't want anything to change, either. But he doesn't say that. Instead, he kisses the left side of my cheek and whispers into my ear, "Don't worry so much. It will all work out as it should." He grins. "I just hope we don't find out that you're married to a male model who just happens to be away for a lengthy catalog shoot in Milan."

I laugh, then turn back to the window and watch, deep in thought, as the rolling green hills whiz by.

Another castle. Another sheep.

· · ·

"Oh, Victor, it's beautiful!" I exclaim as he pulls our rental car into the gravel driveway. The house is exactly as I'd imagined, with its stone façade and casement windows with sheer white curtains. Lavender and rosemary everywhere. I grab the paper sack from our brief stop at a market along the way as Victor carries our bags to the door.

Inside, soothing neutrals abound: white slip-covered sofas, ashy wood coffee table and dining set. "That's it," I say. "I'm moving in for good."

"Isn't it great?" He reaches up to dust away a cobweb from the ceiling above him. "Such a shame it doesn't get more use. My friend works in Spain half the year, so it just sits empty."

I point ahead. "Look at that kitchen!"

He nods. "Oh, I fully intend to find my way in there tonight to make you something very Provençal."

"And the pool!" I throw open the French doors and run out to the patio and back garden, where cypress trees line the perimeter. I pull the cover off one of the chaise longues beside the large rectangular swimming pool and settle in, exhaling deeply. "If anyone needs me, I'll be right here."

"Why don't you go put your swimsuit on," Victor suggests. "I'll make us a drink."

I find what appears to be the master bedroom

and wheel my bag inside, thinking about what it might be like to live in a place like this with Victor, and the scene is a beautiful one: the two of us, breathing in the sunny, herb-filled air, eating delicious dinners, making art and—my cheeks flush—love. I slip on my black bikini and cinch a towel from the bathroom around my waist self-consciously.

"I'll just be out on the patio," I say in the living room, where Victor hands me a cocktail muddled with lavender flowers.

I take a sip as he walks closer. "Let me see you."

I'm nervous as he places his hand on my waist, releasing the towel to the floor. He smiles at my shyness. "You didn't tell me you were a swimsuit model."

"Oh stop," I say, retrieving the towel with flushed cheeks. "I probably look . . . I don't know . . ."

His expression momentarily freezes as he pulls me to him. "I wish you could understand how beautiful you are. I wish you could know . . ." His voice trails off as he runs his fingers through my hair.

Do the words feel strange on his lips? Does he even mean them? Or does he merely pity me, the girl with no memory?

"Let's swim," he says, his smile returning. "I'll go find my trunks."

He returns minutes later shirtless and in sunglasses. Although he doesn't seem to be the sort of man who spends much, if any, time at the gym, his muscles are defined and toned. "Tell me," I tease, "how is it that a chef can have a six-pack?"

He rubs his stomach. "First of all, this is in no way a six-pack. But thank you." He grins. "This bodes well for me when your supermodel husband materializes next week. I'll need to put up my best fight, and it will be stiff competition."

I laugh. "But seriously. How do you eat with such gusto and stay so fit? Are you getting up at the crack of dawn and running up and down the steps of Montmartre or something?"

He removes the cover from the chaise longue beside me. "No. I am much too lazy for that."

"Then what is it? Good genes? Because I have a hunch that if I ate crème brûlée as often as you do, I'd be twice my size."

He lies down in the lounge chair beside me and grins. "It must be my tapeworm, then."

I laugh. "Your tapeworm?"

"Yeah, a godsend, that critter."

"You're pretty funny, you know?"

"I'm glad I make you laugh," he says. "Not everyone gets my humor." His smile fades for a moment, then returns. "Hey, how about some music?"

"Yes, please," I say.

He pulls his cellphone from his pocket. "Let me see if I can hack into this Sonos system. Do you like jazz?" he asks as the gentle sound of a saxophone filters through the outdoor speakers.

"Is the sky *blue?*" I take a sip of my drink, then I close my eyes, rocking my body slowly to the melody. I may be suffering from amnesia, but even so, somehow I know that jazz runs through my blood. "Stan Getz," I continue.

"Nice. One of my favorites as well. You know what I've always said?"

"What?"

"Must love jazz."

"What do you mean?"

"Remember the movie *Must Love Dogs*?"

I nod.

"For me to get serious with anyone, she absolutely must love jazz."

"I guess I pass, then."

"Well, we'll see how you stand when I quiz you on Chet Baker later."

" 'My Funny Valentine'?" I say, taking another sip of my drink while pondering jazz and the absurdity of life. I can identify a Chet Baker song, and yet I can't tell you a thing about myself.

"The sun, the house, the pool, the peace— to me, this is heaven," he says. "When the restaurant takes off in a few years, and I recoup my investment, my dream is to buy a house like this and spend the summers out here, and maybe long weekends in the fall, Christmas."

"I love it," I say.

He stands up suddenly. "Come on, let's jump in!"

"You first," I say.

I watch as he dives into the pool, surfacing a moment later and shaking his hair to the side. He tosses it in a certain way, a familiar way. Like . . . someone else I used to know. The memory surfaces with such intensity, it almost hurts.

"What is it?" he asks.

"The way you turned your head just now, it reminds me of . . ." I take another sip of my drink. "It's nothing."

He looks away.

"Are you worried?" I ask cautiously, walking toward the pool. I sit down at the edge and dip my legs in.

"What do you mean?"

"Worried that . . . there might be someone else in my life, someone who might threaten what we've found?" I remember the shirt I'd discovered in my drawer, with its tropical print. *Who was he? Do I still love him?*

Victor forces a smile. "Of course, I can't deny that it makes me nervous. But like I said at the restaurant, the past has already happened. There's nothing we can do to change that, so let's focus on the present, the life we're living right now."

"Yes, you're right," I say, sliding into the pool. At first the water is shockingly cool, but I acclimate quickly.

Victor moves toward me and wraps his arms around my waist. "But let me just say this: If another man does turn up trying to claim you, I'm not going down without a fight."

I grin, and wrap my legs around him under the water as he kisses me softly.

The phone rings inside the house, and Victor hesitates at first, then leaps out of the pool to answer it. "I better get it, just in case it's the caretaker. My friend said he might call."

I climb out and return to my chaise longue, where I take the last sip of my drink and reach for my bag, retrieving my sketchbook and pencils. As I begin to sketch the scene in front of me, I hear Victor's voice, hushed and low, in the kitchen. I can only make out bits and pieces.

"I told you . . ."

". . . she's fine . . ."

"No, no . . . no . . . wait a bit longer."

"Good."

"I'll know soon."

"Who was on the phone?" I ask when he returns.

"Oh, just the restaurant," he says. "You'd think they could leave me alone for one day, but no." He sighs.

I nod, returning to my sketchbook, but when

the breeze rustles through the palm in the corner of the garden, I don't hear wind chimes, or catch any glimpses of buried memory. I remain firmly planted in the present.

For dinner, Victor makes roast chicken, potatoes, and a simple but elegant mâche salad, all with the ingredients we picked up at a market earlier.

"The chicken," I say, after taking a bite, "is *so* good."

"Just sea salt, olive oil, garlic, and a little rosemary," he says. "People overcomplicate chicken. That's really all you need."

Later, after the dishes are washed and put away, we take our wineglasses outside and sink into one of the outdoor sofas. Victor switches on the gas fireplace. The flames are mesmerizing, but the stars overhead are even more so.

"I'd wager that there isn't anywhere in the world where the stars are as grand," he says, pointing to the sky. "They're so close, you can almost touch them."

"I'll take Jupiter, then," I say.

"Technically a planet, but anything for my lady." He reaches up, makes a plucking motion with his fingers, then places the imaginary planet in my hand.

"Why, thank you, sir."

He grins, looking up at the sky again. "Now, you know what you really need?"

"What star might that be?"

"The North Star."

I giggle.

"To help you find your way, your compass." He clears his throat and rises to his feet. "Now, this one will take a little more wrangling, but . . . there it is." He reaches higher. "Almost have it. Almost! There!" He proudly places the North Star in my palm.

"I think it's fair to say that no man has ever given me a star." I grin. "I've never met anyone quite like you."

He nods dramatically. "Victor Lamont. Making good food and bad jokes since 1969."

I grin. "You're eight years older than me."

"Indeed I am." He weaves his fingers into mine. "Too old, you're thinking?"

I squeeze his hand. "Just right, I'm thinking." I study his face for a long moment. "How can you . . . like me," I ask, "if you don't *know* me?"

He searches my eyes. "But you're mistaken," he replies. "I do know you." He points to each of my eyes. "In there, deep down, I can see you."

"Can you?"

"Sure I can. I know that you're kind and compassionate, joyful and creative. And I also know that my heart is completely captured by you."

I feel a wave of emotion wash over me when he presses his lips to mine, kissing me softly at first, then passionately. He lifts me into his strong arms, carrying me to the bedroom. Starlight filters in through the window as he sets me on the bed, first unbuttoning his shirt, then crawling toward me, kissing me again, before pulling my cotton dress over my head and letting it fall to the floor. His hand traces the outline of my legs, my breasts, and I relent to his touch, gasping as he pulls me to him. His breath quickens as he kisses my neck, looking into my eyes as he moves closer. "Trust me," he whispers, pressing himself between my legs. "I promise not to hurt you."

"But what if . . ."

He presses his finger to my lips and shakes his head, kissing me again. "No what-ifs." I can feel his desire—a hot fire, burning wild and free, and with it, I feel free, too. Safe, somehow. I close my eyes and pull his mouth to mine, yielding to him, our bodies entwined.

I open my eyes when I hear the phone ring the next morning. It's still dark, and can't be later than five A.M. Victor is still asleep; a sheet covers the lower half of his naked body. He doesn't budge, so I decide not to wake him. Instead, I quietly slip out of bed, tiptoeing to the door, narrowly avoiding tripping on my suitcase.

"Hello?" I whisper into the phone in the living room, but there's a thick static on the line, and I can barely hear the caller. "Hello?" I say again.

"Vic?" It's a woman's voice. "Vic, is that you? It's Emma."

The hair on the back of my neck stands on end as I slowly let the handset drift away from my head, then place it back into its cradle.

Who is Emma? Victor hasn't mentioned anyone by that name. And why would she be calling him here, and at this hour? I slip back into the bed beside Victor, relieved that the phone hasn't rung again. He rouses, rolling onto his side and then pulling me to him. Within minutes, we are making love again, and I forget all about the telephone.

"I hate to leave," Victor says later that morning as he packs his suitcase. He woke early and made us breakfast, which I smelled the moment I opened my eyes. I wrapped myself in a robe and walked to the kitchen to find a beautiful frittata on the counter, hot from the oven. A moment later, I spotted Victor hovering over the side of the pool, stick in hand, attempting to rescue what looked like a butterfly on the verge of drowning. I watched as he carefully dipped the stick into the water for the little creature to climb onto. In a few moments, its yellow wings flapped away in the morning breeze.

"An excellent rescue operation," I said, smiling from the patio.

He stood up, a little startled. "Oh, good morning. I didn't think you were up."

"Just now," I said.

He looked back at the pool, then pointed to the kitchen as the butterfly ascended over a cypress tree. "Good, breakfast's ready."

"I wish we could stay another day," I say now, taking a final glance around the bedroom.

"Me too," Victor says. "But I have to get back to the restaurant."

"I know," I say, with a smile.

We tidy up the house, then load the car and set out for the train station. We'll be home in Paris by one o'clock, with plenty of time for Victor to return to Jeanty for dinner service.

On the train, Victor naps while I gaze out the window thinking about how perfect, even healing, it had felt to be in his arms. So why did I get the sense that he seemed off this morning? *Am I misreading things?* I stare out the window for a while until my eyelids get heavy. Without warning, I hear the wind in the palm trees again, the wind chimes. This time, I'm in an art studio of some sort. There's an easel and canvases stacked up in the corners of the room. My jeans are splattered in paint of every imaginable hue. On the wall in front of me is the painting that hangs in my Paris apartment: the one of the California backyard scene. It's hot, and I wipe a sweaty wisp of hair from my brow before lifting a fresh canvas and setting it on the easel. I reach for a brush, swaying to soft piano music coming from somewhere near, or faraway.

A man's voice calls my name. "Caroline. Caroline."

I open my eyes. Victor is sitting next to me on the train, smiling. "Wake up, sleepy girl. We're home."

I rub my eyes. "Wow, I must have fallen asleep."

Victor nods. "You were out for a solid hour."

We disembark, and Victor kisses me before hailing a taxi outside the station. "I have to drop off my bags at my apartment and change before going to the restaurant. Will you be able to manage from here?"

I remember that his apartment is on the other side of town, making a shared cab ride back a logistical problem. "I'll be fine," I assure him.

He hesitates, glancing at his watch. "I should take you home first."

I shake my head. "No. I know you're anxious to get back to the restaurant. I'll be fine."

"Okay," he says, kissing me once more.

A dark-haired woman walks by, and I am struck with a familiar feeling that I know her somehow, but before I can get a better look, she's disappeared around the corner.

"I'll be working late, but I'll call you when I get home, if you'll be up," Victor says, as his cab approaches.

"Yes," I say, smiling. "I'd like that."

He blows me a kiss from the window as the taxi whisks him away.

• • •

I find the spare key I left under the doormat and let myself in. "Margot?" I call out into the apartment as I set my bags down, but there's no reply.

I unpack, make myself a snack in the kitchen, then sort through the mail in the living room. The flowers on the entryway table have wilted, and a dozen or so petals have fallen to the floor.

I kneel down to clean them up but stop, suddenly struck by the unexpected beauty in what might otherwise be considered debris in need of a broom and dustpan. I reach for my sketchbook and pencils and begin capturing the scene as I see it, a perfect, beautiful mess.

"What do you think?" I ask Inès later that afternoon at the art studio. She lowers her dark-rimmed glasses, examining my progress on a painting I've been working on for the last few days. Inès looks particularly pretty today with her hair piled up into a high bun like a little island perched atop her head. Her blouse has been swapped out for a sweater, her sandals exchanged for boots, with jeans, ever so delicately distressed, cuffed just above the ankle. To me, she is the epitome of a woman who has complete control of her life. I long to feel that way about mine.

"I think it's . . . perfection," she says, leaning

in closer, then stepping back for a more global perspective. "A lotus, definitely," she says, pointing to the canvas. "Look at the way you captured the petals here, and the use of shadow and light. You should be very proud."

I smile, feeling better than I have in a long time, with or without my memory. "Thanks."

"Have you given any more thought to participating in the art show? With this lotus, you now have three paintings to exhibit, and time to complete more."

"I don't know," I say, looking over the painting again.

"Please," she says. "I think it would do you some good."

"Is it fancy? Will I have to talk?"

"Everything's fancy in Paris," she says, grinning, "and no, you don't have to talk. Go find a dress, and you'll have a ball."

"Don't you have to be a *real* artist to have an art show?"

"But you *are* an artist," she says. "And, I think, a born one at that." She takes off her glasses. "As women, it is critical that we own our identities, our stories."

"Easier said than done for me," I say.

"I know," she continues, aware of my accident and memory loss. "But when you obtain bits and pieces of information about yourself, like this painting, you should celebrate them."

I stare at the painting for a long moment, hoping that the canvas will somehow unlock a clue about my life, a past memory, a shard of remembrance dislodged and pushed to the forefront of my cerebral cortex that will all at once make sense of, well, everything. *"Aha,"* I'll say, *"that's who I am!"* I squint harder, scouring my work for something, anything. And yet, all I see is a . . . lotus.

"I don't know what there is to celebrate here," I say with a sigh.

"This," she replies, pointing to the canvas. "Whether it makes sense or not, it's a beautiful creation that came from you. Your brain conjured it up. Just think, maybe in your past you were struck by the beauty of a lotus you saw in Bali, or some other exotic place. Or maybe as a child your mother planted them in the garden and you noticed the way they caught the sunlight in the late afternoon. Or maybe," she pauses and her eyes get big, "you're the lotus."

I shake my head. "I don't understand."

She smiles. "Just think about it."

I nod. "Inès, can I tell you something?"

She pulls up a stool and sits beside me. "Sure."

"I've been having these . . . flashbacks," I say. "At least, that's the best way I can describe them. They're moments when I feel like I'm transported to other times in my life. My past, at least I think." I take a deep breath. "Well, I had another one today, on the train. I was in an art studio. *My* art studio, as far as I can tell."

"I'm not surprised in the slightest," she says, smiling big. "I knew you were gifted the moment you picked up a paintbrush."

I swallow hard. "You said you were stuck once. May I ask . . . what was your trauma?"

She takes her glasses off and exhales deeply. "I married my true love, a boy I'd known since primary school. Evan." She sighs. "We got married straight after college and had two blissful years before he was diagnosed with lung cancer. He died four months after the diagnosis. Never smoked a day in his life."

I place my hand on my heart. "I'm so sorry."

She nods. "I thought I'd never recover. I was plagued with grief. But a funny thing happened. That grief, that horrible grief, broke me open."

"Broke you . . . open?"

"Yes," she says. "I didn't know how closed off I was before, how little value I placed on the things that truly matter in life. Grief helped me change. Art helped me heal." She smiles. "It's why I started this studio, and it's why I believe that you will find your way, too, just as I did. If you told me that I'd be here today, remarried, a mother, thriving, after losing Evan," she pauses and shakes her head, "well, there were many years when I wouldn't have believed you." She nods. "We all have pain we carry around with us.

247

Some worse than mine, some less. I learned long ago that there's no point in wallowing in it. All wounds heal, even the deepest ones. So I decided one day that I had two choices: either I could stay stuck and succumb to the grief, which in my case would let cancer claim two lives, or I could move forward and choose life." She smiles. "You can probably guess my choice."

"That's beautiful," I say.

"Thank you," she says, turning back to my painting. "It's truth." Her eyes light up. "Hey, I forgot to ask you . . . was that you who I saw today at the train station with a particularly handsome gentleman?"

"Oh," I say. "Yes. I thought I recognized you from across the station, but I didn't have my glasses on."

"Did he give you the flowers yet?"

I shake my head. "I don't understand."

"Your boyfriend," she continues. "The one at the station."

"I don't understand."

"I saw him at a flower shop near Jeanty. He was buying an enormous arrangement. At least a few dozen roses." She places her hand over her mouth. "I hope I didn't ruin the surprise."

I shake my head. "But . . . I didn't get any flowers." I pause. "Maybe they were for a sick friend, or his mother, or—"

"I highly doubt that," she interjects. "Nobody

gives red roses to his *mother.*" She nods confidently. "They're for you, *mon amie.*"

I stare at her blankly. "We don't have plans tonight."

She rubs her arm nervously. "Listen, I shouldn't have said anything. If it was a surprise, I've ruined it."

A surprise, or a . . . revelation? I remember the call in Provence from the woman named Emma.

"It'll all be fine," she says. The bells on the door jingle as two people enter the studio: a man in his midforties and a little girl with pigtails.

"Mama!" she cries, running to Inès, who scoops her up and spins her around in a little tornado of love. I think about what Inès had just said about choosing *life.*

"Sweet child," she says, pointing to her daughter's mouth. "What is this? You lost a tooth!"

As I watch the precious exchange between mother and daughter, something deep inside of me aches, like a surge of phantom pain from a missing limb, long since amputated.

I smile and turn to the door. "Good night," I say softly to them all.

There's a chill in the air outside, and I pull my sweater tighter around my body as my phone buzzes in my purse.

"Hello," I say.

"Caroline, it's Dr. Leroy."

"Oh, hi," I say.

"You haven't returned the messages I've left at your apartment, so I thought I'd try your cellphone."

"I'm sorry," I say. "I was . . . out of town."

"And how are you feeling?"

How am I *feeling?* A cacophony of words come to mind: overwhelmed, scared, unsure, worried, frustrated, insecure. But somehow, I am unable to settle on one.

"I feel . . ." I say, my voice cracking a bit, tears welling up in my eyes. "I don't know. Lost, I guess."

"I'm so sorry," she says. "We've done all we can for you medically, but I think it would do you good to talk to someone. I know a therapist who specializes in memory loss. His name is Louis Marchand. He has an office not too far from you—a few streets up from the rue Cler, if I'm not mistaken. I'll text you his phone number. Why don't you call him, make an appointment?"

"I don't know," I say.

"I promise, he won't bite," she continues.

I sigh, remembering Inès's words. "Okay, I'll call him."

"Good," she says. "Oh, Caroline, I've been wondering, have you . . ." Her voice trails off.

"What?"

She pauses for another moment. "Oh, it's nothing." She clears her throat. "Take care of yourself, my dear."

As I walk ahead, I think of what Victor said the other day about living in the moment, focusing on the present, the here and now. He'd asked me to trust him. Could I?

As the sun sets, it casts a glow of orange on the city. Everyone, it seems, has a place to be, or belong. A mother and her little boy scurry across the street to the bakery just ahead. A dog and its owner scale the steps to an apartment to my right. A woman on a bicycle chimes her bell as she passes, probably eager to meet her boyfriend or husband at a quiet bistro somewhere.

But what about me? Where do I belong? I veer right toward my apartment. Margot will be there. I'll stay up and have a cup of tea with her. But when I hear church bells ringing in the distance, I freeze. Somehow, I feel compelled to seek them out. I look overhead to see if I can locate a steeple, a spire, anything churchy. And then I spot an ancient-looking building at the end of the block, with a bell tolling on top. A small elderly woman stands at the entrance, welcoming people as they walk in.

I inch closer, but stop before climbing the steps to the entrance.

"Well?" the old woman says to me a few

moments later. "Have you made up your mind yet?"

I turn around to see if she's talking to someone behind me, but there is no one else.

"I'm sorry," I say, confused. "Made up my mind?"

"Yes," she continues. "About whether you're going to come in for the service or not. We don't bite, you know."

I smile, taking a step forward, then another.

"Good girl," she says when I reach the top of the steps. "Take any seat you like."

I nod, then sit down on a pew in the very back. Everyone is singing hymn number forty-seven, so I pick up the little book in front of me, find the right page, and sing, too. When everyone kneels, I kneel. When they pray, I pray. And when I close my eyes, I . . . hear the palm trees.

I am, at once, eight, plus or minus, in a blue gingham dress and white patent-leather buckle shoes. My hair is in braids and I'm holding my mother's hand. She is beautiful. Very thin, in a gold dress, with wavy blond hair, parted at the center and cascading down each side of her face.

"Mama, why are we going to this place?" I gaze up at an enormous building with a bell at the very top.

"It's called church," she says, smiling at me.

I peer up at the building inquisitively. "What do you do there?"

She kneels down so her eyes meet mine. "You learn about God, honey, and you pray, and sing."

I nod as if this all makes sense, but it doesn't.

"When I was little," she continues, "my mama took me to church, just like I'm taking you now. And I learned an important lesson."

"And what was that?"

"That there is no problem so big that Jesus can't solve it."

Even at the age of eight, I am acutely aware of what Mama's "problem" is.

I reach for her hand. "Can God fix Daddy, Mama?"

She doesn't answer the question, not directly. Instead she hugs me and takes a deep breath. "Ready?"

I nod, and together we scale the steps to the entrance. There is lots of singing, and so many big words I don't understand. And then everyone bows his or her head and prays. Mama closes her eyes tightly and folds her hands. I'm praying, too, that Mama is right. That no problem is too big for God to fix.

When I open my eyes, the church is empty. I am on my knees, hands folded. A teenage boy is near the altar, snuffing out candles. Startled, I reach for my bag and head for the door.

The older woman at the entrance is waiting for me.

"I prayed for you tonight," she says. "That you will find your way."

"*Merci*," I say, blinking back tears. Outside, I reach for my cellphone and find the therapist's phone number in a text from Dr. Leroy, then give him a call.

CHAPTER 16

CÉLINE

"Get up," Reinhardt barks, jerking my arm upward, forcing me to stand. "You said it's a nice day for a walk, so we'll walk."

"Where are you taking them?" I cry, turning back to the street down which the vehicle that carried Papa and Cosi sped off. "What will you do with them?"

He appears unconcerned with my anxiety. "Now don't you worry your pretty little head about that. We treat our prisoners with dignity."

"Prisoners?" I cry.

"Why yes, that's what they are."

"But they've done nothing. You must let them go. I beg of you."

"I'm afraid you're wrong about that," he says with a sinister smile. "They were *born* wrong. You were too."

"Please," I continue. "Spare them. I'll do anything."

"Anything?" he asks, amused. "I'll have to consider that."

We walk a few blocks ahead. What would our neighbors think? Could anyone help us? I notice someone looking at us from an upper window. A woman. But just as soon as our eyes meet, she pulls her curtains shut. How I long to be back in the comfort of my apartment with Cosi and Papa, just as we were this morning, just as it all used to be.

"We're almost home," he says, tightening his grasp on my arm.

I shiver as he leads me back to the rue Cler, but we're not going to my home. The apartment building in front of us is one of Paris's fanciest. Two of our clients have homes here. I'd made the deliveries myself when Nic had been ill, peeking inside only briefly when a housekeeper or maid signed for the order.

Before Reinhardt leads me inside the building's entryway he gestures to the grand structure, pointing at the top floor. "It's already the most exquisite penthouse in Paris," he brags, tightening his grip on my arm. "But I think it needs a bit more . . . *decor.* You'll help me with that." My legs move as we enter the building and proceed to the elevator, but I don't feel as if they are walking, not really. I merely float.

He pushes the button to summon the elevator and smiles. "Bet you've never lived in a building with one of these."

I don't respond, and only stare ahead as he leans in close to me, placing his large hand on the small of my back. The pace of his breath quickens as he pulls my body toward his.

I feel nothing. I am numb.

Suddenly Reinhardt's attention is diverted from me to the street, where something catches his eye. Outside a young mother carries a small child who is having a tantrum. The elevator bell chimes and the door opens. "Hold the lift," he says, eyes filled with rage. I watch as he goes and opens the door to the street and shouts at the woman, "Are you aware of the time? Shut that child up or I'll do it for you!"

It's a moment, I suppose, to run. But where to? Defeated, I hold the elevator as instructed as Reinhardt stands in the building's open doorway, continuing his interrogation of the poor woman. I glimpse a small figure slipping into the lobby through the tiny space behind Reinhardt. Between beats of my heart pounding in my chest, I notice a flash of dark hair, and then feel a cold hand on my leg beneath my skirt. I gasp, knowing in an instant it's Cosi. By some miraculous chance, my daughter has found her way to me.

"Cosi!" I whisper.

"Mama, I escaped!" she says in her quietest voice. "Papa opened the door of the truck. I jumped out and I followed you."

Adrenaline surges through me. My baby is here, but how can I protect her now? Reinhardt is fiddling with his keys by the front door.

"You have to go, honey," I say quickly.

She shakes her head. "I want to stay with you."

I don't know what's the better choice: send her out to fend for herself, with Germans on every street corner and Reinhardt looming, or find a way to smuggle her upstairs and protect her inside the apartment.

I can't bear to part with her again, so I choose the latter, pointing to the stairwell in the corner of the lobby. "Run to the top floor," I say. "Be quick, and look for me at the top of the staircase. I'll distract him and somehow find a way to get you in. Run!"

She dashes to the stairwell just as Reinhardt turns to walk back to the elevator. "Now, let's hope she's learned her lesson," he says indignantly. "If there's one thing I despise, it's a mother who can't control her offspring. Let's go." He joins me in the elevator, the doors close, and it jerks upward as his eyes burrow into my flesh. I pray that Cosi makes it there in time. Will Reinhardt see her? Can I find a place to hide her? *Run, little birdie, run.*

And when the elevator doors open, depositing us on the fourth floor, there she is, her little face peeking out of the door that leads to the stairwell. Reinhardt doesn't notice, thankfully. He's focused on his key ring and the three separate locks fixed on the outside of the door. The apartment, it seems, is a veritable jail cell. Reinhardt opens the last lock, then precedes me into the apartment; Cosi runs to me, hiding behind me as we walk in. When Reinhardt turns his gaze to the entryway table, she makes a dash down the hallway.

"What do you think?" he asks, turning to me with a proud smile, as if he'd built the place with his bare hands. "Do you like it?"

I only stare ahead.

He frowns, touching my arm lightly. "Come now, it's rude not to answer my questions."

I nod.

"Ah, you do like it." He smiles. "I knew you would. Let me give you a tour."

Before he can begin, a phone rings in another room, and he disappears to answer it.

"Cosi," I whisper down the hallway.

She runs to me, and I frantically point to the coat closet. "Wait there until I say."

"I'm afraid of the dark, Mama," she cries, Monsieur Dubois in the clutch of her little hand.

"You're not alone," I say, patting her bear on the head.

Reinhardt's voice carries through the apartment, sending chills through my body. He's speaking in German, and whatever the subject of the call, it has angered him.

I close the closet door as his heavy steps return to the entryway.

"I'm afraid I must go. Important business that must be attended to." He walks to me and traces the outline of my lips. "I'll be home tonight, and we'll get to know each other then."

I wince at his touch but do my best to remain calm.

"Your bedroom is the third door on the right. Make yourself at home. And don't get any ideas about escaping. My housekeeper, Madame Huet, resides here full-time. She's taking her nap now, but she's the type who sleeps with one eye open, if you know what I mean." He smiles. "She's aware of your presence and will be watching you. Further, there are only two exits. This door, which I keep triple bolted from the outside, as you've already seen, and . . ." He pauses and points to the expansive balcony beyond the living room. The building seems so much taller than ours, somehow. Being on the fourth floor feels as if we are up in the clouds. "Well," he continues, "you wouldn't want to do that to yourself, now, would you?"

He shuts the door behind him, carefully latching the outside locks, each making a terrifying click. When I no longer hear his footsteps, I run to the closet and reach for Cosi's hand. "Come," I whisper. "I'll take you to the bedroom. We have to hurry. Someone else lives here, too. A housekeeper."

We rush down the hallway together. The apartment is much larger than ours. I feel disoriented as I peer at the doors that line the walls. Did he say the second room on the right or the third? Or was it the left? I can't remember, but I decide it must be the third. Yes, the third.

I open the door and its old hinges let out a creak that sounds like a high-pitched scream. The room is small and plain, with only a double bed, a small desk, and a shabby-looking tweed chair by the window. I pull the drapes open and light streams in. The walls look as if they haven't seen the sun in a very long time and are starved for it.

"Is this where we'll stay?" Cosi asks softly, touching her hand to the blue wallpaper, which is peeling at the edge.

"I think so," I say, kneeling down to face my little girl. "But until we find a way out of here, we must hide you. No one can know you're here. Do you understand?"

"Yes, Mama," she says in her sweet voice.

I open the closet, then shake my head. This would be the obvious place to hide her, but it isn't safe. What if the housekeeper came in and found her? No. I point to the bed and tell Cosi to sneak under it, until I can find another place.

"Don't worry, Mama," she whispers a moment later from under the bed. "I'm good at hiding."

"I know you are, sweet child," I say, my voice cracking. I lie down on the bed above her. I am weary, but I must be strong for her. And I will be. We will make our way through this. Together.

Moments later, I hear footsteps approaching in the hallway outside the door. "Shhh," I whisper to Cosi, leaping to my feet. "I think someone's coming."

A moment later, a stern-looking woman opens the door. She is quite tall, several inches taller than my five-foot, three-inch frame. At least sixty, maybe older, she wears a crisp blue dress and a white apron. Her hair is pulled back into a severe bun beneath her white hat. Frown lines punctuate her face, and her mouth forms a deeper scowl when her eyes meet mine. The housekeeper Reinhardt had told me about, obviously.

"I'm Madame Huet," she says, looking me over the way one might examine a roast at the butcher shop, before rejecting it for a better cut of meat. "You're different than the last one. She didn't hold my attention long." The housekeeper stares at me for another long moment before turning on her heels. "Dinner is at five. Don't be late."

After the door is closed and the sound of her footsteps fades down the hallway, I whisper to Cosi, "You can come out now, honey." She cautiously pokes her head out from beneath the bed.

"I can't decide, Mama," Cosi says to me, obviously deep in thought about something.

"About what, love?"

"That woman," she says. "I can't tell if she's mean or just . . . sad."

I love how my little girl's natural inclination

is to consider the good in others, even this cross housekeeper with a heart of veritable stone.

She bounces Monsieur Dubois on her lap. "Papa says that some people seem mean, but they're just sad inside."

Tears sting my eyes, but I blink them back. I think about my poor father, slumped over in the back of that German truck. The thought of it is more than I can bear.

"Yes," I say, collecting myself. "Papa is right about that, dear one. But I don't know about this Madame Huet. She may be sad, or she may just be . . . mean, through and through. Just the same, we need to be cautious."

Cosi nods. "Will the *bad man* come back?"

"Yes, and perhaps soon."

She shakes her head. "There isn't any good in him. Not one drop."

"I'm afraid you're right about that, love. So we must not let him find you."

"Mama," she whispers. "I have to go to the bathroom."

A sense of panic comes over me. *How will this ever work? How will I keep Cosi safe and undetected in this tiny room?*

I open the door as slowly as I can, to minimize the sound of the creaking hinges, then tiptoe to the hallway. I'm relieved to find the bathroom just across, and I rush Cosi inside, locking the door behind us.

"Hurry," I tell her.

She nods, doing her best to finish quickly, before flushing the toilet. I notice a ceramic pitcher beside the sink and reach for it, filling it with water before we sneak back to the bedroom. Inside, I set the pitcher on the floor on the window side of the bed. "It will be good to keep water here, just in case I leave the room and am . . . gone for a little while."

Cosi nods.

"And after you drink the water, you could use the pitcher to . . ."

She giggles. "Mama! That is *not* ladylike!"

I smile. "Well, in case of an emergency, is all I'm saying."

She runs to the window. "Look! From up here you can see everything, Mama! You can see the market and, look, you can see my school, too! I wonder if it's time for arithmetic or spelling? I feel like a bird, Mama!" She flaps her arms playfully. "I could actually . . . fly away."

I am so lost in thought that I hadn't considered that Cosi could be seen from the window. "No, honey," I say. "Come away from the window at once. What if someone sees you?"

She steps away from the window and nods gravely. "They could tell *the bad man.*"

"Yes," I say. "And we can't take that chance."

She sits on the bed beside me and leans her head against my chest. "I'm worried about Papa."

"I know," I say. "I am too. But you know what?"

"What?"

"He wouldn't want us to worry about him," I say. "He would want us to be smart and to find a way out of here."

She nods. "Like secret spies."

"Yes, like secret spies. He'd want us to put all of our energy into that."

She nods again.

"And do you know what my mother would do, your grandmother, if she were here?"

"What?" she asks, looking up at me with her big, green, curious eyes.

"She was always so good at finding the positive side of a bad situation. You're a lot like her, you know?"

"I am?"

"Yes, very much. I wish you could have known her. She was . . . sunshine, even on the rainiest day. She made everything wonderful."

"Like you do," she says, squeezing my arm.

I smile. "Mama could make the most painful tasks fun. Like doing laundry, or washing the dishes, or peeling potatoes, which I always hated. She made games out of everything, and it was magic." It feels good to reminisce, to return to a time when life was uncontaminated by fear, to remember the way Mama's face lit up when I ran into the room. "That's what we're going to do here. We're going to make this an adventure. And you know how we're going to do it?"

"How?"

"We're going to pretend."

Her face brightens. "I will be a princess, and this is my tower. You are the queen."

"Yes," I say.

"And our knights are out fighting a war against barbarians, but we are safe here in our castle," she whispers. "The king will return soon, my father and your husband, and he will bring me a hundred new dresses and . . . a puppy!"

I smile. "And in the meantime, we will wait patiently and braid our hair and eat cake." I hand her an imaginary plate, and she reaches for it, taking an imaginary bite.

"Mmmmm," she says.

I know she's hungry. I am, too. But we have our cake, and our pretend little world, and for now, that is the very best I can wish for.

All day, I expect Reinhardt to return at any moment. I pace the floors anxiously, fretting about what will happen when he does. I prepare for the worst. He'll unlock the front door and shout my name. I can't let him come into the room. He might see Cosi, or worse, Cosi would have to listen to what he will do to me. It would traumatize her beyond words. I can't let that happen. I'll tell Cosi to stay under the bed, keep the dust ruffle pulled down while I go to the main room and face him there.

But he doesn't return, and by the time the little clock on the desk reads five o'clock, I remember Madame Huet's warning not to be late for dinner.

"I won't be gone long," I whisper to Cosi as she crawls under the bed.

"Okay, Mama," she says. She found a pen in the desk drawer earlier, and it might as well have been a rare gemstone. She loves her little journal so, and I delight in seeing her record her sweet drawings and stories inside its pages, especially now, when her imagination is all she has.

I lift the dust ruffle to peek at her before I go. "I'll be back before you know it."

"Yes, Mama," she says. "I know. You are going to a very important ball. There will be music and dancing and delicious things to eat. Everyone's waiting for you and they will bow and curtsy when you arrive down the grand staircase. Hurry—you mustn't keep them waiting."

My eyes well up with tears. Yes. This is how Cosi and I will survive. Just like this. "Yes, my sweet princess."

I go out the door and find Madame Huet standing in the hallway, so near the bedroom, it's almost as if she materialized there. "You're late," Madame Huet says, hands firmly placed on her hips.

"I, I . . . I'm sorry," I stammer, startled to see

her. *How long has she been waiting there? Did she hear Cosi and me talking?*

"Don't let it happen again," she says, walking ahead. I follow her to the dining room on the other side of the apartment, with walls made of dark mahogany panels and a large table with at least a dozen chairs. I imagine many high-ranking Germans have dined here.

"Sit," the housekeeper says, pointing to a chair at the end of the table.

I take my seat as she disappears through a door, then returns a moment later with a tray, which she places in front of me. I haven't eaten all day, and at this point, anything edible would do, but this is much better than edible. I inhale the savory aroma on my plate—roasted potatoes, carrots, and a fine cut of steak that is breaded in a way I have never seen. It looks divine.

"Thank you," I say, reaching for my fork and taking a bite.

She watches me from the doorway to the kitchen.

"It's . . . very good," I say.

The housekeeper frowns. "Flattery will get you nowhere with me."

I have to find a way to smuggle food back to the room for Cosi. Could I wrap some of the steak in a napkin? Too messy. Instead, I eye the basket of dinner rolls as Madame Huet steps back to the kitchen for a moment, then tuck two into the bodice of my dress. Instead of swallowing the last bite of steak, I hold it in my mouth, then stand, eager to return to the bedroom.

"Finished, I see?" the housekeeper says. I can't tell if she's pleased or irritated by my clean plate.

I nod, walking back to the bedroom and closing the door behind me. I pull the bit of meat from my mouth and exhale deeply.

"Cosi," I whisper.

Her little head peers out from under the bed.

"Look what I brought back from the ball," I say, handing her the bit of meat and roll. "I'm sorry it isn't much. The . . . count and countess of Luxembourg have enormous appetites, you know."

She smiles, wolfing down the scraps I've brought her without a single complaint, then drinking a little water from the pitcher on the floor. I wish I could give her more. I'll try harder tomorrow, maybe sneak into the kitchen while Madame Huet naps. I'll find a way.

Hours pass, and Cosi dozes off in the bed beside me. I let her sleep like that for as long as possible, with a cautious ear peeled, before moving her beneath the bed. I hate the thought of her spending the night on the cold, hard floor, but it's the only way. At any moment, Reinhardt could return.

And, just as the arm on the clock points to eleven o'clock, I hear the front door open, and heavy footsteps on the floor.

CHAPTER 17

CAROLINE

"Good morning!" Margot says the next day, greeting me with her little boy attached to her hip. He's no more than two, with the sweetest cheeks and wispy brown hair.

I smile. They'd both been asleep when I came home last night. "I'm so happy you're here. Did you find everything you need?"

She nods. "This apartment is amazing."

I look around. "It is, isn't it? Though a little ridiculous for one person to have such an enormous space, I suppose." I grin. "It'll be nice to share it with you."

I can smell something delicious coming from the kitchen.

"I'm making breakfast," Margot says. "Not anything like Jeanty, I assure you, but . . . if you're hungry."

"That sounds wonderful," I say. "Thank you."

We have breakfast on the balcony, a delicious egg and vegetable hash, then move to the living room and sip our coffee while Élian plays with a stack of plastic measuring cups I brought out from the kitchen. He giggles and claps his hands as he stacks them this way and that, then bangs them together.

"Élian is such a great name. I don't think I've heard it before. How did you come to name him that?" I ask, taking a sip of my coffee.

"I saw it on a World War Two monument when I was a girl," she explains. "It was one of thousands of names of victims of Nazi hate crimes in Paris during the occupation. For some reason, the name just jumped right out at me. I was instantly smitten."

"Fate," I say.

She nods. "I decided then and there that if I had a son, that's what I'd name him." She looks down at her mug. "Jacques never liked the name. He said it . . ." She pauses for a moment, her face suddenly awash with worry. "Never mind."

I reach for her hand. "You're here now. You're safe."

She nods.

"Anyway, I wanted to honor the past, but also give the name new meaning, new life." She watches her little boy playing happily on the floor. "I'm not sure I've done that." The bruise under her left eye is healing but still visible.

"What do you mean? Of course you've done that!"

Her eyes well up with tears. "I wanted so much for him." She shakes her head. "Instead, he got an alcoholic father and a broken mother."

"You are not broken," I tell her. "You are a wonderful mother, and though you may not know it, you have such strength. One day Élian will understand that you fought for him." I smile. "It will only get better from here."

"Do you think so?"

"I know so."

She smiles. "I feel terrible admitting it, but I wasn't so sure about you for a long time."

"It's okay," I say.

"I remember when you started coming into the restaurant, about three years ago. You seemed . . . so sad. I tried to talk to you several times, tried to cheer you up. But you were . . . I don't know . . . it was almost as if you were *unreachable.* Like a stray cat in need of medical attention, but if anyone got too close, you'd scratch them. And then Vic bought Jeanty, and he was so enamored with you, and you barely gave him the time of day."

I sigh. "I'm sorry. I don't know why I acted the way I did. My past remains a black hole, I'm afraid."

"Then, after your accident, you came in again, and I expected more of the same, but you had . . . well, you'd changed. It took me a while to see that. I had no idea you could be . . ."

"Normal?" I say with a smile.

"No, I mean that I didn't know you had such warmth, such kindness under all those layers."

I kneel beside Élian and tap two of the measuring cups together, and he giggles.

"Sometimes it takes the worst to bring out the best in us, I guess."

"You bring out the best in Victor, you know," Margot adds.

"Do you think?" My mind wanders back to Provence, the strange phone calls. Emma. The flowers I never received. I haven't heard from him since we returned. Not even a text.

"Yes," she says. "But I . . ." She pauses for a moment, then begins again, "I just wonder if . . ." Her voice trails off.

"Wonder what?"

Élian waddles toward the balcony, and Margot stands up quickly to scoop him up. "Time for your nap, my little friend," she says, planting a kiss on his cheek. "I may take a snooze with him," she continues. "I didn't sleep much last night, and this mama is exhausted."

"After all you've been through, you need the rest."

She disappears down the hall to the far bedroom, and I think about the box of letters I found in the closet, just as the doorbell rings. I run to answer it, my heart fluttering, thinking that it might be Victor. Instead, I open the door to find Estelle.

"Hi," she says. "Is this still a good time?"

"Oh yes, yes," I say. The appointment I'd made had entirely escaped my mind. "I'm sorry. Please come in."

She sits down on the sofa and sets the letters I gave her on the coffee table. "These letters were"—she pauses, shaking her head as if astonished—"an unbelievable find."

"I'm pleased to hear that," I say.

"While Céline was smart not to give away too much detail in her writing, her letters do link her, as I suspected, to this apartment. They also impart a sense of desperation. She was in trouble, that was obvious. The question is, did her beloved, Luc, ever come to her rescue?"

I sigh. "What more have you discovered?"

Estelle nods. "I had some luck reading the pages of Esther's memoir under the ultraviolet light I told you about. Some passages were too badly damaged to make out, I'm afraid, but the puzzle is coming together. Céline—a widowed mother of a young daughter—and her father owned a flower shop, right here on the rue Cler. After her father was roughed up by a German soldier, they went to Esther for medical help. The rest is a bit fuzzy, but from what I can piece together, the family suddenly went missing. Esther writes that she had hoped they had escaped, but from what I can make out, that was not the case."

I shake my head. "Then what happened?"

"Well," she continues, "my theory is that Céline was detained by a Nazi soldier, right here, and possibly with her little girl."

I cover my mouth.

"I'm still combing through the databases to see if I can trace her father to any of the work camps, but so far I haven't come up with any matches. As hard as historians have worked to identify all victims of the Holocaust, they estimate that thousands remain unnamed, their stories untold."

"I know this happened so long ago," I say, rubbing my forehead. "But there has to be someone in the neighborhood who was young enough at the time to remember . . . something."

Estelle shrugs. "If you know of anyone, I'd love to talk to them."

"Wait," I say, recalling Monsieur Ballard. "Hey, would you like to join me for a late lunch at Bistro Jeanty tomorrow? There's a regular there who might prove himself useful to you. We could see if he's there. He's a treasure trove of knowledge. Maybe he'll have a nugget for your project?"

Estelle's eyes are big. "I'd love that!" She glances down the hallway toward the bedrooms. "I wonder if you'd mind if I had a look around."

"Of course not," I say. "But I have some guests staying with me, and I'm afraid they're asleep at the moment."

"No problem," she says. "I'll come back another time."

"Anytime," I say, standing up. "I'm sorry. I need to leave soon for an appointment, but I'll see you tomorrow at Jeanty."

"Yes," Estelle says, tucking the items on the table into her bag again. "Thank you, Caroline. You've been so very helpful."

As I collect my coat and purse, I think about the possibility of Céline being held hostage in this very apartment by a monster, maybe even with her little girl, and I shudder. No wonder Monsieur de Goff despises these walls. No amount of new paint could cover the dark stain of evil. But then a burst of sunlight filters in from the windows, casting a playful shadow on the door, and I remember there is power in the light. I pray that Céline found it.

I take an elevator up to Dr. Louis Marchand's third-floor office, where a receptionist offers me a cup of tea and tells me my therapist will see me soon. Dr. Leroy had made the recommendation, but I'd been skeptical. How could a stranger, even with a PhD, access the boarded-up passageways of my mind?

"He's the best in Paris," she'd promised. "It's at least worth a try."

And so, here I am, trying.

I'm escorted into a room down the hall, where I take a seat on a burgundy velvet sofa. On a table beside me is a box of Kleenex and a book about Tuscany. The cypress trees on the cover remind me of something, but, of course, I don't know what.

"Hello," a man says, walking in the room. "You must be Caroline."

"Yes," I say, with a nervous smile.

"I'm Dr. Marchand, but please, call me Louis."

I nod. "Louis." He's at least sixty, maybe older. His smile is warm, his eyes kind. I imagine the thousands of people who have shed tears on this sofa.

"Tell me about yourself," he says, crossing his legs and reaching for a notebook and pen on the table beside him.

"Well," I say. "That might not be that easy."

"Ah, yes," he says. "Dr. Leroy sent your file over."

I shrug. "I don't even know where to begin."

He nods. "Let's start with now."

"Okay," I say hesitantly, looking around the room, pausing a long moment before I shrug and take a deep breath. "My name is Caroline, and I live at eighteen rue Cler. The rest?" I sigh. "I have no idea."

"Ah," he says, smiling at me as if I've amused him a great deal. "I hate to act like a smart-ass, Caroline, but you do."

"I do?" I shake my head. "I do *what?*"

"Know the rest . . . about yourself."

I sit up higher on the sofa, clutching the pillow beside me. "Monsieur, I mean, Dr. Marchand, I mean, Louis, perhaps you don't understand. I was in an accident. I lost my memory."

He nods. "Yes, I'm aware. And you were very lucky."

"If you call *lucky* losing your memory." I proceed to tell him about my present state, Victor, the apartment, Margot—bits and pieces of a life I am stitching together, like squares of a patchwork quilt.

"I know you must be frustrated," he continues. "But if you take anything away from this session, I want it to be this: you may have lost your memory, but you haven't lost yourself."

I blink hard, letting his words marinate.

"You're still you," he says. "Even without the encyclopedia of your past. You're still authentically you." He uncrosses his legs and leans in closer. "And, frankly, to know yourself in the raw state that you are in, without any baggage from the past, well, that in and of itself is quite a gift. A strange one, but a good one."

We talk for another half hour, and he gives me a series of breathing and cognitive exercises that are supposed to help unblock my mind. "Remember," he says, as I stand to leave, "you may feel as if you've lost everything, but that's not the case." He points to his head. "It's all in there."

In the kitchen, Margot asks, "How was your day?" and hands Élian a sippy cup, which he offers to his stuffed bunny.

"Good," I say. "The appointment with the therapist was . . . interesting."

"Any progress on your memory?"

I shake my head. "Not really, but I think I had a few revelations."

"That's promising," she says, before grinning. "Victor's called a few times."

My eyes widen. "Oh?"

"He wants to know if you're coming to the restaurant tonight." Her eyes are bright. "He really wants to see you."

"I don't know," I say. "Maybe I should just . . . stay home."

Margot shakes her head. "Caroline, there's a time and a season for staying home. I get it. In fact, before Élian, when I was single, there's nothing I used to love more than a quiet night at home. I didn't have to cook for anyone, even myself. I'd just have a cigarette and an apple, and it was heaven."

I smile. "A cigarette and an apple. I love that." I pause, considering my own perfect solo night in. "I'd have peppermint bark and a glass of red wine."

She laughs, nodding. "I totally get it. But tonight," she shakes her head, "this is a . . . *moment*. And it could be a crucial one in the story of the two of you." She squeezes my hands. "Trust me. You have to go."

"You really think so?" I ask wistfully.

"I do."

• • •

Margot coaxes me into putting on a sweater and a skirt before heading out. I'm so lost in thought that I hardly care about the wind and what it might be doing to my hair, or that my heels have gotten caught in the cobblestones more than once. And when I see Jeanty in the distance, my heart beats faster. I wish I had Margot's confidence. I, instead, have been feeling vulnerable since we returned from Provence. *What if I made a poor choice in trusting Victor? What if his interests in me are purely . . . physical and nothing more?* The last thing I need is heartbreak.

"Hi," he says as our eyes meet inside the restaurant.

I smile as he takes my coat, then leads me to a dim back corner of the restaurant, an area separated from the rest of the room by an emerald velvet curtain and usually reserved for private parties. We slip into a table lit by a drippy candelabra.

"I wanted to create something . . . special for you tonight," he says.

"It's beautiful," I say, tugging on the gold ring on my right finger. I'd found it in my bathroom drawer and slipped it on this morning.

Victor opens a bottle of Italian wine and pours us each a glass. "To new memories," he says, extending his to mine for a clink.

"And old," I say, before taking a sip.

As the courses come out—one beautiful platter after the next—we talk effortlessly, but I don't share my fears, nor do I dare tell him how vulnerable I feel or ask for the reassurance I so desperately need. Instead, I sip my wine and eat my food and try to enjoy the evening. Perhaps I've been too cautious. After all, Victor has been nothing but lovely, and here I am getting ridiculously caught up in that woman's phone call when we were in the south, and something silly Inès said about flowers. As Victor produces and uncorks another bottle of wine, I decide to let it all drift away.

"Let me get us some fresh glasses," he says, standing up. "I'll just be a minute."

I smile as he slips behind the curtain. I take the final sip of wine in my glass. A perfect, light nebbiolo with a tart cherry finish. I wonder if I even like nebbiolo, or at least, if I did before. Or are all of my tastes and preferences newly forged? I eye the mushroom and Gruyère tart on the table and wonder if my former self loved mushrooms as much as I do now, or if these affinities will vanish when my memories return.

Victor had left his cellphone on the table, and it suddenly lights up and begins buzzing. I can't help but notice the name on the screen: Emma. My cheeks burn.

He returns a moment later with two fresh

wineglasses in hand, then pours the new bottle of wine. As he begins talking, I stare straight ahead.

"What's wrong?" he says, noticing the shift in my mood.

"Nothing," I say, avoiding his gaze.

"Caroline, please," he says, "what's bothering you?"

I take a deep breath, wishing I could prevent what I know is to come: an eruption, I fear, of volcanic scale.

"Who is . . . *Emma?*" I say. "She called in Provence, and"—I pause, pointing at his phone on the table—"she called just now."

His eyes blink rapidly. I can tell, whoever she is, it's somehow awkward, and he isn't prepared to talk about it.

"Is she your ex? The one you said you once loved? Is that who you bought the flowers for?"

Victor shakes his head. But instead of being calm and patient, he seems agitated, even a little annoyed. "I invited you here because I wanted to have a special night with you. Why would you think I would have any other intentions?"

"Then who is that woman and why does she keep calling you?" I hate how my voice sounds. Insecure. Like a scared schoolgirl. But there's no masking how I feel.

He clears his throat. "She's . . . no one." He pauses. "Wait, why are you acting this way? Listen, Caroline"—he sets his napkin on the table and looks deep into my eyes—"I don't know what I must say for you to trust me."

I look around the dimly lit space. There are no flowers in sight. Perhaps he's already given them to Emma, or some other pretty woman he was with the night before. I sigh, rising to my feet.

"I would never hurt you," Victor says, lifting his hand to my cheek.

"That may be true," I say, wiping away a tear. "But I'm too fragile right now to know if I can believe you or not." I swallow hard, taking a long look at him. "I'm sorry. I should go."

"Please," Victor says. "Caroline, don't leave."

He reaches for my hand, but I don't let him take it. I slip outside the curtain, weave through the restaurant, and find my coat before heading outside. I'm equal parts embarrassed and upset. But mostly I'm just lost, so sorely lost.

When I wake the next morning, Margot and Élian have already left. The details of last night hit me like a hammer to the head as I fumble to make myself a cup of coffee in the kitchen. With each sip, I remember more of what I'd said to Victor, how I'd left with a heavy heart. I swallow hard, wishing the night had ended in a different way. But for what? To be deceived? To be fooled into believing that I was in a relationship with someone who really cared about me, as opposed to someone who merely felt sorry for me?

I shower and turn to my sketchbook; I'm staring at an image of a palm tree I've created when the phone rings.

"Does one o'clock still work?" It's Estelle, and I've completely forgotten my promise to meet her for lunch.

"About that," I begin. "I'm—"

"I'm sorry," she says. "I'm on the train, and it's so loud. I can barely hear you. I just wanted to say that I'll be a few minutes late, okay?"

"Okay," I say with a sigh.

Estelle waits for me outside of Jeanty, looking chic in a pair of dark skinny jeans and a tan sweater. She smiles when she sees me, then kisses my cheeks. "I must have passed this bistro a thousand times; I can't believe I've never had a meal here."

The warm air hits my face as she follows me inside. "You'll love it," I tell her, as I look around cautiously. "*Bonjour*," I say to Lorraine, one of the waitresses who's helping out at the hostess desk until Margot returns. I glance back at the kitchen timidly. "Is Victor in?"

"Oh, he just stepped out," she says. "But he shouldn't be too long. Just a quick trip to the market. We're out of potatoes."

"Potatoes," I say with a smile as I wave to Monsieur Ballard, then motion to Estelle to follow me to his table. "That's the man I want you to meet."

"Bonjour, Monsieur Ballard," I say, smiling. "I'd like to introduce you to a friend of mine. This is Estelle Olivier." I explain her project as he leans in with interest.

"Please, sit, both of you," he says, pushing his newspaper aside. He motions to one of the waiters to bring out two more espressos. "How are you feeling?"

"Fine," I say.

He takes a long look at me. "I don't think you're being entirely forthcoming."

I sigh, glancing at Estelle, then back at Monsieur Ballard. "How do you know?"

"I've learned a great deal about reading faces in my time, and your face tells me that you're . . . conflicted."

"I suppose I am."

"Well," he continues, "if I could give you any bit of advice worth its salt, I'd tell you what I wish someone would have told me when I was your age."

"And what would that be?"

"Stop worrying all the time."

I smile. "Easier said than done."

He sighs and throws up his hands. "Dear, I can't tell you what to do, but I can tell you what I wish I would have done."

"Then let's hear it," I say, exchanging a glance with Estelle, who appears equal parts amused and curious.

He nods. "I would have turned down that damn accounting job and gone to Italy, to Portofino, just like I wanted to. I would have kissed the girl I should have kissed when I had the chance." He pauses, and his eyes drift off. He clears his throat. "I would have spent more weekends with my children when they were young. I would have spit in that German officer's face when he insulted my mother on the street, even if he gave me a bloody nose. And I would have . . ." His voice trails off, and so do his eyes, to the little cabinet in the far wall, and perhaps to a memory long ago.

"What?" I ask. "What were you going to say?"

He clears his throat. "It doesn't matter now. The point is, seize the moment. *Your* moment."

"I wish it were that easy," I say.

"My dear," he replies, "it is. I assure you, it is. Life is what you make it. You know what you want." He turns to the door as Victor walks in. "Now go get it."

As Monsieur Ballard begins chatting with Estelle, Victor walks into the restaurant carrying a basket brimming with potatoes. I notice a stalk of Brussels sprouts poking out of the side.

"There you are," Victor says when our eyes meet. He sets down his load and walks over to me, kissing my cheek as if nothing has happened.

"I'm . . . sorry," I say. "About last night. I shouldn't have been so emotional."

"I'm sorry, too," he says. "I . . . shouldn't have been so intense."

I nod, searching his eyes.

"You know," he continues, "you don't have to be afraid with me."

"I know," I say, smiling. "At least, I think so."

He reaches for my hands. "I'm not going to hurt you. I promise."

I smile.

"And your memory today?"

"Same."

He exhales, squeezing my hand. "I miss you."

"I miss you, too," I say, cracking a smile, wondering if I've been too cautious.

He leans in closer. "When can I see you?"

I think of the flowers again, along with my other lingering doubts, and decide I *am* being too cautious.

"How about right now?" I say.

He grins. "Yes, right now."

"What do you want to do?"

"First I want to kiss you," he says.

I grin.

"And then I want to take you to this new restaurant that opened across town."

"Okay," I say, unable to stop smiling.

"I'll just go let the staff know I'll be out until dinner service."

I say goodbye to Monsieur Ballard and Estelle, who are engaged in deep conversation.

"I'll call you in a few days," Estelle says.

I grin as Victor takes my hand. "Anytime."

"The restaurant is a bit of a walk," he says, eying a map on his phone. "Maybe we should take a taxi?"

"I really don't mind walking," I say. "And it's such a nice day. But if you're in a hurry . . ."

"No, we'll walk," he says, taking my hand and glancing at me a moment later. "What's on your mind?"

"What do you mean?" I ask.

"You're mulling something over," he says. "I can tell."

"Oh, nothing, really," I say. "My art show is this Friday. I guess I've been thinking about that."

"I'd love to come," he says, simultaneously waving to a man across the street. He doesn't stop to make an introduction.

"I know it's a terrible time to break away from the restaurant. You don't have to come."

"I'll be there," he says. "I promise."

"Well, no pressure."

"Now, now," he says, stopping. "Do you think I'd miss my girlfriend's big show?"

I smile, loving the way he's called me his girlfriend.

Twenty minutes later, we arrive at a restaurant called Chez Sol. I peer inside the window. It's lively inside, with colorful décor, and tables packed with people lingering over late lunches and cocktails.

"It looks busy; do you think we can get a table?"

He winks. "I may have a few special connections."

Inside, a man about Victor's age greets him with a hug. There's a line of people waiting to be seated, but he rushes us to a table by the window.

"I take it you're friends with the owners?"

He nods. "They have a restaurant in Mexico, which is where I met them. I helped them find this building, get everything connected."

I survey the menu. "It looks amazing."

"Wait until you try the fish tacos with pineapple salsa."

When the waiter arrives, Victor chats with him for a moment and orders us an assortment of tacos and two mescal margaritas.

"Mescal?"

Before I can place it, Victor fills in the blanks. "It's a smoky tequila," he explains. "Trust me, you're going to love it."

And I do. But I love this moment with him more. I'm glad I didn't close myself off. Yes, I may still have lingering concerns, but I'll sort them all out somehow. Monsieur Ballard is right. It's time to live my life with intention, not fear. I order a second margarita, then look up at

Victor. "I've really loved painting, and I've been thinking about turning one of my spare bedrooms into an art studio."

He smiles.

"I don't know if I'll ever do anything with my paintings, but maybe, someday, I could sell a few."

"I think that's an excellent idea." He holds up his glass. "Cheers to that."

"Thanks for today," I say in front of the restaurant.

He kisses my forehead. "When will I see you again?"

"I don't know," I say, looking out at the street.

"Wait. If you're not sick of me yet," he says, and smiles, "why don't you come to the restaurant tonight, around eight? Julien will be taking over the evening service then. I'll hang up my apron and we can have dinner. Just us. I'll have Lorraine reserve the table in the back."

"All right," I say.

"I'll make it worth your while," he says with a wink. "You'll see."

I smile as he heads back to the kitchen, watching him as he disappears behind the double doors.

I decide to clear my head with a long walk to the chic department store Galeries Lafayette to look for a dress for the art show. Inès described the event as "fancy," and I'm certain there's nothing in my closet that even remotely qualifies. Estelle calls on my walk.

"You were right," she says. "Monsieur Ballard is a trove of information. He is absolutely fascinating."

"Good," I say. "I thought you'd like him. But did he give you anything of use for your project?"

"Yes," she says. "Did you know that Céline was engaged to be married to a man who worked for the Resistance?"

"Really?"

"His name was Luc Jeanty."

My eyes widen. "Jeanty as in Bistro Jeanty?"

"Yes," she says. There's commotion in the background. "I have so much to tell you, but I'm just stepping into class."

"No problem," I say. "Call me another time."

"Okay, I will. Oh, and Caroline, your boyfriend, the chef, is really cute."

My cheeks warm as I smile to myself. "He is, isn't he?"

The Galeries Lafayette is exquisite. With its domed ceiling and countless floors that all open onto an expanse at its center, it's like nothing I've ever seen.

I think about Céline's fiancé and his work with the Resistance as I wander the first floor

291

through a maze of tables splayed with cosmetics and perfumes. Luc Jeanty. I wonder if he could have ever imagined that the Paris he'd fought for would be as beautiful as it is today. I wonder if he'd be pleased. But really, I wonder if he'd been reunited with the people he loved: Céline and her daughter.

Beside me, a very chic-looking woman in a fur vest selects a perfume bottle, maroon and clad in rhinestones, then spritzes her left wrist. I follow suit, then frown, gasping as an intense aroma stings my eyes. Musky and strong—not me at all.

I turn back to the escalators and head up to the first of many upper floors, stopping when I see a black dress on a mannequin in the distance. Short and fitted, with lace detailing around the bodice and a little ruffle at the hem. Simple, but elegant.

"May I try on that dress?" I ask a passing saleswoman, pointing to the mannequin.

"Your size, dear?"

I look down at my body, then up at her again. "I really don't know."

She smiles. "I'll bring you a few to choose from."

In the fitting room, I slip the first dress on over my head and cinch it at my hips, smoothing out the fabric. It's snug, but not overly so. I smile at my reflection. Of all the bodies to wake up from a coma in, I suppose mine isn't so bad. For the show, I'll pull my hair into a tight bun, highlight my cheeks with a little blush. Red lipstick, definitely. And in this dress, I would look just right. Would Victor think so?

"I'll take this one," I say to the saleswoman outside.

I follow her to the counter. Behind her is a high-fashion display with two mannequins in fur and studded leather pants—not my style—with a TV screen playing a black-and-white American film from the sixties, perhaps early seventies. I freeze, unable to take my eyes off the TV screen. I . . . know this movie somehow. But this is not a passive memory, as Dr. Leroy described; this one is deeply seated. I can't explain it, but it is integral to who I am.

The saleswoman's lips are moving, but I don't hear her voice. In fact, I don't hear anything. I am too transfixed by the screen. Suddenly, the world around me comes to a screeching halt as the pieces of my life begin to come together. I feel them shifting in my brain, like the corners of a difficult jigsaw puzzle that give the entire image clarity. I blink back tears, looking up when I hear the saleswoman's voice again.

"Mademoiselle?" she says. "Your card, please."

"I, I'm . . . so sorry," I stammer, reaching into my purse. I hand her my credit card, then look up at the screen again, where a glamorous blond woman cozies up to a handsome actor on a midcentury-modern sofa. They are drinking martinis. I know what will happen next. He'll put a record on. Friends come to dinner. She finds out he's having an affair with one of her friends. She shatters the soufflé in the kitchen. I know it! I know every detail! But unlike the collection of knowledge in my mind—song lyrics, random facts, how I can apparently list the U.S. states in alphabetical order—this is different. I know without a shadow of a doubt that this memory is deeply and inextricably connected to *me*.

"Mademoiselle?" It's the saleswoman's voice again, pulling me from the depths of my memory bank, which feels, somehow, like a locked vault I have only now been handed a key to.

"Your receipt." She turns to the sales floor again, where a woman and her teenage daughter are trying to get her attention.

"Wait, Madame," I say.

She turns around and I point to the TV screen. "That movie, that actor. The man. Do you happen to know who he is? I keep trying to place him, but . . ." I shake my head. "I can't."

She turns to the TV screen, scrunching her nose quizzically.

"Isn't that the American actor . . . Wes Williams?" She watches for a moment longer, then nods. "Yes, definitely him."

I stare at the man on the screen, watching as he lights a cigarette, flashing a smile that oozes charm.

She looks at me like I may as well be from Mars. "I thought every American knew Wes Williams."

As she walks to the other customers, I stare at the screen a moment longer. The thing is, I *do* know him. I know him in the very cells of my body. Wes Williams is my . . . father.

I close my eyes, again hearing the sound of the breeze rustling through palm trees, the wind chimes making their haunting clanging sound. This time, I am young, not more than seven. I am running around the lawn in the backyard of a home in California. San Diego. It's the same home as in my prior visions, but years earlier.

Beside the pool, a beautiful woman reads a magazine in a chaise longue. I run to her and wedge myself into the small space to her left.

"Mommy," I say, fingering the gold bracelet on her wrist. "When is Daddy coming home?"

She takes off her large sunglasses; I can see that she's been crying. "I don't know, dear one," she tells me. "But soon, I hope."

Time skips forward. And suddenly I am ten, maybe eleven, in corduroy pants and a turtleneck. I'm licking a Popsicle on the lawn outside. I hear shouting in the kitchen. A man's voice. A woman crying. A glass breaks.

"Wes, stop! Please stop!"

I run inside and watch my mother on her knees,

begging my father not to leave. "I'm sick," she says. "You can't leave me. I . . . won't know what to do. Think of Caroline. Wes, don't do this to us!"

At once, they both notice me.

"Darling," my mother says, standing up, collecting herself as best she can. "Your father and I were just having a . . . disagreement."

"That's right, kitten," my father says, walking toward me. He's older than my mother, by at least fifteen years. He pats my shoulder, then lights a cigarette. "Why don't you go run along and play."

"Mama," I say, rushing to her. "Are you really . . . sick?"

"Oh, I'm fine, honey," she says. "Nothing that the doctor can't give me medicine for."

I look at my father, then at my mother, and I know that while my life hasn't exactly been normal, it will now never be the same.

I burst into tears. The breakup shatters my world; so does my mother's cancer. A miserable slideshow of images—IV tubes, endless pill bottles, hospital beds—flash through my mind. And then I'm a teenager, standing beside my father at my mother's funeral. There's a large mound of dirt to the right, and two men are lowering her coffin into the ground. I'm holding a red rose in my hand, and I toss it on top of the coffin as it makes its descent.

My father and I stand there a long while before I turn to him and ask, "Do you think she'll be happy in heaven?"

"Sure, kid," he says, lighting a cigarette. "Hey, I've been meaning to tell you that I have to be away for a few weeks. Filming a new project in Utah." I nod. "There's someone who'll be coming to look after you. Her name is Julia."

Julia. The name reverberates in my ears. "Julia is great," he says. I notice the sparkle in his eyes. "I think you'll find her to be an awful lot of fun. And, who knows, maybe she'll be able to live with us on a permanent basis."

The dirt hasn't even settled on my mother's grave, and my father is already talking about another woman. I look out the window of his 1977 Porsche and cry all the way home.

"Excuse me," a woman says, brushing past me, jarring me back to the present, where I'm standing between racks of women's dresses at the Galeries Lafayette. I feel dizzy, nauseous.

The fog is finally lifting, and as it does, my world comes into focus.

I know who I am.

My mind is so busy, processing so many things, that I'm hardly aware of my journey back to the rue Cler. I float into the elevator, materializing in my apartment like a ghost. Every bone in my body is struck with a deep exhaustion, and my eyelids are heavy as I find my way to my bedroom and let my head fall on the pillow. My brain, it seems, can no longer handle the weight of my memories, downloading with such intensity. I close my eyes. Sleep is my only escape.

When I open my eyes, hours may have passed, or maybe only minutes, but I am jarred from slumber by the phone ringing in the kitchen. Startled, I jump out of bed and run to catch it on the fourth ring.

"Ms. Williams?" It's an American man, whose voice I don't recognize.

"Yes," I say, disoriented.

"Please," he continues. "I need to speak to you. It's about a highly sensitive matter."

"Okay," I say, cautiously.

"My name is Edward Stern," he continues. "I work with a firm in Los Angeles that represents your late father Wes Williams's estate. I understand that you became estranged from him in your teen years, which is why you might have missed this."

"Missed what?" I ask.

"I'm getting to that," he says. "Now, when your parents split up, he signed over the deed of the home in San Diego to your mother, and when she died, she left that to you."

"I don't understand."

"Bear with me. I'm getting to my point. At the

time of your father's death, eight years ago, the will we had on file didn't mention anything about him having a daughter."

"I guess that's not much of a surprise," I say with a sniff, my mind awash in memories from my childhood, many of them sad ones. "Fatherhood wasn't high on his priority list. Womanizing, on the other hand, was."

"And that's just it," he continues. "Without next of kin to locate, the bulk of his estate, after fees were paid out, went into a trust, where it remains now. Money just sitting there, with no one to claim it." He clears his throat. "You knew your father had passed, correct?"

"Yeah," I say, more shards of recovered memories hitting me like shrapnel. "I saw it on the cover of *People* magazine."

"As I'm sure you know, your father fell into severe dementia in his later years."

I feel a lump in my throat, and I swallow hard. Perhaps that's why he never reached out. "I actually . . . didn't know."

"Anyway, all this to say, after his death, a lot of women came forward claiming they deserved shares of the Williams estate. It was an absolute circus. But in all of it, one woman, Julia Benson, had the strongest claim."

Julia. "Oh, I remember her," I say. "She came to 'take care of me' after my mother died, which boiled down to her throwing away all of my mother's things and then convincing my father to send me to boarding school."

"Well," he continues, "Ms. Benson came forward with a copy of what seemed like a legitimate will. It appeared to be signed by Mr. Williams, and it left his entire estate to her."

"I've never expected anything from my father, and I never will, but that woman . . ." I shake my head, remembering the way she had mocked one of my mother's dresses while cleaning out her closet. "She shouldn't get a penny."

"That's just the thing," he says. "She's not going to. The will fails to stand up legally, as it isn't notarized, nor does it contain signatures from witnesses, but it led us to you."

"What do you mean?"

"Ms. Benson's forged will includes an entire clause about you, specifically stating that your father wished to cut you out of any potential inheritance. Now, it doesn't matter what she claims your father wanted; the point is, in her falsified documents, she revealed the rightful heir to Wes Williams's estate, and that person is you."

"Me?"

"You're an awfully hard person to find, you know. No Facebook. Nothing of significance online. When we finally realized you were in Paris, I hired a private investigator to find you."

"That explains the phone calls," I say. "I knew someone was following me."

"We didn't mean to frighten you," he says. "We only wanted to find you. Anyway, I'll have all the paperwork couriered to you this week. We'll need you to sign, and after my team in New York makes the final authorization, I can present you with a check. That could take a week, maybe a little more." He pauses for a moment. "Your father was a very successful actor. Some forty films to his name, is that right?"

"You'd know better than me," I say.

"You're inheriting a significant amount of money. It's none of my business, but if I were you, I'd seek out a financial advisor you trust and get this money wisely invested. I'd also be careful about who you tell. There's a certain type of man who preys on women with money."

I nod, feeling a chill come over me.

"Well," he says, "I'm glad we were finally able to connect. And I certainly don't want to upset you, but the private investigator we hired, well, he . . ." His voice trails off. "I know you had an accident and all, and I'm not sure how to say this."

"What?"

"Well, that man, Victor, you've been spending time with . . ."

My eyes widen. "Victor? What about Victor?"

"It's just that you should know that . . ."

"Know what?"

"Listen, I only mean to say that . . . I don't think he's exactly who you think he is."

I shake my head. "Are you telling me not to trust him?"

"I've overstepped my bounds," he says abruptly. "I'm sorry. It's your life, and you'll sort it all out. Best of luck, Ms. Williams. Truly."

I stare out my kitchen window, my mind reeling, my heart racing. None of this feels real, and yet somehow it is.

"You look awfully pale," Margot says, studying my face as she walks into the apartment sometime later. "Are you sick? I heard the flu is going around."

I shrug. "Just a lot on my mind."

"Please," she says, reaching for a plate. "Let me make you something to eat."

I shake my head. "Thanks, but I'm not hungry."

"Well, you have to eat, or else you'll—"

"Can you do me a favor?" I say, interrupting her.

"Of course, anything."

"Can you call the restaurant and tell Victor that I'm not coming in tonight? He's expecting me for dinner at eight, and I . . . I just can't make it."

"But don't you think you'll feel better in a few hours? Maybe after you lie down for a bit? Victor will be—"

"Please, just call him for me," I say with an exhausted sigh. "I just can't. I can't."

"Okay," she says softly. "I will."

I walk to my bedroom and close the door, sinking into my bed without bothering to change my clothes or wash my face. My phone buzzes on the bedside table, but I don't answer it or look at the texts. I know it's Victor, but I can't bear to face him just yet. Right now, I can't bear to face anything.

CHAPTER 18

CÉLINE

He's come back. I leap to my feet and place my hand on the door, opening it slowly so as not to wake Cosi, then slipping into the dark hallway. I see him in the distance, taking off his coat. He's a large man, and not just in height; his limbs are long and muscular. And in the darkness, with only the light of the moon filtering through the windows, he looks bigger and more frightening than ever.

I don't want to face him. I don't want to imagine what he might do to me. But I do not want any of it to happen where Cosi is. Therefore, I must walk into the lion's den.

"Hello," I mutter. My hands tremble so violently I have to clasp them together to steady them.

He doesn't seem to hear me, so I say it again, a bit louder: "Hello."

This time he turns around. He sees me. I am in the center of the den now, and he walks toward me with precision. He is the predator, and I am the prey.

"Here you are, so eager to see me," he says, running his heavy hand along my cheek, down my neck, along the side of my left breast and then down to my waist, where he grabs me and pulls me closer to him. He reeks of cigarettes and alcohol. "I thought I'd have to wake you up in your bed tonight. That might have been fun. Imagine your surprise to find my body pressed against yours, my hands touching you in places—"

I gasp in terror as he thrusts his hand between my legs, plastering his lips on my face like leeches.

"You like that, don't you?" he says, amused, fumbling with the buttons on the bodice of my dress. His patience gives way after a few seconds and he rips the top half of my dress open, sending the buttons flying. I hear one hit the hardwood floor and roll to a stop. He tears my undergarments off, too, revealing my bare breasts, before taking a step back.

"No," he says. "Not here. Not the first time. We'll go to my bedroom."

He lifts me into his arms as if I'm a mere feather and carries me, like an animal he's slain in a hunting expedition, to the first door on the right. He tosses me onto his bed. I blink back tears as he places his hands on me, then close my eyes and . . . pretend.

At once, I am no longer in the lion's den—I'm sipping tea in the countryside far, far away. Cosi is picking wildflowers while I read a letter from my king. Luc is coming home soon. "Give my love to our princess," he writes. "I miss you both terribly."

I hardly notice what he does to my body, for I am not in it. I am somewhere else, somewhere safe, where he cannot find me. And when he is finished, I lie there, in a frozen state, until he rolls over and begins to snore, at first lightly, then so loudly I imagine the sound must rattle the windows.

Slowly, I creep out of his bed and onto my feet, doing my best to collect my clothing without making a sound. I take a step toward the door, and the floorboard beneath my feet lets out a menacing creak. I make a note of it and take another step, timed to the rhythm of Reinhardt's snoring, which muffles another creaky spot in the floor. Just three more steps. Two more. But then his snoring stops altogether, and he gasps for breath. I stand naked in the darkness until he rolls over and begins snoring again.

I manage to open and close the door without waking him, then go to the bathroom. I can barely look at my reflection in the mirror. My body aches. There are angry welts on my stomach and thighs, which will surely become bruises tomorrow. I wipe away the blood between my legs then slip into my dress. It's badly torn and will need to be mended, as I have nothing else to wear. Perhaps Madame Huet has a needle and thread?

I want to take a bath, to wash Reinhardt's filth off my body, but the noise from the pipes might wake up Madame Huet, or worse, him, so I tiptoe back to my bedroom, to Cosi. I pray she didn't hear my cries three doors down. I pray that she slept through the assault I endured.

My legs ache as I kneel down beside the bed, lifting back the dust ruffle to check on her, but to my horror, she's . . . gone.

"Cosi?" I whisper, terrified, into the darkness. I check the bed, then look around me. "Cosi!" I whisper again.

I sit down on the bed, sinking my head in my hands. It was a mistake to bring her here. A selfish mistake. I wanted so desperately to keep her with me, to protect her. But that's not what I've done. I've brought her into the lion's den with me. How could I have been so foolish? She would have been better off out there. She might have found some nice family to take her in. She'd be safe now, instead of held captive in this prison.

Where could she have gone? I told her to stay under the bed. It isn't like her to disobey me. I consider the fact that her hunger might have gotten the better of her, and she might have snuck to the kitchen to find something to eat. I'll check there.

I stand and walk to the door but stop suddenly when I hear a strange sound, almost like an animal scratching the inside of a wall. *Probably just a rat.* I ignore it and reach for the door handle, and then another sound. This time it's different: a very quiet knock. One, then another, and another. I listen carefully and trace the sounds, which appear to be coming from . . . under the bed.

"Cosi?" I whisper, falling to my knees again, but she is not under the bed. The knocking sound persists, however. I crouch at the foot of the bed and pat the floorboards. One gives a little, and I'm able to wedge my fingers into a gap and pry the edge up, pulling a large, square section from the floor. A secret door. I gasp when I see that there's a little room beneath the floor, and my heart bursts to find Cosi sitting in it.

"Cosi!" I cry. "Are you all right, honey?" She's been scared of the dark her whole life, but if she is frightened now, she chooses not to let on.

"Yes," she whispers. "Mama, look what I found! A hiding place!"

I don't know what to make of the dark space beneath the bed. I am too tired, and too grateful that Cosi hasn't gotten herself into trouble, to consider it further.

"This will be my room," she says cheerfully, "until the war's over and Papa and Luc come home."

I suppose it's not a bad idea. She'll be undetectable here, as long as Reinhardt or

Madame Huet don't already know about it, though that's unlikely. I can't hide her under the dust ruffle forever.

"All right," I say. "Is it cold in there?"

"A little," she says, "but I'll be fine."

"Here," I continue, pulling the cover off my bed. "Take this blanket." I lower it into the dark space below the floor, and she wraps it around her small body. "Knock if you need anything, and I'll help you open the hatch."

"I will," she says. "Good night, Mama."

"Good night, sweet one. *Ne pas s'envoler, mon petit oiseau.*"

Don't fly away, my little birdie. I secure the floorboards back in place and climb into bed. We've survived our first day in our castle on the rue Cler.

Sun streams through the window the next morning. I open my eyes briefly, then close them again. For a luscious moment, in that strange place between sleep and waking, I have no idea where I am. But then reality creeps in like a cancer, and I remember everything, every terrifying detail. I sit straight up in bed. Everything aches, especially my legs.

"Cosi," I whisper. *Is she okay?*

I kneel down and pry the hatch open, and there is my little girl looking up at me. The morning light pierces through the dark space below, and she squints a little until her eyes adjust. "How long have you been awake?" I ask. "Did you knock?"

She shakes her head. "I've been up for a while. I don't know how long. I wanted to let you sleep."

I extend my arm and help her up into the room. "How is it possible that my daughter is an actual angel, sent from heaven?" I say, smiling.

But she doesn't return my smile. She looks horrified. "Mama, what . . . happened to you?" She runs to me and points to my face. "There's blood on your cheek."

I look down at my dress and see the torn bodice, which I'd forgotten about. "It's nothing, nothing at all, honey," I say, placing my hand over my chest. "Don't you worry. I'm just fine."

"Did the bad man do that to you?" she asks, touching my arm lightly.

"Don't you worry, love," I say quickly. "Now, I suppose I ought to find something to wear and some breakfast for us."

She smiles. "Princesses get hungry."

"Yes, they do."

After Cosi is safe in her little room beneath the floor, I venture out to the hallway. The door to Reinhardt's bedroom is open, and I'm relieved to see that he isn't there. Madame Huet has obviously already made the bed. The pillows are fluffed, and the coverlet pulled tight. Did she see my blood on the sheets?

Cautiously, I walk into the living area. I'm grateful not to see his shoes by the door. Just then, I notice something I didn't see before: an interior lock bolted to the door. For some reason, it isn't latched, so I jiggle the handle on the chance that it might open, but it doesn't. I sigh. Obviously locked from the outside.

"Don't bother," Madame Huet says behind me.

Startled, I turn around to find her standing a few feet away.

"I . . . I was only . . ." I begin to say, attempting a response.

"Only trying to escape?" The older woman rolls her eyes at me. "Pointless. When he leaves, he locks the door from the outside. When he's home, he locks it from the inside. And only the two of us have the key." I search her face, looking for any fragment of kindness, but am unsuccessful.

"Now," she continues, turning toward the kitchen. "I suppose you must be hungry."

I nod.

She notices my torn dress and frowns. "In the closet in the second bedroom, you will find a change of clothes, and any undergarments you'll need are in the dresser. They belonged to the others. But surely you'll find something that will fit. Reinhardt likes his women looking smart."

I turn to see about finding a new dress, as the

housekeeper clears her throat. "Take a bath first, for heaven's sake. Towels are in the cabinet beneath the sink. Don't dawdle. Breakfast will be ready in a half hour."

I make my way to the other bedroom and open the closet, which smells of a nauseating mix of assorted perfumes. I run my hand along the dozens of dresses and various shawls and nightgowns inside. *Whose were these? What did Madame Huet mean by "the others"? Where are they now?* I lift the hanger of a striking red dress and hold it up to my body. It's about my size, and very fashionable. Just the sort of thing I might have worn on a date with Luc. It feels as if a decade has passed since that night together, or maybe a century, and yet the thought of it still makes my heart swell.

I examine the red dress more carefully and see that the neckline is far too low-cut, so I put it back. I consider others until I finally settle on a simple blue dress, belted at the waist.

Inside the dresser drawers I find an assortment of neatly folded lingerie and an array of panties, some silk, which I'd never been able to afford. I try not to think about the other bodies who wore these things. I quickly select a few items and shudder as I close the drawer on the dark secrets it keeps.

I draw a bath as Madame Huet instructed and plunge into the tub. No amount of soap can take away the horror of last night, but it feels good to be clean again. I dry off, put on the new dress, and head to the dining room, where the housekeeper is waiting.

"Much better," she says with approval, pointing to my chair, but I don't sit down.

"I'm sorry, Madame Huet," I say as sweetly as I can. "It's just that . . . I'm not feeling *well* today. I'm sure you can understand. I'd prefer to take my breakfast in my room this morning."

An obvious creature of habit, she is displeased by my request.

"You see," I say, "I have a . . . sensitive stomach, and I'd hate, ever so much, to soil this beautiful rug."

"I understand," she says quickly. "I'll be back with a tray."

Five minutes later, I return to Cosi, who enjoys her first proper meal in our castle.

Reinhardt doesn't come home that night, or the next. I am told by Madame Huet that he has been called to the south for an urgent matter. I hope he never comes back, but he does, and I endure more of his terror. He is sometimes rough and brutal, and sometimes emotional, asking me to hold him like a mother would a little boy. I do as he says, always while transporting myself elsewhere in my mind. When I am with Reinhardt, I am not there. Sometimes I even feel as if my spirit is detached from my body in such a real way that in certain moments, it's as if I'm actually standing above the bed watching him as he rapes me.

I hate it with every bone in my body. But as the months pass, I come to anticipate his patterns and do what I need to do to please him. This is how we will survive, Cosi and me.

We have a certain rhythm to our days. I almost always manage to bring her something for breakfast and smuggle her to the bathroom. Lunch is more difficult, but there is a window during Madame Huet's afternoon nap to sneak something from the pantry. Cosi's little room is fairly well stocked with dry goods like oats and nuts. She was particularly happy with the bag of raisins I found in the back of the pantry. I also cautiously collected other items of comfort for her from around the house: A pillow and an extra blanket from one of the spare bedrooms that would never be missed. A flashlight from Reinhardt's drawer for dark nights, and a stack of books and magazines. When I found a ball of yarn, then paired it with two skewers from the kitchen for knitting needles, she immediately set out to knit Monsieur Dubois a scarf. It's almost done.

We figured out some of the more practical problems, too. I repurposed a lone bucket on the balcony for more water storage, just in case. And, while she hasn't needed to use it yet, a bowl for a toilet—and some paper, should there be an emergency in the night or when I am not in the room.

Yes, we are managing in this prison of ours. Cosi busies herself drawing and writing in her journal or making believe in her imaginary world, but I know she is growing weary of living this way. I am, too.

Isolated from the world outside our windows, I have no idea of the state of France, or of the world. Hitler might have taken up residence in Versailles for all I know. But I don't think so. Reinhardt seems more anxious than ever. The phone rings at all hours of the night, and he wants less of me, which is the greatest relief, and also my greatest concern.

I think about the others before me that Madame Huet has alluded to more than a few times. *Where did they go when he lost interest in them?*

I need to hold on a bit longer, keep his interest, until the war's over. France will be liberated, and with it, Cosi and me. If soldiers can fight in the battlefield, I can fight here.

When I lie awake at night, I think of ways we might escape, but Reinhardt's prison is impenetrable, except, say, by suicide. After his assaults, I limp back to my room, then open the window and gaze longingly at the cobblestone streets below. I could just . . . jump, and end this pain forever. But then I always think of my sweet

Cosi, cuddled up with Monsieur Dubois in her little room under the floorboards, and I know I must keep on.

Some days are harder than others. Like when Madame Huet finds a raisin on the floor of my bedroom.

"What's this?" she asks, reaching down and picking it up for inspection. "Is this a . . . raisin?"

"I don't know."

"It is," she says. "How did it get here?"

"I have no idea."

"I only use raisins for Monsieur Kurt's muesli, but he hasn't requested that in months." She looks at me suspiciously. "Have you been *stealing* from my kitchen?"

"No," I say. "Of course not."

Just the same, she reports the raisin incident to Reinhardt later that night. Afterward, he pulls off his belt and whips me with it. "Little thief," he shouts. "A lashing for every raisin. How many did you take? How many?"

I beg him to stop, but he doesn't relent until I slump over on the floor. Afterward, my back is left bloodied and bruised. Madame Huet doesn't apologize, but she does bring an ice pack to my bedroom that night. And after that, I have the feeling that things have shifted between us. While I will never trust her, I like to believe that some of the ice in her heart has begun to melt.

Christmas comes and goes like any other day. It

doesn't snow, but frozen rain pelts the bedroom window. There will be no presents for Cosi, nor Papa's challah, warm from the oven. Reinhardt departs in the early hours of the morning to the south, which is, perhaps, the greatest present of all.

January bleeds into February, and Cosi and I forge on as best we can. By March, with news from Reinhardt that the Allies are losing their handle on Europe, our spirits plummet. While the human spirit may be capable of enduring most anything, it cannot carry on without hope—and our stores are rapidly depleting.

I see it in Cosi's eyes. Life has gone from a joyful adventure to a dark disappointment, an exhausting labyrinth with no end. Just as I, on late nights after suffering Reinhardt's assaults, stare longingly out the window to the cobblestone streets below contemplating a swift end to my pain, Cosi considers her own exit strategies. One day, minutes before Reinhardt, always punctual for dinner, is due home, Cosi wanders into the hallway and stands, staring at me defiantly. Fortunately, Madame Huet is busy in the kitchen, and I am able to whisk Cosi back into the bedroom before Reinhardt's return.

"What if they'd seen you?" I scold, blinking back tears.

Her cheeks, once rosy, have grown ashen over the months. "What if they did?" she cries.

"Maybe they'll send me away! Anything would be better than being trapped in this room."

Tears sting my eyes for my daughter's pain. I notice the way she watches the birds fly by outside the window—creatures with more freedom than she has.

"My sweet girl," I say, kneeling down beside her. "I know you are suffering, and I hate it so. But believe me when I say that what lies beyond this is far, far worse than you can imagine."

She nods, staring off into a corner of the room despondently, before I tilt her chin back to me. "Don't fly away yet, little birdie," I say through tears. "I know it's hard, but you'll fly again, someday. I promise."

Her small smile is enough to fortify me with hope as I tuck her into the dark space beneath the floor, even if my heart is already heavy with a terrifying secret I've kept to myself for months now. I am pregnant, and I won't be able to hide it much longer.

When I finally tell Reinhardt, he laughs at first, which frightens me, but then a stillness comes over him. He walks to me and places his hand on my belly. I tremble, as I always do, at his touch. But he instructs me not to be scared. "My heir," he says as I shudder inwardly.

The baby growing inside of me is as much mine as it is his, and yet I am torn with worry. How will I ever be able to explain to him or her who their father really is?

In some ways, the pregnancy is a blessing. After learning the news, Reinhardt leaves me alone, for the most part. But if I'd expected any warmth from Madame Huet, I was mistaken. "Don't flatter yourself," she had said with repugnance. "You're not the first one he's impregnated."

Cosi has noticed my growing belly, of course, so I have no choice but to tell her, and she's delighted. Each morning, she nestles her head on my belly and talks to the baby in whispers. "Do you think he'll like me?" she asks one morning after breakfast, nibbling scraps of food I've smuggled back.

"Him?"

She nods. "I've always wanted a little brother."

I pause to consider who this child could be, studying Cosi's big eyes, so filled with love and kindness, just like her father's. Could the son of an evil man be born . . . good?

I turn to the door, suddenly, when I hear the doorbell ring. "Stay put," I whisper to Cosi as I peer into the hallway to have a look.

"Shall I just sign here?" Madame Huet asks.

I tiptoe closer until I can make out the face of the deliveryman standing on the threshold. *Nic!*

His eyes meet mine, but after a tiny flash of recognition, he nods coldly at the housekeeper.

"Thank you, madame," he says curtly as she hands him a coin.

Does he understand that I am being held captive in the apartment? I stare down at my swollen belly. *Surely he doesn't think I am here of my own free will.* My heart races.

I think about those few moments for days, turning the encounter over and over in my mind until, two days later, the doorbell rings again, just after breakfast.

I follow Madame Huet to the door, and my heart practically bursts at the site of Nic again. Like last time, he keeps our association to himself. But I am bolstered by new hope. *Maybe Luc has come home. Maybe he can get a message to him.*

"But you must be mistaken," Madame Huet says, shaking her head. "I didn't place this order."

Nic looks a little worried but keeps his cool. "It's a . . . gift from my boss, Gabriel. He wishes to thank you for your business."

"Oh," Madame Huet says, taking the sack Nic extends to her. "Well, in that case, tell him that we thank him for the gesture."

"I will," Nic says cheerfully before casting a cautious glance my way. Our eyes lock for a moment, and with my gaze, I try to impart everything: *"Nic, we are in trouble. Cosi and I need your help!"*

It's not clear whether he understands, or even

cares. And maybe he's only trying to protect himself. After all, how well do I really know him? In these times, even the seemingly nicest people have only the energy to look out for themselves, as evidenced by our own family physician.

But then Nic gives me a final glance, and I know, just know, that he has greater character and a bigger heart than that. "Oh, be sure to try the *pains aux raisins*," he says. "They're our *specialty*."

After Madame Huet has closed and relocked the door, she heads to the kitchen with the pastries.

"Wait, do you think I might have a pastry . . . now?"

She looks at me quizzically. I can't tell if she hates me or pities me, or both. "But you only just had breakfast."

"I know," I say, clutching my belly, "but I didn't eat a lot at dinner last night and I'm still a bit hungry."

"Suit yourself," she says, handing me the bag. I spot two *pains aux raisins* and select both of them.

"My, my," she says, eying me critically.

"It's just that . . . well, I'm famished this morning."

"Hungry indeed," she continues. "But if I were you, I'd be careful. Reinhardt won't be pleased if you gain too much weight."

"Yes, of course," I say, turning back to my bedroom. "Thank you, madame."

I shut the door and Cosi crawls out from under the bed. "Look," I say. "Pastries!"

She climbs up onto the bed beside me, her eyes bright. "Oh, Mama, let me touch them. Are they real?"

"Of course they are, love," I say. "But first, before we eat them, we have to look for something."

"For what?" Cosi asks, confused.

"A message. From a friend." I can't bear to tell her that Nic has just appeared at the door. She'd weep at the thought of missing him, and it would only sharpen her pain. "I think there may be hope for us."

"Really?" Cosi asks eagerly, leaning in as I carefully pull the layers of sweet bread apart. There is nothing in the first one, and I wonder if I've simply imagined all of this—or, worse, if Nic believes I am willingly living in this apartment, a volunteer mistress to a German soldier.

I reach for the second pastry and pull it apart carefully, until I see a tiny slip of white paper, folded into a tiny speck. I open it eagerly, as Cosi looks over my shoulder. It reads: "Are you in trouble? Weds. ten A.M."

"What does that mean?" Cosi asks.

"I think he wants me to give him a sign, to let him know if we need help."

"Will you?"

"Yes," I say, smiling. "This friend put himself at great risk doing this for us."

"Mama?" Cosi says, her face beaming the way it used to when she'd race home from school with some exciting thing to tell me. "When we're rescued, can I bake your friend a cake?" She smiles. "To thank him, for rescuing us."

"Yes, my love," I say, returning her smile. If only it were that simple. I reach for a scrap of paper on the desk. "Cosi, will you get me your pen?"

She climbs down to her little room, which she's gotten so good at maneuvering into, though not out of. She isn't quite tall enough to hoist herself back up, so I offer my hands.

"Here, Mama," she says, handing me the pen.

I write on the piece of paper, careful to avoid Cosi's gaze: "In trouble. Help. Pregnant. Find Luc, or Esther in my building. Talk to no one." I don't mention Cosi. It's too risky. *If Madame Huet, or Reinhardt, intercept the message*—I shudder, not allowing myself to think about the possibly grave consequences.

Cosi looks at me with a hopeful expression. "Do you think it will work?"

"I hope so, love."

I pretend to be interested in plucking dead leaves from the houseplants in the living room on

323

Wednesday at ten o'clock, but fifteen minutes pass and Nic still hasn't arrived. When Madame Huet comes through with a basket of freshly folded laundry, she casts an annoyed glance my way. "What on earth has gotten into you? You're destroying the plants."

"I was only . . . getting rid of some of the dead matter," I mutter. "We own a flower shop . . . or at least we used to." I swallow hard. "Deadheading is good for plants." My heart pounds in my chest like a gong—so loud, I wonder if Madame Huet can hear it. *What if Nic doesn't come? What if . . .*

My heart seizes when the doorbell rings.

"Who on earth would that be?" Madame Huet says, setting the laundry basket down with an annoyed huff, eying me suspiciously.

Nic stands outside the door again. "Hello," he says to Madame Huet, who looks, again, confused by his presence. "I was just"—his voice falters a bit, but he regains his steadiness—"making my rounds, and it seems that one of our employees mistakenly sent me with an extra order. Anyway, I was making a delivery nearby and thought of you." He smiles a bit nervously and extends the bag. "Here."

Madame Huet isn't taking his bait. "No thank you," she says, stepping back. "My boss doesn't like charity. When we want pastries, we'll order pastries. Good day."

I run ahead, reaching my hand through the crack of the door before it closes.

"Wait!" I cry, grasping the bag in my hand as Nic takes the note tucked inside my palm. "We'd love them."

Madame Huet closes the door and scowls at me. "You shouldn't have done that."

"Done what?" I ask, looking in the bag for a *pain aux raisins*. I see one and pull it out, along with a chocolate croissant for Cosi.

"Carried on like that," she continues. "He might want trouble."

I shrug. "A bakery delivery boy?"

"In these times, we can't be too careful." She clutches the key she keeps on a chain around her neck, and for the first time, I detect fear in her eyes. "What if he has been working with the enemy? Reinhardt would put a bullet through my head, and yours."

"I'm sorry," I say, taking a step back toward the bedroom. "It just seemed a shame to let those lovely pastries go to waste."

"Just the same," the housekeeper sneers at me, her momentary vulnerability gone, "stay in your room until dinner. I can't risk you causing a scene when the laundry is delivered this afternoon."

"Yes, madame," I say, walking quickly to my bedroom before she can snatch the pastries from my hand.

"Cosi," I whisper, opening the hatch. There

325

is no movement below, and I wonder if she's sleeping. "Cosi!" I whisper again. A moment later, her sweet face appears in the light. Her face looks paler than ever. "Are you feeling all right, honey?"

She nods, but her grasp is weak as I pull her small body up into the room.

"Look," I say. "Pastries!"

She seems unusually disinterested as I pull out the *pain aux raisins* and dissect it until I find the scrap of paper inside. My heart beats faster. It reads: "Hold steady. Help on the way."

I smile at Cosi, my eyes welling up with tears. "Do you know what this means, honey?"

She doesn't respond, and instead sets her head on the pillow.

"They're coming for us. We'll be rescued! And soon you can bake that cake."

She smiles.

"Here," I say, handing her the chocolate croissant. "Eat."

She shakes her head. "I'm not that hungry, Mama."

"Really? I've never seen you turn down a chocolate croissant." I place my hand on her forehead. "Honey, you're burning up!"

I tuck her under the blankets beside me, holding her close as her body shivers. Her fever worsens through the afternoon, and by dinner she is delirious and refuses to take sips of water.

When dinner comes, I tell Madame Huet I am ill and prefer to take my dinner in my room.

She nods, but as she dishes up my plate, larger servings than normal, I can tell her suspicions are piqued.

"Funny," she says, handing me the tray and smiling curiously. "You don't seem to have a cough."

I clear my throat as the hair on the back of my neck stands on end. "It . . . comes and goes," I say, patting my chest. "Anyway, thank you. And . . . sorry for the trouble."

I feel her gaze burning through my back as I leave the kitchen, wondering if she knows. And if so, if she'd tell Reinhardt.

I hold a spoon to Cosi's lips but she recoils, turning her back to me, just as she does when I offer her a sip of water. I can't bear to send her down to the cold, damp space beneath the floor. Not tonight, not in this state. So I tuck her close to me and hold her until we both doze off.

My eyes flash open, sometime in the night, at the sound of a door slamming, and then heavy footsteps in the hall. *Reinhardt.* There isn't time to get Cosi beneath the floor. She's weak and delirious as I tuck her beneath the bed instead. "Don't make a sound," I whisper. "He's coming."

Reinhardt opens the door a moment later as I pull the blanket up around my body. He stares at me for a long moment. Outside the window,

327

a cloud shifts, and moonlight streams in, illuminating his face—tense, with dark shadows around his eyes, and a heavy layer of stubble on his jawline. He's drunk. I can smell it. And as he takes a step toward my bed, I tremble. *Not here. Anywhere but here.* I can't bear to think of Cosi being a witness to what Reinhardt has planned for me.

Instead, he stops and clears his throat. "I'm going away for a month. Important war business."

I nod as he leans closer, pulling the cover, then the sheet, off my body and setting his gaze on me like a leaden blanket. His breathing is heavy as he places his large hand on my belly, the sour smell of whiskey and stale cigarettes heavy in the air.

He plants his wet lips on mine, thrusting his tongue into my mouth. The taste of his breath turns my stomach, and the stubble on his face burns against my skin, but I hold still, and a moment later, he pulls back.

"That's all," he says, closing the door.

I wait for several long moments, heart racing, before I peer down below the bed.

"Is the bad man gone?" Cosi mutters. "Did he hurt you?" I feel her forehead and gasp. Her fever has worsened. With Reinhardt here, she isn't safe in the bed, but I can't bear to send her down to the cold darkness below. Instead, I crawl down beside her under the bed, tucking the blanket around us, her shivering body beside mine. If Reinhardt returns, I'll leap to my feet the moment I hear his footsteps, and lure him out of the room. With any luck, he won't suspect Cosi.

I say a silent prayer as Cosi drifts into a feverish sleep beside me—for our protection. For Papa. For the Allied forces to be victorious. And it is answered—well, in part—moments later, when I hear the sound of a woman's laughter down the hall. Though I ache for any woman who shares Reinhardt's bed, I am grateful he isn't sharing one with me. He'll be snoring soon—I know his pattern well—and then he'll be gone. *Important war business.* With any luck, we'll be rescued before his return.

I'm able to persuade Cosi to take a sip of water, but no more, and she coughs loudly afterward.

"Shhh," I whisper. "You mustn't make a sound. Someone will hear."

I'm able to quiet her, but then, a few minutes later, her cough persists, croupy and deep chested. Her breathing is shallow and she wheezes for air. I hold her to me, stroking her hair until she finally falls asleep, which is when I hear footsteps in the hall again. And this time, a knock at the door.

"Yes?" I say, inching out from under the bed and opening the door.

I peer into the hallway, but no one is there. The sounds of Reinhardt and his female companion have faded as well. And then something beside my feet catches my eye. I kneel down to find a tray on the floor. I cautiously lift it and close the door behind me, then set it on the bed to have a look: a glass of milk, a plate of buttered toast, two washcloths rolled up over a bowl of ice, and warm tea beside a bottle of aspirin. And, next to the plate, a little bowl of raisins.

Madame Huet. I blink back tears.

I offer Cosi a sip of tea and coax her to swallow an aspirin before pressing a cold compress to her forehead. *Lord help us. Let us make it through this night.*

CHAPTER 19

CAROLINE

The next morning, I open my eyes before sunrise, dress quickly, then make a cup of coffee in the kitchen. Careful not to wake Margot or Élian, I grab my sketchbook and tiptoe to the balcony, where I watch the sunrise. My memory, once locked shut, encapsulated, feels as if it's been punctured by tiny pinholes, allowing a little light to shine into the darkness. Yesterday's revelations have been monumental, and yet there are still so many shadows, so many dark corners of my memory waiting to be illuminated.

I pull my sweater tighter around me. Mornings are as chilly as they are beautiful. As the sun peeks up over the horizon, it casts a pink-orange glow on the sky, bathing the city in a soothing, rosy warmth.

I turn to my sketchbook. I can feel another memory coming. A big one. And I've been waiting for it for so long now.

I hear the palm trees, the wind chimes. I steady myself . . .

Alma. I can hardly believe that my little girl is turning seven. It seems like only yesterday that I'd found out I was pregnant. I stared at the pink line on the test strip for a solid hour. That spring, I painted a mural in her nursery, the natural thing to do when you are both an expectant mother and a professional artist. Peonies, roses, tulips, daffodils, zinnias. I wanted her to see flowers when she woke up and flowers when she closed her eyes at night. Of all the paintings I made in my career, the mural is one of my favorites.

"Make a wish!" I say, just before my little girl blows out her candles.

"Okay, Mama," she says, pausing for a moment to consider her wish, then nodding assuredly. "Got it." She closes her eyes, then takes a deep breath before extinguishing each of the seven flames.

After the presents are opened, the dishes are cleared and loaded in the dishwasher, and the last guest has gone, I ask Alma if she'd like to see her final present.

"Yes!" she cries expectantly.

I lead her around to the side of the house, to a sunny plot of land. I've already prepped the soil, and waiting for her are a fresh pair of pink garden gloves, a small trowel, and a few other garden tools. I have painted a sign, posted in the ground, that reads: ALMA'S GARDEN. Next, I hand her a stack of seed packets and point to some herbs and flowers in plastic containers.

"Are you ready to plant your very first

garden?" I hand her the set of pink garden tools with matching pink gloves.

She wraps her arms around me. "Oh, Mama, this is my favorite gift of all!"

I love to make Alma happy, and I know this garden will. She'll be out here at all hours, weeding, picking, admiring—watching her plants grow and change with the seasons, just as my mother and I had done together, so long ago. She'd have loved Alma, I know—just as much as I do.

When the garden is planted, we clean up and Alma asks if we can go swimming.

I'm tired, and there are a million things I have to do, but it's Alma's birthday. "Sure, honey," I say, and I go change into my swimsuit.

"Let's pretend we're mermaids," she says in the pool a few minutes later, splashing around beside me.

I play along, marveling at her imagination but also noticing that her long blond hair is falling into her eyes.

"Honey, let me get you a scrunchie for your hair."

"No, Mama, mermaids don't use scrunchies!"

I grin. "Sure they do, sweet girl."

"Mermaids like to be free," she explains. "Their hair, too."

It makes sense, I guess. Oddly, almost everything Alma says makes sense.

We play, splash, we conquer the octopus king before I towel off and glance at my phone and notice that it's getting late. If I'm going to get dinner on the table, I'll have to run to the grocery store, and soon.

Alma looks displeased. "Mama, why are you getting out? The prince is coming on his ship!" She watched *The Little Mermaid* once when she had the flu last year, and ever since, it's been mermaid central around here.

"Honey, I have to run to the store. Maybe Daddy can swim with you?"

I sigh, thinking of the fight Victor and I had last night. He slept on the couch as a result, and we barely spoke at Alma's party. Am I being too hard on him? No. I shake my head to myself. While I can appreciate all the travel we did before Alma was born, times are different now. We can't up and move to Mexico, just because he has the bug to start a new restaurant there. Alma loves her school, and my art career is thriving here. I've had three new installations just this month. And besides, what's wrong with Café Flora? The restaurant has been a hit since he opened it three years ago; it has even recently been written up in a local magazine as the best-kept secret in San Diego. Why can't he just be satisfied with that? I look around at our beautiful home, the very one I grew up in, and wonder if any of it, or we, would ever be good enough for him.

When he walks out to the patio from the living room, I look away.

"Hi," he says. "You did a great job with the party."

"Thanks," I say.

He walks closer, reaching for my hand, which I let him take. When he pulls me close, I melt in his embrace, the way I always have since the first time he held me, that night in Paris so many years ago.

"I'm sorry about last night," he continues. "You're right. It's completely off base of me to suggest that we move to Mexico."

I sigh. "Do you really mean that?"

He nods.

"Because, Vic, I don't want you to resent me. I don't want you to ever think that I held you back." I look up into his big dark eyes. "I don't want to have a boring life, either, but," I glance back at Alma, splashing happily in the pool, "our life is *here.*"

He nods. "It is."

"You know how rocky my childhood was." I blink back tears. "I don't want that for Alma."

"You're right," he says, squeezing me tighter. "We'll stay put. I'm sorry."

I nod, pulling the towel around my body. "We can talk more about this later. I need to shower and head to the store." Since Victor cooks so much at the restaurant, I try to do most of the

335

cooking at home. "Can you keep an eye on Alma?"

"Sure," he says.

"Daddy!" our little girl cries as he walks toward the pool, diving in beside her.

After I shower, I pull my hair into a quick bun and slip on a comfy cotton dress. "All right, you two," I say, reaching for my keys. "Does salmon sound good?"

"Great," Victor says.

I look for my purse in the living room, then remember I left it in my studio, where I find it lying next to a painting that's still drying from this morning. I got up before sunrise to work on my latest, a commission from a couple in New Zealand.

Victor is drying off on a chair by the pool when I walk out to the patio again. "Don't take your eyes off her, honey," I whisper, kissing his cheek. We are both protective of Alma, but I can sometimes err on the side of being overly so. She's taken swim lessons since infancy, and we have little to worry about.

"Don't worry," he says, leaning back in the lounge chair and reaching for his book. "I'll stay right here."

"Back in a flash."

Salmon. Chard. One lemon. A baguette. Some red potatoes. Oh, a pint of ice cream for Alma. Milk.

Anything else? I survey my cart as I wave to one of the moms from school, whose name escapes me, then head up to check out. The lines are long. I should have known better than to go shopping right at the dinner hour.

On the drive home, I think of Victor's apology and smile to myself. Every relationship has its bumps in the road, and I can be grateful that our journey hasn't been a rocky one. Victor is nothing like my father. He'd always do what's best for Alma and me. I know that in my heart, even if my vulnerabilities sneak in once in a while, like they did last night.

I take a shortcut past Alma's school, recalling how I'd taught the second graders an art lesson earlier in the week. Alma had been so proud. Four more blocks, then I turn into our little neighborhood, but slow my car when I notice a strange sight: a crowd of people standing in the street. I recognize Alma's piano teacher, Mrs. Wayfair, immediately, her red hair standing out in the crowd. As my car inches closer, I see that she's crying; so is Greta, the older woman who lives on the corner and walks her dog, Muffie, three times a day. There are others I don't recognize, and also three police cars, parked haphazardly along the road, one in the driveway of . . . our home, beside an ambulance. Sirens flash.

I slam on my brakes and jump out of the car,

running through the crowd to my front door and inside, where the scene before me makes me fall to my knees.

Alma lies limp on the living room floor. A team of paramedics are administering CPR, alternately compressing her chest and blowing air into her mouth. Unable to stand, I crawl to my little girl, gasping for air. Screaming for answers. "What happened? Will she be okay? What can we do?"

She's dripping wet. Water pools on the floor beneath her body. A chunk of her hair has been cut or ripped from her scalp. I scream, and a police officer touches my arm. "Ma'am," he says, "please. Let the paramedics do their work."

I nod, shaking from head to toe. *Where is Victor?*

"Ma'am," the police officer continues. "Your daughter's hair appears to have gotten caught in the pool's filtration system."

I shake my head. "No, no. I, I, I just had it cleaned last week."

"I'm afraid that cleaning doesn't make a difference. It's just these old pools. Their suction—they can be very dangerous."

And then my eyes meet Victor's. He's weeping, just as I am. He runs to me, and together we fall to the floor, holding each other in our grief.

We remain suspended in a numb place, waiting for our little girl to sit up, cough, and take a deep breath. But she doesn't. Her face is blue. The lead paramedic finally stops the chest compressions, then lowers his head.

"I'm so very sorry," he says. "We couldn't save her."

"No!" I cry, running to Alma's side and pressing my cheek against hers. "Can't you do something? Can't you . . ." I am hysterical.

"Ma'am," the officer says, touching my arm. "There's nothing more anyone can do. Please, let her go."

"No!" I scream. "No!" Victor tucks his arm around me, pulling me up to a stand as the medical team lifts Alma's limp body onto a stretcher. "Don't let them take her, Vic." I pound on his chest as he pulls me to him. How could this happen? "You promised to keep her safe," I say, sobbing.

Victor is crying, too, in as deep a state of shock as I am. He shakes his head, as if trying to make sense of the horror that has just happened. "I, I only looked down at my book for a moment, and she was . . . gone. I dove in. She was under the water, in the deep end. I'd never seen anything like it. Her hair was caught in the filter." He falls to his knees. "I got her out. I called 911. But . . ."

"But you were too late," I say, shaking my head, through more tears. "I'll never forgive you!" I scream. "Ever, as long as I live."

If he's speaking, I don't hear him. There's nothing he can say, anyway. The paramedics cover my sweet daughter with a sheet and wheel her away, forever.

CHAPTER 20

CÉLINE

The next morning, I awake to Cosi's face peering over me. My back aches, and I groan as I turn over on the hard floor. "Hi, Mama," she says cheerfully. The baby in my belly shifts as I yawn, then open my eyes. "I'm not sick anymore."

I place my hand on her cool head. *Thank God.* Her fever must have broken in the night. Keeping her with me was dangerous, yes, but I couldn't bear to send her below, not when she was so ill. But we survived, and Cosi is well again. That's all that matters. We crawl out from under the bed and I quickly get her some water and yesterday's pastry, which she takes an eager bite of. I study the *pain aux raisins*, which remains on the desk in pieces, and I think of the message inside. Am I foolish to believe that Nic could actually mobilize a plan to rescue us? What if Luc hasn't returned? What if Nic couldn't find Esther? I scold myself for not writing her address on the note I'd given him. He'd never been to our home, though Papa and I had talked about having him to dinner many times. How would he know where to find her? There could be hundreds, thousands,

341

of women with the same name in Paris, let alone in our neighborhood. And even so, how could Esther, a nurse, mobilize a rescue mission? I sigh.

Cosi turns to me after she's finished her pastry. "I'm ready to fly, Mama."

I smile. "I know you are, love. But not quite yet."

She nods. "Luc will come."

"Yes," I say, smiling back at my daughter and willing myself to embody her resolve. "Yes, he will."

When I catch Madame Huet's gaze at dinner, I smile. "Thank you," I say. "What you did last night . . . it was incredibly—"

"I don't know what you're talking about," she says, frowning, returning her gaze to her plate.

I nod. "I'm sorry." Whatever kindness was shown would remain unspoken.

While the war rages on, Reinhardt's absence brings some calm to our lives, but it hasn't persuaded Madame Huet to aid in our escape. She continues to keep the door locked and treat me, more or less, like a prisoner she merely tolerates, perhaps for reasons of self-preservation—Reinhardt could come home at any moment, and then what?—but I like to think that somewhere beneath that icy exterior of hers lies a tiny wedge of kindness; I got a rare glimpse of it the night Cosi took ill, which is why I let my guard down from time to time, allowing Cosi to linger for longer stretches in bed in the morning, or in the bathtub when she begs me to let her play with the bubbles just a few moments more. One afternoon when Madame Huet is napping, I even let her go into the living room. She touches the sofa's upholstery and runs her fingers along the coffee table as if they are rare artifacts from a Greek archeological dig. To her, after all these months, leaving the confines of the bedroom feels like stepping out onto another planet or feeling the rush of cold water in your throat after days crawling through a desert.

Paris is glorious in June, and I'm not sure who is more miserable to be confined indoors, Cosi or me.

"I wish I could run through the park like I used to," Cosi says.

"You will, soon," I reply.

"Will I?" she asks. "Or are you just saying that?"

I swallow hard. "Of course you will, love."

"Then why don't we get out of here? Right now. We can get that mean old housekeeper to give us the keys."

"Honey," I say, "it's not that easy." I touch my belly. "And not in my state."

She nods. "I just keep thinking." She looks to the window. "What if this is all the life I am going to get? Just here in this room."

I shake my head. "No, love. This is not all the life you're going to get."

She nods. "Well, I've decided that it will be okay if that's what happens." She sighs. "I will always miss Papa, and I suppose I'll be sad that I never got to kiss Nic," she pauses with a grin, "but I get to be with you, Mama."

I clench my teeth, trying to keep the tears from coming. "And I get to be with you, love."

"Then I guess we're lucky, right?"

I nod, thinking of the little boy in knickers who was pulled from his mother across the street from our apartment.

Cosi squeezes her teddy bear. "And I have Monsieur Dubois, too." Her smile quickly fades as she turns back to me. "Mama, if . . . anything happens to me, will you make sure Monsieur Dubois is safe? Will you always look out for him?"

I shake my head, unsuccessfully trying to blink back the rogue tears that spill out onto my cheeks. "Oh love, nothing is going to happen to you."

Her eyes are steadfast, determined. "Just promise."

I nod, clutching Cosi's sweet teddy bear to my chest. "I promise."

• • •

Madame Huet announces at breakfast that Reinhardt will be detained longer. More important business in the south, again, she explains. She knows I'm pleased, and I suspect she is, too, but we each keep our cards close to our vests, until a week later, when I mistake the tray of sweets and glass of milk (for Cosi, of course) for kindness. That evening at dinner, I smile and say, "Madame Huet, will you please let us go?" I pause and place my hand on my belly, "Before he returns. Please?"

"What do you take me for, a fool?" she says, clutching the key around her neck. I'm reminded of how Reinhardt has warned me he's equipped his housekeeper with a gun.

As time passes, I begin to wonder if Reinhardt has been killed—shot by the Allies, or better, taken to prison, where he will rot in a cell for the rest of his miserable life.

But then, on a particularly sweltering Thursday, the seventeenth of August, I hear the front door open and heavy footsteps on the wood floors.

"Where is everyone?" he shouts into the apartment. "When a man comes home, he expects to be greeted properly." Even through walls, his deep voice reverberates. Cosi and I exchange a worried look as I quickly tuck her into the room below the floor, straightening my hair a bit before taking a deep breath and opening the door. What will he think of me now, a woman pregnant to full term, with swollen ankles?

Madame Huet stands at attention beside Reinhardt. He looks larger than I remember, and I steady myself as his gaze falls on me.

"Look at you," he says. "Practically the size of a horse."

I lower my head and place a protective hand on my swollen belly as he tosses his coat at Madame Huet. "I'm starving. When's dinner?"

"As soon as you like, monsieur," Madame Huet says dutifully.

He nods.

"I trust your business in the south was successful?" the housekeeper says.

"Indeed so," Reinhardt replies, looking only at me. He walks closer and scours every inch of me with his eyes. "I have a present for you, Céline." He reaches into his pocket and pulls out a small pouch, tossing it at me. It hits the floor before I can catch it, making a loud clink on the ground. I bend to pick it up, carefully opening the little sack.

Inside is a man's watch. At first I don't understand. Nothing makes sense to me anymore. But then I recognize the worn leather band, the shape of the hour and minute hands, the inscription on the back, from my . . . mother. *Papa's watch.*

I fall to my knees. "Where did you . . . get this?" I cry. "What does this mean?"

Reinhardt smiles smugly, brushing past me

346

toward his bedroom. "Is that all I get? Not even a thank-you?" He shakes his head. "I should have just tossed it in the pile of junk with all the others." He slams the door behind him.

I don't tell Cosi. Instead, I tuck Papa's watch under the mattress and dry my tears before I hoist her up from her little room beneath the floor. The news would break her, just as it has broken me, and I can't do that to her. In her little journal, she keeps lists of all the things she wants to do with Papa once we're rescued, including visiting Normandy, just as I promised her we would.

That night we both go hungry because I am too grief-stricken to go to dinner, where I'd have to face him, but Cosi doesn't complain, nor does she protest when I tell her she must sleep in the darkness of her little room instead of in bed with me, as she's grown accustomed to doing while Reinhardt has been away. She simply kisses me good night, tucks Monsieur Dubois under her little arm, and climbs down to the dark space below. The flashlight has long since run down its batteries, and with that, we've lost almost all our remaining rays of hope. Luc and Esther have not found us. Papa is gone, and inside me, a strange child stirs, readying itself to be born into a world far crueler than I've ever known, a world, I fear, that even a lotus flower wouldn't survive in.

CHAPTER 21

✤

CAROLINE

I glance at the clock, shocked that it's already after ten A.M. I've been so embedded in my returning memories that I've completely lost track of time. I promised Inès I'd drop into the studio and help her set up for the art show. I stand up, quickly, then sink back into my sofa again with an exhausted sigh. Dr. Leroy said this might happen: rapid-onset remembering. It feels a little like waking from a dream, that strange, ethereal sense of being neither here nor there, nor anywhere, and yet all the while having a deep and all-consuming notion that nothing will ever be the same.

My eyes are heavy again, and when I rest my head on a blue velvet throw pillow at my right, I can hear the palm trees rustling, and I give in to the newest memory flooding my mind.

There I am, in the house in San Diego, with boxes everywhere. From the living room window, I see a moving truck backing out of the driveway and heading away. The renovation took longer than expected, but after nine long months, we have a brand-new kitchen, hardwood floors, and a master bathroom. The apartment we rented was fine, but it's so good to finally be home.

There's a man in the distance, the same one from before. His back is turned to me, and I am overcome with an emotion I can't place at first. A moment later, I recognize its shrill, hot edges. Anger.

We are fighting. He promised to be home this weekend, to help me unpack and set up the house, but instead, he's driving to LA for some food industry event, and I am furious. I rub my swollen belly—I'll be twenty-two weeks pregnant on Monday—and head out to the patio, where I sink into a chaise longue and sulk.

A few minutes later, I feel a warm hand on my shoulder. "Hey," he says. "Can we talk?"

I don't want to talk to him. I just want him to be here. To help me unpack all these twenty-six thousand boxes. I sigh, staring straight ahead.

"Remember our honeymoon?" he says, kneeling beside me. "Those incredible tacos we found in that little place along the road?"

I nod, still looking straight ahead, arms folded, holding my ground.

"I still think that pineapple salsa is one of the best things I've ever eaten."

"Me too," I say softly, the memory disarming me somehow.

"I'm sorry I have to go this weekend," he continues. "If it weren't such an important meeting with these investors from New York, I'd bag the whole thing and stay here with you.

It's only for two nights. Just leave the boxes until I'm home." He tucks a lock of my hair behind my ear. "Hey, how about I make tacos tonight?"

"Okay," I say, cracking a smile. He kisses my cheek and heads to the kitchen.

It's hard to stay mad at him long, this husband of mine. I close my eyes tightly, remembering our honeymoon. At once, there we are in Tulum, Mexico.

Victor looks perfect in his new shirt, linen with a tropical banana-leaf print. A little zany, maybe, but when I saw it in a shop window a few weeks ago, I couldn't resist buying it for him to wear on the trip. Every man should have a tropical shirt in his closet. I smile to myself in the backseat of the taxi, watching him study a map of Mexico as the car barrels along the road, half-dirt, half-paved in places, a thick forest of palm trees and tropical vegetation on either side of us.

The driver slows down and pulls over in front of an unmarked road. "Do you think this is it?" I ask skeptically. It's hard to believe that just yesterday we exchanged vows at that little church on Coronado Island.

"*Husband.* It's such a funny word, isn't it?" I said to him on the plane.

"So is *wife,*" he said, laughing.

We might have new titles now, but we're still the same, Victor and I. Two people madly in love, embarking on the beginning of our lifetime together.

In the beginning, his family in Paris had been less than thrilled with the idea of his marrying an American and moving to San Diego, but they came around, especially after that first visit when they saw the house we'd eventually be living in, my childhood home. When his mother set her eyes on the pool, I think she actually wanted to move right in. "Might we come for a week in the fall?" she asked sweetly the day they flew home. "Paris is so miserable in October."

I smile to myself as Victor checks his phone. "Yep, the address is correct. Look," he says, pointing to a sign that's partially obscured by a palm branch. THE ALMA INN.

We carry our luggage up a sandy pathway to an open-air check-in desk. "Welcome," a woman says, handing us each a cocktail of some sort. "Mescal margaritas."

"Mescal?" I ask.

She smiles. "It's a smoky tequila. Try it; I think you'll like it."

I take a sip and nod. It's indeed smoky and just a bit sweet—perfectly balanced.

She hands Victor our room keys, then leads us down a winding path that leads to the beach. Nobody seems to be wearing shoes here, so I kick off my sandals.

"Here we are," she says, pointing to the most

charming little thatch-roofed bungalow, so close to the ocean you could practically leap right in from the front steps.

"Vic," I squeal. "It's perfect!"

"I'll leave you," the woman says, smiling shyly. "Congratulations."

I walk toward the door, but Victor stops me. "Not like that," he says, scooping me into his arms. "Like this."

He carries me over the threshold of our little bungalow, where we will spend the next week in each other's arms.

"I'm the happiest man in the world," he says.

"And I'm the happiest lady." I smile, reminiscing. "Remember the day we met, in Paris?"

He nods. "You thought I was, what did you say, a Casanova?" His English is perfect, but I still think it's cute the way certain words he pronounces come out sounding distinctly foreign.

"Yeah," I say. "I thought you were a player, like all the other Frenchmen I met that summer."

"Well, I thought you were cocky."

I smile, reaching for his hand. "It was about time you found a woman who could hold her own."

He smiles as I hold up his hand, twisting his gold wedding band around his finger. "Do you want to look now?"

He begins to pull his ring off. Inside its inner edge is a surprise inscription I've left for him. There's one inside my ring, too. Our wedding gifts to each other. We decided to wait until the first day of our honeymoon for the reveal.

"Now?"

"Wait," I say, inching closer to him. We both hold our rings expectantly. "Remember that day we stumbled upon that magical little garden in Montmartre?"

"How could I forget?"

"And how we drank wine and watched the sunset and stayed there until the stars came out?"

He nods.

"Remember what you said, about how the stories of our lives are . . ."

"Written in the stars," we both say at the same time.

He smiles. "Look at the inscription on your ring."

My arms erupt in goosebumps. "You too."

Together we hold them up, reading the words we have left for each other.

I smile, misty-eyed. "Of course we'd pick the same thing."

"Written in the stars," I say.

"*Écrit dans les étoiles,*" he repeats in French.

The waves crash loudly onto the shore outside. I slip my ring back on and quickly change into a swimsuit before casting a playful glance in Victor's direction. "Race you to the beach!"

He jumps to his feet, but not fast enough. I've already gotten a head start and reach the water's edge first. Salt water sprays my face as he wraps his arms around my waist, picking me up and spinning me around.

I lean my back against Victor, his arms draped lovingly around my waist as we stare out at the turquoise sea, transfixed by its beauty, soft waves crashing at our feet.

"You know what I think?" I say.

"What?"

"I think if we have a little girl, someday . . . that we should name her Alma, after this place."

"Alma," he says, the ocean breeze picking up his voice and sending it down the shore and beyond, like a message fit to broadcast to the world. "Alma it is."

I feel a cool hand on my arm, and my eyes flash open. Margot is hovering over me as I lie on the couch. "I'm sorry to wake you," she says cautiously. "It's just that you've been sleeping so long. I thought I'd make sure you're feeling all right."

"Yes," I say, sitting up, startled. "I mean," I begin, swallowing hard as I blink back tears. I can't find my words.

Margot sits beside me and squeezes my hand. "Everything's going to be okay," she whispers.

A draft of cold air wisps against my skin, and I shiver, wondering how anything could ever be okay again.

CHAPTER 22

CÉLINE

AUGUST 24, 1944
Paris, France

My water breaks at half past three. Not a slow trickle, like the birth stories of other women I know, friends who've shared nostalgically as they sipped their espressos. Nor does this feel like anything I experienced at Cosi's birth. No, this . . . this is entirely different. The pain rushes through me now as fluid surges down my legs like a violent waterfall, staining the rug in the bedroom. I'll be punished for that, of course. Maybe a cigarette burn on my inner thigh, like the time I dropped an expensive crystal vase in the dining room. It cracked in three places, sending a river of water and mangled tulip stems onto the wood floor. And while Reinhardt raged about the priceless vase, deliberating about what my punishment would be, I could only stare at the purple tulips and think of Papa. How I miss him, especially now.

The stain on the rug is the least of my worries. The baby is coming, and fast. Reinhardt won't be home for at least three hours, maybe longer, if he stays out drinking with the other officers. The reality of pregnancy displeased him, and the larger I got, the less he summoned me to his bedroom, choosing to pass the time with other women—many other women.

I've heard their screams from our bedroom at night, Cosi too. I clutched my pillow, both comforted and frightened by the alternate moaning and screaming. As awful as it was, at least it meant a reprieve from Reinhardt's terror.

The ten months we've been held hostage have been a nightmare, to say the least. But I've learned to survive the repeated assaults by detaching from my body and slipping into the garden in my mind. Luc's there; Papa and Cosi, too. There are peonies and roses, hydrangeas and lilacs. Tulips in the spring, alliums in the fall. Flowers for all seasons. Flowers to drown out the agony.

And there is no shortage of agony. Just after dinner last night, Reinhardt poured himself a glass of whiskey and summoned me to the sofa to buff his boots.

"I saw a friend of yours today," he said with a smile.

When I remained silent, he spoke again. "Aren't you going to ask me who?"

It could have been anyone; I just hoped he hadn't done anything to Luc.

When he prodded me with his right boot, I nodded in compliance. "Who?"

"That little tart Suzette."

My eyes widened. He must have followed me that day we had lunch together.

"No, I didn't lay a hand on her, if that's what you're wondering. Would've been impossible, anyway." He laughed, shifting his scuffed left boot so I could get a better angle. "You see, I got a call this afternoon from some of my men. There'd been a terrible disturbance in the street, down in the ninth arrondissement, that needed to be . . . taken care of." I looked up at his face, which I rarely did unless forced to. There were dark circles under his eyes. "The little bitch jumped off the roof of her building."

I gasp, covering my mouth.

"Have you ever seen what a body looks like all splayed out on the street?"

I felt a surge of nausea rise in my body as my eyes erupted in tears. *Oh, Suzette. Not like this.* In my mind's eye, I saw her beautiful face, her joyful blue eyes, the two of us skipping through the park after school, our hair in braids tied with ribbons. I thought of our last conversation, and how I'd hoped we'd persevere the way lotus flowers do. But, sadly, Suzette had succumbed to the murky waters below. She never found the light, as I had hoped for her, for us. *Would I?*

Suddenly, I feel my first contraction, mild at

first, then slowly radiating through my mid-section. Reinhardt stands up abruptly, as I clutch my belly, preparing for another wave of pain. With each passing minute, it only intensifies.

On one drunken night, Reinhardt threatened to kill me, to plunge a knife in my belly, carving out two lives in one fell swoop. Sometimes I wish he had just gotten it over with. The termination of terror. Though a violent death, it would be quick enough. My baby, if a girl, wouldn't be subjected to rape and torture in the way I had. She wouldn't ever know what a wretched place the world had become right before my very eyes.

But there are three of us, not just two. Who would see to Cosi's safety in her little room below the floor? How would she ever escape? The news of Suzette's death has unsettled me deeply and nearly depleted my scarce reserve of strength. But I must find more. Just a little more.

In my bedroom again, the contractions keep coming, one on top of the next, like the strong waves on the beaches of my childhood. I close my eyes and try to remember how I giggled and screamed, running in and out of the surf, as my mother and Papa watched from a blanket in the distance. But these aren't Normandy waves. They crash into my body with great force, and I cry out in agony.

What would Luc think, I wonder, to find me

like this? Would he still love me? Or would he be disgusted by my state?

Another bolt of pain surges, this one worse than the others, as Reinhardt's heavy footsteps pound down the hallway and to the front door. I hear it creak open and then slam shut, and I am grateful that he has gone, at least for now.

There is more blood now. Too much blood. I feel weary, dizzy. The August heat is sweltering, and sweat drips from my brow. I lie down on the bed, blood quickly soaking the sheets beneath me. I don't have much time left, I know that. I open my mouth to cry, but nothing comes out.

"Cosi," I say, forming my daughter's name with my parched lips, but my voice is only a whisper, not nearly loud enough for her to make out. I don't have the strength to stand, and my breathing is very shallow. I hear my beloved daughter moving around in the little room below the floor. Hours have passed. She must be terrified. "Cosi," I say again, with my last thread of strength, before my eyes close.

It's not clear how much time has passed when I am roused by the sound of the door hinges. My eyes flutter open, just for a moment. It's no longer night, and light streams in from the window. Hovering over me are two familiar faces: Esther and . . . Luc!

I don't know if I'm awake or dreaming. I close

my eyes, then open them again, blinking back tears at the sight of the man I love.

"We finally found you," Luc says, tears welling up in his eyes. "The housekeeper let us in, on her way out. She was carrying a suitcase. I don't know whether she's working with the Germans or not, but at least she had the decency to let us in before she fled. She said we'd find you here."

Information is coming at me so fast, I can barely take it all in. Nic, he continues, had come through, as I'd always hoped, sending word to Esther of my whereabouts. Together, they'd planned the rescue. Luc had anticipated a confrontation with at least one German, so he'd come armed.

I open my mouth to speak, but no words come out. Luc is crying. He tucks his hand in mine as Esther lifts up my skirt and pulls my legs open. Usually steady and composed, her face is ashen as she looks up at Luc. "We need to get her help. Now."

The room is spinning. I'm so very weary. My eyelids feel like two heavy bricks, but I will them to open. I must tell them about Cosi, that my little girl is hiding in a space beneath the floorboards. Cosi can hear them now, certainly, but, with the floorboards muffling sound, she won't be able to make out Luc's voice, or Esther's. She has no way of knowing whether the people above are here to help or hurt her, so she will do what I instructed her to do, always: stay quiet and wait for the signal, three knocks, that all is well.

I know this is what Cosi is doing now, and it breaks my heart. I look up at Luc, terror stricken. "Cosi," I whisper, my voice hardly detectable. "The . . . room."

Luc and Esther exchange glances. "I think she's trying to tell us something," he says.

Esther shakes her head. "She's delirious. She's lost too much blood. If we don't get her to the hospital soon, we might lose her, and"—she swallows hard—"the baby."

As Luc carries me through the door and to the elevator, I reach my arms back to the apartment with every ounce of my remaining strength. "Cosi!" I cry. This time, my weak voice registers, and Luc nods.

"I know," Luc says. "We'll find her. I promise."

They don't understand that Cosi is just steps away, locked in a prison beneath the floor. And as they rush me into the elevator, I can only weep, whispering my daughter's name over and over again—though all Esther and Luc can hear are muffled moans.

I have no strength left, not even an ounce. As my eyes close, I see Cosi's little face. She is clutching Monsieur Dubois, in the apartment with Papa. They are talking about Normandy. I can hear her voice, like a comforting melody.

"Will you take me there? Someday? And can we

get a tarte normande, the kind you used to love as a little girl?"

"Yes, sweet child."

"And can we look for treasure on the beach, and throw rocks in the water, and look for starfish in the tide pools?"

"I promise."

CHAPTER 23

CAROLINE

"Come on," Margot says. "You went to all the trouble to buy that gorgeous dress and now you won't go?"

I sink into the couch with an exhausted sigh. Since the avalanche of memories returned, I have little interest in attending my art show this evening. "I just don't feel up to it."

"I've seen your art," she says. "You have talent." She picks up the dress on the hanger and holds it up. "And you have a beautiful dress. Get up, girl! Let's get you ready!"

I've been dodging Victor's phone calls for days. I'm definitely not ready to see him, especially now that I *know*. I have so many unanswered questions—most notably, why he's kept the truth from me. It feels like a betrayal. But I'd told Inès I'd attend; besides, my name is already printed in the program.

"Okay," I say, standing up.

"That's the spirit," Margot says.

She curls my hair into loose waves, then applies my makeup. I barely recognize myself in the mirror afterward.

"You look like a million bucks," she says, grinning in the doorway as I zip up my dress.

"Thanks," I say, skeptically, as I reach for my purse. I only wish I *felt* like a million bucks. The truth is, I feel like ten cents.

"There you are!" Inès exclaims as I walk through the door. The studio is packed. I scan the crowd and am relieved when I don't see Victor.

"You look amazing," she says, kissing each of my cheeks.

"So do you." She's wearing a long, red silk dress, short sleeved, with a yellow sash around the waist—a look only Inès could pull off.

"Would you like a drink? Perrier? Wine?"

"Wine," I say quickly.

She returns with a glass of white wine, and I take a big sip of it, then another, as guests mill about eying our work. I see my paintings across the room, clustered together with a sign that shares my name and photo.

Inès leans in to me. "You wouldn't believe how many people have been inquiring about your paintings."

I nod, noticing Margot chatting with a particularly handsome man in a suit. I smile to myself. For the first time in a very long while, she's gotten a babysitter for Élian.

"I have no doubt all of them will be sold by the end of the night," Inès continues.

I should be happy, thrilled, but I can barely muster a smile.

She frowns. "Is something wrong?"

I shake my head, then take another big gulp from my wineglass. "No, no, everything's fine. Great."

She's unconvinced. "You don't seem like yourself."

"Well, I have all this makeup on," I say.

"No, it's not that." She looks at me quizzically.

"I got my memory back," I say through tears.

"That's great!" Inès says.

I shrug. "Not really."

She looks at me, confused, as I wipe away a fresh tear. "Inès, three years ago, I was an artist, living a happy life in San Diego. I had a husband and a daughter. I had a thriving art career."

"What happened?"

"My baby died," I say, trying my best to compose myself. "I don't think there's any amount of art therapy that can help a person get over that."

Inès reaches for my hand, stunned. "I'm so sorry," she whispers. She's the person who always seems to have the solution for everything, and I can tell the wheels in her mind are turning. "You know what?" she says a moment later. "You should talk to my mother."

"Your mother?"

She nods. "She's not in the best health, sadly, but she's as sharp as a tack, and the strongest person I know. She might be able to give you some interesting perspective on grief."

I shake my head. "How so?"

"Trust me," she says. "Just talk to her."

"Okay," I say, reaching for another glass of wine.

An hour and a half later, I've lost track of my wine consumption, and I feel light and numb all over. Several Bistro Jeanty regulars came, including Monsieur Ballard, which made me smile. Before he left, he said, "No more formalities between friends. My name is Nicolas. Please just call me Nic."

You could say that it's a perfect night, I guess. But as much as I worry about the possibility of seeing Victor, for some reason his absence hurts now. Surely, after everything, he'll at least show up, look me in the eye, offer an apology, even if I can't accept it. I sigh. *How can I ever accept it?*

At nine-thirty, I decide to call it a night. Margot has already left to have a drink with handsome-suit guy. Good for her. But for me? It's time I go home.

"I'm sorry he didn't come," Inès says, kneeling down to retrieve a plastic cup from the floor.

"It's okay," I say with a sniff. "It's for the best."

And then the door hinges creak and a blast of cold air pummels in: Victor. He's standing just ahead, smiling nervously.

"Oh no, is it over?" he asks, rubbing his forehead. "Did I . . . miss it?" He's out of breath, his face awash with worry. He peers at his watch, then runs a hand through his thick wavy hair.

My heart surges with emotion.

"The restaurant was a nightmare tonight," he explains. "One of our ovens broke, and Julien is out with the flu." He pauses, taking a cautious step toward me. "Wow, you look . . . beyond stunning."

Inès disappears to the back room as he continues to speak, but I don't hear his words. I merely watch as his lips move. For a moment, I don't feel any anger or sadness.

He looks at the west wall of the gallery and touches my arm, and the audio comes into focus again. "Those must be yours?"

I nod, my eyes fixed on Victor.

"You've always been such a gifted artist." He smiles at me, his eyes misty. He knows I know.

"It was you," I say. "It was always you."

He approaches slowly, wiping away a tear. "Yes, my love."

I swallow hard.

"After . . . everything, and then the divorce," he says, "I couldn't bear it. I wanted so desperately to reach you, to break through your walls. I moved to Paris, bought the restaurant—all so we could try again. Start over. But you wouldn't, or couldn't." He rubs his forehead. "It killed me. And then you had your accident. I was beside myself. I came to the hospital each day, pretending to be a concerned stranger. I thought I'd lost you." His voice falters. "But then you pulled through. And I know it sounds crazy, but I couldn't help but wonder if your amnesia was an opportunity, in a sense. A chance for us to start fresh. When you came into Jeanty that morning, it was like I'd been given the most miraculous gift. You were . . . you again."

I look away, wiping a tear from my cheek.

"I just thought," Victor continues, tears spilling from his eyelids, "I just thought that if I could have one more shot, one more chance to get through to you, to court you all over again, that maybe, just maybe, you'd see that . . . we were and are and will always be . . . *written in the stars.*" He touches my cheek lightly. "Caroline, can you blame me for wanting to take that chance?"

I shake my head, my heart teeming with conflicting emotions. "But why couldn't you have told me the truth?" I take a step back. "You kept me in the dark for your own benefit."

He looks as if I've just punched him in the face. "I was there all along," he says. "After the accident, I made sure you were okay." He looks deeply into my eyes. "My love, please, try to understand that I did this all for *us.*"

I shake my head. "And what if I never regained my memory? That happens sometimes. Then what? Were you ever going to tell me about our daughter? Or would you keep her memory hidden from me because it was in *our* best interest?" I burst into tears, thrusting myself to the door and out to the street.

"Caroline!" he exclaims, following me outside.

I turn around. "You'll be happy to know that I just inherited my father's entire estate. But you already knew that, didn't you?"

He shakes his head. "What are you talking about?"

"It doesn't matter," I say. "Just tell me who the flowers were for."

"The flowers?"

"The flowers you bought the day we returned from Provence. Inès saw you with them."

"Caroline, they were for *you!*" He sighs. "That night you stormed out of the restaurant, I was going to . . ." He pauses when his voice cracks. "I was going to tell you everything and then ask you if you'd be willing to start over with me."

I look at him for a long moment. "Victor, even if that's the case, even if you are telling the truth, how can I get over the fact that our daughter died right before your very eyes?" Tears stream down my face. "Couldn't you have done something? Anything? Couldn't you have . . . saved her, Vic?" He pulls me to him, and I yield to his embrace, my makeup-tinged tears soiling the lapel of his navy jacket. I weep, clutching his chest.

"My love, don't you know that I carry the weight of that every day? I feel it right here"— he points to his heart—"when I wake up in the morning and when I go to sleep at night. There is no escape from that pain." He takes a deep breath. "And, my darling, I did try to save her. I tried with all my might. I've turned the scene over and over again in my mind, maybe a million times. I've talked to experts and therapists, the police detectives who were at the scene. And while I may never be able to forgive myself, I know now that there was nothing I could have done to prevent what happened."

I step back and take a deep breath, looking up into his eyes. He reaches his hands out to me, but I don't take them. I can't.

"Caroline," he pleads. "Let me love you."

"Oh, Vic," I say, my voice cracking, tears stinging the corners of my eyes. "I wish I could. I wish it so badly. But I just . . . can't."

We each failed our daughter; this is the price we had to pay. I take a step back, drape my coat over my shoulders, and walk ahead into the night, alone. Victor doesn't follow me. And with each step, I feel the familiar thorny vine growing around my heart. No more red lipstick. No more walks to Montmartre, or silly paintings and sketches.

All these weeks, I'd merely been dreaming. And now I'm awake—wide awake.

CHAPTER 24

AUGUST 25, 1944
Paris, France

Reinhardt wakes with an aching head. The insolent sun pierces brightly through his bedroom window, only making it worse. "Madame Huet," he shouts. "Come close my drapes at once!" When she doesn't appear at his door, he calls out again. "Madame Huet! I said get in here!" He holds his head in his hands and stumbles to the window, closing the curtains himself. "Damn housekeeper," he says. He ought to kill her like he did the rest of the women who'd lived here. Worthless, the lot of them.

He falls back into bed as last night's events come into focus like a bad dream, and he remembers that Madame Huet has left. Last night, he came home to find the apartment door gaping open. Madame Huet's room was empty and the suitcase under her bed gone, along with Céline. The only trace of her, in fact, was the bloodied sheets. "Whore!" Reinhardt had shouted, kicking the wall beside the bed.

He'd taken a heavy swig of vodka and wandered down to the street screaming Céline's name, like the angry owner of a dog who'd run away and, when found, would be severely punished. He roughed up a few passersby for information, but it was no use. Céline, it seemed, had vanished.

The streets of Paris felt different somehow. Germany was losing the war, and with it, its grip on the city. But he would still take what was rightly his. And when he saw that Bistro Jeanty was closed for the night, he laughed to himself. With a swift kick of his boot, the door hung flopping on one hinge, and he stumbled inside like a wild boar, knocking over tables and shattering polished wineglasses on his way to the bar, where he grabbed a bottle of scotch.

She wasn't supposed to leave. Not like that, without his permission, and bleeding all over the bed, too. He shook his head. *She* probably killed his child, the bitch. She wasn't strong enough to carry it. Weak. But that was his fault, after all. He should never have impregnated a Jew. All wrong. He needed a strong German woman. She'd have delivered a healthy child. She'd have given him an heir.

And yet, in some twisted way, Reinhardt loved Céline. He loved the way she smelled and tasted. He loved the pitch of her nose, the shape of her body in the moonlight, especially the deep curve that extended from the side of her waist to her hip. He also loved her spirit, even though it drove him crazy that she didn't fear him the way the other ones did. Yes, she cried out when he took his belt to her, but pain is different than fear, and Céline did not fear him. He could coax other women into submission, but not Céline, not even after all this time. And for that, she gave him a thrill unlike any other woman he'd had in Paris. She was his favorite. And now she is gone.

It's half past ten in the morning, and Reinhardt is alone in the apartment. He walks to the living room and finds on the table a telegram from one of his superiors that he didn't notice last night. The envelope is torn; Madame Huet probably read it before she left. Her departure shook him as much as did Céline's. He would have wagered money on the housekeeper's loyalty. But, it seems, she is having the last laugh.

Reinhardt holds the telegram in his trembling hands—just six brief words, but they tell him everything he needs to know: "The Allies are on their way."

He looks out the window, surveying the street below. His peers are piling into vehicles right and left; he recognizes one of them with whom he'd had dinner just two days ago. A teenage boy stands in the middle of the square waving a French flag. Reinhardt instinctively considers running for his rifle in the hall closet and planting a bullet in the idiot's skull, but it would draw attention. He knows he must go before it's too late, though it is already too late.

There isn't time to pack a bag or bring any

of his accumulated treasures from Paris—the priceless paintings, the clothes, the gilded mirrors he pilfered from the apartments he brutally raided. A shame to leave it all behind for thieves to loot. If Madame Huet had any sense, she'd have taken the silver, and maybe she did. There isn't time to check.

He dresses quickly in plain clothes so as not to be detected, then tucks a revolver under his belt before heading to the safe. Inside are piles of assorted watches, jewelry, and gold coins he's accumulated during his tenure in Paris. He stuffs as much as he can into his bag, then gives the apartment a final look. This isn't how he imagined things ending, in defeat. But he'll make a new life in Berlin, just as grand as the one he's had here. Yes, just as grand.

He begins walking to the door but pauses when he hears the muffled cry of a . . . child. *Strange,* he thinks; there aren't any children living in this building. He takes a few steps down the hallway, and the cries become louder; in fact, the sound seems to be coming from . . . Céline's room.

He pushes through the doorway, recoiling when he sees the bloody sheets. His stomach turns. And there it is again—the sound. A child, a little girl, crying out in desperation. "Mama," she cries. "Mama, please let me out!"

He smiles as he kneels down to the floorboards and listens to the muffled cries that emanate from just beneath. He'd almost forgotten that Céline had a daughter. He'd seen her in the flower shop, of course, and then his officers had captured her with that Jewish father of hers, or . . . had they?

Rage surges in him like a stoked fire. She'd hidden her daughter in here somehow. All this time. How had she deceived him like this?

"Please," the girl sobs. "Mama, please."

Her crying displeases him, and he wants to make it stop. He pats his hands along the floorboards, pressing on them until one gives a little. A hidden floor. He's heard about things like this, people hiding Jews in cellars and false rooms, where they live in darkness like rats. He shakes his head. He'll get this rodent; he'll put a bullet through her head.

It won't be a difficult task, not for Reinhardt. He's killed children before, women too. So many women. Some right here in this very apartment. Killing this one will feel especially good—his final duty for the Fatherland before he flees.

What a delight it will be when she squeals in terror. His fingers are too thick to wedge into the groove of the flooring, so he retrieves a crowbar from his bedroom, its edges flecked with dried blood.

"Mama!" the girl cries out again, as Reinhardt sets his revolver on the floor, at the ready.

"Shut up, you little bitch!" he shouts, digging

the edge of the crowbar into the floor as he stumbles and loses his balance.

"Shit," he says, picking himself up, even more determined to exterminate what lies below.

The bedroom window has been left propped open, and he pauses when he hears commotion on the street below, prompting him to have a look.

To his horror, an armored tank barrels past, followed by another, and another, with American soldiers marching beside them. He knows he must leave. This cat and mouse game with a silly schoolgirl might be one he would enjoy winning in other times, but not now.

Reinhardt retrieves the revolver, then runs to the living room, where he stands on the balcony that overlooks the street below. He knows that if he runs, he'll be a sitting duck—shot in the back and flayed like a . . . His heart beats faster. And if he stays . . . He pauses, hearing the sound of heavy footsteps outside the apartment.

He imagines his homeland, the life that had been promised to him—the one he's never had. He's sacrificed everything for Germany, and Germany has failed him. Or has he failed Germany? A tear falls from his eye as he grips the revolver tightly. He pushes the gun's barrel deep into his mouth. Today, the only recipient of his bullet would be him. And in his final act for the Fatherland, Reinhardt pulls the trigger.

CHAPTER 25

CAROLINE

Days pass, then weeks. Victor doesn't call, not that I expect him to. I've said my goodbye, and I meant it. There is no use pretending anymore, for either of us. Surely he sees the value in that, of each of us getting on with our lives without causing each other further pain.

I avoid Bistro Jeanty, opting for another nearby café for my meals. It's not nearly as good, and the coffee is bitter, but I . . . won't go back.

Margot has found childcare for Élian and has returned to the restaurant. I told her that she can stay in the apartment as long as she wants as long as she doesn't mention Victor; she agreed.

I bought some new furniture, booked a trip to Italy in November. Margot says I should pick up yoga, and I promise her I'll give it a try.

While my memory first started coming back in a slow trickle, it now feels like a raging faucet that I can't shut off. Just this morning, I remembered the password to open my laptop screen: "Peony."

After breakfast, I type in the word, and like magic, I have access to the inner sanctum of my laptop, which turns out to be quite boring.

No emails of significance, no racy online dating profile, no Pinterest board. But then a Word document in the upper right corner of the desktop catches my eye. It's titled "Letter to Victor." I click on it.

September 19, 2007

Dear Victor,

I'm living in Paris now. I figured that after everything, I should write to you. I realize I left suddenly, and I hope you can understand that it was just too painful for me to stay in our house. I want you to know that you may stay there as long as you like. Forever, even.

I like living here. I like that no one knows me. I like that people don't come up to me at the market and ask how I'm doing or look at me as if I have cancer.

It's strange being here without you. I think a lot about the day we met, of all the happy memories we've shared here. Those moments seem so long ago, so far away.

I could have never predicted this for us. Losing Alma. The divorce. Sometimes I wake up at night in a cold sweat, believing that it's all a horrible dream. And then reality rushes in, and I realize the bad dream is my life.

You always said that we have little control over the paths our lives take, that they unfold as they will. If that's the case, then let's do that, let them unfold, without forcing or fighting things. I don't know where my life will lead me. But, as you always say, it's already written in the stars. Whether the story of us has a happy ending or not, only the stars know.

This is very hard to write, but I need to ask you to let me go. I can't bear to see you. It's too painful. Please do not write or call, either.

I will always love you, always think of you, always wish I had been strong enough to keep holding your hand.

I'm so very sorry.

Love,
Caroline

I close my laptop, stunned by my own words. I don't remember writing the letter. If he'd actually received it, it must have wounded him deeply. But even so, he came to Paris. He tried.

I look out the window, blinking back tears as I glance at the clock. I'll have to hurry. I've promised Inès that I'd meet her at her mother's apartment at one o'clock for coffee. I'll be late if I don't leave soon.

• • •

I sigh as I bypass the elevator and climb the stairs to the second-floor apartment where Inès's mother lives, on a quiet, shady street about a ten-minute walk from the art studio. She'd insisted that talking to her mother would do me some good, and while I resisted for a time, I was no match for Inès's determination. "She wants to have coffee with you on Tuesday at one o'clock," she'd said. "You don't want to disappoint an old lady."

Inès greets me at the door and invites me in to the small, but beautiful, apartment. She takes my coat and gestures toward the sunlit living room, where dozens of family photos hang over the fireplace. By the window, an old woman with white, wispy hair sits in a reclining chair. "Come," Inès says. "Meet my mother.

"Mama, Caroline is here. The woman I've been telling you about."

The old woman's eyes light up. "My daughter told me you are quite the talented artist."

Inès nods. "She even has a studio in California."

"California!" the old woman says. "There are palm trees there."

I smile as Inès brings me a cup of coffee, and I take a seat in a chair beside her mother.

"We had a trip planned last year, but Mom got sick," Inès says.

"I'll be well by spring, and we can plan another," the old woman counters.

I smile, admiring her tenacity.

Inès's phone rings, and she excuses herself to the kitchen to take the call.

"Now," the old woman says. "Inès says you've had a painful past."

"Yes," I say.

"That makes two of us," she says, looking out to the street. "I was just a tiny thing when the German Army marched into Paris and changed our lives forever. I lost my whole family in the war."

I place my hand on my heart. "I'm so sorry."

"A part of you never really gets over that sort of pain, but after all these years, you know what I've come to learn?"

I shake my head.

"Pain and grief want to do one thing: suck you down with them." She makes a fist. "And when you do, they win. Now, who would want that to happen?"

I smile.

"I know what you're thinking: that I'm just an old woman with silly ideas."

"No, I—"

"It's okay. I probably do seem silly. But the beauty of old age is you start to care less about what others think of you, and instead focus on what really matters." She reaches for my hand and squeezes it tightly. "Inès says that you're hurting. She told me your story."

I swallow hard.

"That sweet daughter of yours wouldn't want you to drown in your grief. Keep swimming to shore. I promise, you can make it. I did."

I wipe away a tear as Inès returns from the kitchen. After that, our conversation remains light, and a half hour later, we say our goodbyes. Inès's mother looks out the window. It's started raining. "I hope you don't have far to walk, dear. It's a monsoon out there."

"Not far," I say.

"Caroline lives on the rue Cler," Inès adds, "not far from the studio."

"Oh, where?"

"Eighteen rue Cler," I say.

Her eyes brighten. "Yes, I know the concierge there."

"Monsieur de Goff?"

She nods. "Like me, he was torn from his family during the war. A German soldier ripped his teddy bear from his arms, not far from your apartment." She takes a deep breath. "You may not know it, but underneath all those layers of pain, there's a wonderful man inside, with the purest heart. He's been a good friend to me, and a confidant."

I wonder if the two were ever romantically connected, but decide not to ask.

"Well," the old woman continues, "be well, Caroline. Remember what I told you."

"I will," I say, smiling, then hugging Inès before heading to the door.

I look for Monsieur de Goff when I return, but he's not at his post. Inès's mother's words linger as I head to the elevator, just as Estelle barrels through the door. I wave. I'd almost forgotten that she was coming over today.

In the apartment, she sets her bag down on the coffee table, beside my open sketchbook, which Margot must have been looking at and left open, as I'd long since tucked it away.

"Wow," she says, "is this . . . yours?"

I nod, quickly closing the book. "It's nothing."

"No," she continues. "It's really good. I didn't know you were an artist."

"I'm not," I say. "I mean, I used to be, but I'm not anymore."

Her face is serious. "With all due respect, I don't think anyone can stop being who she truly is."

"Then I'm an artist who stopped making art," I say. "Better?" There's a sharpness to my voice that didn't used to be there. I notice it at the market when I talk to the vendors, or in the morning when Margot and I are in the kitchen together and she attempts to make small talk.

"I'm sorry," she mutters. "I didn't mean anything by—"

"No," I reply. "*I'm* sorry. I . . . haven't been myself lately."

"It's okay," she says.

"How has the project been going?"

"Great," she says, opening her bag to retrieve her notebook and pen. "I have so much to tell you, but first, do you mind if I have a look in the back bedrooms?"

"Sure," I say, leading her down the hallway to the bedroom where Margot and Élian are staying. I switch on the light. "It's not much, but . . . here you are."

"This is it," she says, taking it all in. "This is the place. I can feel it."

"What do you mean?" I ask.

She silently surveys the room, studying each curve of the plaster, each nail in the trim around the window before looking up at me again.

"With the help of some of my friends in the chemistry lab, I was able to salvage more of the pages in the nurse's diary. Those, coupled with written accounts and all of my interviews . . . well, I can finally paint an accurate picture."

I nod.

"Imagine this," she continues. "It's the late fall of 1943. Your name is Céline, and you and your father own a flower shop nearby, just on the rue Cler. Paris is occupied by the Germans, and you must look over your shoulder everywhere you go. Your father is part Jewish, but with a French last name. It shouldn't matter, you tell yourself. Your family's last name is Moreau. Nobody will give you trouble. And so you send your little girl to school each day, and you tend to your flowers. Cosette, Cosi for short, is eight. She is your world."

"Cosi," I say, smiling.

Estelle takes a deep breath and nods. "Then, one day, out of nowhere, a high-ranking German officer living at eighteen rue Cler takes an interest in you. He can have any woman, by force, but he wants you."

I feel a chill creep over me.

"He threatens you. Tells you that your father will be imprisoned if you don't obey his wishes. You call his bluff and attempt to escape, but he intercepts your plan. He arrests your father and little girl. And you watch them drive away in a Nazi vehicle."

I place my hand on my mouth as Estelle continues to pace the room.

"But, in an unexpected twist of fate, your little girl breaks free from her captors and follows you to eighteen rue Cler, where you have two choices: send her running into the streets alone, German soldiers at every turn, or smuggle her into the apartment, where you can do your best to protect her."

I swallow hard, listening to her every word. I know bits and pieces of the story already, of course, but as Estelle speaks, she fleshes out more details, and the story of Céline and Cosi doesn't just feel familiar, it somehow feels a part of me.

"You choose the latter. As the weeks progress, your life is a . . . nightmare. The German officer keeps you locked in the apartment with an evil housekeeper who sees that you don't escape. You are raped and brutalized. All the while, little Cosi hides, tucked away in this very bedroom, dependent on any water or nourishment you can smuggle in for her. Then, one day, you discover an indentation in the floorboards at the foot of the bed." Estelle kneels down and pats her hand around the floor. "You suspect that there's a space of some sort beneath the flooring, a hidden room." She runs her finger along a narrow groove between two floorboards. "And you wedge your fingers between it and pry the panel open. You and Cosi gaze into the dark expanse. It's cold and dark, but it means safety for Cosi. She bravely climbs down, and you give her your blanket to keep her warm. She doesn't complain. She's a brave little girl."

I wipe away a tear.

"Your abuse continues, worsening, even. One day you discover you are pregnant. As the child inside of you grows, your hope fades. You obsess about ways to escape, how to outsmart the housekeeper, but to no avail. But then the German officer leaves for an extended period of time. The baby is coming soon. And on a sweltering day in August, you know it's time.

You're in a great deal of pain, but you try to hide it from Cosi. You must be brave for her. But when the contractions surge like knives through your back, radiating down your legs, you know you don't have much time left. And then help comes. The nurse, Esther—the woman who lives below you—and Luc, your love. You don't know if you're hallucinating or not. You've lost a lot of blood. But their faces seem so real. They must be real."

I hang on her every word.

"And they are real. And they lift you from your bloodstained bed, and they carry you out of this godforsaken jail cell. But without Cosi. She's quietly waiting in the little space beneath the floor. It's too difficult for her to let herself out, as hard as she tries. Maybe if she were nine, a big girl. But she's eight now, and not nearly tall enough to push the little hatch open. And you are not strong enough to tell your rescuers that they must rescue one more soul. Your Cosi. Your sweet Cosette."

"Good Lord," I say, weeping.

"You've lost too much blood. You try to tell them, but you have no voice. You're somewhere between here and there, life and death. All you can think of as you're carried to safety, to a hospital bed where doctors will attempt to save your life, and the new life inside of you, is that you have left your little girl behind."

"My God," I say, running to the foot of the bed and falling to my knees. My cheeks are stained with tears. Estelle and I exchange glances. "Do you think she's . . ." I look down at the floor.

She squeezes my hand. "I don't know, but it's time someone tried to find out."

"Wait," I say, my heart beating fast. "I don't know if I . . ." But then I pause and think of Alma. What if this had happened to *us?* What if she had been left this way? What if she had . . . perished here? I'd want her to be found, to be laid to rest. I'd also want her to be *remembered.* "It's . . . okay," I continue. "Go ahead."

Estelle nods, prying the edge of the flooring up. Cautiously, we both peer into the darkness below. Estelle reaches for a flashlight in her bag, carefully scouring each corner.

"It's empty," she says.

We're both equal parts relieved, confused, and disturbed.

"Do you think she . . . survived?" I ask.

Estelle sits down on the bed. Élian's stuffed bunny is just behind her. "I'm not sure. We aren't the first to pry this hatch open." She glances at her watch. "But I'm going to find out. You gave me the phone number of the couple who bought the apartment years ago and remodeled it." I think of Monsieur de Goff, and all of his reasons for being the way he is. "Thankfully, the woman agreed to speak to me. You should come."

"But it's your project," I counter. "Wouldn't I just be intruding?"

"Not at all," she says. "It might sound silly, but I have a feeling that you are meant to be there."

CHAPTER 26

CAROLINE

Maybe they're not home?" I say to Estelle after she rings number 304 on the callbox a third time.

"I'll just try once more," she says, undeterred.

This time a woman answers.

"It's Estelle. May we come up?"

"Oh dear, yes," the woman says. "I'm sorry to keep you waiting. I was on the phone and lost track of time."

Marcella, tall, with curly dark hair, greets us at the door of her third-floor apartment. She wears leggings and an oversized sweater, her right wrist clad in assorted gold bracelets.

"Please, sit down," she says, pointing to the couch.

I introduce myself and explain my connection to Estelle's project.

"Ah, it's a grand apartment, isn't it?" she says, reminiscing the way one might about the one that got away.

I nod. "It is."

"I will always wonder if we made the right decision letting it go when we did. But I just had to keep coming back to that day . . ."

Estelle leans in and opens her notebook, pen at the ready. "Tell me about it."

Marcella's eyes flutter a bit, as if straining to remember the pain of an unrequited love.

"We'd gotten married the previous summer and had been looking for a home in Paris for the better part of a year. You might say we were picky, but we knew exactly what we wanted. A balcony for me, and sufficient kitchen space for Manuel. He hates galley kitchens." She takes a deep breath. "Well, it was one disappointing listing after the next. Until . . . eighteen rue Cler."

Estelle and I exchange glances. "The apartment had sat empty for almost fifty years until it came on the market that day," she continues. "No one knows the full story, but the agent at Sotheby's provided some details in the listing notes. During the occupation of Paris, a high-ranking German officer had reportedly fancied the address and chosen it as his home, sending the residents, a Jewish family, to a work camp, where they all eventually perished. After the war, the French government did their best to return properties like this to their rightful owners, but in many cases, the owners had long since passed, and next of kin often couldn't be located." She shakes her head. "Properties sat empty, in trusts, which was the fate of eighteen rue Cler until Parliament passed a new law dictating that such unclaimed properties be sold, with all proceeds going to specific humanitarian and government programs. As awful as it was to learn that a Jewish family had been ripped from that home, and had endured unthinkable things, we couldn't do anything about it. But we could buy the apartment and allow our funds to go to good use. To us, that felt redemptive, somehow, even if in just a small way."

Estelle nods as Marcella glances out the window, lost in thought. "Well, we fell in love with it immediately, which isn't a surprise. Our real estate agent, Monsieur Petit, who, by the way, had a substantial gut"—she pauses to pierce the air, thick with memories, with a nervous laugh. "Anyway, he tried to talk us out of buying it. It needed so much work, he said, and the permits would take forever. It would be years before the renovation would be complete." She shakes her head. "But we wouldn't listen. We had to have it. But when we got into the remodel, we learned that our real estate agent was right. The apartment needed new, well, everything. It was a monster of a project, but at the time, we were up for the challenge. I stopped in every day to check on the construction progress, and it was a delight to see it slowly transform into the place we envisioned it to be, until . . . one day."

Estelle's gaze narrows. "What day?"

"I don't remember the exact date, just that it was in August. It was so hot. I'd bicycled over, like I always did, after work. I brought Eduardo, our contractor, takeout." She pauses, frowning. "I'll never forget the look on his face."

"What sort of look?" Estelle asks.

"Shock," Marcella replies. "He came out of the far bedroom holding a crowbar, covered in dust and debris. He looked like he'd . . . seen a ghost." She swallows hard. "He told me there was something important that I needed to see. I wish it had been something like ants, or even rats." She shakes her head. "But it was far worse."

My heart beats faster.

"Ed had been prepping the floors for sanding when he noticed a loose floorboard, concealing a hidden room beneath." She covers her mouth. "I can still remember the smell, that awful, musty smell."

Estelle's gaze remains fixed on Marcella. "What are you saying you found in there, exactly?"

"At first, I didn't know what I was looking at," she says. "Ed's hand was shaking so badly."

"Did you find . . . remains?" Estelle asks cautiously.

I cover my mouth.

"No," Marcella says. "But it was obvious that a child had been kept there, for a long time, perhaps. It's possible that her remains had decayed, been destroyed by an animal, or had been disposed of years ago, quietly. Or maybe she was rescued in the end. I just don't know."

"She?" I ask. "How do you know the child was a girl?"

"Ed recovered a few items, including a moth-eaten dress." She pulls a wooden box from beneath her coffee table and lifts the lid. "And these." Inside is a very ragged brown teddy bear, which she hands to Estelle for examination, followed by a weathered, and quite water-stained, leather diary of some sort.

"It was hers," Marcella says. "Cosi's." She opens up the diary and touches one of the pages. "She must have been an angel. You can tell, just by reading her sweet words. And to be kept in the dark that way . . ."

"Did you find anything else?"

"No," she says. "I mean, nothing of importance. I think Ed also mentioned a broken pitcher and a flashlight. We notified the police, of course, and they were able to verify that a German officer had once lived in the apartment." She nods decidedly, turning back to the box of relics from so long ago. "I couldn't bear to turn these over to the police. Somehow, it didn't seem right for a child's most precious possessions to be locked up in a lonely police department. So I kept them. For her." She hands them to Estelle. "But I'd like you to have them now." She smiles.

Estelle smiles. "It would be an honor."

"After all that, my husband and I decided to say goodbye to eighteen rue Cler. We sold it soon after, to a real-estate management company that wanted to finish the renovation, then put it into a portfolio of short-term rentals for Americans looking for chic Paris apartments." She shrugs. "We couldn't sell it fast enough."

"I can understand completely," Estelle says.

"Oh," Marcella continues. "I almost forgot about the necklace."

"The necklace?" I say.

"Yes. We narrowly missed it, but Ed found it in a corner." She shakes her head. "How he had the courage to go down there like that I don't know." She runs to an antique bureau across the room, selects a small envelope from a drawer, then opens it, depositing the contents in Estelle's hand: a locket on a little gold chain. The clasp is stiff, but she's able to pry it open. Whatever was once inside is now gone.

"All of this is just . . . extraordinary," Estelle says, obviously moved.

I fan through the pages of the diary, reading Cosi's sweet musings about her little world, her hopes, her dreams, her fears. And then my eyes stop on a page toward the back. One passage in particular catches my eye:

I've had so much time to think down here, and I want to say that I think that the most important things in life are thankfulness, forgiveness, and love. Mama taught me to always be thankful. And when you say thank you it makes other people feel happy. And forgiveness, because, life is too short to be cross. It's also not fun. And, last but not least, love—because when you have love in your heart, nothing and no one can take it away from you.

"You're crying," Estelle says to me. Her eyes are misty, too.

"I've always hoped," Marcella says, "after all the unspeakable things Cosi may have endured, that her story could help someone, somehow."

I nod. "It already has."

Estelle and I sit at a nearby café for a long time after we leave Marcella's apartment. "Do you think Cosi survived somehow?" I ask, taking a sip of my second double espresso. "Do you think she could still be living today?"

"Maybe," she says, eying the little teddy bear. "Though, sadly, I think it's unlikely."

The sky is undecided: one part sun, one part dark clouds, and like the present and the past, both are battling for their presence to be known. The outcome is still unclear.

Estelle entrusts the little box to me before she leaves for class. I linger at the café a moment longer, unable to stop thinking of Cosi. I lift the lid of the wooden box and pull out the diary.

"Today is my half birthday," one entry reads. "Papa will sing, and Mama and I will get a croissant at the bakery." These are the words of a child from another era, a soul I will never know, and yet, I can hear her voice, loud and clear, as if she's sitting right beside me on this bench, legs dangling just like Alma's would have been.

I read, and I read, and I read, of her hopes and her dreams, of the way she worries for her mama when she hears her screaming in the other room with the "bad man." And then I come to the very last page. Her handwriting is different here, fainter, messy, unsteady. It's a farewell, I can see that. "I think today may be my last day. I will tuck away this little book and hold on to Monsieur Dubois and pray for heaven."

I wipe away a tear, pulling her beloved teddy bear from the box. Monsieur Dubois.

CHAPTER 27

COSI

It's been four days since they took Mama. I know because of the tiny ray of light that streams through the floorboard, signaling when day becomes night. She's probably had her baby by now. A little sister would be nice, but so would a brother. I'd teach him how to play jacks and tell him never to pull girls' pigtails. We'd call him Theodore, or Teddy, for short. I pull Monsieur Dubois to my cheek. "That would be a nice name, wouldn't it?"

When the gun fired, it frightened me, but I didn't hear the bad man's voice after that, or his heavy footsteps. It's all quiet now. Too quiet.

I long for someone to come, anyone. And when they do, I'll cry out. I'll use all of my remaining strength to make sure I'm heard. And then they'll take me to Mama, and everything will be fine again.

I lay my head on the cold floor, wishing there was still water in the pitcher, even just a tiny drop to quench my parched throat. But the water's been gone for days now. So are the last of the raisins. I feel strange, achy all over and very tired. I'm afraid that if I close my eyes, I may not have the strength to open them again.

I worry about Mama. Something must have happened. I heard a man's voice in the room above. He came to rescue her, but why didn't she tell him about me? Why didn't she send him back to get me? Something must have happened. I squeeze Monsieur Dubois tighter.

I once asked Papa about heaven, and he told me he'd always imagined it to be like his home in Normandy: the scent of apple blossoms dancing in the salty air, fish roasting on the stove, and waves crashing on the shore. I may never see Normandy, but Papa's description of heaven makes it okay. I imagine him waiting for me there in his red chair by the fire, with a pipe in his jacket pocket and his hands, scarred by rose thorns, folded on his lap.

"Welcome home, Cosette," he'll say, arms stretched out wide to me as I leap into his lap. "I've missed you so."

I'll find Mama in the kitchen, apron tied around her waist, singing a little song as she prepares dinner. "My darling girl," she'll say as I wrap my arms around her.

I blink hard, but no tears come. I am like a tulip in the flower shop deprived of water.

My eyes are heavy, too heavy. I am no longer able to keep them open. "We're going to go to heaven," I whisper to Monsieur Dubois.

• • •

I don't know if I'm awake or dreaming, or even if I'm on this earth anymore. I smell the crisp sea air as it whips against my cheeks. There are apple trees in the distance, too, just as I'd imagined. I fix my eyes on a perfect red orb hanging from a branch, and I imagine sinking my teeth into its flesh, when I hear my name.

"Cosi?"

I turn around, but the voice isn't coming from anywhere near. It's somewhere else. Somewhere far away. The wind rustles the apple tree and I turn back, standing on my tiptoes and extending my hand higher.

"Cosi!" the voice calls again, but this time it's closer, and *familiar.*

My eyes flutter, then close, and when I open them again, the apple tree is gone. There is only darkness, and heavy footsteps above me.

"Cosi? Are you down there?"

Luc. It's Luc!

"Luc!" I cry, but whatever voice I once had has been reduced to a mere whisper.

"Cosi!" he calls again.

I sit up, using every ounce of my remaining strength, desperate to be heard, to be rescued from this horrible darkness. I feel around for the pitcher, and when my hands clasp its handle, I force my legs to a stand, then crash it against the side wall. It shatters, just as I expected it to, making a loud crash that would be impossible to miss.

"Cosi!" Luc calls out again. I hear his hands patting the floorboards above me, and then beams of glorious light pour into the darkness. I squint as I look up, and my eyes meet Luc's.

"Sweet child," he says, leaping down into the space beneath the floor and taking me into his strong arms. "I've found you, and I am never going to let you go."

CHAPTER 28

CAROLINE

That evening, I tell Margot about my day, the story of little Cosi, and she gasps. "To think she was . . . right there, in the bedroom I'm sleeping in."

We decide to stay in and make pasta, but I realize I'm out of marinara sauce. Élian is playing happily in the living room. "I'll run out and grab some," I say. "I'll be back in a sec."

Monsieur de Goff is in the lobby, locking up the little room where he keeps his supplies. He must be getting ready to leave for the day.

"Hi," I say, walking toward him.

He nods at me. "Monsieur de Goff," I say, eyes welling up with tears. I have no words, and before I can think twice, I wrap my arms around his neck, hugging him tightly, as if the strength of my arms somehow possessed the power to cure the pain each of us carries. But then I realize that I have gotten lost in a moment of emotions. "I'm sorry," I say, quickly stepping back. I wipe tears I didn't know were there.

The old doorman looks at me, a little stunned.

"I . . . met Inès's mother," I explain. "The owner of the art studio across the way. She told me your story, about when you were a little boy."

His eyes don't leave mine.

"I'm so sorry."

For the first time, at least in my presence, the corners of his mouth turn upward, forming a smile.

"I understand now," I say, "why my questions about the past were so hard for you to answer."

He's quiet for a long moment. "They ransacked our house, took everything, even our lives. I was the only one to survive. My sisters, my mother, father. They all died in the camp. I don't know how, but I lived. I was skin and bones and covered in lice when an American soldier carted me out of that godforsaken camp on his shoulders."

I gasp, overcome with emotion.

"I ended up returning to the rue Cler, living with a great-aunt who'd managed to survive the occupation," he continues. "We pretended that nothing had changed, when everything had. You could always tell who'd endured terror, though. You could see it in their eyes. Still can." He shifts his stance. "The summer I turned thirteen, I met a girl a few years older than me. She told me her story, how she and her mother had been held captive by a German, right here in this building."

I place my hand over my mouth.

"Cosi," I say.

He nods. "The girl looked different than I'd remembered. She was nearly a woman by then, but it didn't take long for me to connect the dots. Sadly, her mother died in childbirth shortly after she was rescued. But my friend wouldn't have survived had it not been for her mother's care and sacrifice. And Luc."

"Tell me more."

He nods. "After Céline was rescued, right before she died, Cosi waited to be freed, but it took days before her mother's fiancé, Luc Jeanty, connected the dots."

Jeanty.

"An old school friend of his had lived in a similar apartment on the rue Cler, and they'd often played in a hidden compartment in a back bedroom. He had a hunch that Céline might have hidden Cosi in a similar place. And can you believe it? He was right. He got to her just in time. Skin and bones, barely clinging to life."

I swallow hard as he continues.

"Luc took her in, raised her like his own. The most admirable fellow I'd ever met. Anyway, when I came to work here, Cosi asked me to make a promise to her."

"What was that?"

"That I would make sure that no child suffered within these walls the way she had."

"You are a good man, Monsieur de Goff," I say, searching his tired eyes. "Is Cosi . . . still in

Paris? I would love nothing more than to meet her."

The old man smiles. "But, mademoiselle, you already have."

I shake my head. "I don't understand."

"Mademoiselle," he says, "Inès's mother . . . is Cosi."

My heart beats fast as I cross the square to the market, so lost in thought as I purchase a jar of marinara that I hardly notice the cashier giving me back my credit card.

On the way back to the apartment, I spot Inès in the distance, locking up the art studio. I wave, and she walks toward me holding a stack of canvases.

"Can I help you with those?"

"Oh, thanks, but I don't have far to go. I'm meeting my husband for dinner at a restaurant around the corner." She smiles. "He has bigger muscles than I do. I'll make him cart these home from there."

I pause for a long moment, contemplating how to tell her the mammoth-sized story I've just pieced together, but I don't know how or where to start.

"Everything all right?" Inès asks. "You look like you have something big on your mind."

My arms erupt in goosebumps.

I smile through misty eyes. "Yes, I do, and yes,

I'm fine. Listen, it's a bit of a long story. You're off to dinner, so why don't we meet for lunch tomorrow and I'll tell you."

"Perfect," she says, blowing me an air kiss before turning around again. "Oh, I forgot to tell you that I sold *all* of your paintings after the art show."

"Wow, really?"

"Yes, every one," she continues, with a sparkle in her eye. "And all to the same customer, too."

"The same customer?"

She nods. "Victor. He bought them all."

I swallow hard.

"Oh, come on, don't look so surprised. The man obviously is in love with you, silly." She grins. "Okay, I'll see you tomorrow."

I wave at her as she dashes off.

A raindrop hits my cheek as I look back at my apartment building. Monsieur de Goff has just stepped out to leave for the night. I watch him raise his umbrella and think of what he said about his promise to Cosi, and the kinship between those who suffered during the occupation.

Another raindrop hits my face, with another close behind, and then a torrent falls down from the sky. I would normally run for an awning to wait out the onslaught. But not now. Something in me has broken, or maybe, as someone wise said, broken *open*. I look up to the sky, letting the storm wash over me. For the first time in so long, I am not afraid.

"Alma," I whisper, the rain mixing with my tears. "I miss you so much, baby. Your daddy does, too. Oh, love, we never wanted this to happen. But you know what? I think I know what you'd say to us right now if you could. I think you'd tell me to go give Daddy a hug, wouldn't you? And forgive him."

"Mademoiselle," a man passing by says. "Are you all right?"

"Yes," I say, laughing and crying at the same time. I'm drenched, and I probably look like a lunatic. Maybe I am. I don't care.

"Yes," I say again. "I'm fine."

As I run to Bistro Jeanty, I hear young Cosi's voice in my ear, words she hadn't wavered from all her life: *I want to say that I think that the most important things in life are thankfulness, forgiveness, and love. Mama taught me to always be thankful. And when you say thank you it makes other people feel happy. And forgiveness, because, life is too short to be cross. It's also not fun. And, last but not least, love—because when you have love in your heart, nothing and no one can take it away from you.*

CHAPTER 29

CAROLINE

By the time I reach Jeanty, I am soaked, and also . . . crestfallen. The restaurant's lights are dim. The door locked. A CLOSED sign hangs in the window.

"No!" I cry, pounding on the door. "Victor!"

The man who runs the charcuterie next door is locking up his shop when he looks over at me as if I've quite possibly lost my mind.

"Excuse me, monsieur," I say, unable to remember his name. "Do you know why Jeanty is closed? Where's Victor?"

He regards me with suspicion. I must look like a disaster, soaked the way I am, but I don't care.

"Did he say anything to you?" I continue. "Anything?"

The man shrugs. "I've owned my shop for more than forty years, and the bistro hasn't been closed a single day. And then an American woman comes in and sends everything into chaos." He throws up his arms. "What will I eat for dinner tonight now?"

As he storms off down the street, I detect movement inside the restaurant and run to the door again, knocking loudly against the glass door as a figure moves closer.

The handle turns, and the door creaks open. But it's not Victor who greets me. Instead, it's a woman in a fitted blue dress. She's blond, tan, and . . . beautiful.

"Emma?" Victor's voice is coming from the kitchen. My heart sinks. "Oh," I say, taking a step back. "I'm sorry, I . . ."

"Wait . . . Caroline?" She squints. "I'm not wearing my glasses. Is that *you?*"

I nod, confused, looking at her more carefully. *Do I know her?*

She wraps her arms around me. "I'm sorry; Victor told me about your accident. Maybe you don't remember me. I'm Emma. Victor's cousin from Nice."

I smile, nodding. "Of course!"

"I came to your wedding," she continues. "I know it's been a long time. And I got my hair highlighted." She runs her fingers through her honey-colored locks. "But anyway, I'm so happy you're here! Come in! My boyfriend, Antoine, and I are in town for a few days on our way to Rome, and Vic invited us to come stay."

"Why is the restaurant closed?" I ask.

She looks at me quizzically. "You haven't heard? Victor has decided to sell it."

I gasp. "What?"

"I know, a tragedy," she continues. "See if you can talk some sense into that cousin of mine."

She continues chattering on, but I tune her out

410

when I see Victor sitting at a table at the back of the restaurant, quietly sipping a glass of red wine by candlelight.

As I walk past Emma into the restaurant, our eyes meet, and mine well up with tears. In all of my anger, I'd forgotten that Victor's heart hurts just as much as mine does. I may always grieve, but it is time to forgive.

"Oh, Victor," I cry, kneeling beside him. His eyes light up and he caresses my rain-soaked hair.

"I love you so much," I say. "I'm . . . so sorry that I . . . I'm so sorry for everything."

"I'm sorry, too," he cries, cradling my face in his hands.

"It's my fault," I say. "I should have pulled her hair back before she got in the pool that day."

"I should have had the pool inspected," he says, shaking his head. "I had no idea the filtration system was a hazard."

I fall into his arms and we both weep in each other's embrace.

"Will you forgive me, my love?"

I nod. "Will you forgive me?"

"Yes," he says, looking into my eyes. "Can we start again? Can we, please?"

"Yes," I say, tears streaming down my cheeks. "Yes."

CHAPTER 30

CAROLINE

TWO YEARS LATER, SPRINGTIME
Paris

"Just one more," the photographer says, camera in hand. "Maybe hold up the book a little higher. There, just like that. Now look out over the city, and smile!"

"Doesn't Estelle look great?" I whisper to Victor, who stands beside me. She's invited us to a special luncheon to celebrate the publication of her book about Cosi and Céline, and I couldn't be prouder of her, and her accomplishment.

I turn to my left and take in the view from the top of the staircase in Montmartre. Paris has never looked lovelier. Cherry trees in bloom, flowers bursting to life after a long winter slumber.

I glance at the book in my hands, admiring its beautiful cover and title: *All the Flowers in Paris*. The French edition comes out in a week, the U.S. edition, next month. The publisher decided to use my painting of peonies for the cover. I'd been shy about it at first, but now, as I hold the final product in my hands, it fits.

My life finally fits, too. Victor and I exchanged marriage vows for the second time, then honeymooned in the Greek islands. After moving out of the apartment at 18 rue Cler, we bought an apartment in Montmartre, not far from the little garden with its patch of wooly thyme, and we're happy there with our sunny balcony overlooking the city. We even converted one of the bedrooms into an art studio, where I paint every day.

It was harder than I thought it would be to leave the old apartment. It sat empty for a long time, but the release of Estelle's book has brought a lot of interest, and I hear there's talk of a group of charitable investors who want to convert it into a museum, much like the Anne Frank House in Amsterdam.

The money from my father's estate helped me fund a small nonprofit organization for women in need (an ironic but happy coincidence, which I would have loved to share with my mother if she were here right now; I'd make her president). After much consideration, I named the organization the CCA Alliance after Céline, Cosi, and Alma. We have a hotline for victims of domestic abuse and offer meals, advice, job training, housing, and other assistance through a network of volunteers throughout Paris. We're not looking to win the Nobel Prize, but if our work can make one teddy-bear-clutching little girl feel safe when her world is falling down around her, then it's all worthwhile.

Vic didn't end up selling the restaurant after all, but he's offloaded many of the day-to-day tasks to Julien, who's proven to be a very reliable and talented understudy, which gives us the freedom to travel as often as we like. Victor has his eye on Iceland next; I'm thinking Costa Rica.

Monsieur Ballard (Nic) passed away in January. But I will always feel good about one thing: he got his kiss, and even more. The lifelong friendship he'd maintained with Cosi had sparked into something more in Nic's final years, but I think the flame had been there all along.

"It's funny," Cosi had said to Inès. "I had a crush on him my whole life, and he finally noticed me when I became an old lady." Notice her he did. In fact, they shared two happy years together before Nic became ill.

After the funeral, Victor hosted a lunch in his honor at Jeanty. We still keep his favorite table waiting and miss him dearly, but no one more than Cosi.

But old love breathes life into new, and shortly after the funeral, Margot's handsome-suit guy proposed. He loves Élian as much as he loves her, and his family, which owns the largest office-supply company in France, has welcomed them both with open arms. Just the same, Margot insists on staying at Jeanty.

Monsieur de Goff finally retired from his post at 18 rue Cler, his promise of protection kept. I'm happy to hear that he's in good health and has taken up bingo.

Cosi made that trip to California she'd always dreamed of, though, sadly, without Nic. While her health has been failing of late, she made it to the book-launch party and handled questions from the media with grace, reading passages from her journal. She'd given Estelle her full support and even wrote the book's foreword. Her sentiments made me weep.

"Thank you," Inès said to me, wiping away a tear, just as the party was wrapping up. "I could never have predicted that one of my own students would give my family the clarity and healing that we didn't know we needed." For whatever reason, Cosi had never shared her story with her daughter, and the truth had brought them closer together than ever. "Just tell me," Inès continued, pressing her hand against her chest. "Has your heart healed?"

"Oh," I had said, glancing at the doorway, where Victor stood waiting for me. "I don't know that my heart will ever heal. Maybe not completely. But I'm better. I'm whole again."

"You did great today," Vic says, squeezing my hand.

All the Flowers in Paris is Cosi's and Céline's story, of course, but in some small way, it's also mine, and Alma's.

I smile. "Thanks." Estelle has done a marvelous job with the book, unearthing so many details of Cosi and Céline's struggle, which culminated in a story that was both tragic and heartbreaking, but also redemptive and triumphant. Apparently, Madame Jeanty had a change of heart, too. Though she succumbed to cancer shortly after the war, before her death, she'd renounced her ties with the Germans and begged her son's forgiveness. Francine and Maxwell Toulouse, the neighbors who had turned in Céline and her father to the Nazis, would forever be banned from Jeanty.

The wind picks up, sending a gust that rattles an old cherry tree to our right, its branches heavy with pink blossoms. We stop for a moment and watch as thousands of tiny petals dance and swirl in the breeze. For a magical moment, it looks like a veritable pink blizzard.

"Alma would have loved that," I say, grinning, after the wind has settled.

Victor nods. "She would have."

We can talk about her these days without it sending us into an emotional abyss. In fact, we talk about her a lot, like what she would be like as a teenager (spunky), whether she'd like Paris or not (definitely), what she's doing right now at this very moment in heaven (stockpiling cotton candy—duh).

"We'll see her again," Victor said the other

day. It was just a passing comment in the kitchen, a response to some insignificant thing I said about her old ballet slippers, the ones she used to insist on wearing everywhere. His reply gave me such comfort. Because he's right. We *will* see her again. That's what love does. It binds people together, with ties that are stronger than time, stronger than war and destruction, evil, or pain.

I look up to the sky, thinking of Céline and Cosi, and my own sweet daughter, as a single pink petal goes rogue from the pack and lands on my cheek. I catch it and hold its silky softness between my fingers.

The truth is, all the flowers in Paris—every last petal—could never fill the void that Alma left, and I know I may always grieve. But I have come to learn that we can never lose what we love deeply and truly. It becomes a part of us.

I close my eyes and think of our old house in San Diego. Yes, Alma had taken her last breath there on that tragic day, but she'd also taken her first steps under that roof, and danced and sang and gave us a million beautiful memories there. I let my mind recall the big, sunny kitchen. All of our jazz records. The garden. My art studio. Even the pool.

"Vic," I say, blinking back tears.

"Yes, babe?"

"I think I'm ready," I continue, swallowing hard, "to go home."

My husband tucks his arm around my waist as I take a deep breath, then exhale, blowing the little pink petal back into the air, surrendering it to the breeze.

ACKNOWLEDGMENTS

This story was born, in part, from conversations with two very wise women in my life: my longtime literary agent, Elisabeth Weed, and my editor at Ballantine Random House, Shauna Summers, both of whom pushed me to set one novel-in-progress aside to focus on this one. Scrapping a project that you've put a lot of time into isn't easy, but both Elisabeth and Shauna had the savvy and foresight to know that this was *the book,* and they were so very right. Thank you both for weathering the creative process with me as this story took shape!

There's another rock star who deserves mega-gratitude from this author: my foreign rights agent, Jenny Meyer. Smart and fiercely loyal to her authors, Jenny has been a champion of my books since the beginning. Because of her, my novels are sold in more than twenty-five countries, and I've become a bestseller in many. I still pinch myself for that, and, Jenny, I am deeply and forever grateful for your representation and friendship.

I couldn't have written this book without the moral support of my parents, especially my mom, who talked me down from the ledge a few times when life got stressful and book deadlines tight.

I realize what a gift it is to have a mother who is truly your friend. Dad, you're pretty great, too!

To my boys, Carson, Russell, and Colby Jio, you're still young and you may think your mom is a little weird, but, guys, look on the bright side: It builds character! And when you grow up, I hope you'll look back and think that all those bedtime stories I told were pretty cool. But even if you don't, I will always love you. Being your mom is the greatest joy of my life.

Also, shout-outs to my awesome stepkids: Josiah, Evie, and Petra. You guys rock! And thanks, Petra, for introducing me to your sweet friend Cosi, whose name inspired the character in this book.

Thank you, too, to the terrific team at Ballantine—marketing, publicity, sales, copy-editing, and everyone behind the scenes—you guys are the best!

And, last but not least, I want to thank my husband, Brandon, who's selflessly journeyed around the world to accompany me on my book tours and research trips, who's lugged my heavy bags, taken thousands of photos, made me laugh until I've narrowly avoided peeing my pants, kept me hydrated, and best of all, made me feel loved—wholly and unconditionally. Finding you in this second chapter has been a dream come true.

ABOUT THE AUTHOR

SARAH JIO is the #1 international, *New York Times*, and *USA Today* bestselling author of ten novels. She is the host of the *Mod About You* podcast and also a longtime journalist who has contributed to *Glamour*, *The New York Times*, *Redbook*, *Real Simple*, *O: The Oprah Magazine*, *Bon Appétit*, *Marie Claire*, *Self*, and many other outlets, including NPR's *Morning Edition*. Jio's books have been published in more than twenty-five countries. She lives in Seattle with her husband, three young boys, and three stepchildren.

sarahjio.com
Facebook.com/sarahjioauthor
Twitter: @sarahjio
Instagram: @sarahjio

Books are produced in the United States using U.S.-based materials

Books are printed using a revolutionary new process called THINKtech™ that lowers energy usage by 70% and increases overall quality

Books are durable and flexible because of Smyth-sewing

Paper is sourced using environmentally responsible foresting methods and the paper is acid-free

Center Point Large Print
600 Brooks Road / PO Box 1
Thorndike, ME 04986-0001 USA

(207) 568-3717

US & Canada:
1 800 929-9108
www.centerpointlargeprint.com